Camilla Isley is an engineer turned writer after she quit her job to follow her husband on an adventure abroad.

She's a cat lover, coffee addict, and shoe hoarder. Besides writing, she loves reading—duh!—cooking, watching bad TV, and going to the movies—popcorn, please. She's a bit of a foodie, nothing too serious.

A keen traveler, Camilla knows mosquitoes play a role in the ecosystem, and she doesn't want to starve all those frog princes out there, but she could really live without them.

You can find out more about her here: **camillaisley.com** and by following her on Instagram, Facebook, or TikTok.

@camillaisley
facebook.com/camillaisley

tiktok.com/@camilla.isley

By The Same Author

Romantic Comedies

Standalones
I Wish for You
A Sudden Crush

First Comes Love Series
Love Connection
I Have Never
A Christmas Date
Opposites Attract

New Adult College Romance

Just Friends Series
Let's Be Just Friends
Friend Zone
My Best Friend's Boyfriend
I Don't Want To Be Friends

FIRST *Comes* LOVE

A romantic comedy anthology
BY CAMILLA ISLEY

This is a work of fiction. Names, characters, businesses, places, events and incidents either are products of the author's imagination or are used fictitiously. Any resemblance to actual events or locales or persons, living or dead, is entirely coincidental.

LOVE

Connection

A second chance romantic comedy
BY CAMILLA ISLEY

One

Two Weddings

♥♥♥

Saturday, June 10—New York, JFK Airport

"You've been staring at those two plane tickets for almost an hour now. My role as bartender compels me to ask: what's the big dilemma?"

I stare at the guy behind the bar for the first time since I sat on this stool an hour ago. He has a broad smile and a friendly face.

"If you stop pretending to be drying glasses just to peek at my tickets and pour me another drink," I say, "I'll tell you."

"Sambuca, with ice?"

I nod and shift my attention back to my tickets. Maybe if I stare at them hard enough, the letters will magically move and spell out a solution for me. In the background, I can hear ice tinkle as it hits the bottom of a glass, then crack when the bartender pours the Sambuca. These sounds mingle with the general noises of the airport: flight announcements, passengers chatting, and luggage rolling on the floor.

"Here you go." The bartender sets my drink on the glassy surface of the bar in front of me.

"You added coffee beans," I observe. "Nice touch."

"Pleased to please. But isn't 7 a.m. a little too early for double heavy spirits?"

"I'm on U.K. time, and believe me, I need the double heavy spirits."

"Which brings us back to the tickets. I've earned an explanation."

I sip my Sambuca and take a closer look at the guy's face. Young—mid-twenties, I'd say. Short sandy hair, intelligent eyes, and always the big smile. He's back at his occupation of drying glasses that don't need drying. Probably one of those people incapable of standing still with nothing to do.

On the screen behind him, a report about a fire at Miami International Airport is taking over the news. The screen reads that the fire has been contained with no casualties, but the airport will sustain heavy delays throughout the day.

"Looks like they're having troubles in Miami," I say, jerking my chin toward the screen.

"Trying to change the subject, are we? You're not going to make me beg for your story, are you?"

I swirl the ice in my glass. "Is this on the house?"

"On the house, along with the free advice."

"All right. One ticket's for San Francisco, the other one for Chicago. There're two weddings today, and I need to choose which one to go to."

"Two close friends?"

"You could say that."

"Oh, okay. Let's see, do you have a particular role in one of the weddings? I mean, do both your friends expect you to show up? Don't you usually need to RSVP months in advance for this kind of thing?"

"Mmm, this wedding…" I push the Chicago ticket forward. "I'm supposed to be the maid of honor. This wedding…" I slide the San Francisco ticket next to its twin on the countertop. "I'm not invited."

The bartender snorts. "Seems pretty straightforward to me. Why would you want to bail on a friend to go to a wedding you're not invited to?"

I look him in the eyes. "To stop it from happening."

"Woo-oh. And the plot thickens. My morning just got a lot more interesting than I was expecting. Is it about a guy? Is he the one who got away?"

"Yep." I take another swig of Sambuca; it burns my throat as I swallow. "You don't make burgers here, by any chance? I'm starving."

"Burgers at seven in the morning?"

"I told you, I'm on U.K. time. And burgers are my favorite."

"Sorry, but the kitchen's closed. I can give you some tortilla chips." He opens a new bag and pours them into a wooden bowl. "So, what's his name?"

"Jake."

"Jake." The bartender pauses. "The name has appeal."

"Not just the name." I sigh.

"You want to tell me what happened?"

"We first dated in high school. After graduation, he wanted to go to Stanford, and I wanted to go to Harvard."

The bartender whistles. "The war of the Ivy Leagues. What do you guys do?"

"I'm a lawyer. He's a surgeon."

"So what happened? You fought over schools, went your separate ways, and drifted apart during college?" he asks, his tone saying, *"Same old, same old."*

"No. I went to Stanford instead, to be with him. He assured me we'd go to Harvard for grad school."

"Oh. I sense that promise didn't come true. So you stayed together through college as well. And…?"

"Stanford offered him a scholarship for Med School. Everything paid for. No student loans, no living expenses. It was an offer no one could've refused."

"And that's when you broke up?"

"No, not yet. I hadn't applied to Stanford Grad School, so for me, it was either lose one year or move to Boston. Harvard was my dream, Stanford his. It wouldn't have been fair for either of us to have to give up our dream school."

"So you left?"

"Yeah. We spent the summer in California and I moved to Boston at the beginning of the fall term. We thought three years apart would be manageable. That's when we found out why everyone says long distance relationships don't work. School was demanding for both of us and catching a six-hour flight over the weekend became more and more difficult. We settled on leading different lives. We were used to sharing everything. Every day, every moment. Suddenly, we both had this huge chunk of life with different things in it. Things the other couldn't understand or get excited about. It was hard. We started arguing, and…"

"And?"

"Depends who you ask. If you asked Jake, he'd probably tell you it was a miscommunication issue. He'd say I overreacted to him telling me about a job offer he'd received in San Francisco. If you asked me, I'd give you a slightly different version…"

"Was your career really that important?" the bartender asks.

"It wasn't that I valued my career over my relationship with Jake. It was the sensation of always coming in second after *his* career. I'd given up my college dream for him. I'd waited all of graduate school… it was his turn to put me first. To put *us* first."

"If he's still in San Francisco, what's made you change your mind now about being together?"

"I'm not sure I *have* changed my mind."

"So why buy a ticket to San Francisco if you're not even sure you want to try to work things out with him?"

"It was a rash, stupid decision. When I found out Jake was getting married, I panicked. My first thought was that I couldn't let him do it."

"So what's changed?"

"I cooled off and thought about it."

"And?"

"And I realized flying to San Francisco and confronting him was crazy. I mean, what are the odds, really, of us getting back together? I live in London, and he lives in San Francisco. I haven't seen him in forever. I know nothing about his life. We ruined everything once already. How can we possibly make it work this time?"

"And yet here you are, staring at a ticket to San Francisco and contemplating crashing his wedding."

"I can't stop asking myself the 'what if?' question. I'm tired of living in a world of what ifs."

"Meaning?"

"I might've been a tad unreasonable after our break up," I admit.

"As in?"

"As in I moved to the other side of the world and ignored all his calls, emails, and messages. I wanted a fresh start, so I cut him out completely."

The bartender grabs the now-empty wooden bowl and refills it with tortilla chips. "Why?" he asks.

"I was sure he could talk me into moving back to San Francisco if I gave him the chance."

"And you didn't want to quit your job for him?"

"I couldn't. I owed it to myself to make the best choice for *my* career. But the fact remains that moving to the other side of the world didn't help much in forgetting him. I'm still in love with him. He's the only one I ever loved."

"How long ago was this?"

"Three years."

"And you haven't seen him or spoken to him since then?"

"I'm a mess, I know."

"How did you find out he was getting married?"

"Amelia told me—my best friend, the other one getting married today. Amelia, Jake and I are all from a small town near Chicago. She moved to London after getting her bachelor degree and she lives there with her soon-to-be-husband William. But she wanted to get married at home. Anyway, Amelia and Jake had some guests in common, they told Amelia about Jake's wedding as they'd already RSVP'd 'Yes' to him."

"Do you know the woman he's marrying?"

"No." I shake my head decisively. "I don't know anything about her, and I've forced myself not to search Google for intel."

"Aren't you curious?"

"*Yes*. But I can't give her a face. I'd never be able to crash her wedding if I did. She has to stay a ghost."

"When are the weddings?"

"This afternoon."

"Whoa. What's so special about June 10 that everyone wants to get married today? And you're hard-core. Shouldn't you have tried to talk to the guy a little sooner? Are you literally going to barge into the church and yell 'STOP!' in the middle of the ceremony?"

"I'd decided not to go at all."

"But you brought the ticket all the way from London, just in case."

"I did. Having the ticket, even if I knew I wasn't going to use it, made me feel calmer."

"And now you've changed your mind?"

"I don't know. I have no idea what I'm doing."

"When does the plane leave?"

"Which one?"

"Tell me both times."

"San Francisco's eight thirty. Chicago's ten forty-five."

"So you have less than..." He pauses to look at his watch. "Twenty minutes before they start boarding for San Francisco."

"That's correct."

"What's Amelia's take on the situation?"

"She got mad at me at first for even thinking about ditching her wedding. But then again, she's always been a huge fan of Gemma and Jake."

"Gemma?"

"That's me. We all grew up on the same street, and we've been friends forever. Anyway, she's marshaled a back-up maid of honor and she told me to follow my heart."

"And what does your heart say?"

"My heart's telling me it loves Jake. But this is too big. As you said, I can't run into the church and beg him to cancel the wedding."

"What time's the wedding?"

"Six p.m."

"What time does your plane land?"

I look at the ticket. "Noon."

"So you'd have plenty of time to get there before the ceremony starts."

"Mmm, I'm not so sure. The wedding's in some fancy winery in Napa."

"That's barely an hour's drive. You'll still have all the time you need to get there and talk to him before he goes to the altar."

"But what am I going to say?"

"Say that you love him."

"And?"

"Nothing else. If he's in love with you, it'll be enough."

"Say he doesn't laugh in my face and tell me to leave. Say he admits he still loves me. It doesn't change anything. I'm still in London, and he's still in San Francisco."

"You'll figure something."

"I'm not so sure."

"You said it yourself: you don't want to live in a world of what ifs, right? So it seems pretty obvious you have to try."

"But I'm so scared."

"Do you have anything to lose?"

"No, not really."

"Then why not go?"

"What if he doesn't love me anymore?"

"Then he doesn't, and it will suck, but at least you'll have your answer. But if you don't go, and you don't ask, you'll never know, and you'll regret it for the rest of your life. If you love him, go."

My face becomes suddenly hot and an electric prickle spreads from my heart to my fingertips. "Right. What's the worst that could happen?"

"They could arrest you for crashing a private party. Or the bride could sue you for emotional damages. Or…"

"I'm a lawyer; I can take care of myself in the law department. Are you on my side or what?"

"Of course I am. So, what's the next step?"

"A car. I'm going to need a car in San Francisco. I need to rent a car." My pulse is racing. I pick up my phone and tap away frantically. "Uhhuuuhhhu. It's done. I did it. I've booked a car. I'm really doing this. Oh gosh. I'm doing it! Is it too lame if I want to high five you?"

"No, not at all." He raises his palm. "Shoot away."

I slam my hand into his. "I have to tell Amelia so she can get her maid-of-honor-plan-B rolling."

"All passengers. Flight UA 730, with destination San Francisco, is beginning boarding at gate B 25. We're going to start boarding families with small kids and passengers with special needs. Then, we're going to board first and business class passengers. And finally, all other passengers…"

"That's your flight they just announced."

"It's my flight. I'm going." I fumble with my bag and carry-on luggage and almost fall from the stool. "How much do I owe you?"

"It's on the house."

"Everything?"

"Yeah. You go tell your man you love him. Go catch your love connection."

"Thank you. Thank you so much." I hurry toward the gate.

"Hey," the bartender calls after me. "Let me know how it goes! I'm on Facebook."

"What's your name?" I shout back without stopping.

"I'm Mark Cooper. And you?"

"Gemma Dawson."

Two

One Choice

◆◆◆

Saturday, June 10—New York, JFK Airport

"…Isn't 7 a.m. a little too early for double heavy spirits?"

"I'm on U.K. time, and believe me, I need the double heavy spirits."

"Which brings us back to the tickets. I've earned an explanation."

I swirl the ice in my glass. "Is this on the house?"

"On the house, along with the free advice."

"All right. One ticket's for San Francisco and the other one for Chicago. There're two weddings today, I need to choose which one to go to."

A female flight attendant with long strawberry hair interrupts me.

"Please don't talk to me about weddings. Not today." She plonks herself on the stool next to mine and says, "Mark, can I have a drink? Make it strong, please."

She's remarkably beautiful. Tall, with amazing lips and flawless skin. But her blue eyes are filled with so much sadness.

"What's up with you ladies and drinking so early in the morning?" the bartender asks.

"I don't give a damn about the time," the flight attendant says. "I've changed so many time zones in the past week, I'm not even sure if it's day or night for me."

"Did I miss something?" Mark asks in mock shock. "Is I-can-drink-at-7-a.m.-because-I-have-jet-lag the new black?"

"I just need something to calm my nerves and survive the day," the flight attendant pleads. "Make it a shot, please. Quick and painless."

"What happened to you, love?" Mark asks her. "You've got a dark aura today."

They seem to know each other well.

"The whole of Miami Airport almost went into shutdown today. An idiot started a fire, but the firemen caught it before it spread and everything was solved quickly. Otherwise, I would've been stuck in that swamp for the entire weekend."

"Oh, come on, darling. Miami's hardly a swamp. What's really up with you?"

"Nothing. Is my drink ready?"

"Give me a sec." Mark starts fumbling with various bottles and a shaker. Who knew you could put so much work into a shot? "Aren't you supposed to go home, honey?"

"Too depressing. I might drink myself to death if I go home now. At least here you can keep tabs on me."

"Will do, but for now… here's your drink. A pink starburst shot for the nerves."

I'm kind of jealous. My Sambuca, albeit with coffee beans, looks a little beginner problems-of-the-heart-at-7-a.m.-drinker next to the pink starburst. At least, I'm assuming the flight attendant is going through a heartbreak. Nothing else could drive a seemingly non-AA woman to drinking so early in the morning. I should know.

Anyway, I don't have much time to admire the pretty pink starburst. As soon as Mark puts the glass on the bar, she grabs it and drains it in a single swig.

"Better?" he asks.

"A little bit."

The vodka did add some color to her previously ghastly cheeks.

"Is this dark mood about your professor?" Mark prompts.

The word professor has barely left his lips before the flight attendant starts sobbing her heart out. She's hiccupping one word for every two or three sighs.

"Never… if… mine… engaged all along… wedding… today… she blonde…"

Mark looks at her, eyes wide, mouth slightly open. "You may have to repeat that, sweetheart."

I should be offended that my own wedding troubles have taken a back seat in the conversation, but this woman seems to be doing a lot worse. Plus, I could use a break from my ticket staring.

"Tissue," she pleads.

Mark offers her a paper napkin, and she blows her nose loudly. After a few more sobs, she seems calm enough to speak.

"William," she says, spitting the name in a way that tells me she hates and loves the guy at the same time. "He's been engaged all this time. Never had the guts to tell me until he was practically at the altar. Too bad men don't wear engagement rings. We should shackle a band on their fingers—an irremovable one—the moment they propose. At least that way they couldn't walk the world free to string along perfectly innocent, stupidly over-trusting naïve women like me."

Ouch. She's really having it rough.

"Engaged?" Mark asks. "But how's that possible? You've been with him… how long?"

"A year!" the flight attendant wails. "Twelve months down the drain. Bam, just like that. A year of my life, wasted. I was already seeing him as the father of my unborn babies, and he's probably going to make one with another woman. Tonight!" If she were a cat, she'd be wheezing. "He always said he couldn't stay in New York for the weekends. Remember how he always flew back to London the minute his last class of the week ended? It was because he had a fiancée to go back to. And she's blonde."

"Do we hate her?"

"No, we don't hate her. She doesn't have any fault in this. She's getting married to a lying, cheating, sorry excuse for a man, and she doesn't have a clue."

"Don't you think she *should* have a clue? It sounds to me as if she's marrying a man she doesn't know. How could she not suspect anything?"

"Same applies to me. I didn't suspect anything. I didn't have the slightest clue. Believe me, he's that good."

"Esther, I'm so sorry," Mark says. "I thought the professor was The One."

"Me too."

"How did you find out?"

"The bastard told me. Two weeks ago. He just said it: 'I'm sorry, I'm getting married in two weeks. I thought I'd have the strength to call it off, but I don't. I love you, but I can't see you anymore.' That's what he had the guts to tell me. More or less. In one awkward conversation, I was gone from his life."

"But you really never had a teeny tiny suspicion? Didn't you check his Facebook profile?"

"He doesn't use Facebook. He says it wouldn't be dignified for a professor."

"Ah, never trust a guy who doesn't have a Facebook profile."

What a bastard. How can anyone do something like that? Why get married if you're already cheating? It doesn't make sense. It's like adding Mexican chili peppers to a dish when you can't digest spicy food.

"And he said he loved you."

Esther nods.

"Do you think he was lying?"

"The worst part is that I'm almost sure he wasn't."

"But, darling, this whole story doesn't make sense. If he says he loves you, why would he go get married to another woman?"

"He said he's been with her for a long time. He said he tried to call it off, but every time he was about to tell her, he panicked. In the end, he said he just couldn't do it. So today, he's marrying her in Chicago. She's from a small town nearby. I Googled her. She *does* have Facebook. Her name's Amelia. She's blonde and beautiful. And today she's going to become Mrs. William Reilly."

Amelia and William Reilly. As she says the names, a bolt of electricity runs through me. Amelia, my blonde best friend, is getting married today in Chicago to William Reilly. He's a professor at London Business School. He also has a job at Columbia University where he teaches Financial Markets one week every month. And he doesn't use Facebook because he thinks it wouldn't be dignified for a scholar. It's one coincidence too many.

I try to stay calm and not show the shock on my face when I oh-so-casually butt in.

"What did you say this guy, the professor, taught?" I ask.

The bartender and the woman turn toward me as if they've both just remembered I'm here.

"Excuse me. Who are you?" the flight attendant asks, unable to keep the hostility from her voice.

"Gemma Dawson, nice to meet you," I say with a warm smile. "I apologize for interrupting, but I couldn't help overhearing your conversation."

"Esther Porter." She offers a manicured hand, which I shake. "And *I* should apologize. I'm being rude for no reason."

"Mark Cooper," the bartender chips in.

We do an awkward round of nice-to-meet-yous.

"Why did you want to know what he teaches?" Esther asks. "What difference does it make?"

Since I can't exactly tell her the truth, I blab the first excuse that comes to my mind. "I read this study once, which said people who work with numbers—finance people in particular—have a tendency to live duplicitous lives." I can't believe the load of crap that's exiting my mouth. But I need to know for sure if she's talking about Amelia's William.

"That's absolutely true!" Mark exclaims. "Didn't your professor teach Financial Markets at Columbia?"

"Yeah," Esther confirms. "I'm glad to know there's a clinical explanation for his being a cheating, double-crossing bastard."

My heart sinks. How many William Reillys commuting from London to New York to teach Financial Markets at Columbia could there be? Just one, I'm afraid.

"All passengers. Flight UA 730, with destination San Francisco, is beginning boarding at gate B 25. We're going to start boarding families with small kids and passengers with special needs. Then, we're going to board first and business class passengers. And finally, all other passengers..."

I hear the announcement for the San Francisco flight and my heart plummets. I can't go. I can't abandon Amelia and let her marry that scum. If I needed a clearer sign Jake and I aren't meant to be together, this is it. I'm not going to San Francisco; I'm not stopping his wedding. I feel my heart break in my chest and I lean on the bar countertop for support.

"Are you okay?" Mark asks me. "You look as if you've seen a ghost!"

"Yeah, yeah. I'm fine. I just need to use the restroom. How much do I owe you?"

"Don't worry, it's on the house."

"Everything?" I ask, surprised.

"Yeah, don't worry," he says with a big smile. "Hey, we never finished our chat about those plane tickets."

"It doesn't matter anymore," I tell him, tearing the ticket for San Francisco in two and throwing it in the bin at the end of the bar. "The universe just decided for me. Thanks again." I wave goodbye to Mark and turn toward Esther. "I know it's not much, but I hope you'll find someone who deserves you."

"Thank you," she sighs. "Have a safe trip."

I wave goodbye again, grab my hand luggage and shuffle away from the bar toward the screens with the Departures information.

"This is the last call for Flight UA 730, with destination San Francisco. All passengers, please go to gate B 25 for boarding. The gate will be closing in five minutes. I repeat, this is the last call for flight UA 730 with destination San Francisco."

Hearing the announcement is like having a jackhammer pointing to my chest and digging into my heart. It's shattering everything it finds in its way, leaving nothing behind. Just a giant empty hole. I'm letting Jake go, I realize with a flip of my stomach. I wipe a single tear from my cheek and stare at the screen, shaking the heartbreak away. I don't have time to mourn the loss of the love of my life right now; I have a job to do. There will be plenty of time to cry later—like, the rest of my life.

Right. I stare at the panel. The flight for Chicago departs from Gate A 47. I head there. While I walk, I take out my phone and search on Google for the phone number of Columbia University. Before I crash into Amelia's wedding screaming, "He's a cheater!" I need to have my facts straight.

After some pushing around of privacy laws, I finally manage to speak directly with the Business Department Dean. He confirms that only one William Reilly teaches Financial Markets at Columbia and commutes from London once a month.

I sit on a plush chair at the gate and text Amelia to tell her I'll make it to her wedding. I tell her to wait for me at all costs before she starts the ceremony. She texts back a shower of smiling emoticons and I can't help but feel miserable for being about to ruin her life. Only, I'm not the one ruining her life. The bastard is. Right. I'm saving her from living unhappily ever after. This is the attitude I need to keep for the rest of the day. There's no way stopping her wedding isn't the right thing to do. She will understand. She has to. I just hope she's not going to hate me for it. I was never a believer in, "Don't shoot the messenger."

Three

Speak Now

❤❤❤

Saturday, June 10—New York, JFK Airport

"Good Morning, ladies and gentlemen, this is your captain speaking. I'm glad to inform you we're about to take off. The weather's clear today and we should be able to land in San Francisco right on time. I wish you a pleasant flight."

I relax back in my seat, relieved to hear we're on schedule. I don't have much of a buffer as it is—if I want to get to the winery before the ceremony starts, everything needs to go smoothly. I just wish I weren't trapped on a plane for six hours with only my crazy thoughts to keep me company. My body might start a rebellion. I haven't slept in a day, and the idea of crashing Jake's wedding is pumping so much adrenaline in me, I'm ready to explode. I feel worse than a beer can in an automatic shaker. I grab the armrest as the plane gathers speed on the runway and takes off.

As soon as the seatbelt sign switches off, I fish in my bag for a notepad and a pen. I like to organize my thoughts in writing. When I have a speech to give, I always prefer to follow a script. Speaking off the cuff makes me nervous, so I start jotting down some marry-me-instead speech ideas.

Dear Jake,

Mmm, I'm not really writing a letter, though.

Jake,

Yeah, that's better. A strong, assertive start.

Jake,
I've known you my entire life and I've been in love with you for most of my adult life.

Adult life? Who says adult life? It's not romantic enough. I need to remind myself I'm not writing a harangue but an undying love declaration.

Jake,
I'm just a girl standing in front of a boy...

Overkill? Maybe I should keep it simpler and less cheesy.

Jake,
Ditch the biatch and marry me instead!

Short, concise, says all one needs to know. Pity I can't really use it.

***

By the time we land in San Francisco, I've reached speech draft number eighteen and I've still no clue what I'm going to say to Jake. On the other hand, my brain's positively fried. As I don't have to claim any luggage—I'm traveling light—I head straight to the car rental to pick up my car.

At the concierge, there's a bit of a line—five people before me in total. Damn. I hate waiting in line. Especially after the traveling and lack of sleep. I hope all the good cars won't be gone by the time my turn arrives. The clerk seems a super slow and fastidious one. It takes her forty-five minutes to sort through the customers before she finally gets to me.

"Good morning. I need your name, driving license, and credit card, please."

"I'm Gemma Dawson; I've made an online reservation."

"Yes, I have your booking in the server for a three-day rental. Is that correct?"

"Correct."

"Just a second." She types away at her keyboard. "Would you like to add insurance, ma'am?"

"Yes, please."

"All right, your credit card has already been charged for the rental amount when you booked online. I'll add insurance and charge a deposit fee of five hundred dollars. The deposit won't be withdrawn from your account, but it'll be on hold, meaning it won't be available for you to spend. Once you return the car, the amount will be made available to you in two business days to a week. Is that okay with you?"

"Yeah, sure." Deposit, plus insurance, plus the rental itself, plus the plane tickets. These will max out my credit card. I should have brought more cash.

"Okay, the credit card's taken care of. You can have it back." She slides it across the counter. "I just need to input the last few details for the insurance…"

"Sure."

"Oh."

Oh? What is she oh-ing about? I want 'very well' or 'here are your keys', not 'oh.'

"Is there a problem?" I ask, on edge. This is taking way too long.

"I'm afraid so, madam. I apologize; I should've checked before. Your driver's license appears to have expired."

"What do you mean, 'expired'? That's impossible!"

"Madam, it says here it expired a month ago."

I check the expiration date. "Oh, gosh!" My palms get clammy at once.

"Have you been driving with this?"

"No, no. I live in London. Nobody drives there."

"A U.K. driving license would be fine too."

"I don't have a U.K. driving license; I'd never be able to drive on the wrong side of the road with no casualties."

"If you don't have a valid license, I can't rent you a car."

"But I need to go to Napa! How will I get there without a car?"

Why is this happening to me? Today of all days.

"I'm sure you'll find a cab outside. It shouldn't cost you more than the rental. I'll need your credit card back to issue a refund."

"Here." I take the card out of my wallet and pass it to her.

A minute later, she hands it back. "The refund has been issued and the funds will be available to you in two business days to a week."

"Two business days?" I exclaim, bewildered. "You mean to say that my card's still maxed out?"

"If today's charge maxed it out, yes. It will stay that way until Tuesday at the very least."

"Can't you issue a refund in cash?"

"No, madam, we're not an A.T.M."

"So now I don't have a car, and you've taken the money to pay for the cab. What am I supposed to do?"

"There's a train to the city, and I'm sure you'll be able to find a bus to Napa, but we're not a tourist office. Now, I kindly need you to step aside so I can serve our next customer. Have a nice day."

"You too," I say. *Rot in hell*, I think.

***

Two trains, three buses, and four hours later I finally arrive in Yountville, the town in Napa where my final bus stops. With all the connections, I barely managed to close my eyes for half an hour here and there. I'm exhausted. But I'm not giving up. I'm a woman on a mission.

I look around the deserted bus stop to see if I can find a taxi station. Jake's getting married in some sort of fancy castle in the area, and I need someone to take me there. Yountville looks like a cross between an Old West outpost, a French country town, and a Disney park—thanks to a garden of stone mushrooms on the side of the main road. Maybe tapping one would turn them into the cutesy trolls from *Frozen*.

Mushroom trolls aside, the town looks desolate. No cars zooming on the street, no passersby, no one. The only open place seems to be a red brick building with an ivy-covered wall that looks like a shopping mall. I head there to ask for some information and enter a chocolate shop with the cutest truffles you'll ever see on display. A nice looking woman is standing behind the counter leafing through a magazine. She looks up as a bell above the door chimes, announcing my arrival.

"Hello. How may I help you today? Are you looking for a present?"

"Err, no. Actually, I was wondering where I could find a cab."

"Oh."

Another oh. I don't like ohs.

"You won't be lucky today," she says. "It's wedding season, and all the taxis are working as shuttle services, booked way in advance. You'll hardly find one passing by."

"But how do people get to weddings if they don't have a car?"

"Ah, well. Usually, transportation's arranged by the bride and groom. Are you going to a wedding?"

"Yes, at the Castello di Amorosa."

"What hotel are you staying in?"

"I'm not exactly staying in a hotel. I just arrived."

She gives me a puzzled look.

"I wasn't supposed to come," I explain. "I changed my mind at the last minute, but I need to get there quickly. The wedding starts in one hour."

"You're going dressed like that?" she asks even more suspiciously, narrowing her eyes at me.

I stare down at my crumpled blouse, jeans, and traveling flats. "*Yes*. I'm going dressed like this because, guess what, I'm not a guest. Okay? I'm not even invited if you really must know." All the stress, the fatigue of the past twenty-four hours, is finally bubbling out. The shaken beer can has been opened. "But I need to get to that wedding before it starts. And I need to get there fast as it's my intention to steal the groom *before* he gets married. So if you could please tell me if there are any means of transportation I could use to get there, I'd be eternally in your debt."

The woman claps her hands and squeals, "You should've told me that in the first place. Nothing this exciting has ever happened to me." I refrain from pointing out that nothing's really happening to *her* and let her babble on. "You're going to be the talk of the town. Stealing the groom, like in the movies. This is so romantic!"

"So, can you help me?"

"Of course. I'm Jody, nice to meet you."

"Gemma." I shake her hand.

"Let me call my brother. He has to go there to deliver some hay; there's a pretty farm near the castle. I'll see if he can give you a ride."

***

"Are you all right back there?" Jody's brother, Mike, shouts from the cab of his tractor half an hour later.

"Yeah, I'm fine," I shout back. At least as fine as I'll ever be riding on the back of a noisy tractor, perched on a stack of hay bales. It turns out Jody's brother drives a one-seater tractor.

If this was a chick flick, I'd be thoroughly enjoying watching the adventures of the female lead as she struggles to reach her one true love. But I've never been more aware of how much TV can make anything appear cool, when *it's not*. Like riding on the back of a tractor. And this not being a movie, I'm not even sure it won't all have been for nothing.

As the castle gets closer, I worry less about if I'm going to get there in time, and more about what Jake's reaction will be. Does he still love me? What will he say? Will we look into each other's eyes and run away into the sunset, holding hands? I hope he'll look me *only* in the eyes, as the rest of my body can't be much to look at right now. I probably smell too, and the hayride isn't helping.

The tractor stops. "All right," Mike shouts, killing the engine. "We're here. I can't go up the hill with this, but there's the parking lot, and the entrance is just behind it."

I hop off.

"You need help with the bag?" Mike asks.

"No, I'm fine, thank you," I say, pulling my trolley bag off the hay. "Thanks again! You saved my life."

"Good luck," Mike yells, before restarting the tractor and blowing a dark cloud of exhaust on me. Just about all the freshening up I need.

I check the time on my phone; it's already past six. The ceremony must be underway. There goes my plan of a discreet talk before everything started. I guess it'll be "burst inside and yell in the middle of the ceremony" instead. I hurry up the hill, dragging my hand language behind me, and reach the castle's entrance.

There's a guy guarding the door.

"I'm sorry, madam, we're closed for a private event today."

"Yes, I'm here for the wedding," I say nonchalantly.

The guy eyes me suspiciously. "You have an invitation?"

"Sure," I lie, and open my trolley to pretend to look for it inside. "I can't seem to find it right now… I'm already late. Is there any chance you could let me pass? The ceremony must've started by now."

"I'm sorry, madam, I need to see an invitation before I can let you through."

"Sure, I'll find it. I'm sure it's here somewhere." I try to appear calm and unconcerned, but inside I'm panicking. What if this guy doesn't let me in? Will I be on the other side of the wall while Jake says, "I do"? How pathetic would that be? No, it can't happen. I came here from the other side of the world; I won't have this stupid, sorry excuse for a bouncer keep me out. I need a distraction; just a few seconds to have him drop his guard so I can slip through the door.

I'm still rummaging inside my luggage when an idea hits me. I position the trolley bag so that the wheels are facing downhill and push it. The bag rolls down the slope, sprawling some of my clothes along the way. I yell in surprise and bouncer guy instinctively runs after the rolling bag. As soon as he turns his back, I duck inside the castle.

I run down a random corridor, having no idea where I'm going or where the ceremony's being held. Someone shouts behind me, but I don't turn around. I keep running through a pair of wooden doors, under an arcade, and through another door, until I find myself in a square courtyard crowded with many elegantly-laid round tables. They must be for the wedding reception. I'm getting closer, but where is the ceremony?

"You stop right there, miss," bouncer guy yells from under the arcade. He's running toward me at a menacingly fast pace.

A bunch of closed doors overlooks the courtyard. I slalom through the tables and launch myself at the door straight ahead of me, bursting inside just as bouncer guy catches up with me. I've made it into a frescoed room full of people.

Someone's speaking.

"Should anyone here present know of any reason why this couple should not be joined in matrimony, speak now or forever hold your peace…"

I made it. I'm in.

"Gotcha." Bouncer guy grabs my elbow forcefully.

"STOP!" I yell. "You have to stop! Let me go. Let me *go*."

Bouncer guy has grabbed me from behind, lifting me from the floor, and he's carrying me outside while I'm kicking my legs furiously in the air. "Stop!" I scream again. "You have to stop. I speak! I want to speak now! STOP!"

"Gemma?"

The groom turns toward me and the entire room falls silent. I freeze, one leg kicked out in midair. If ever someone could master the make-you-feel-like-the-only-person-in-the-room stare, Jake was your man. Suddenly, I don't seem able to talk anymore.

Four

Not Holding Peace

♦♦♦

Saturday, June 10—Chicago Area

"Should anyone here present know of any reason why this couple should not be joined in matrimony, speak now or forever hold your peace..."

"STOP!" I yell at the top of my lungs as I run up the aisle. "I need to speak. Stop. You have to stop." I'm drenched in sweat and panting.

"Gemma?" The groom turns toward me, and the entire room falls silent. I freeze in the middle of the aisle and suddenly I don't seem able to talk anymore. *Because I want to kill the bastard!* I don't trust myself with getting any closer to him.

"Gemma?" Amelia blinks, perplexed. She's resplendent in her white gown. My heart breaks for her. "You made it! What happened to you? I got your text saying you were coming, but you disappeared. You should've landed hours ago. What happened?"

"Long story." I try to catch my breath. "Expired driving license, maxed credit card, public transportation, traffic, chicken trucks..."

The journey here was a nightmare. The resort where Amelia's getting married is lost in the country in the middle of nowhere. I'd tried to rent a car to come here, but it turned out my license had expired and my credit card maxed out. I didn't have enough cash on me for a cab all the way from Chicago, and once I got to the closest town by bus, *there were no cabs*. So the only passage I found was in a truck transporting chickens. I'm sure I still have feathers on me.

"Are you okay?" Amelia asks.

"Mostly…"

"Err-hem." The minister clears his throat in the background. "If you don't mind, miss, we're in the middle of a ceremony here."

"Right." Amelia seems to realize for the first time that I've just interrupted her wedding. "Why don't you take a seat and we can talk later?"

"Actually," I mumble, twisting my fingers, "I need to talk to you right now."

"Can't it wait until later? I'm kind of in the middle of something here," Amelia says, annoyed now.

"Don't you think I know? I need to talk to you *before* you go through with the something. It's important."

"Okay then, say what you've come to say so we can get a move on."

"It'd be better if you could step aside for a second and talk to me in private."

"Gemma, I love you. But I'm getting married, right now. I'm not stepping aside for a girl talk."

Mr. Taylor, Amelia's father, grabs my elbow and drags me gently to the side. "Come on, dear, this can wait until later."

"Let me go," I protest. "Let me go! Amelia, I need to talk to you, seriously, please. Give me five minutes."

"Gemma, I know you have a taste for drama, but today is not the day. We will talk *after* I get married."

"Nooooo!" I scream as Mr. Taylor revives his efforts to drag me away. "You can't marry him, you just can't."

"Have you gone mad?" Amelia screeches. "Why have you decided to ruin this day for me? First, you say you're going to be my maid of honor, then you dump me to run after your ex-boyfriend, then you change your mind again, get here half an hour late, and try to stop the wedding. Why? *Why*?"

"I really think we should talk about it in private."

"If you have something to say, just say it, for goodness' sake."

Amelia's dad chimes in. "Young lady, I've known you your entire life and I've never been more disappointed in you."

"Mr. Taylor, I'm sorry, but I assure you I have a very good reason. Amelia, please. I have something serious I need to tell you, but it's better for you if I don't say it in front of everyone. Trust me on this."

"I've had enough," she snaps. "Dad, can you please take her outside? I'll talk to her later." She turns to talk to the minister. "You can go on."

"Hem, technically…"

"What?" Amelia spits.

"The ritual imposes that when a claim is made, I am to listen to it."

"It's nothing serious, I can assure you," Amelia says caustically, shooting me a furious look. "My friend's jetlagged. We can move forward." Amelia turns to her brother. "Malcolm, get her out of here."

Amelia's brother joins their dad and grabs me from behind, lifting me off the floor. I try to resist, but I can only kick my legs uselessly in the air while he drags me outside.

"Stop, let me go. Even the minister says I should talk. Amelia, please listen to me. You can't marry him. You can't. Let me go!"

As we near the exit door, I panic. They're going to drag me out in five seconds, and Amelia's going to marry that bastard. I can't let it happen. So I blurt my secret out in the worst possible way.

"He's a cheating, lying bastard!" I scream.

There's a general intake of breath from the guests, and Amelia's brother drops me to the ground. I shake him off with some indignation and walk back up the aisle.

"Why are you doing this to me?" Amelia asks, close to tears.

"Because it's true." I'm about to cry myself. "Her name's Esther, she lives in New York, and she works as a flight attendant. He's been having an affair with her for a year, and he called it off two weeks ago because he didn't have the guts to leave you even though he's in love with her. He's been living two lives since he got that teaching job at Columbia. One with you in London and one with her in New York."

"I don't believe you," Amelia hisses.

"If you don't believe me, ask him," I say quietly.

All heads turn toward William. He looks like a corpse. Ghastly skin, bluish bags under his eyes, and hollow cheeks. He doesn't look like someone who's getting married but more like someone who's walking down death row.

"Tell me it's not true," Amelia squeals. "Tell me."

William stares at her, petrified.

"William?"

He finally breaks.

"I'm sorry…"

"Sorry? You're *sorry*?"

"I didn't know how to tell you."

"Tell me? Tell me what, exactly? That you don't love me? That you're in love with someone else? That you cheated on me for a year?"

"I-I'm sorry…"

"No. *NO*. You don't get to be sorry, you bastard."

That's when she goes Carrie-Bradshaw-after-Mr.-Big-leaves-her-at-the-altar crazy and hits William on the head with her bouquet. "You humiliated me," blow. "You cheating," blow. "Lying," blow. "Loser," blow. "I hate you," blow.

Petals fly everywhere. When there's nothing left of the bouquet, Amelia throws it away and stares at the room, disoriented. She catches my gaze and something switches on her face. She runs toward me and I'm afraid I'm going to be next on her hit list, but instead she grabs my hand and pleads, "Get me out of here. Get me out of here as quick as you can."

Hand-in-hand, we run out the door, down the long, carpeted hallway, and burst onto the grassy lawn.

"I don't have a car," I say.

"How did you get here?"

"On a truck full of chickens. Trust me, you don't want to know."

A whistle resounds behind us, and we turn to see Amelia's brother running after us.

"Dad says to take his car." He throws the keys at me and gathers Amelia in a bone-crushing hug. "Call us when you're a little calmer—promise?"

"I promise," Amelia says. "But now I just want to get the hell out of here."

I follow her panicked gaze to the chapel's entrance door where the first guests are streaming outside. I catch a glimpse of my trolley lying against the wall.

"My bag," I say to Malcolm. "I need my bag."

"I'll get it. You get the car around." He hugs me and whispers in my ear, "Thank you, and sorry. We owe you."

I wave him away, embarrassed and close to tears again, and follow Amelia to the car. Malcolm puts my bag in the trunk and bangs his hand on it twice to signal we can go. I push my foot on the accelerator, sending grit flying under the tires as I steal the bride away.

I look at her. She's staring out of the window and I can't see her face.

"I'm sorry I had to tell you this way."

"I can't talk about it. Not yet." Her voice is broken, as is my heart for her.

"Where do you want me to take you?"

"Away. As far away as possible."

"Okay."

I'm not sure what she means, but I'm okay with driving the car until we have a better idea of where we're going. That is until I remember my driving license has expired. I hit the brakes. We're on a road in the middle of a crop field. There's no police here, but once we get to the main road, I can't risk being arrested.

"I'm sorry, but you'll have to drive. My driving license's expired."

"Of course you'd come to steal the bride with an expired license."

Amelia shakes her head, amused. She steps out of the car and becomes immediately serious again as she looks down at herself in her wedding gown, which becomes the next victim of her blind rage. She tears, trashes, and screams. This time, instead of petals, there's crinoline and tulle flying everywhere. When she's accomplished the look of a zombie bride from *Dawn of the Dead*, she starts pulling at the dress like a mad woman.

"Help me. Get it off me. I need it off me."

I run toward her and start undoing all the tiny hooks and buttons on the back.

"It's taking too long. I can't breathe."

"This dress has a thousand buttons."

"I don't care about the buttons—tear it off. Get me out of it."

I rip the fabric apart with some satisfaction and help her slip out of the zombie dress.

She takes a couple of calming breaths before saying, "Clothes. I need clothes." She's wearing only her bridal lingerie. Thank goodness we're in the middle of nowhere. "My honeymoon bag should be in the trunk with yours. I slept at my parents' yesterday."

I open the trunk and fish in her bag for a pair of jeans and a black tank top. She throws off her shoes to get into the jeans, pulls them on, and bends forward to pick up the shoes, which she curve-balls into the field. Okay, I'm going to let it slide and not give her a lecture about littering. Instead, I go back to the trunk and pass her a pair of flats.

She gets out of the field and into the car, I mount shotgun, and we speed away. The sole memento of our passage in this deserted land will be the cadaver of a white satin dress resting in peace at the side of the road.

As we reach more trafficked streets, Amelia makes one sure turn after another. She seems to have a clear idea of where we're going.

"Ames?" I say uncertainly. "Where are we going?"

"How many days do you have off?"

"A week, stretchable."

"Good."

"Why? Where are we going?"

"The airport."

Five

Wedding Inquisition

♥♥♥

Saturday, June 10—Napa Valley

"Gemma?" Jake repeats. "Is it you?"

Finally, bouncer guy drops me to the ground. I shake him off with some indignation and walk back toward the center of the room.

"Jake," is all I'm able to say.

On the other hand, the bride doesn't seem to suffer from muteness.

"Jake, who is this woman? Security, can you take her away, please?"

Jake appears shell-shocked.

"Is this Gemma, as in your ex-girlfriend?" the bride asks. "What's she doing here?"

"I don't know," Jake says.

"Tell her to go away. I don't want her here."

I find my voice again. "Jake, I need to talk to you."

Jake stares from me to his wife-to-be and back, still at a loss for words.

"Well, we don't want to hear what you have to say. So you can go," the bride says.

I look pointedly at the minister. "I have a right to speak; everyone can speak. I want to speak now."

"Well, technically, she does have a right to speak," the minister says.

"Oh, please!" The bride's voice jumps up a few octaves as she turns toward the minister to argue. "You're the one who told me the 'speak now or forever hold your peace' was an archaic form with no real value, and that it wasn't necessary anymore."

"But you insisted on keeping it, so now she has a right to speak. It's the protocol."

The bride turns around and gives me the stare of death. I ignore her and turn toward Jake.

"Jake." I inhale deeply. "When I discovered you were getting married, my world collapsed. I bought a ticket for San Francisco the same night, telling myself I was never going to use it, that coming here was a stupid idea, that I'd say the wrong thing and humiliate myself. Then today came, I was at the airport with the ticket in my hands, and I couldn't stay away.

"I couldn't live with myself another day if I didn't do this. I wish I had perfect and beautiful words to say to you, but the truth is I don't. I wrote eighteen speech drafts coming here and now none of them seems to make any sense. All I can think about are the things I should've said three years ago, and I didn't say because I was too stubborn, too proud to admit my mistakes. Too proud to pick up the phone when you were calling. Too proud to reply to your emails. Too proud to admit I was wrong and you were right.

"Well, I'm not anymore. I made so many mistakes, and coming here today is probably going to be the biggest one yet. But the one thing I'm sure wasn't a mistake in my life was—*is* loving you. Because that's what I came to say, I love you… and I'm sorry. I'm sorry for leaving you, I'm sorry for all the wrong choices I made, and I'm sorry for choosing the worst possible day to tell you all this. But I'm not sorry I love you. Knowing I was about to lose you forever made me realize that in the past three years, I've lived my life without being really alive. Because you're what makes me feel alive. You always have been. And I don't care if my life's here, in London, or wherever else, because now I understand that *you* are my life, Jake. Not a job, not a place.

"I've tried not to love you—believe me, I've tried. But I just can't. I don't care if this is lame or embarrassing. I don't care about anything other than you… I thought you should know… what I'm trying to say is just that I love you, I'm in love with you, and I want to be with you."

I finish my speech, and the entire room stays wrapped in an eerie silence. Everything seems frozen in time. The guests look like petrified statues, and Jake's face is inscrutable. I keep looking into his gray eyes, trying to decipher what's going on inside his head. I get lost in his gaze of misty winds, ice, and snowstorms.

That's until the bride breaks the spell. "Well, you've said your piece. Now you can go. Jake, tell her to go."

Jake tears his eyes away from me and stares at the bride.

"Jake," she repeats, her voice shaky, "tell her to *go*."

Jake has his back turned; I can't see his face as he's dropped his head to stare at the floor. When he looks back up at the bride, her face scrunches up in a grimace.

"I can't," Jake says heavily. "I'm sorry."

"You bastard," the bride yells, raising her bouquet above her head. I think she's about to go Carrie-Bradshaw-after-Mr.-Big-leaves-her-at-the-altar crazy and hit Jake on the head with the bouquet, but she must have a change of heart midway because she hurls the bouquet at me instead, screaming, "You bitch!", and runs out of the room.

Instinctively, I duck. The bouquet soars above my head, hitting Jake's mom straight in the face. Why did I duck? I should've taken one for the team. This isn't going to gain me any I'm-a-better-daughter-in-law points. *Stupid reflexes*!

I see Jake murmur something to his younger brother, Edward, who walks toward my side of the room.

"Are you okay, Mom?" he asks Mrs. Wilder.

"Yes, yes."

He kisses her on the cheek, exchanges muffled words with bouncer guy, and turns toward me. "You. With me," he says curtly.

I contemplate protesting, but I need someone in the family on my side. I throw one last glance at Jake, who's whispering furiously with the minister and doesn't turn around. So I follow his brother out of the room.

"Where are we going?" I ask Edward as he turns into a narrow corridor and down a flight of steep stone steps.

"Somewhere more private."

Oh my goodness. He's taking me to the castle dungeons. What next? Is the wedding inquisition coming to interrogate me? Are they going to send bouncer guy?

Edward leads me through a labyrinth of corridors and finally lets me into a small room with walls made of thick stone, no windows, and two doors. The room's furnished with two chairs and an old-fashioned table.

"Wait here," Edward says.

"For whom? How long?"

"Jake, and I'm not sure."

"Please don't leave me here alone."

"You're going to be fine; I have things to sort upstairs." He walks through the door, then pauses and pops his head back into the room. "Ah, Gemma?"

"Yeah?"

"That was bad ass." He winks at me and walks away, closing the door behind him.

I pace around the small cell, but there's not really much I can do besides sitting in one of the chairs. I check my phone—no signal here.

Not that I need to call anyone. What's going on upstairs? What's happening? Is the wedding off? It looked that way, but who knows?

Suddenly the door bursts open and Jake storms into the room. With a few flicks of his fingers, he removes his bow tie and sets his gray eyes on me. They're ignited with… umm… emotions. Love? Hate? Anger? Passion? I'm not sure. I can't read his features.

Even with the tortured face, he's impossibly handsome. My eyes flicker over the bow tie hanging loosely around his neck and the open shirt exposing his Adam's apple—too sexy. I move my gaze up to his shaven, strong jaw and back to his icy gray eyes, intimate and foreign at the same time. Three years have chiseled his face, making it even more gorgeous. *Not fair.* No one should look this good.

I make to get up on wobbly knees and go toward him, but he stops me with a raised finger. "Down," he orders, moving the same finger downwards to indicate what I should do.

He starts pacing around the room. He stops, looks at me, and speaks.

"You…" He shakes his head and starts pacing again.

After a few seconds, it's a repeat.

Stops. Looks. Speaks.

"Of all days… *today*!" Shakes head. Starts pacing.

It's like a dance.

Stops. Looks. Speaks.

"Years, Gemma… *years*!" Shakes head. Starts pacing.

Stops. Looks. Speaks.

"Not a word…" Shakes head. Starts pacing.

Stops. Looks. Speaks.

"You're crazy."

He's finally standing still. Umm. I'm tempted to ask if he thinks I'm crazy in a you're-so-cute-because-you're-crazy-romantic way or if it's more of an I-want-them-to-shut-you-in-an-asylum-and-throw-away-the-keys crazy. I make to stand up and join him, but he shows me his index again.

"Down."

"Can't we talk if I stand?"

"No Gemma, we can't. Right now, I need you there at a safe distance. I'm still too mad at you to have you in my air."

"Okay, I'm going to sit down." I feel like Chris Pratt talking to Blue in *Jurassic World*. I'm not sure if Jake is going to tear me to pieces or join #TeamGemma. "But please say something."

"Three years, Gemma. *Three. Years.*" He finally seems able to streamline his thoughts in a more articulate way. "Not a word from you in three years, and you choose my wedding day to have a chat?"

"I'm sorry, Jake; I know my timing's bad…"

"Bad timing, she says. Ah! Your timing isn't bad, it's awful. Why did you wait until I was at the altar?"

"Well, my plan was to catch you before the ceremony started," I explain. "Then there was this rude lady at the airport who wouldn't rent me a car because my driving license was expired, but she maxed out my credit card with the stupid deposit anyway so I didn't have any money left for a cab. I took like five different trains and buses to get to Yountville, and from there the only way I could get here was on the back of a tractor filled with hay. Then bouncer guy wouldn't let me in, so I had to cook up a distraction. I sacrificed my bag, I threw it down the moat, and I ran past security. By the time I was inside, it was too late. The ceremony had already started, so it was sort of a now-or-never moment."

"You came here riding on a hay tractor?" He's trying to keep a straight face, but I can see the corners of his mouth twitch. And for the first time since I got here, hope rises in my chest.

"I did."

"You're crazy."

"I am a bit."

"And I'm crazy."

"Are you?" I ask.

He's looking at me with such intensity, I might pass out. I want to throw myself at him and hug him, kiss him. But I'm afraid I'm going to get the sit-down finger again, so I stick to my chair.

"This morning," Jake says, still looking at me with a fire burning in his eyes, "all I could think about was you. The first thought that popped into my head when I woke up wasn't *I'm getting married today*, it was *today I'm saying goodbye to Gemma forever*. I was about to throw everything to hell. But you'd refused to speak to me for three years. You didn't return any of my calls or messages—*not one*. And I've tried, Gemma, you know I've tried."

"I know," I whisper.

"So I told myself that I didn't know anything about your life today, that you were probably already married to someone else or something, and that I had to move on with my life and leave you in the past. But the moment I saw you, I knew I wasn't getting married today. The truth is, you had me at Jake…"

"I did?"

"You did. And so, yeah, I am crazy… about you. Damn me, I'm still in love with you."

I stare at him. "You mean you're not getting married anymore?"

"No."

A huge smile takes over my face.

"Up," he says, and I get a thumb going upward this time. "Come here," he whispers.

I get so close to him our noses almost touch.

"I missed you," he says, cupping my head in his hands and burying his nose into my hair. Well, he's not going to get a red berry rush, but I hope he won't be too disgusted. "You smell so good; I've missed your smell." Yeah, he's definitely touched in the head or crazy in love with me, because no one in his right mind would think I smelled good right now.

"Gemma?" He nuzzles my neck.

"Umm?"

"Are you having a whole conversation in your head? You know I can't hear you."

"Yeah. I mean, no. I missed you too."

I pull away from him to look him in the eyes, but he holds me close. He slides one arm around my lower back, squeezing me against the solid wall of his chest, and I melt in the warmth of his embrace. I snuggle closer to him, afraid of letting go. He strokes my hair and the side of my face until his hand slips under my chin, lifting my face up toward his. Time holds still as we lock eyes, then it seems to fast forward as he presses his lips to mine in a kiss we've both waited three years to share. It feels simultaneously as if no time and an eternity have passed since our last kiss. It's all so familiar, and yet so new. This is Jake. He still loves me and we're kissing.

After five minutes or an hour, I can't tell, Jake pulls back and buries his head into my neck. "So what now? What was your grand plan after you stole the groom?"

"I didn't plan ahead," I confess. "I'm not very equipped, to be honest. I don't have a car, money, or any clothes. They're all scattered down the moat, and bouncer guy is probably feeding them to the pigs."

Jake roars with laughter. "I forgot how crazy life could get with you. How about I take you to dinner?"

"Dinner?"

"Yeah, you have to eat, right? We can start simple and figure out the rest as we go."

He's more right than he knows—the last thing I ate were the tortilla chips at the airport. I could never stomach airplane meals. I'm surprised I haven't passed out yet.

"Still talking in your head?" Jake asks.

"Yes. No. I mean, I'd love to go to dinner with you."

He takes my hand and guides me outside the castle into a new life.

Six

Honeymoon

♦♦♦

Saturday, June 10—Cabo San Lucas, Mexico

I pick up the bottle of complimentary champagne from the floor and take a swig. I'm with Amelia in her honeymoon suite in Mexico, and we've been sitting on the floor at the foot of the bed drinking champagne since we got here.

"He's married," I say, staring into space. "Jake's married. I can't believe it."

"I'm not married." Amelia takes the bottle from me and gulps down the bubbly as if it were water. "Gosh, I'm such a cliché," she adds when she's done drinking. "How pathetic, going on my honeymoon with my best friend after I was dumped at the altar."

"Ah, well. Technically, *you* left *him* at the altar. And at least, in this case, your best friend's just as heartbroken as you are."

"Were you really going to bust Jake's wedding?"

"Yeah, I would have. You know, if I hadn't met…"

"My ex-fiancé's mistress." Amelia finishes the phrase for me.

"Yeah, her. You really had no clue something was up with William? Not an inkling?"

"To be honest, this past year I've been so busy planning the wedding I wouldn't have noticed a pink elephant sitting in my living room, bellowing. You know what the worst part is?"

"You'll have to change your Facebook relationship status to 'it's complicated'?"

"No." She chortles. "To tell the truth, I'm more disappointed my perfect wedding got ruined. I'm more depressed I'm no longer a bride. It's more saddening than not being William's wife. I keep thinking no one will see the butterflies released."

"Butterflies?"

"Yeah. I had this cute mint-colored birdcage filled with all-colored butterflies, and they were supposed to open the cage when we cut the cake and all the butterflies would've soared in the air above us and it would've been beautiful."

"It would have," I say pensively. "But a wedding isn't really about the butterflies. Not unless they're in your stomach."

"No. I guess not."

"Are you in love with William?"

"I don't know how to answer. I've always taken my being in love with William as a given. I haven't asked myself that question in a very long time, and now I'm too angry and too drunk to give you a reliable answer. How about you? Are you sure you're still in love with Jake?"

"Want to know what the worst part is for me?"

"You got a Brazilian wax and no one's going to see it?"

"No." I smile despite myself. "That I can answer your question in the blink of an eye with no need to think. I'm in love with Jake. I always have been."

"Oh, Gemma, I'm so sorry. You should've gone to San Francisco to stop him."

"*And what, send you a text?* Hi, Ames, I just met your soon-to-be-husband's mistress. Please don't marry him. Talk to you soon. Love, Gemma*?"*

"You could've called."

"Amelia, I love you, but you're getting annoying. I could never have told you over the phone William was having an affair. You would've done the same for me, so cut the crap. Plus, I'm not even sure what Jake would've said."

"You think he would've stopped the wedding?"

"I've no idea, honestly." I take the bottle from Amelia, drink, and pass it back to her. "I last saw him three years ago, and I told him to go to hell, never picking up the phone again to answer one of his calls or messages. Chances are he hates my guts."

"Jake doesn't hate your guts."

"Well, even if he doesn't hate me, he probably doesn't love me anymore. He wouldn't be marrying someone else otherwise. Crashing his wedding would've gone down in history as one crazy-Gemma moment. If I went there pouring my heart out on his wedding day, he would've told me something like..." I do an impression of Jake's voice: "'Nice to see you, Gemma, glad to see you're okay. Now, would you mind? I'm getting married here.'"

"Gosh, Gemma, that's exactly how Jake speaks."

It stings that I remember his voice and lilt so well.

"Anyway, if I'd gone to San Francisco, I would've become an anecdote for Jake and his wife to tell their grandkids." I keep speaking in mock voices. "'Grandpa Jake, do you remember that time your crazy ex-girlfriend tried to stop you from marrying Nana? What was her name?'

"'Gemma,' someone would say.

"'Right, Gemma, what happened to her, anyway?'

"'She got even crazier with old age and now she lives alone with her ten cats.'" I conclude my recital. "So yeah, having to crash your wedding saved me from making the most embarrassing move of my life. I should probably thank you, not the other way around."

Amelia laughs her head off.

"What's so funny?"

"You are. You are literally the only person who could make me laugh on a day like this."

"You can have a spot in my crazy cat house."

Amelia chortles a little longer before she's suddenly serious again.

"Gemma?"

"Mmm?"

"How are you, seriously?"

"It's as if street workers jack-hammered my chest to dig my heart out."

"That good, uh?"

"I'm having palpitations. The thought of having lost Jake forever is giving me a panic attack. I need to stop thinking about it." I take the bottle back and drown my sorrows in Dom Pérignon.

"See, I'm not having palpitations about William," Amelia says. "Just homicidal instincts…"

"Well, Jake didn't cheat on me."

"Is she beautiful?"

I don't need to ask who 'she' is. "She had nothing on you, believe me. Plus, she was as wretched as you are. William pulled a number on her too. Up until two weeks ago, she thought she was dating the perfect guy, not an engaged, cheating scum. And if it's any consolation, she's jealous you're a blonde."

"Why? How does she know? What color is her hair?"

"She's a redhead, and she stalked you on Facebook."

"Give me my phone." Amelia leans over me and grabs it from the floor. "*I* want to stalk *her* on Facebook. What was her name again?"

"Give me the phone; you're not stalking her."

"Why not? She stalked me first."

"It wouldn't do you any good."

"Why?" Amelia narrows her eyes at me. "Is she so beautiful it'd kill me?"

"No, she's not, but it's no good, anyway. Don't torture yourself."

"As if you didn't stalk Jake's fiancée."

"*Wife*. And no, I didn't."

"Really?"

"Yes, really."

"Not even a peek?"

"No."

"Why?"

"Because when I thought I was going to crash his wedding, I didn't want to give her a face, and now—well, it'd only make me cry. Imagine if she looks like Courtney Thorne-Smith in *Ally McBeal*. It'd drive me crazy to know Jake married lawyer Barbie."

"Oh."

"Why are you oh-ing me? Don't you oh me. Have you looked her up?"

"No… yes. Just a little."

"Does she look like lawyer Barbie?"

"No, not really."

"You're lying. Give me your phone, now! I want to see her."

"No, it's not a good idea." Amelia raises her arms above her head and out of my reach. I'm too drunk to stand up and snatch the phone from her.

"Let's make a pact," Amelia proposes when I stop struggling.

"What pact?"

"I'll bear the looks of lawyer Barbie for you if you'll bear the looks of flight attendant Barbie for me. And we promise to never look them up. Never, ever. Deal?"

"Deal. I need this pact to keep my sanity."

"Gemma?"

"Yes?"

"I'm scared." She looks me in the eyes. "I haven't been on my own in forever. What's going to happen to me?"

"You're going to be heartbroken for a while. Then you're going to start dating again and have the time of your life. Until one day, you'll meet your real soul mate and you'll live happily ever after."

"What a load of crap. You hate dating!"

"It's more of a love-hate relationship."

Amelia stares at her left hand. "I used to be so annoyingly smug with my one carat resting cozily on my finger." She shakes her head. "How am I going to show my face at work? I'll be the office joke."

"Hey, come on. No one's going to laugh at you."

"Oh, they will, especially all the single ladies I used to look down on."

"Did you look down on me too?"

"Gemma, I hate to be the one breaking it to you, but you're hardly a single lady."

"Meaning?"

"Meaning men fall for you left and right like flies. It's always *you* pushing *them* away."

"And we finally understand why. No one measured up to Jake. No one ever will. I'm doomed."

"Don't worry. You're going to be heartbroken for a while. Then you're going to start dating again and have the time of your life. Until one day, you'll meet your real soul mate and you'll live happily ever after."

I punch her on the shoulder. "That speech was for you… it doesn't apply to me."

"Why?"

"I've already met my soul mate, and I let him go. Here come the palpitations again; please, can we change the subject?"

"It gives me palpitations that I'll need a new house," Amelia sighs.

My mood instantly brightens. "Oh, that's true. You'll have to move out. It's perfect!"

"What do you mean, it's perfect? With the rates in London, I won't be able to afford a house on my own. I'm going to need roommates again. I don't want roommates! I was supposed to be starting my adult life with my husband, not looking for flat shares."

"Yes, you're going to have *a* roommate, and it's going to be awesome!"

"Are you crazy?"

"No, I'm asking you to move in with me. Naomi's sublease expires in two weeks and I'm kicking her out. I was going to live alone, but having you as a roommate is going to be so much fun!"

"Are you serious?"

"I am."

"Oh my gosh, and you have two bathrooms! I love you."

"Me too."

"Oh."

"Not the oh again. What's going on?"

"My furniture. I'd just finished redecorating the house, and it was so beautiful. And now we'll have to sell it. My home," she wails. "Is it bad I'm more heartbroken over my new furniture than over losing

William?"

"Since you can buy all the new furniture you want, I'd say it's not bad at all. Come on, we're going to have a blast living together."

"Thank goodness you're here. You saved me today, and I know how much it cost you. I'll never be able to repay you."

"Shut up, you're making me cry. Come here." I hug Amelia and she hugs me back. We cling to each other like never before. Because right now, each other's all we have.

Seven

Fumé Blanc

♥♥♥

Saturday, June 10—Yountville, California

I take another sip of wine from my chilled glass. "This tastes wonderful!" I'm having dinner with Jake in the cutest bistro in the core of the Napa Valley. We're dining outside with a view of the sun setting over the beautiful vineyards below us. The atmosphere couldn't be more surreal.

"I'm glad to see it's not just a fancy name," Jake says.

"A fancy name? What do you mean?"

"When Robert Mondavi created the Fumé Blanc, he did it because he was sure he'd made a wonderful wine, and since Sauvignon Blanc had a bad reputation at the time, he changed the name. I was curious to try it after hearing the story. Good to know it's not just an average wine with an expensive name."

"Definitely not average. This place is too beautiful to produce average wines."

"I know. That's why I wanted to g—" Jake stops and looks at me, embarrassed.

"Get married here?" I finish the sentence for him.

He nods.

A server arrives to take our orders, interrupting the tense moment. Once he's gone, I resume the conversation.

"Should we leave the awkward topics for after the appetizers, or rip the Band-Aid?"

"I'm a doctor; my professional opinion is to rip the Band-Aid."

"Rip it is. I'm sure we both have so many questions… how about we take turns?"

"Ladies first," Jake replies with a dashing smile.

"How long have you been with…?"

"Sharon, her name's Sharon."

Oh, what a pretty name. "So, how long have you been with Sharon?"

"Two years, we've been engaged for one."

"Are you in love with her?"

"I thought I was. I wouldn't have proposed to her otherwise. But I always knew she was second best." He gives me a long stare, and my stomach does weird things in response. "I care for Sharon, and I'm sorry I just broke her heart in a horrible way. She probably hates me right now. But it was the only thing to do. It's probably better it happened today than getting a divorce later."

"So you don't—"

"I thought it was my turn now."

"Yeah, it is. Go ahead."

"Are you moving to California?"

"Oh, wow." I should've remembered that about Jake. He likes direct questions. "I haven't planned anything yet. This morning I didn't even know if I was flying here or going to Amelia's wedding instead. But as I said, I don't care where I live. I could pass the bar here. It'd take me a while—I hear it's tough in California, but why not? Would you want me to move here?"

"So you don't care about your job anymore?"

"It's not that I don't care about my job. But I've had time to put things into perspective. I'm not an idealist kid fresh out of college who thinks she'll conquer the world. I love what I do, I'm great at it, and winning a case is still better than sex sometimes."

Jake raises a skeptical eyebrow at this.

"But in the end, a job is just that: a job. A job doesn't hug you when you come home at night, a job doesn't kiss you goodnight, and a job doesn't tell you about the Fumé Blancs of the world…"

"Oh, I see, so you want me only for my wine expertise," Jake teases.

Our orders arrive, and we eat in silence for a while. When I can't stand it anymore, I look up at him.

"My turn again." I take a deep breath and fire the question I've been burning to ask for three years. "Why did you care more about your job than you did about me—about us?"

"I never cared about my career more than I did about you. I just…" He pauses and stares at the sky for a long time before focusing his gray eyes back on me. "I took you for granted. I never thought you'd leave. And when you did… I knew it was wrong to expect you'd always put my needs and my job first. I knew it was my turn to give up something. I would've left. For you, of course I would have. You never gave me that chance. You just disappeared…"

"You knew where I was."

"Yes, I knew. But you completely cutting me out of your life wasn't exactly encouraging! And… I was mad at you for leaving and never looking back."

The conversation's getting heated; I try to smooth the tones. "So, basically, we've both just been very proud and very stupid."

I smile nervously. His jaw relaxes, and he smiles back.

"You haven't answered my question," I say.

"What question?"

"Would you want me to move here?"

"No," he replies, decisively.

Oh. My heart falls into the pit of my stomach.

"It's my turn to haul my ass to where you are," Jake adds.

My heart is immediately back in my chest and pulsating at a crazy tempo. "Are you saying what I think you're saying?"

"I don't know. What do you think I'm saying?" Jake flashes me a wicked lopsided grin. It makes him look like the boy I fell in love with so many years ago. Besides my heart racing, now there's some fluttering in my belly too.

"That you're moving to London?" I ask tentatively.

He winks at me before taking a sip of wine. "The London Clinic contacted me about a research job opportunity a while ago. I didn't give it much thought at the time. But now, it feels almost like it was destiny."

"It does. It'd be so perfect! You could move in with me—I'm kicking out my roommate from hell in two weeks when her sublease expires. I've already given her notice. You could move right in." I stop abruptly and blush bright red. "If that's what you want… if it's too much, too soon." I'm babbling. "If you need some space to… I don't know. What's the recovery protocol after a broken engagement?"

Jake throws his head back and roars with laughter.

"What's so funny?"

He shakes his head. "I'd forgotten…"

"What?"

"What it's like to be around you… how cute you are… how much…" he stops.

"How much w-what?"

He looks me straight in the eyes. "How much I love you."

Eeeeeeeeee. I could die happy now. Jake's stare on me is so intense it fries my brain.

"I love you too. So, so much. I'm so sorry I've waited this long to come tell you… we wasted so much time…"

"We're not going to waste another day. I'd be happy to move in with you."

I beam at him; I've never been this happy.

"So you're not regretting your decision, not even a little?"

"No. I'm sorry for the pain I've caused…"

"Me too," I interrupt him.

"But I couldn't stay. You are who I want. You always have been…"

Unfortunately, my phone rings at this point, interrupting Jake.

"It's my sister," I say. "Do you mind if I pick up? She calls so rarely; it could be important."

"Say hello to her from me."

I mouth "thank you" and slide my finger on the screen to answer.

"Hello."

"Is it true?" my sister asks.

"And hi to you too. Is what true?"

"Did you crash Jake's wedding?"

My eyes widen. "How do you know about that?"

"Gossip travels fast. So, is it true?"

"Mmm-hmm."

She whoops so loudly I have to distance the phone from my ear.

"Are you with him now?"

"Yes."

"Wait, am I interrupting something?"

"Yes, we're having dinner."

"I'll let you get back to your dinner and report to Mom and Dad that you're fine. But call me back soon and let me know if you can spare two days to come down to San Diego since you're already in Cali. I'd love to see you."

"I'll see what I can do. My card's sort of maxed out at the moment, but the balance should refresh in a few days. Now I need to sort out what…" I peek at Jake from under my brows. "What my next steps are going to be."

"All right, I'll leave you to your *sorting*. Have fun and don't do anything I wouldn't do."

"That amounts to more or less nothing."

"That's why I said it. Bye-bye. Love yah, and Jake too."

"Same here. Bye." I end the call.

"So, where were we?" Jake asks.

"Aw, let me see… You were telling me how I was your one and only…"

A ringtone interrupts us again. It's Jake's phone this time. He takes it out of his pocket and looks at the caller ID. "It's my mom. I should probably take this. She's going to be worried sick."

He stands up and says "Hello" into the phone, then walks a few steps away—enough for me not to be able to hear what he's saying. He scratches his head as he talks to his mom. After a few minutes, he's back.

"She wants to talk to you." Jake hands me the phone as he sits down at the table.

I take it with shaking, clammy hands.

"H-hello?"

"Hello, Gemma, my dear."

"Hello, Mrs. Wilder."

"Jake's my eldest son, and he was getting married today."

"Mrs. Wilder, I'm sorry for…"

"No need to be," she cuts me off. "I always knew you were the right woman for him."

"Oh, wow. Thank you."

"But as I said, today was Jake's wedding day… Just know I expect to have grandkids sooner rather than later."

"Aw, well…" I don't know what to say.

"Have a nice evening, Gemma."

"Yeah, you too, Mrs. Wilder."

She hangs up. I stare at Jake, petrified.

"That bad?" he asks. "What did she want to tell you?"

"That she expects grandkids!"

Jake laughs again. "Poor woman, I guess today was quite a shock for her."

"What did she tell you?"

"Oh, just mundane details." He waves me off.

"Like what?"

"Like Edward's going to my house to get all my things before Sharon burns everything."

I bring my hand to my mouth. "Jake, I'm so sorry. I've ruined her life, haven't I?"

From across the table, Jake takes my hand away from my mouth and into his hands. He brushes his thumbs on my palm in soothing circles. "You didn't ruin her life. I did. I did it when I proposed to her knowing that deep in my heart she wasn't the woman I wanted. I did this, not you. In the end, it will be better for Sharon this way. Trust me."

"I feel horrible to be this happy at someone else's expense."

"This one's on me."

A server arrives with the check, and I'm grateful for the interruption.

"Where are you staying tonight?" Jake asks.

"No idea. I didn't book a hotel, I don't have any money, and the only clean clothes I have left are the ones Edward was able to salvage from the moat." Jake's brother was the one who organized our escape from the castle. He retrieved my bag, procured a car, and made sure we made our way out unseen.

Jake chuckles again.

"What about you?" I ask.

"I was supposed to be on my way to Aruba right now and my house is definitely off limits." I tense again. "But, unlike you, I have a working credit card." Jake smiles, vanishing my anxiety. "We can check into a hotel." He wiggles his eyebrows at me jokingly and I blush despite myself.

"I'm not sure I should go to a hotel with you. You look like someone with bad intentions," I say, standing up.

His eyes darken as he stands next to me. "Do I?" he says innocently.

I melt under his stare. "Let's go," I whisper.

Eight

Ashes

♦♦♦

Sunday, June 11—Cabo San Lucas, Mexico

"Make it stop," I moan, as an annoying sound makes my head pound.

"It's your phone. You make it stop," a female someone complains next to me.

I'm on the edge of a double bed with expensive, pristine white sheets, which attack my sore eyes with their brightness as I pull one eyelid open to have a look around to figure out what the hell is going on. I spy a semi-naked woman sleeping next to me. It's Amelia.

I roll over the bed, whining. Last night, drowning our pain in alcohol seemed like the best of ideas. This morning, not so much. I tumble off the bed and crawl on the floor on my hands and knees, looking for my phone while trying to keep my eyes almost completely shut, relying on my hearing instead.

I locate the phone somewhere at the foot of the bed and answer without looking at the caller ID.

"What?"

"And good morning to you too," says a voice that sounds disturbingly like my mother's, but not quite the same.

"Who's this?"

"I should be offended you don't recognize me, but by the slur in your words, I'm assuming you're drunk—or, more likely, hungover, given the time, so I forgive you. It's your dear younger sister."

"Kassandra," I whisper.

"Yep, the one and only."

"What do you want?"

"Where are you?"

"In Mexico."

"Mexico, where?"

"In a honeymoon suite somewhere."

"So it's true, you crashed Amelia's wedding?"

"Mmm-mmm."

"You two are the gossip of Chicago. How is she?"

"Blissfully sleeping and not talking to an annoying sister."

"She doesn't have a sister. Why do you sound so grumpy, anyway?"

"I'm suffering."

"More like you're wasted. Did you get drunk out of solidarity?"

"No, I have my own problems."

"What problems?"

I'm still too drunk to have brain-to-mouth filters, so I just say it.

"Jake got married yesterday."

Silence on the line. I relish the pause. By the time Kassie speaks, I'm almost asleep again.

"I'm sorry," she says.

I half-mumble, half-yawn something unintelligible.

"So you're in Mexico. You went with Amelia on her honeymoon. You're both sad, heartbroken, and drunk. I'm coming over before you two commit suicide. Give me the name of your hotel."

"I'm not giving you anything."

"Gemma Cecelia Dawson." This sounds even more like our mom.

"You're the younger sister; you don't get to Gemma-Cecelia-Dawson me."

"Yes, I do. Because the older sister's acting worse than a pubescent teen. Out with the hotel name."

"I don't remember it."

"What did we send you to Law School for? Use your brains, Gemma. Search for a towel, a pad, or something with the name of the hotel on it."

"You didn't send me to Law School. Hold on…"

I crawl back to the side of the bed, grope the nightstand for a notepad, and read the engraved name aloud,

"Las Ventanas al Paraiso, Cabo San Lucas…"

"Cabo, uh? Cool. How do you spell bentanas?"

"What did we send you to UCSD for if you can't even spell windows in Spanish?"

"You didn't send me anywhere. Okay, I've taken the name down. How long are you staying?"

"Two weeks."

"Perfect. I'll be there in two days, and I'll bring a friend."

"Wait, are you seriously coming over here? Don't you have to study or something? Isn't it too expensive?"

"I can take a break from studying. And it's not Spring Break; flights from San Diego to Cabo are pretty cheap."

"Is your friend a she?"

"Yeah, why?"

"We don't want any testosterone around. This honeymoon is a testosterone-free zone."

"See yah in two days, Gem."

"Whatever." I hang up, climb back into bed and pass out.

***

Kassandra and her friend, Lucy, fly here two days later and they really are a breath of fresh air in our funeral party. They force us to get out of the room—they call it sun therapy, they make us eat our vegetables, they take us to visit the towns nearby, and they give us pot to smoke—they call it laughing therapy. Normally, I would censure this behavior, but if the only thing that can get me in "high spirits" is getting high, I'll cut a break on disapproval.

Kassandra's a free spirit, much more than I was in my wildest days. And I need her vitality, her energy, to pull through these first days of my new Jake-free life.

Two weeks later, on our last night at the resort, I'm having a cocktail with my sister on the patio. We're cozily settled in plush chaise lounges, gazing at the ocean.

"Thank you for coming here." I look at Kassandra. "I know I don't say it enough, but I love you."

"Aw, puh-leeease. I can take a five-star vacation anytime you need me to."

"I know, but I also know you have your life in San Diego. And you can say what you like about this not being Spring Break, but if Mom and Dad give you the same allowance they gave me in college, this must've been a stretch on your finances."

She mumbles something and hides her face in her cocktail glass.

"What's with the guilty face?" I ask her.

"Mom and Dad helped fund this trip," she confesses.

"How come?"

"I told them why you were here and they were worried."

"You told them about Amelia's wedding?"

"No." Pause. "The other wedding."

I laugh despite myself. "Gosh, you sound like *Harry Potter*."

"Why? They had weddings in *Harry Potter*?"

"Just one, but you said the 'other wedding', like the 'other ministry.'"

"Gemma…"

"Uh?"

"You're such a nerd."

"So I get heartbroken and you get a free vacation?"

"Come on, Mom and Dad were just worried. They didn't want you to be alone."

"I wasn't alone."

"Ames was hardly going to play cheerleader. We're family, and I was a two-hour flight away from you, which doesn't happen that often lately. I miss you."

"I miss you too. You should take up my offer and come to visit me in London. It's a fun city, I promise."

"And I promise I'll come, someday. How are you, really? Can I send you back alone?"

"I'm not going to kill myself, I swear. You've done a great job; we would've been a sad party without you. I'm going to be all right."

"Can I ask you something?"

"I'm not going to like this 'something', uh?"

"If you loved him so much, why did you break up with him?"

"I was proud and stupid and didn't realize how much I needed him. Somehow I always thought I could get him back if I really wanted to."

"And in all this time you never realized how much he meant to you?"

"Not until I found out he was getting married. What can I say? Hindsight's a bitch!"

"A real bitch. I'm going to miss you tomorrow."

I hug her from across our chaise lounge.

"Now get up, old you," Kassandra says, hopping out of the chair. "I have wild plans for our last night in paradise." She pulls me up and turns the dock station volume to only-college-kids-wouldn't-think-this-is-too-loud. We get ready inside our room, dancing, singing, drinking, and laughing.

***

I arrive in London in the early evening the next day.

"Are you sure you're going to be okay?" I ask Amelia as the chill—compared to Mexico—air outside London City Airport hits us.

"Yeah. Will said he's going to keep away from the house for at least two weeks, giving me enough time to pack."

I suspect Will's spending those two weeks in New York with Esther, but I don't say anything.

"We'll put the house on the market right away. How about you?"

"I'm going to have a quiet weekend before it's back to life as usual on Monday."

"You want to do something?"

"No, I need a couple of days by myself."

"To mourn Jake?"

I nod.

"Well, the only way to go from here is up. For the both of us." Amelia hugs me and hops into a taxi. I take the one after hers.

As I push the door of my apartment open and drop my bag to the floor, I feel like a failure. Naomi moved out while I was in Mexico, so the apartment's completely empty. I stroll into her room and take in the mess she's left behind; she didn't bother to clean. Garbage and no-longer-wanted clothes are scattered everywhere on the floor. But I'm too depressed to get angry, and anyway, I'm so glad she's out of the house that I don't care about the amount of trash she's left for me to clean.

I walk back to the kitchen and open the fridge. The only things inside it are a huge ice cream tub and some cans of diet Coke. I couldn't have hoped for anything better. I don't care that massively enlarging my derriere with ice cream probably isn't a good idea. I need comfort food. I sit on the couch and scarf down as much cookie dough as my stomach can hold. High on sugar and fats, I wander into my bedroom and take a box out from under the bed. On the lid, I've glued a picture of a jukebox. Where the word 'jukebox' should have been, a name's spelled out of letters cut from magazines: Jakebox. I know, my teenage self had a cunning sense of humor.

I take the Jakebox into the living room, put 'Since U Been Gone' by Kelly Clarkson on replay on my iPod, light a fire in the fireplace, and sit in front of it. I take a deep breath before lifting the lid of the Jakebox. My heart starts beating violently as I stare at all the mementos of my life with Jake, years' worth of memories. I'm glad I have physical things I can burn. What do teenagers who have grown up in the era of Facebook do when they break up with the love of their life, plan an assassination on Mark Zuckerberg?

On a first look inside the Jakebox, I see some solid items I can't burn, so I take the trash bin from the kitchen, bring it back to the love-bonfire, and start sorting items.

First out of the Jakebox are the tickets from our first movie night, *Kill Bill: Volume II*. Also the night of our first kiss. *Fire.*

The *Kill Bill: Volume II* DVD itself is the next item. *Bin.*

Next is a sheet of crumpled paper Jake passed me in class the first year we dated. On top, it says, "*Prom?*" Below are two choice squares, one says, "*Yes,*" and the other says, "*Yes.*" I marked both of them and stamped a lipstick kiss underneath. *Fire.*

Next, little plastic golden miniatures of the Little Mermaid and Prince Eric from a Happy Meal surprise. I was obsessed by the Little Mermaid miniature because I couldn't find it anywhere and Jake ate

McDonald's for a month to get me one. *Bin*.

Next, a blank card sprayed with his aftershave. I made it when I moved to Boston. I remember sniffing it whenever I missed Jake. I lift it to my nose. It's faint, but Jake's aftershave's still there. *Fire*.

Next, a ton of photos. I leaf through them, scattering them on the floor. There's everything: proms, graduations, concerts, vacations, everyday life. One, in particular, catches my eye. It's my favorite picture of Jake. I took it the first night we made love. We were at his parents' cabin at the lake. It's a shot of him from the chest up. The photo's a bit dark because Jake had the sun behind him, but his face is still visible. He's shirtless and has one arm raised above his head, braced on a tree branch. He's wearing a surfer necklace, a present from me for his birthday, which he thought was super cool. He never took it off all that summer. His face is tilted to the right, and he's smiling a crooked smile. I'm not sure why I love this picture so much, but it's… it's just Jake. My Jake. He wasn't posing or anything; he'd just looked up at me calling him when I shot this and it's as if his face is lit with love, happiness, and youth. I drop the picture back on the pile on the floor, staring at it, still overwhelmed. That's when I start sobbing. Tears blind me and rain down on the pictures. Out of rage and scorn, I collect the photos in my arms and throw them all in the fire.

Next, I pick up a stone in the shape of a heart. From a vacation somewhere. I hurl it at the bin.

Next, a sheet of paper where Jake copied the lyrics of *I Want to Know What Love Is* for me. *Fire*.

Next, a bunch of tickets: planes, movies, school dances, and concerts. Different years, different cities… still us. *Fire*.

A CD compilation Jake made me. We still used CDs, bless us. *Bin*.

A postcard of Hawaii. We promised we wouldn't go there, not until we got married and we went on our honeymoon. *Fire*.

Seashells from a day at the beach. *Bin*.

A letter. I can't open it. Jake sent it after we broke up, pouring his heart into it and begging me to take him back. I honestly don't understand how I could not have replied. Why did I let him go? Why was I so damn proud and stupid? Why? *Fire*.

A page from my old diary. Despite my better judgment, I read this one.

> Dear Diary,
>
> For the first time in my life, I'm in love. How can I tell I'm in love for sure? Because Jake asked me to come watch his soccer practice and you know I hate soccer. It's soooooo boring. But today instead of being bored out of my mind, I'm just happy. And soccer seems like the best thing in the world.
>
> I'm happy for the way Jake's eyes search mine on the stands before anyone else after he's scored. I'm happy for the little flutter in my belly I get every time he waves at me. And I'm happy because last night Jake kissed me, and it was the best kiss ever. Not that I've kissed anyone else before, but I'm sure Jake's the best kisser in the world.
>
> I love him soooooo much. I love him sooo, soooooo much. I told him last night after the kiss. And he said it back. I'm in love. We're in love. I'm soooooooooooo happy.

Underneath there's a Gemma-loves-Jake doodle. But Kelly Clarkson is my queen, and the only thing I'm *soooooo* going to do right now is move on. *Fire*.

Next is the first rose Jake gave me, exsiccated. Can I burn this? Better not take chances. *Bin*.

Lining the bottom of the Jakebox is the wrapping paper from the first Christmas present he gave me. I can't believe I kept this. *Fire*.

That's all, folks.

I tie a couple of tight knots on the black garbage bag resting inside the bin. I run outside to throw it in the trash before I can change my mind and try to retrieve something. When I get back inside the apartment, the only thing left is the actual Jakebox. I burn the bottom first. I take the lid in my hands and trace Jake's name with my fingers and then I throw the cover in the fire too. It stays there unscathed, suspended in time for a few seconds before the letters start to blacken and blur—I'm not sure if it's due to the fire or the tears in my eyes, or both. It doesn't matter anyway because, in five minutes, it all turns to ashes.

Nine

Dinner Talk

♥♥♥

Thursday, June 29—London

In my apartment, I cup Jake's face and kiss him. "I can't believe you're really here." It took him three weeks to settle all his things in California, pack his stuff, and join me in the U.K. Meanwhile, I went to visit my sister in San Diego and I got back to London in time to clean the mess Naomi—my former roommate from hell—had left hanging around.

"I can't wait to show you London. You're going to love it."

"Not as much as I love you." He kisses the tip of my nose.

"Were you able to bring everything?"

"I've brought the essentials, my mom's selling whatever I've left in Cali, and the rest's arriving by cargo ship next month."

"You have much? Because my place isn't that big."

"Don't worry; I won't steal your closet space."

"So, err… Sharon didn't burn anything?"

"No. She didn't."

"Did you see her?"

"I did."

"And?"

"She was tanned. She went on our honeymoon with her bridesmaids."

"That's not what I'm asking."

"She was fine, really. Hurt, but on the mend. I apologized; I owed it to her. She's very rational; she understands what happened. She said it probably saved us from divorcing in a few years."

"I wish I could apologize too."

"She's rational, not a saint. You'd better steer clear for at least twenty years."

"I feel horrible for what I did to her."

"Come here." Jake grabs me and I melt into his arms. "She'll be fine. She's going to meet the right guy for her, and when that happens, she'll be grateful to you too."

I let him soothe me. "Was your family upset you're moving here?"

"No. It's a bit farther away than San Francisco, but it's not like I was exactly living at home even before. So it's not much of a change for them. A couple more hours on a plane when they visit. That's all."

"So they don't hate me for ruining your wedding and hauling you to another continent?"

"No, definitely not. My mom was happy. She'd given me a speech about 'unresolved things' before the wedding. And I see now she was probably talking about you."

"You think?"

"I'm pretty sure. She said she knew I wasn't going to marry Sharon the moment you burst into the room, followed by security."

"Aw, gosh. Don't make me think about bouncer guy. So your family's happy about us?"

"If I'm happy, they're happy." Jake leans in and kisses me again.

After the kiss, I decide to change the subject and shake off the moping mood. "Are you jetlagged?"

"No, not too much. Why?"

"Amelia invited us to dinner at her place tomorrow night. I know you just got here and that you begin work on Monday, but I haven't seen Amelia in forever and I ditched her wedding to… well… crash yours. So it'd be great if we could go. But if you don't want to, I can tell her to rain check for next week."

"No, tomorrow's fine. I want to see Amelia; it's been ages for me too. And her husband could become a good friend."

"Are you missing California already?" I ask, worried.

"No, but I've lived there for a decade. Most of my friends are there. It's weird living in a city where I don't know anyone except you and Amelia."

"London will swipe you in like a tornado. You'll see. There are so many people here, it's impossible not to make friends."

***

The next evening we're standing in front of Amelia's door with a bottle of wine and a handful of good expectations for the night. But as William opens the door to let us in, all my optimism is crushed.

William's being perfectly nice and polite. He smiles, shakes Jake's hand with an attitude of male comradeship, hugs me, offers us wine… but something's off. I can feel an emphatic wave of awkwardness coming from him. As perfect as all his gestures are, they don't feel sincere. It's as if he wishes he were anywhere but here. I'm probably over-analyzing as always and he's just tired after a week at work. Maybe tonight he wanted to stretch on the couch watching a movie instead of having to entertain guests.

"Gemma." Amelia launches herself at me and crushes me in a hug. Now, this is a heartfelt greeting. "I've missed you so much!"

"Me too. Ames, I'm so sorry I missed your wedding."

"Don't. You don't need to apologize; you had a very good reason." She lets me go and shifts her attention to Jake. "Come here, you very good reason," she tells him. "I've missed you too." They hug. "It was about time you two came to your senses and stopped wasting your lives."

"Still bossy, are we?" Jake teases.

"As always. Please sit down; I'll bring the appetizers in a second."

As the night proceeds, I can't shake the sensation that something's off between Will and Amelia. It's nothing they do, more what they don't do. They never touch, they never kiss—and I'm not saying they should make out at the dinner table, but I expected a newly wedded couple to be at least a little overbearing in the PDA department. They never look at each other, like *at all*. I try all evening to convince myself it's just my imagination, and that I'm reading signals where there's nothing to read—at least until William drops a conversational bomb on the table.

"So Jake," he says, "would you say calling off your wedding was the best decision you could have made?"

I stare at him dumbfounded. Did he really just ask that? I look at Jake; he's taken aback by the question, but he's recovering fast.

"It was the best decision I could have made given the circumstances. I should probably have realized I was making a mistake way sooner than the day I walked down the aisle."

"Mmm," William presses him. "But even after you realised it was a mistake, didn't you feel the pressure of your family, her family, your friends?"

Why's Will insisting so much on this topic? What's he playing at? Why does he keep asking Jake about his once-was-wife-to-be? As if she wasn't enough of a skeleton in our closet already. I know Jake doesn't have any regrets, but the less he thinks about Sharon and what we did to her, the better.

"Will, maybe Jake doesn't want to discuss this particular topic over dinner," Amelia chides her husband.

"No, it's okay," Jake says. "I guess it was the elephant in the room." I love him so much for how he owns the situation. "And to answer your question, I didn't have much time to feel the pressure. It was a split second decision. I knew what I should do, what I wanted to do, and I did it."

"T-that's admirable," William says. Then he grabs his glass of wine and downs it.

The awkwardness at the table has spiked to new heights.

"Well," Amelia says, looking mortified. "It's time to serve the main course." She gets up and starts collecting our empty salad plates.

"I'll help you," I say. I take my and Jake's plates and follow her into the kitchen. "Hey."

"Hey."

"Is everything all right?" I ask.

She stares at the sink for a while before answering. "Yes, and no. Everything seems perfect on the surface. But deep down, something's wrong."

"Is it William?"

"He's a big part, but it's not just him. It's… not right. It's hard to explain. It's like I've spent the last year on a wedding planning high. And now that my perfect wedding's over, my marriage is… I don't know."

"You don't know, as in?"

"Like yesterday, for example, I tried to think about the last real conversation I had with Will. And I can't remember one that didn't involve flowers, venues, hors d'oeuvres, or some other wedding-related thing."

"But what about the honeymoon? Did you guys have a good time?"

"It was… lovely," Amelia says in a tone between sad and spiteful.

"But it wasn't passionate, or intense, or exciting. It was just mature."

"Was it you, or was it him?"

"It was the both of us. He didn't make an effort. And I couldn't be bothered to make an effort either. I'd rather read beach novels in peace by the pool than make an effort to talk to my husband. And he seemed content looking at his phone all day instead of talking to me. He seems to be attached to the thing these days. He takes it everywhere he goes, even to the bathroom. I might've become jealous of his phone."

"But was this just the honeymoon, or was it also before, after? Maybe you need to relax after all the stress of the wedding."

Amelia bites her lower lip. I read indecision in her features.

"What, honey? You can tell me."

"I've no idea how it was before. It's awful. I've spent the last year obsessing about the wedding, and with work and everything else… I didn't notice Will at all. I'm a horrible person."

"No, you're not. You guys just need some time to adjust."

"I don't know, Gem, I'm having thoughts someone who just got married shouldn't have."

"Like?"

"Like it was a huge mistake. Last night I was having drinks with my colleagues after work, and even though I can't stand half of them when the night was over, I found myself dreading coming home. I didn't want to. What does that say about me? I'm the worst wife ever."

"Come here." I hug her. "It doesn't say anything; it's not as bad as you think, I promise. You love Will. Talk to him. I'm sure you guys can fix whatever's going on with you two."

"Yeah, yeah. You're right; I'm being silly and getting too much into my own head. Okay, let's bring the main course out or the boys will start wondering where we went."

***

"That was…" Jake pauses to find the right word. "Interesting." We're outside, walking toward the Tube to get back home. "But to be honest, I don't think William will become my new BFF."

"You didn't like him, did you?"

"The guy didn't do anything wrong per se. It was just weird."

"Definitely weird."

"What was with all those questions about canceling my wedding?"

"You mean he asked more?"

"While you ladies were in the kitchen, he kept grilling me with all these personal questions. It was crazy."

"I'm so sorry. This probably wasn't the evening you had in mind, uh?"

"What did Amelia say? Is she okay?"

"No, she's not. She senses something's off too. She said she's been neglecting Will for a year to organize the wedding and she feels bad about it. She said he seems more attached to his phone than to her lately."

"Meaning?"

"She said he takes his phone everywhere he goes, even to the bathroom."

Jake lets out a low whistle.

"Why are you whistling?"

"I hate to be the one to break it to you, but when a guy is that attached to his phone, it's because he's got something to hide."

"To hide? Like what?"

Jake throws me a side stare.

"You think there's another woman?"

"I won't lie to you. From the way he kept asking me how I felt for following my heart and, I quote, 'freeing myself from the chains of family's expectations'—yeah—he was talking like a guy who wished he'd done the same thing."

"And left Amelia at the altar?"

"Or before. Or he's thinking about doing it now."

"Did he say something else?"

"Yeah, he asked if it was good to be with the woman I really loved…"

"And you don't think he was talking about Amelia?"

"Somehow, I'm pretty sure he wasn't."

"Oh gosh. And I told her everything would be fine."

"It will be. If they're not right for each other, the sooner they realize it, the better. Believe me, I talk from experience."

"I hope you're right." I stop in front of a set of steps leading underground. "This is our station. Let's go home."

Ten

Team Building

♦♦♦

Wednesday, June 28—London

It takes a lot of work to clean Naomi's mess, but it's as good a distraction as any to keep me busy on the weekend or after work. Any activity is better than no activity as my stupid heart tends to take over and voice its complaints whenever I'm idle. So I'm keeping busy and working myself to exhaustion, both at the office—taking on more cases than any one person could handle, and at home—rubbing clean every small crevice of this apartment until it shines as new.

Right now, I'm helping Amelia move her final boxes into her room. As I deposit the last cardboard box on her bed, Amelia appears on the threshold looking like a human Christmas tree of bags. She comes into her room, kicks a box out of her way with a stiletto-clad foot, and drops all the bags on top of some other boxes before collapsing on the bed.

I take a bottle of white wine out of the fridge, grab two glasses, and join her.

"Celebratory drink?" I ask, offering Amelia one of the glasses.

"What are we celebrating?"

She seems off.

"You moving in with me?"

"To moves!" She clinks her glass against mine with an undecipherable smile and takes a gulp of wine slightly too large to be healthy.

"I sense some bitter-sweetness here. What's going on?"

"William's moving to New York to be with the flight attendant."

"She took him back?"

"Apparently they're soul mates, destined to be together."

"So, are you… mmm… jealous?"

"More bitter." She takes another long sip of wine. "It doesn't seem fair that he gets to cheat on me for a year, ruin my life, and live happily ever after with his mistress. It just isn't fair."

"It isn't fair."

"No. It adds insult to injury. I'd much rather he be miserable and suffering. Am I a horrible person for wishing that?"

"No, just human."

"It's just that, at this point in my life I'm supposed to be shopping for ovulation predictor kits, not I'm-close-to-thirty-single-and-desperate shoes!"

"You bought new shoes?"

"Yep."

"Can I see them?"

"Sure." Amelia gets up and brings to the bed one of the many bags she carried into the apartment. "Here they are."

"Oh my gosh, Ames!" I take the shoes out of the box and they're the sexiest pair of black stilettos I've ever seen. They're wrap-around sandals made of a net of crystal-covered leather. The motif looks like sparkly fish scales. "These aren't I'm-single-and-desperate shoes, these are I'm-smoking-hot-and-you'd-be-lucky-to-kiss-my-toes shoes. Any special occasion?"

"Tomorrow evening I've got drinks with my colleagues. I hate those things, but they're supposed to be for team building, so I've to go. Oh, and you're coming with me."

"Am I? Why?"

"I need a friend there. There's this guy at the office. I hate him, he's worse than William."

As she says this Amelia turns purple.

"Worse than William?" I wonder what a dude could've done to be classified as worse than William, given present circumstances. He must've sunk pretty low. "What did he do?"

"He stole one of my accounts, then he made me cry, and then he kissed me." Amelia pouts and I almost choke on my wine at the kissing part.

"He kissed you?"

"Yeah, the guts of him."

I smirk; something tells me Amelia didn't exactly dislike the kiss.

"Good kisser or bad kisser?"

"Good. I mean, average."

"Uh-huh. And how did you go from the client stealing to the crying to the kissing?"

"He announced the account change this morning at the staff meeting. In front of everyone, *the bastard*."

"He sounds a bit jerky. Is it office policy to steal each other's clients?"

"It's accepted. The partners think it keeps the working environment more lively."

"So he what? He waited for you to be on your honeymoon to steal one of your accounts?"

"Precisely."

"What a D-bag. But why you? Did he want to be mean to you?"

"Yes."

"Why?"

"I guess it was payback."

"Payback for what?"

"For me stealing his biggest client last month," Amelia replies, unconcerned.

"Amelia! You made it sound like he was bad, and you're worse than him."

"At least I had the class not to gloat about it in his face."

"Is that how he made you cry?"

"No, much, much worse."

I stare at her interrogatively.

"Once the meeting was over, he came into my office to gloat. He asked me if I'd liked my wedding present."

I stop mid-sip, shocked. "He didn't."

"He did."

I squeeze her knee.

"That's when I lost it. He was there, standing on my threshold all arrogant and smug, and I'd just found out Will was moving to New York… I threw the first thing I found—a mug—at him and I-I started crying. Ugly, hysterical crying. I couldn't stop myself. I kept sobbing and sobbing."

"And what did he—what's his name?—do?"

"Dylan, his name's Dylan. He came into the office and closed the door."

And the plot thickens.

"He had the nerve to ask me why I was crying. I told him that stealing my client was okay; it was fair game. But mocking me about my failed marriage, or non-wedding, wasn't cool."

"Yeah, not cool."

"Then he asked me what I meant by failed marriage. And I said he could stop pretending he didn't know. Then he asked what was it he was supposed to know. So I screamed in his face that my husband-to-be had cheated on me for a year and that my maid of honor had to tell me while I was at the altar…"

"Yep, I'm familiar with that part of the story. So what did he do then?"

"He asked me if I was married. I said, no. Then he asked me if I was engaged, or seeing someone. And I asked him if he enjoyed being a sadist, and that's when he kissed me."

"Just like that?"

"Just like that. I was yelling at him and he grabbed me by the shoulders and kissed me."

"And you?"

"At first I was so surprised I didn't know what was going on. Then, I might've kissed him back a little bit before I came to my senses, pushed him away, slapped him in the face, and threw him out of my office."

"How's this Dylan in the looks department?"

"He's okay, I guess."

"Mmm. Interesting."

"What's interesting?"

"So you hate the guy?"

"Yes, definitely hate him."

"Even if he's hot, a very good kisser, and clearly into you?"

"He's not into me."

"Why would he kiss you the moment he finds out you're not married or engaged if he's not into you?"

"Maybe it was the only thing he could think of to make me stop screaming at him. And after I slapped him, he's obviously going to hate me even more than he did before."

"Have you seen him after the kissing incident?"

"No, I steered clear of him all day."

"Mmm, I don't know. I'll have to meet him before I can form a complete opinion. Actually, it's good you have a date with him tomorrow night. I can't wait to meet Dylan the kisser."

"It's not a date. It's office drinks."

"Yeah, and that's why you bought take-me-to-bed shoes especially for the occasion."

Amelia smothers me with a pillow.

"What are you going to wear?"

"No idea. You want to help me choose?" she asks, getting up from the bed.

"Sure." I offer my hand, and she pulls me up.

We start digging outfits out of her suitcase. I love girls' nights. And this is such a perfect one I almost don't think about Jake at all. *Almost.*

***

At six-thirty the following evening, we're pushing our way into a posh bar in central London. Amelia's wearing her new shoes and a simple-but-sexy LBD. And since last night we were going through Amelia's wardrobe, I borrowed my outfit from her closet. I'm wearing—drum roll here—a stretch-jersey print dress. A big change from my usual color palette of monochrome boring.

"Let's go to the bar, I need a drink," Amelia suggests.

"Is the kisser already here?" I ask. I can't wait to see this guy.

Amelia takes a quick scan of the room. "No, not yet."

"Drinks it is then." I take her hand and shoulder my way into the crowd.

When we finally reach the bar, I order two martinis and two shots. Amelia needs to loosen up a little. As for me, the more alcohol in me, the less I think about Jake on his honeymoon; Jake moving into his new house with his wife; Jake making love to her… you get the gist.

"Here, shots first!" I take the two glasses and pass one to Amelia.

"I'm not doing shots. Are you crazy?"

"Why not?"

"I don't want to get drunk in front of all my colleagues. I'm already the office joke for what happened with Will. The last thing I need is to embarrass myself further."

"I'm sure no one's making fun of you for what happened."

"No? You're going to find out very soon. Flotsam and Jetsam are coming this way so you can see for yourself how charming my female colleagues are."

"You named them Flotsam and Jetsam? After the Sea Witch minions in *The Little Mermaid*?"

"Yes, Flotsam's the blonde," Amelia whispers before parting her lips in a big, fake smile. "Felicia, Jackie… you made it."

I turn around and choke on a chuckle. If Flotsam and Jetsam had to drink a magic potion and transform into deadly mean girls, Felicia and Jackie would make an excellent representation. They're two thin Prada-clad evil-smiling minions. They even have their arms intertwined just like the eels' tails in the movie, and apparently, they speak in unison too.

"Amelia, so good to see you," they say in high-pitched voices, air kissing my friend.

"And who's your friend?" Jetsam asks.

"Gemma, nice to meet you." I wave to avoid having to shake their hands.

"We were just doing shots." Amelia downs hers and I follow her lead. "You want to join us?"

"Now, Amelia. Shots? Seriously?" Flotsam asks. "Isn't it a jot juvenile?"

"But now that you're newly single," Jetsam picks up the snarky banter, "you're up for a bit of wildness."

"So you two gals are married?" I jump into the conversation.

"No, we're too concentrated on our careers," they reply in chorus.

"We don't want to keep you from your team building then," I say.

"It was so nice meeting you," Flotsam says, moving away.

"So nice," Jetsam echoes and they're gone.

I goggle my eyes at Amelia.

"Told yah. And thanks for the shot—I needed it to survive *that*."

"We can move on to less juvenile drinks." I do an impression of Flotsam's shrill voice and pass Amelia her martini. She grabs the glass and turns around so quickly, her drink sloshes on the bar.

"Hey, careful. You're spilling your drink."

"He's here," Amelia hisses.

"The kisser? Where?"

"Two tall guys at the door, he's the one on the right."

"Who, David Beckham doppelgänger in a suit?"

"He's not David Beckham's doppelgänger!"

"Mmm, I bet he wouldn't look too bad in an underwear ad."

"You're the worst. Next time, you're staying at home. What's he doing?"

"Looking around… as if he's searching for something, and… he's found it!"

"How do you know he's found it?"

"Because he's coming over here."

I watch David Beckham whisper something to his friend before moving decidedly in our direction. I turn around to face the bar as Amelia's already doing.

"What? Talk to me so he'll have to go away."

"Nope. You'll have to talk to him. And I'll be here discreetly listening to all you guys say."

"You're the worst friend ever; you were supposed to come here to…"

"Amelia?" A deep voice coming from behind us interrupts her babbling.

"Dylan," she says coldly, turning around to face him.

I make myself as small and inconspicuous as possible while I hang onto their every word.

"I wanted to talk to you about what happened yesterday."

"Good. I'm glad you came here to apologize."

"Apologize? Why should I apologize? You're the one who slapped me. *You* should apologize."

"You deserved the slap. You stole my account, you made me cry, and then you kissed me!"

"And tell me you didn't like it."

Even though I'm not watching them, I sense he's moved forward, nailing Amelia against the bar. The guy's bold. I like him.

"Of course I didn't like it." She's trying to have an indignant-professional tone, but she's achieving more of a meowing-kitten one.

"So why did you kiss me back?"

"I didn't." There's a moment of silence before Amelia crumbles. "Okay, it was an instinctive reaction. I didn't expect you to kiss me. Why did you kiss me?"

"I've wanted to kiss you since the first day you set foot inside the office."

"But you've never said anything before."

"You've never been single before."

I don't hear Amelia's comeback as I get distracted by a guy next to me.

"Hi, I'm Richard Stratton. I'm supposed to keep you entertained while my mate Dylan chats Amelia up."

I turn toward him. Rumpled dark hair, on the longish side. Dark eyes, strong jaw covered in five o'clock shadow, and his lips are parted in a wicked smile. Is every single one of Amelia's coworkers so damn sexy?

"Gemma Dawson." I give him my cocktail-free hand. "Shouldn't wingmen be more discreet? And you're late. I've already been eavesdropping on their entire conversation."

"What conversation?" Richard throws me a mischievous smile and I turn around to see that indeed Amelia isn't having a conversation anymore. Instead, she's shamelessly making out with Dylan the kisser who's living up to his name. I should probably remind her that she isn't playing seven minutes in heaven in a private closet and that she's in a very public bar with all her colleagues watching. I peek at the back of the bar and immediately spot Flotsam and Jetsam staring at the couple, stone-faced. The green of their envy makes them even more similar to their fishy counterparts. Maybe I should let Amelia have her fun.

I focus on Richard. "You're right. It seems your job here is done."

"So eager to get rid of me?"

"No, sorry. That's not what I meant. I didn't mean to be rude at all."

"And you weren't. You want another drink?"

"Yes, please. A martini."

"So how do you know Amelia?" Richard asks me after ordering

our drinks.

"High school. I moved here a couple of years after her."

"What do you do?"

"I'm a lawyer. You?"

"Wow, tough. I work with Amelia, same marketing agency."

"Of course, sorry, this is supposed to be your office night. I'm the intruder. What do you do at the agency, are you in sales like Amelia?"

"No, I'm head of digital. But, really, it's a bit of everything from client management to searching new business opportunities to managing digital delivery, and I run a tight commercial ship. I work directly with Amelia from time to time."

"Oh, so you're a big shot."

"Nah, not really." He shrugs.

Good-looking, charming, *and* modest.

"What do you think of these team building nights?"

"I guess some have taken their bonding more seriously than others." He chuckles, throwing a look behind my shoulders.

"Right, I feel weird standing here while they make out. Would you mind if we moved to find a table?" I smile at Richard.

"It's going to be difficult here, but if you want, we can go somewhere else. Our friends are not going to miss us."

"Aw, well. I'm not really… I didn't mean it like that. I—uh—don't think it's a good idea. It's totally my fault, not yours."

"Did you really just give me an 'it's not you, it's me' speech five minutes after meeting me?"

Despite the awkwardness, Richard manages to make me smile. "But it really is me and not you. I am a mess."

"How come?"

"How about we move outside *this* bar and I can tell you all about it?"

Richard smiles and shows me the way with his left arm. "After you."

***

"So you wanted to crash your ex-boyfriend's wedding," Richard says. He seems amused by my story. "But you ended up having to crash your best friend's—my colleague Amelia's—one instead. Then you went on her honeymoon with her and now you're roommates. And all of this happened when?"

"In the past three weeks," I chime in. "So you see, it really is me. I've just said goodbye to the love of my life for good and I'm not open to anything new at the moment."

"Amelia was just left at the altar and she doesn't seem to be having much trouble moving on."

"Well, it turned out Amelia hasn't been in love with her fiancé for the longest time. So you see how that might speed up things. Whereas for me, I still have a broken heart."

"And that's why you won't go out on a date with me."

"You never asked me on a date," I protest.

"But if I were to, would you really say no? Not even for a bite or a friendly drink?"

I'm saved from answering by Amelia bursting out of the bar. "There you are." She looks as flustered and in disarray as someone who's been making out in a crowded bar should. "I've been looking for you all over."

"You mean when you were pausing to breathe," I whisper in her ear.

"Richard." She nods at him.

"Amelia, enjoying the office bonding?" he teases.

"Not funny," she mouths at him.

"Dylan, my mate." Richard greets his friend who's also joined us outside. He looks… well, there's only one way to say it: like the cat who got the cream.

"I need to go to the ladies." Amelia tugs at my arm. "We'll be back in a sec," she tells her colleagues and then drags me away.

As soon as we enter the restroom, she starts pacing around with both her hands in her hair, adding to the look of general dishevelment. "Gosh. Oh, gosh. What did I do?"

"Behaved like a horny teenager?" I offer.

"Everybody saw us."

"Yep."

"I'm never going to be able to show my face in the office again. I'll have to change jobs."

"Now, that seems a bit extreme. I'm sure office flings are pretty common."

"*Why*? Why did I do it? I don't even like the guy!"

"Actually, he's not that hard on the eye," I tease. This is the understatement of the year. Dylan's a looker and we both know it.

"You're not helping. And I wasn't talking physically. I literally can't stand the guy. I hate him. So what on earth made me do that?"

"I have three answers for you. Number one: vodka. My fault. Number two: animal instinct. Your fault."

"And number three?"

"The thin line that divides hate from love… it's an easy one to cross. But I'm told hate sex can be interesting. You should give it a try."

"You're definitely not helping. You know me, I'm not this person."

"What person?"

"The person who behaves on impulses without thinking. I've always been good, calm, squared…"

"That doesn't mean it isn't time to become round."

"Are you calling me fat?" Amelia smirks.

"No. I'm just saying the way you've been all your life is not the only way. And you definitely don't *have* to keep behaving a certain way if you don't want to. You can be whoever you want and date whomever you like."

"Easy to talk. But what about you?"

"Me?"

"Yes, you and Richard."

"Uh?"

"Well, he's not hard on the eye either."

"He's just not my type."

Amelia takes a comb out of her clutch bag and pauses in front of the mirror to tame her hair. "How come he's not your type?"

I'm about to say, "*He's not Jake*," when she anticipates me.

"And don't tell me it's because he's not Jake. I want serious reasons."

It's my turn to pace around the bathroom.

"Okay, I don't have any good reason, except that he's not Jake. But don't you see? That's more important than all the good reasons in the world. He's just not him."

Amelia turns around and takes my hands in hers. "Honey, Jake's married. He's gone. He's starting a family with someone else. You've got to let him go."

"I'm not ready."

"You're never going to be ready unless you start. And Richard's a good guy, I promise."

"Well, I've already told him all my Jake drama, so I don't think he's too keen on me right now. Plus, he'd only be a rebound. It wouldn't be fair on him."

"If you've already told him about Jake, it shouldn't be a problem."

"How come?"

"Richard's an adult." She stares in the mirror. "If you told him about Jake, he knows he's risking being a rebound and he's willing to take that chance. So, if he asks you on a date, will you say yes?"

"He's not going to ask." I don't tell Amelia I practically made it clear that I'd say no.

"What if he does?"

"What about Dylan? If he were to ask you on a date, what would you say?"

"That's a completely different matter. I can't start something with a colleague."

"It might be too late for that. So?"

Amelia nods at her reflection and puts away the comb, then looks me straight in the eyes through the mirror.

"I'll say yes to Dylan, if you say yes to Richard."

"He hasn't asked me," I repeat.

"Neither has Dylan. So do we have a deal? If they ask, we both say yes?"

I roll my eyes at her in the mirror. "Deal."

Maybe she's right. I do need to move on eventually, so why not start tonight? At the thought, my body goes through a super concentrated version of a panic attack. In five seconds, my heart skips a beat at the thought of having lost Jake forever. Then my pulse starts racing, bringing along a blind panic that spreads from my stomach to my throat. That's when a shiver goes through me and I force myself to calm down and shake away the feeling. And with that shake, I'm finally back to normal.

As we're exiting the restroom, Flotsam and Jetsam stroll in.

"Amelia," Jetsam speaks first. "We thought you might need to freshen up."

"You really have gone on a wild spree," Flotsam sneers.

I can already see their comments putting doubts in Amelia's pretty head, so I take over. "Excuse us, ladies, but we've got to go back to our dates. You should try one of those. They're *fun*, I promise."

And with that, I push Amelia out of the door and leave Flotsam and Jetsam to stare at their outraged, obnoxious faces in the mirror.

"Oh gosh," Amelia says as we push our way back out of the bar. "I'm never going to hear the end of it. They're going to make my life at the office a nightmare. But did you see their faces?" Amelia giggles. "Totally worth it. I love you."

"And I you."

"And when we were about to despair, they came back." Richard greets us as we get outside. "Ladies, we were thinking about grabbing a bite for dinner. Would you like to join us?"

I look at Richard first, his rumpled brown hair at odds with his square jaw. An open expression on his face, a twinkle in his crinkly eyes. Why not? I need this. I need a handsome guy with an honest face. Even if it's just going to be for a night, a month, or whatever.

Before answering, I observe Dylan and he appears hungry. He's looking at Amelia as if he'd rather have her for dinner. I giggle inwardly. "I'd love to join you for dinner," I say. "But only if we can have burgers. They're my favorites, and I'm craving one."

Richard laughs. "Burgers it is, I know just the place. It's not too far away, we can walk there."

Amelia follows the exchange, slightly taken aback, then smiles and agrees. "Yeah, I could use a burger too. Let's go."

Eleven

Hack Me

♥♥♥

Monday, July 3—London

"Sprinkle the chicken with a generous amount of curry, then submerge it entirely in broth." I read aloud the recipe instructions.

Now that Jake's here living with me, I'm more inspired to be homely, so I'm making us a proper dinner as opposed to my usual of milk and Cheerios. I add the curry and the broth and my next step is… let it rest for half an hour. That's easy!

Fifteen minutes into the resting phase, I hear the key turn in the keyhole.

"Honey, I'm home." Jake appears on the threshold, and for one second I'm overwhelmed all over again by the fact that he's here, living with me. That we're back together. My stomach contracts with a pang of joy and I launch myself at him, kissing him senseless before he even has a chance to close the door behind him. Who knew this much happiness was possible?

As we break the kiss, I bombard him with questions. I'm so anxious for him to fit into his new life.

"How was your day? How's the research center? How are the people? Did you make any friends?"

"Whoa, can I at least get my coat off?"

"Yeah, sorry. I'm just a bit over eager."

"What's this smell? Are you cooking?"

"Yep. Chicken almond curry."

"Why, no milk and Cheerios?"

This reminds me I don't get to do "first impressions" with Jake. He knows me too well. "Not for your first evening back from work." I smile at him. "So, how was it?"

I put the plates on the kitchen bar and Jake starts setting the table without me saying anything. Just as we used to do when we lived together in college. The familiarity of it all puts a warm fuzz in my belly.

"Work was great. It actually went beyond my expectations. The research lab's cutting edge, and the funding is unbelievable. Everyone there is top notch, it's intimidating."

"Means you're top notch too." I give him the glasses. "So did you make any friends?"

"I guess one day is too early to say."

"So no one stood out?"

"No. Well, except for one that I'm pretty sure is going to stick."

"Is he a doctor?"

"No, she's a feisty little thing."

"She?"

"Yeah, she."

"Is *she* beautiful?" I'm menacing him with a wooden spoon.

"Remarkably so."

"And you're telling me this… because?"

Jake comes around the kitchen bar and ruffles my hair. "Because I love messing with you."

"And how exactly is telling me about your feisty and attractive colleague messing with me?"

"She's not a colleague."

"What then? Nurse? Patient? Admin?" I'm trying to think of all the love stories that have ever taken place in *Grey's Anatomy* to evaluate the possible combinations. I know I shouldn't be jealous, but I can't help it. I feel more possessive of Jake than ever before. I'm not sure if it's because I'm older, or because now that I know how it feels to lose him, I don't want to go through it ever again.

"Neither."

"And where did you meet her?"

"In the parking lot."

This doesn't sound right.

"So she's not a colleague, or a nurse, or a patient. Who is she?"

"The right question would be: what is she?"

"Meaning?"

"She's a cat."

"You—horrible you." I start protesting and swatting him, both with my wooden spoon and my free hand, but he suppresses my rebellion, grabbing me by the waist and planting a playful kiss on my lips. "You had me worried there for a second."

"I told you I loved messing with you." He ruffles my hair again and leans in to give me another kiss.

"And you made friends with a cat, how?"

"When I went outside to eat my tuna sandwich lunch, she was standing there in a green patch in the parking lot just outside the hospital. I sat on a bench to eat and she followed me."

"You or the tuna sandwich?"

"Both I guess. Anyway, I patted her, and she purred. Then she started staring at me, keeping the purring going."

"And you fell victim to the purring-staring combo?"

"I did."

"Happens to the best of us. It's impossible not to crumble under the pressure of a kitty stare. So you gave her some of your sandwich."

"Worse. I gave her so much I had to go in and buy a new one, and I ate it in the canteen because I knew that if I went back out, I'd give her my second sandwich too."

"You're so cute." My heart swells with love. What did I do to deserve this man? He's gorgeous, a doctor, and feeds stray cats. He's impossibly kind and very much in love with me. If this is a dream, I never want to wake up. Now that I have Jake back in my life, I could never imagine living without him. A shiver goes through me as I imagine what could have happened if I'd chosen to go to Chicago instead. How horrible and lonely would my life be right now? I shake the thought away.

"You think she's a stray?" I ask.

"Yeah. She was so thin, she looked famished."

"You want to bring her home?"

"I'd say yes, but what if she has kittens hidden somewhere? They'd die without their mom."

"Then I'd better start buying meal sized bags of cat food. You'll have to feed her every day now."

"Do we have something she can eat tomorrow?"

"Here." I give him a can of tuna. "This will do for tomorrow."

"Thanks." He takes the tuna and puts it in his work bag.

"What color is she?"

"Stark white. She's beautiful."

"Did you give her a name?"

"No."

"You have to."

"Okay. She had a regal look, so how about a queen's name? Victoria?"

"It doesn't sound like a kitty name."

"Marie Antoinette?"

"Nah!" I make a disgusted grimace.

"Sisi?"

"Who's that?"

"The Empress of Austria."

"Sisi… it has a good ring to it. Sisi the cat—yeah, I like it."

"Sisi it is then."

"Now, are you ready for your first homemade meal?" I ask, bringing the fuming pan to the table.

"I look at it this way: at the worst, I already work in a hospital."

"Shame on you for making fun of me."

"You always were a good tease, and this smells delicious."

"I still am a good tease. Open the wine."

"Yes, madam. But I can't have more than a glass otherwise I'm toasted in the morning."

"Who, keg-stander Jake?"

"That was nineteen-year-old Jake; this is an older model."

"Still gorgeous."

He gives me a mischievous smile.

"You know, sometimes it's weird how we're the same people, but in a different way," I say.

"You still narrow your eyes when you're trying to say something deep."

"And you still pull up the corner of your mouth whenever you're teasing me."

He pours the wine and raises his glass. "What should we toast?"

"The same people and new beginnings."

"Same people and new beginnings."

As our glasses clink, my phone rings in the background.

I take a sip of wine. "Sorry, I forgot to turn it off."

"Aren't you going to answer?"

"Nah, not during dinner. I'll check it later. It'll stop in a minute."

And it does. Only, a second later it rings again. I shift uncomfortably in my seat, worried it could be work. I don't want to go into the office on my first normal-life night with Jake.

"I don't mind you picking up," Jake says.

"But I do. If it rings a third time, I'll pick up."

It does. I get up.

"It's Amelia. I hope nothing's wrong. Ames?"

"Will's cheating on me."

"Oh, gosh. Are you sure?"

Jake raises his eyebrows at me interrogatively and I twirl my index in a *later* gesture.

"I hacked his computer, I'm pretty sure."

"What? How? With whom?"

"Some woman in New York. He's over there right now… I don't know what to do."

"You want to come over? You want me to come over?"

"Is Jake there?"

"Yes."

"Good, I need the point of view of a guy. I'll be there in twenty."

"All right, sweetheart, see you soon. Bye."

I end the call.

"Amelia's coming over. Will's cheating on her."

"I hate to say I told you so. How did she find out?"

"She hacked his computer."

"You girls want to be alone?"

"No, she said she needs a guy's perspective."

We finish our meal mostly in silence.

"What's bothering you?" Jake asks after a while.

I bite my lip. "This was our first 'new life together' night… I'm sorry it ended so soon."

"Hey, Amelia's our friend, and she needs us. Plus dinner was delicious, thank you for preparing it."

"You really liked it?"

"Cross my heart. And don't worry; we've got all the evenings in the world from now on… I'm not going anywhere."

"How do you know I want to live every moment to the fullest for fear of losing you again?"

"'Cause I feel the same. After all this time, finally being with you feels too good to be true, and I'm scared to death something horrible is going to happen. But it's not. We're here. We're together. Nothing bad is going to happen."

"You promise?"

"I promise."

The doorbell rings.

"All right, let's do this. Could you please clear the plates and pour another glass of wine? Amelia's going to need it."

***

"Read this." Amelia bangs a piece of paper on the now cleared dining table before sitting next to me.

I take the offending document—it's an email print out—and read it.

```
Date: Sun, July 2 at 6:07 AM
From: william.reilly@hotmail.com
To: esther.porter@gmail.com
Subject: Forgive me
```

Esther,
I know I'm probably the last person you want to
hear from, but I couldn't stay away. I can't be
without you. I've been thinking about you every day
since I broke your heart. A part of my body is
missing when I'm not with you. I'll never forget
the first time I saw you; you were crossing the
airport hall, walking briskly in your blue uniform,
your flaming hair bouncing behind you. You were
breathtaking. I fell in love with you from the
first moment I set eyes on you. And I'm sorry for
what I did to you. I'm sorry for not being able to
resist you. I'm sorry for not telling you I was
engaged. And, most of all, I'm sorry for not being
able to follow my heart and be with you. Because
that's where my heart is. In New York, with you.
Not at home with a wife I never talk to. I can't
live trapped in a marriage I don't want with a
woman I don't love. Esther, please forgive me. I
made a mistake. I chose wrong. I can't live without
you, I don't want to. I need you by my side. You're
the only woman I want. I'll figure it out. I messed
up, but I can fix it. I will fix it. Please wait
for me. I'm going to make it right. Please give me
another chance.

Yours always,

William

I reread the email twice before passing the sheet of paper to Jake and looking up at Amelia.

"I really don't know what to say. How did you find this?"

"It wasn't difficult. He left his computer on stand-by. He *wanted* to be caught. This way I'm leaving him and he won't have to do the dirty work."

"Ames, I'm so sorry. When did he leave for New York?"

"Yesterday, at noon. He always leaves on Sundays so he can be in class Monday morning."

"And when did you find this?"

"Last night, but I couldn't call you right away. It was… it was… too much. The way he talks about me. A woman I don't love. Trapped in a marriage… I didn't force him to propose, it was his idea to get married. Then he saw a redhead strolling by in an airport and suddenly I'm the clingy wife."

"Did, hum. Did err… she reply to this?"

"Yes."

"Did you print her answer?"

"No need to. It was a one-liner."

I wait for Amelia to tell me the one line. I have a feeling it's nothing good.

"Her reply was, 'Are you in New York?'"

"Did he reply?"

"No, he must've called her. They're probably making up right now."

"So what are you going to do?"

"All I want to do is yell at him, and he doesn't even have the decency to be here to be yelled at."

"But how do you feel?"

"I'm mad. I'm so angry… I want to smash everything I find in my path."

"Honey, I know you must be heartbroken…"

"I'm not heartbroken."

"What do you mean you're not heartbroken?"

"I told you, I haven't had a real conversation with Will since he proposed. I've been in love with my wedding for the past year and the groom was just an accessory."

"You don't mean that."

"If I'm being honest, yes, I do mean it. I'm afraid my relationship with Will was over a long time ago, only I didn't notice. He noticed, and instead of coming forward and saying it, he chose to have an affair behind my back."

"So all you feel is anger?"

"Anger, bitterness… I'm scared. I don't have a life-plan anymore. I feel cheated of my future and stupid for not knowing something was so terribly wrong. How could I not know? How could I not see it?"

"You're not stupid." It's the first time Jake has spoken since Amelia got here. "Listen, sometimes we're our own worst enemy. We're able to tell ourselves all kind of different lies to keep our heads cozily hidden in the sand. Look at me. I told myself I wasn't in love with Gemma anymore. I was ready to marry someone else just to prove it and force myself to move on. You probably knew something was wrong, and instead of addressing the problem head-on, you subconsciously chose to shift your concentration onto the wedding planning. It's not stupid, it's human."

"So are you saying what Will did was him being human?" Amelia asks viciously.

Jake knows better than to defend William in this particular circumstance. "No, that was evil…"

He smirks. And Amelia, despite herself I can tell, cracks the first smile of the evening.

Suddenly, she gets up, fluttering her hands in the air. "Oh, but I'm not going down quietly. Oh no. I already cheated on him."

My mouth falls open. "You did?"

"You betcha."

"With whom? When? For how long?"

"Oh, nothing serious. It was just a colleague in my office this morning."

"You had sex in your office, *today*?"

"No, I didn't have *sex*. There's this guy I work with, he pity-kissed me."

"Pity-kissed? Explain."

"This guy, Dylan." She starts pacing around the table. "He's a bit of a D-bag, to be honest. Anyway, today during the general staff meeting he announced he'd stolen one of my clients."

"Is that normal?"

"Encouraged even, but that's not the thing. If you steal an account from a colleague, you do it with class. You don't gloat about it."

I have some reservations about Amelia's work ethic, but I don't voice them.

"Instead, just a few sleepless hours after I read that," she points at the incriminating email, "he came into my office and asked me if I'd liked my wedding present."

"No!"

"Yes!"

"What did you do?"

"I threw a mug at him, missed his head by an inch… and then I lost it. I started crying and screaming about cheating bastards."

"And how did you go from the mug-throwing and crying to the kissing?"

"It's a bit confused. Somehow he managed to have me tell him the whole story, then he told me my husband was an idiot and then he pity-kissed me."

"That wasn't a pity-kiss."

I look at Jake for confirmation. He shakes his head, *no*.

"Oh please, I was such a mess it had to be a pity-kiss."

"Probably more of an I'm-into-you-and-I-can't-wait-for-you-to-be-divorced kiss."

"Don't say the D-word," Amelia shrieks. "Twenty-eight and already divorced. I'm worse than Ross in *Friends*."

"I'm sure Ross was already on his second divorce by twenty-eight."

"That hardly makes it better."

"Come here." I pull her onto my lap and hug her. "You're going to be fine. We're going to get through this."

Amelia starts sobbing on my shoulder. "I'm so glad you're here."

"I'm always here for you."

"Listen, can I stay here tonight? I don't want to go back to that house."

"Of course you can stay." I throw an apologetic glance at Jake, but he's nodding his head approvingly. And in this moment, I feel even luckier he's here by my side and more in love than ever.

Twelve

Terminate

♦♦♦

Friday, July 28—London

The working week is over and I'm ready for a cozy night in watching romcoms. I'm already settled on the couch. Amelia has "plans." She didn't tell me what they are, but by the amount of time she's spent in the bathroom, I'm guessing they involve a certain David Beckham doppelgänger.

Ping.

My phone bleeps. I unlock the screen and see with a jolt that it's Richard. This is a surprise. We exchanged numbers the night we met, but I've never texted him, and up until today, he's never texted me either. After a month, I thought he wasn't going to.

I read the text.

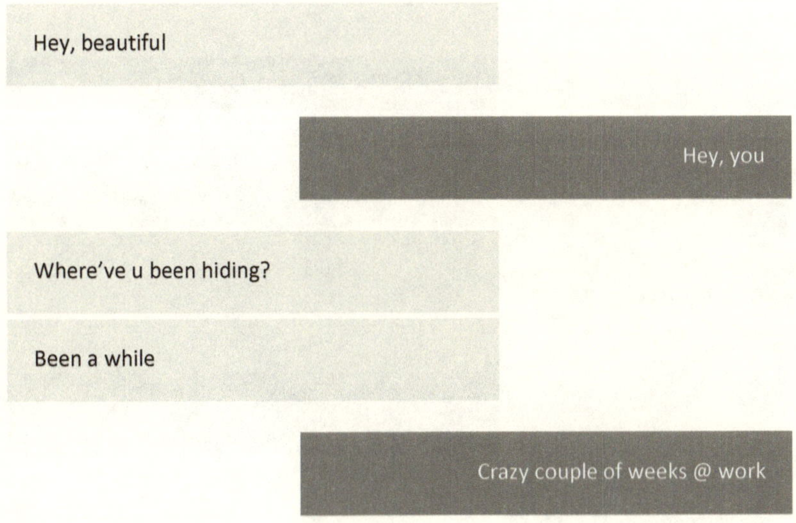

It's as good an excuse as any.

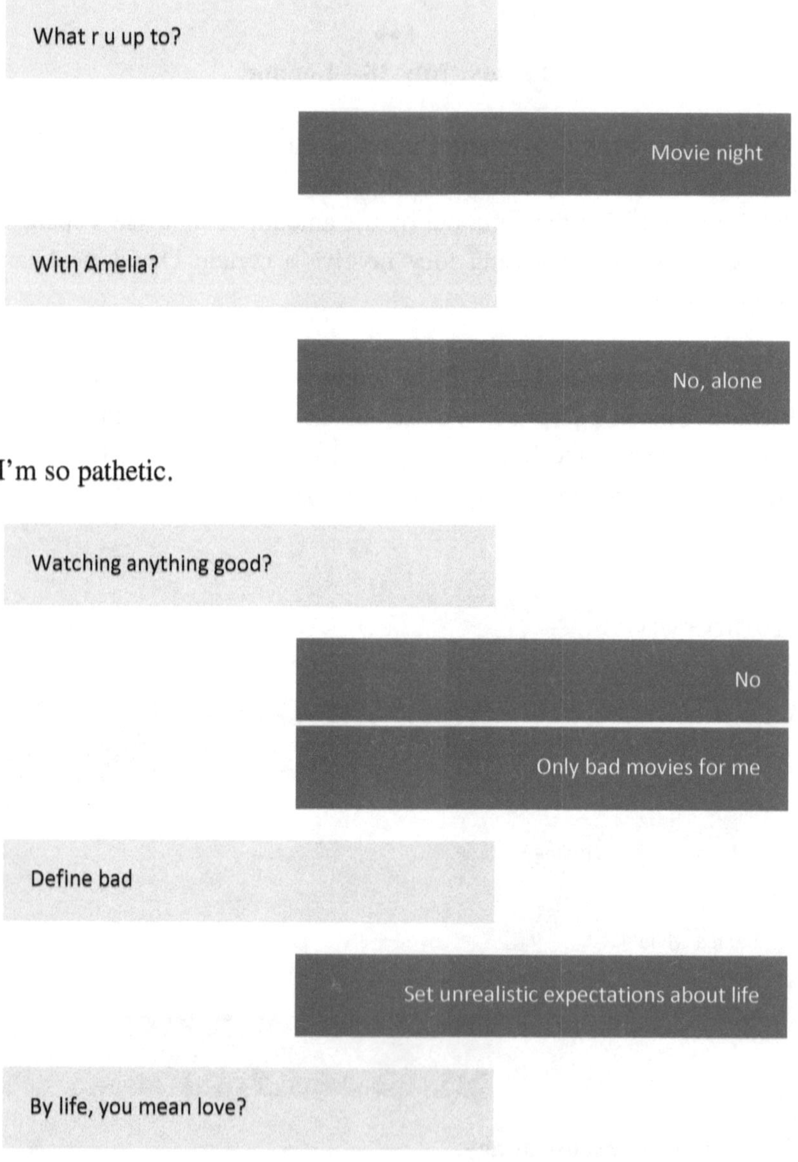

What do I reply? The only thing I can think of is hello, but it seems pretty lame. I bite my lower lip, trying to decide what to write when Richard saves me by texting again.

I'm so pathetic.

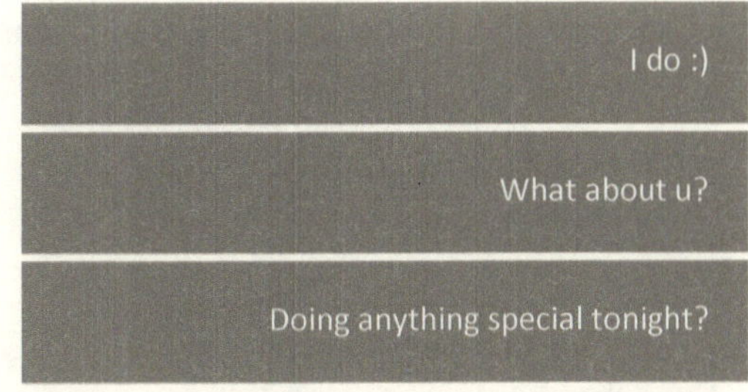

I'm distracted from the screen by Amelia appearing on the living room threshold looking devastatingly hot in an illusion-yoke lace dress. I wolf whistle at her.

"I see we've brought out the heavy artillery. What's the occasion?"

Ping.

"First official date with Dylan," Amelia says, out of breath.

"Oh, so you've finally stopped sneaking to the copy room and made it official?"

"You think I'm wrong? I'm so nervous… This is crazy. I'm crazy. He's a coworker, and it's definitely too early for me to be out there dating. I should cancel. Yeah, I should definitely cancel. This was a bad idea."

Ping.

"It wasn't a bad idea, and you didn't spend two hours getting ready to cancel. Where's the kisser taking you?"

"Stop calling him that. And I don't know, he said it was a surprise."

Ping.

"Who's sending you all these texts, anyway?" Amelia asks.

"Oh, no one."

"No one, uh? Does no one work with me, by any chance?"

"He may. Why? You know something?"

"I may. Let me see."

"No."

We both make a dive for the coffee table, but, stiletto heels notwithstanding, she's quicker in reaching the phone. Her eyes navigate the chat, and before I can stop her, she's typing.

"What are you doing? Stop typing. Give me my phone back."

I'm ready to wrestle it out of her hands when she gives it back.

"There, you're all set for the night."

I quickly read the last three messages from Richard and her reply.

> I was hoping to watch bad movies with a beautiful woman

> Also, I happen to be at Tesco and I've just bought popcorn

> ...Any ideas what I should do with it?

> Why don't you come over?

"You didn't just do that. It makes me seem so forward."

"I so did. You were flirting already on your own. I just gave you a little push."

"Down the cliff. What am I going to do now?"

"I suggest you make your casual homey attire a little more casual-chic and perhaps put on a bit of makeup."

Ping.

"What does he say?" Amelia asks.

"That he'd love to come over. Did you say something about me to Richard?"

"No. He kept asking about you, and I told him that if he wanted to see you all he had to do was ask."

"And when did you decide to use my phone to have me ask him instead?"

"That was a whim."

"Now I'm screwed, and you're the worst friend ever!"

"Now, instead of a night spent moping, you have a hot date. Have fun and don't stay up too late."

She puts on her coat, grabs her bag, and exits the apartment with a wink.

Aaaarrrghhhh! I could kill her.

I rush into the bathroom and throw my pajama top on the floor, kicking it under the sink. I quickly wash my face and armpits, spray myself with deodorant, and apply some concealer and blush. In my room, I switch my sweatpants for skinny jeans and put on a super simple white blouse. I run back into the bathroom, throw my head forward and ruffle my hair with my fingers, hoping to obtain some volume. Amelia, the nerve of her! She spends two hours getting ready for her date and leaves me a twenty-minute warning at best.

The doorbell rings, interrupting my mental bashing of my best friend.

I jerk my head backward and fluff my hair to achieve a perfectly styled messy look. I check myself out in the mirror, and when I'm satisfied with my appearance, I go to open the door.

On the landing, Richard's smiling, holding a Tesco bag in one hand and a paper parcel in the other. Something smells like burgers.

Richard greets me with a smile. "I come bearing gifts."

"What gifts?"

"Oh. I was passing this little kiosk I love; they make the best burger sliders, so I thought I'd buy a few."

"You brought me burgers?" I'm already salivating. "This is *unfair* play, but I like your style." I usher him inside and hug him, feeling slightly awkward.

This is the first time I've seen him after the night we met. And even if that night was cool, we stayed solidly on just-friends territory. I had fun with him, but we didn't kiss or anything. So I feel nervous being alone in my apartment with him. Is this really a date?

I let Richard go, but not before relieving him of the burgers bag. I open it and I'm hit by a divine fragrance of grilled meat. "Can we eat them right away?"

"Sure, I'm a wise man. I wouldn't deny you burgers."

I point at the big table. "Have a seat."

I empty the bag of deliciousness onto a plate and bring two more to the table along with some paper napkins. I don't even wait to be seated before I munch on half a slider.

"So you bring burgers to all your women or is it just me?"

"I'll admit they usually prefer roses, but with you, it seemed a safer bet."

"It was. I'd pick burgers over roses any day. And you should know I'm much more amiable on a full stomach; I haven't had dinner yet."

After dinner, Richard sags onto the couch. "So what are we watching?"

I put a bag of butter popcorn in the microwave and walk toward the TV stand. "Mmm, Amelia bought me a DVD set of eighties movies with Molly Ringwald—she's my favorite actress. So we have: *Pretty in Pink*, *Sixteen Candles*, and *The Breakfast Club*. Any preference?"

Richard smiles bravely and shrugs. "Not really."

Pop. Pop. Po-Pop. The popcorn explodes in the background.

"I'm joking. I wouldn't really subject you to Molly Ringwald night." I smile. "I'm not that evil."

"You had me there. I was scared."

"As for men friendly movies, we have Netflix or," I brush my finger over the DVD shelf, scrolling titles, "I can offer *The Terminator* collection, or we can watch something by Tarantino—I have all his movies except *Kill Bill*." 'Cause I trashed the DVD as it reminded me too much of my ex. No, Jake's a taboo thinking topic tonight. "Or there's the entire *X-Men* saga."

"Since you were set on the eighties, why not watch the first *Terminator*?"

"Great!"

When the popping ends, I put the popcorn in a huge bowl and pass it to Richard. Then, I put the DVD on, turn down the lights, and sit next to him on the couch.

I try to concentrate on the movie, but Richard's presence beside me is too distracting. What's going to happen when the movie's over? What should I do?

I still have feelings for Jake, deep ones. I can't undo them. But if I can't be with him, and that boat has definitely sailed, why not be with Richard? I know I'm not going to fall head over heels in love with him overnight, my stupid heart won't let me. But I could give it a push. I could move on physically before I have emotionally. I've always believed it would be the other way around, but I believed in so many things that in the end weren't true.

I throw a sidelong glance at Richard—his broad shoulders, dark hair, very kissable lips. There's still a giant hole in my chest that seems to grow bigger, instead of smaller, every day. Maybe Richard could fill this hole. Or maybe I don't have the faintest clue who I am or what I need anymore. Or maybe I never knew. Or maybe I need to stop over-analyzing everything and just kiss him.

Tonight I feel stupid and reckless enough to choose the latter option.

***

The next morning Amelia walks back into the house with a smile so wide stamped on her face it makes me want to puke for sugary overflow.

"So," I smirk, thoroughly enjoying her walk of shame, "how was your date with the love maker?"

"Love maker? Seriously?"

"You told me to stop calling him the kisser, and I assume after last night you've evolved to more serious bonding." I grin. "Am I assuming correctly?"

"I don't kiss and tell."

"If you don't, I won't either."

"Wait, you kissed Richard?"

I shrug oh-so-casually. "Maybe."

"No! Tell me everything." She joins me at the kitchen table and I pass her a coffee mug.

"He arrived twenty minutes after you left and he brought me burgers."

"I knew the guy was smart."

"We ate dinner, we watched *Terminator*, and while all the Sarah Connors were being killed, I kissed him."

"You made the first move?"

"I did. But Richard didn't seem displeased about it."

"Is he a good kisser?"

"He's a wonderful kisser."

"Was it only kisses?"

"There was heat, but we stayed solidly on clothes-on ground. He sensed I wasn't one hundred percent ready yet."

"Are you seeing him again?"

"Yes, we have a date next Saturday."

"So you like him?"

"Of course I do. What's not to like? He's handsome, easy going, and he brought me burgers."

"And he kissed some sense into you, apparently."

"He did. Jake's still there in the back of my head. But at least I'm not thinking about him all the time."

Amelia rolls her eyes.

"What about you and Dylan?"

She smiles wickedly and tells me about her night of passion.

Thirteen

Lucky

♥♥♥

Friday, July 28—London

Jake's first month in London doesn't go as smoothly as it could have. My apartment's a bit cramped with three people living in it. We step on each other's toes more often than not, and it isn't exactly the romantic love nest I'd hoped for. But I can tell Amelia's glad she isn't alone in her darkest hours. She needs us after her confrontation with Will. She needs us after meeting with the divorce lawyers—I refer her to the best divorce counselor in town. And she needs us when the house she loves and has invested in so much emotionally, is put on the market.

Lately, Amelia has been more cheerful than one would expect, given the circumstances, and she finally found a nice one-bedroom apartment to rent last week. She seems eager to move out of my apartment and move on with her life. She's already moved most of her things from her old house—which sold three days after they put it on the market—to the new apartment. Right now, I'm helping her pack her last bag of clothes in my spare room before a black cab comes to pick her up in an hour.

"Are you sure you're going to be all right on your own?" I ask her.

"Yes, I'm sure, and…"

She mumbles something unintelligible.

"What was that again?"

"I said Dylan might pop over."

"Dylan the kisser?"

"Mmm-hmm."

"I didn't know he was still in the picture."

"Well, he's been really nice to me since, you know, I threw a mug at him."

"Pottery-throwing is a sure way to a man's heart."

"Anyway, we had a drink the other night after work. And we might've kissed again," she says with a mischievous smile.

There's the reason for the positive attitude. Amelia has a crush!

"Is that the night you came home outrageously late?"

"Yep."

"And here I was worrying they were overworking you at such a stressful time. Instead, there you were making out in bars."

"Guilty as charged. And I may have kissed him at the office a couple more times too. Or a lot more times."

"Oh, gosh. You're having an office romance, this is wonderful. Just what you needed after, err…"

"You mean filing for divorce and waving my ex-husband off to New York to live happily ever after with his mistress?"

"I-I, that's not what…"

"Don't worry, it's okay. We can talk about it. I can even say the word divorcee without shivering too much."

"So this Dylan guy, are we going to meet him?" I steer the conversation away from divorce talk.

"Let me see where this goes. I'm not sure if he's a rebound fling or something more."

"You mean you could potentially see it getting serious?"

"I've no idea, but he makes me feel as if I'm a teenager again. I'm kissing him all over the office, in the halls, outside the restrooms, in the copy room. It's like making out in high school when you had to avoid being caught. It's been so exciting, and he's a breath of fresh air."

"Does he have a Facebook profile?"

"Yes, why?"

"I want to see a pic. Put a face to a name."

"Oh, all right." She takes her phone from the bed where we're folding clothes and taps happily into it. "Here, this is him." She gives me the phone.

"You pulled up David Beckham's fan page."

She takes the phone back to check. "No, this is Dylan's profile picture."

I snatch the phone from her. "You're joking!"

"I'm not."

"Well, well, well… you're in trouble."

"I might be." She blushes.

"You're making out at the office. That's so fun. Have you ever been caught?"

"Yeah, definitely."

"That's not too bad."

"It is. We were spotted by the worst office gossips ever. Flotsam and Jetsam."

"Named after the Sea Witch minions?"

"Yeah, Felicia and Jackie. Two charming ladies, you should meet them. Anyway, it's not all bad they saw us. They were giving me a hard time about the divorce."

"Were they?"

"Yeah, it was mortifying."

"So they've stopped now?"

"Yep, they're too busy spreading the news they caught me having wild sex in the copy room."

"Did they… I mean, were you?"

"No. Of course, not."

"And you don't mind?"

"It's better than divorce sneers, and," Amelia smiles a naughty smile, "Dylan might've caught them gossiping. He told them off pretty harshly. They've been quiet and subdued for a while now. I suspect they both have a crush on him."

"The more you talk about the kisser, the more I like him."

"Well, don't get your hopes up too much. I'm still not sure where it's all going."

"But have you slept with him?"

"No, not yet."

"You plan to?"

"Eventually, if things keep going. I'm a bit scared; Will's the only guy I've slept with in so many years."

"I'm sure Dylan would be more than happy to tutor you." I chuckle.

Amelia swats me playfully. "*If* he sticks."

I don't tell her, but from the way she's radiating happiness, I predict Dylan's going to go a long way.

Amelia closes the zipper on her last bag and we walk to the street corner where we wait for the black cab. When it arrives, I hug her and see her off, telling her to call me if she needs anything and to have as much fun as she can tonight, even if somehow I don't think I need to tell her—Dylan's taking care of that.

When I get back inside the house, Jake has returned from work and he's sitting, shoulders hunched forward, on the couch with a miserable air about him.

"Hey you, why the long face?" I ask, shutting the door behind me. "Is it the prospect of being alone with me again?"

He looks up at me and I see he's white as ash and has a grave expression.

"Jake, what's going on?" I ask, worried.

"Mew." A furry black bundle replies from his lap.

"Who's this little guy?" I do a silly talking-with-babies voice and pick up the black kitty from Jake's lap, bringing it close to my face. "Hello you, you're so cute. Oh, you're so cute." I lower the kitten onto my lap and scratch it behind the ears. It kneads my jeans for a while, purring, then settles in my lap. "Jake, please talk to me. How come you've got a kitty and look so sad? What happened?"

"It's Sisi."

"The hospital stray cat?"

"Yes. She-she died today."

"Oh. How?"

"Hit by a car, but I can't be sure. She was waiting for me in her usual spot. I knew something was wrong at once because she was standing a bit lopsided and she was holding this little guy in her mouth. I crouched down to pat her, and she collapsed almost immediately. She nudged the kitten toward me with her head and she was gone."

"Jake, I'm so sorry."

"I don't know why I'm so sad. Bad things happen every day at work. But the thought that she waited for me, that she trusted me with the most precious thing she had…" Jake shakes his head.

"Pets have a way of getting under our skin in such a powerful way… We're going to take care of this little guy the way Sisi wanted."

"You're all right with keeping him?"

"Him? You're a boy?"

"Mew."

"Can he stay?" Jake repeats.

"Ah! Asking a woman if she wants to keep a kitten is like asking kids if they'd like more toys, or…"

"I get it, I get it. You're okay with the kitten." Jake's furrow relaxes a bit, and he leans on me to pet the tiny cat.

"We should name him," I say.

"I want to call him Lucky."

"You want to call a black kitten Lucky?"

"Yes, because he *is* lucky. He's going to be the most spoiled cat in the world."

"That he is. Lucky, you like it?" I ask the kitten.

"Mew."

"I'll take that as a yes." I scratch him again. "We need to do so many things," I say, turning toward Jake. "We must accessorize the house for kitten needs and we need to find a vet…"

"Come here." Jake pulls me in a side-hug. He brushes the hair away from my forehead. "I love you, you know?"

"I love you too."

"Mew."

"Yes, and we love you too," I say to Lucky.

A warm fuzz spreads in my chest. The family's expanding already, my family with Jake.

Fourteen

After You

◆◆◆
Saturday, August 5—London

The night of our first official date, Richard picks me up in a black cab. I greet him with an embarrassed peck on the lips, blushing madly as I do. I'm a shy person. I know we've kissed already, but this is still too new for me to be completely comfortable or relaxed around him. We get in the car and Richard gives the driver an address in Peckham.

"Where are we going?"

"Since we both love eighties movies, I thought you'd enjoy another one."

"There's a movie theater showing eighties movies?"

I love how I can always discover new things about London.

"Yes, it's an open-air rooftop, actually. They're showing *The Blues Brothers* tonight. You're from Chicago, right?"

"Yes, a small town nearby. I miss Chicago sometimes and I love *The Blues Brothers*!"

"They also have a great rooftop bar, so we can have a casual dinner there too."

"Sounds amazing."

And it does turn out to be amazing. The place, the movie, the sky, the food, it's all perfect. The theater is on top of a tall building with stunning panoramic views of London's skyline, watching one of my favorite movies under the stars, is incredibly romantic. It almost feels like Richard bribed the sky to stay clear of clouds and wink down at us from a million sparkly dots.

We're seated in beach-like chairs that don't allow too much closeness, but it's all right. I'm still debating where I want tonight to end. And being too close to Richard would be distracting. Every now and then, I throw a side-glance at him, taking in all the different expressions he makes that I still don't know. The way his eyes sometimes pop in surprise or the grin pulling at his lips when he's amused but not laughing yet. He's a great guy who's taken me on a perfect first date. Any woman should call herself lucky to be with him. So why can't I stop categorizing him as plan B?

When the movie's over, Richard leads me toward the elevators and we catch an empty one. As soon as the doors close, Richard's lips are on mine. He presses me against the elevator's back and lets go of me only seconds before the doors open again on the main floor. Well, he's definitely not shy. I walk outside, confused, and follow him onto the street where we jump into another black cab.

On the taxi ride home, I've as much buzzing in my belly as in my brain. My lips are still swollen from the kiss, spreading tingles of excitement through me, but the excitement is verging on panic. I have so many questions fluttering in my brain. Like, when we get home should I invite Richard in? Am I ready for third base? Will I ever be ready? Is sex third base or is there a fourth? I always get confused by the bases.

All this second-guessing is weird because I've already been with another man after Jake. His name was Michael, and we dated for a year. So it's not as if sleeping with Richard will be my first time with someone else after I broke up with Jake. Then why does it feel that way? Maybe because last time I'd deluded myself I was over Jake, whereas now I'm painfully aware that no matter how much time has passed, I'm still in love with him.

Richard chooses this moment to brush a thumb over my hand and all my rational thinking gets sidetracked. It feels, mmm, I'm… conflicted. This is one of those classic situations where body and mind—or heart in this case—don't agree. Okay, let's calm down and put the jigsaw pieces together.

Evidence number one: I'm in love with Jake.

Evidence number one-b: Jake's married to another woman and probably making love to her right at this moment.

Evidence number two: Richard's a great kisser, he knows what he's doing, and there's chemistry between us.

Evidence number two-b: I don't need to be already in love with him to sleep with him. I need to let myself fall in love with him one small step at a time. Rome wasn't built in a day.

Evidence number three: I'm not committing to anything for life. It's just one night. Yeah, I should take things on a day-by-day basis from now on. That should be my new life mantra.

Final piece of evidence: Amelia's staying at Dylan's tonight and we could have the apartment all to ourselves.

When the black cab pulls up in front of my building, Richard asks the driver to wait for a second while he says goodbye. Ever the gentleman. I exit the car, chanting in my head over and over again:

To invite him in, or not to invite him in? To invite him in, or not to invite him in?

Richard rounds the car and is at my side in a few quick steps.

To invite him in, or not to invite him in?

"I guess this is goodnight." He cups my head with both hands and gives me the softest kiss.

To invite him in, or not to invite him in?

"I should get going now; want to do something next week?"

To invite him in, or not to invite him in?

"I… yes, I mean. Wait here."

Acting braver than I feel, I walk past Richard, lean forward, and knock on the cab's window. The driver immediately rolls it down.

"Yes, miss?"

"You can go," I tell him.

"You still need to pay me."

"Aw, oh. Yes, sure. Of course…" Why do I always make a fool of myself? I'm fumbling desperately in my purse to find my credit card when Richard pulls out a bill and passes it to the driver through the open window. The driver takes it and zooms away into the night.

"Thanks," I mumble.

He smiles. "You're welcome."

What do I do now? My split-second bravado is already gone.

"So," Richard says.

"So what?"

"You tell me." He chuckles. "You're the one who sent my taxi away."

"I did. Well, I guess now I can't leave you here alone in the street."

"That would be truly cold-hearted."

I take a deep breath. "Would you like to come in?"

"I'd love to."

I smile. "Great."

Move on, I say to myself, *you need to move on*. My new life begins tonight.

Fifteen

Our First Date

♥♥♥

Twelve years before—Chicago area

Gemma placed a black top dangling from its hanger against her chest and stared at her reflection in the mirror. "Black top..." She paused to switch hanger. "Or pink one?"

Amelia, head resting on her hands while she lay on Gemma's bed, scrunched her pretty face at her friend before providing an answer. "The black top makes you look more sophisticated."

"I don't care about sophistication. I want to know what top will get Jake to kiss me."

"You think he's going to kiss you tonight?"

"I thought he was going to kiss me the other night, but he didn't. So what do I know?"

"But last week it wasn't a real date. You just had a walk and sat on a blanket for a while."

"And what's more romantic than sitting by the river stargazing? I still don't know why he didn't kiss me. You think he likes me?"

"Of course he likes you. He wouldn't have asked you on a real date otherwise."

"You're right, this is our official first date. I'm so nervous..."

"Why? I wish I were about to be kissed!" Amelia said, rolling on her back, her gaze lost on the ceiling, daydreaming.

"You would be if you'd agreed to go out with Teddy Parker."

"I don't like Teddy Parker. I want to date Brian."

"But he's dating Priscilla Walsh."

"The hag! I hate her. But I've heard they might break up soon. I want my first kiss to be with Brian."

"Okay, but let's worry about my first kiss for now. Pink or black?"

"Mmm... pink. It makes you less intimidating, more approachable. Utterly kissable."

Gemma put the black V-neck back in the wardrobe and pulled the pink crop top over her head. It left the hint of her belly button visible above the waistband of her high waist jeans.

"I'm pulling my hair up." Gemma used a matching pink band to tie her hair. "Strawberry lipstick. Aaand... I'm ready to be kissed." She turned toward Amelia, who jumped off the bed squealing and crushed her in a bone-tight hug.

"You have to go now," Gemma said. "Before Jake gets here."

"I'm stealing my dad's pager. Page me when you get back. I'll sneak out and come back here so you can tell me everything."

"I will."

Gemma waited in her room for the bell to ring. She had to keep drying the sweat from her palms on her jeans. What if Jake wanted to hold hands? She couldn't have sticky palms. She put an extra packet of tissues in her purse just in case. That's when the doorbell rang. Gemma braced half her body against her room's doorframe to listen to what was going on downstairs.

Her father's voice drifted up the stairs as he asked Jake to join him on the porch for a quick chat. Oh gosh, her dad was giving Jake the you-are-dating-my-daughter-be-good speech. Gemma covered her face with her hands, hoping it'd be over soon. She waited five minutes before hopping down the stairs to join them on the porch. As expected, her dad was sporting his most intimidating scowl. Jake's face was ashen, but his features were set on brave and determined. He looked so handsome in his football jacket.

"Hi." Gemma's eyes sparkled as they met with Jake's. "Can we go, Dad?"

"I want her home by eleven, not a minute later," Mr. Dawson said, still scowling at Jake.

"Yes, sir. We won't be late."

As they walked toward Mrs. Wilder's car, Gemma could feel her father's eyes still on them. Jake opened the passenger door for her, and she waited for him to get in the car with her before she spoke.

"Sorry about my dad. What did he say to you?"

"He—mmm, we're cool."

"Oh, okay. It's great your mom let you borrow the car."

"Yeah. By the way, if she asks, we went to see Harry Potter."

"Okay—yeah, my dad wouldn't be too happy about us watching Tarantino either. He doesn't know I've seen the first Kill Bill. I still

want to see Harry Potter, though. We could go another time." At that instant, Gemma realized Jake hadn't yet asked her on a second date. "I mean, not that we have to go together."

"I'd love to go with you." Jake placed a hand on her knee, sending Gemma's nervous system into overdrive.

***

"For a moment there I thought she was going to forgive Bill," Gemma said as they walked back to the movie theater's parking lot.

"Nah. After all, the movie's called Kill Bill.*"*

"You're right."

Jake opened the car door for her again and Gemma slipped in. They didn't say much on the way home. Gemma's palms kept getting sweatier and sweatier. The date had been perfect. Jake had bought her popcorn, and halfway through the movie, he'd wrapped one arm around her shoulders. But still no kiss.

Jake took a right turn, and Gemma wrinkled her nose. "We need to go left."

"I'm not taking you home. Not yet."

Gemma's belly fluttered. "Oh."

Jake pulled up in a parking lot overlooking Lake Michigan. The view was spectacular, and Gemma's palms were the clammiest of the entire night. Jake killed the engine and turned to look at her. This was it. He was going to kiss her. Gemma watched Jake lean in closer to her with a pounding heart, unable to move, paralyzed with both fear and anticipation. Jake's lips pressed onto hers and all her worries melted as a warm fuzz spread in her chest and belly. Jake's kiss was tentative at first, soft and sweet. Until his hand wrapped around the nape of her neck, pulling her in closer, and suddenly they were kissing for real. Gemma felt her breath catch in her throat, her chest aching with how much she loved Jake. She pulled back to look at him.

He frowned. "Did I do something wrong?"

"No, it was perfect. Jake Wilder, I-I love you."

Jake's eyes widened before a smile spread on his lips. "I love you too, Gemma Dawson."

Then they were kissing again, and Gemma found herself hoping eleven o'clock would never arrive.

♥♥♥
Saturday, August 5—London

"Didn't I just kick you out of this house a week ago?" I ask Amelia.

"You did."

"So what are you doing here?"

"I'm dressing you."

I look in the bedroom mirror, perplexed. "Tell me again why I'm wearing this?"

Amelia rolls her eyes at me. "I've told you. I bought these on a whim, changed my mind, and asked for a refund. But they won't take the clothes back at the store. So, I thought they'd fit you better."

"They're like a present for me?"

"More a hand-me-down. What do you think?"

She gave me a nice pair of high waist jeans and a silky blush top to wear. "A bit retro, but I like it."

"Now pull your hair up."

I obediently scrunch my hair up into a messy bun.

"No, no. Let me do it." Amelia takes control of my head. Brushing, tugging, and finally tying my hair in a high ponytail. "Perfect. Now close your eyes." She's smiling too much; something's going on here.

I narrow my eyes at her. "Why?"

"Trust me."

I do as she says and let her pull me by the hands around the apartment. I'm familiar with the geometry of the place enough to orient myself. She's pulling me out of the bedroom, along the hall, and across the living room to the front door. A brush of cool air hits me when she opens it to drag me outside.

"You can open your eyes now."

I do. Jake's waiting outside the house, propped up against a car wearing his old high school football jacket. He's beaming at me and my mind swirls a little with the strongest sense of déjà vu.

I turn from Jake to Amelia. "What is this?"

She squeezes my shoulders. "I'm going to play with Lucky for a bit and I'll let myself out. Have fun." She winks and disappears back inside the house.

I hop down the few steps to the curb where Jake's standing.

"So?"

"Gemma Dawson, will you go on a date with me?"

"A date?"

"Yes. I haven't taken you on a real date since we got back together."

He's right. We went to a restaurant after I crashed his wedding, and we went to that horrible dinner at Amelia's house before she found out Will was cheating on her. But those hardly qualify as dates. Then Amelia moved in with us, and we haven't had much alone time since.

"Where did the car come from?"

"I rented it."

"Are you sure you can drive on the left side?"

"We're going to find out very soon."

"And why the fuss from Amelia about these?" I flick my hands over the clothes she's made me wear. "And why the football jacket?"

Jake smiles a wicked smile. "Because I'm taking you to watch *Kill Bill*."

Kill Bill. Our first date. Our first kiss. Our first I love you. My heart wants to explode with the same aching love of that night so many years ago. I squeal and throw my hands around his neck to kiss him, but he pushes me back.

"Now, now. That will have to wait until the end of the night. We're doing things properly here."

"All right, Mr. Wilder. You're the boss."

I give him my hand and let him walk me to the other side of the car and open the passenger door for me. I slip inside and a stupidly happy smile spreads across my lips.

Six Months Later

Sixteen

Something Special

♦♦♦

Friday, March 2—London

Up for something special tonight?

It's Richard.

Special, uh?

Like what…?

It's a surprise

I'll pick you up at seven

I didn't say yes

But now you have no choice

'Cause you're too curious to say no

You know that's going to make me die of
curiosity

I know

I'm evil like that!

Yes, you are

See you tonight, x

Something special, uh? I wonder what it could be. After six months of dating, Richard and I are in a good place. We have an easy, uncomplicated relationship with no drama whatsoever. We're in love and it's great. I never thought I'd say, "I love you," to anyone after Jake, but Richard made it so easy for me to fall for him.

I spend half of the day imagining what this big surprise is going to be. So far, Richard hasn't been the surprise-type. I check the calendar, but I haven't forgotten my birthday or his birthday. It's just a regular Friday night, nothing special about it. So what's up with him?

When I get home, Amelia's waiting for me with a keen expression on her face.

"How was your day, honey?" she asks.

I shrug. "Mostly like any other."

"Oh, it's going to get better."

"What do you mean?" Why are people talking in riddles today?

"There was a delivery for you."

"Where is it?"

"In your room."

I dash into my room. An amazing dress is draped on my bed with a Post-it note on it that says, "*Wear me.*" Next to it, there's a dock station with another Post-it saying, "*Play me.*" This is a surprise date version of *Alice in Wonderland*. What are we celebrating, my Very Merry Unbirthday? I wonder if a white rabbit with a ticking clock is going to make an appearance soon to tell me I'm late, which I kind of am considering it's already six. Well, at least I won't have problems choosing what to wear. I'm intrigued. Where's Richard going with this?

I push play on the dock station and it's *The Blues Brothers* soundtrack. I smile, thinking back on our first date at the film club.

To the sound of 'Everybody Needs Somebody To Love', I hop in the shower while dancing and singing like a maniac. I'll give it to Richard: he knows how to set the right atmosphere.

I quickly blow-dry my hair and step back into the room. Now, 'Do You Love Me?' is on and I can't help but shake my booty to the melody.

"Having fun?" Amelia asks, leaning against the doorframe.

"Much. Did you see this dress?" I slip it on. "It's a dream." It's a navy midi-length dress with a see-through hem and shoulder straps. It has blue floral appliques and beads all over. It's gorgeous. "My blue suede pumps will look great with it."

"Yeah, I think that was the idea."

I twirl in front of the mirror, excited. "What do you say, hair up or down?"

"Up, but loose. If you give me a comb, a hair band and ten bobby pins I can pull the perfect bun off in five minutes."

"Yes, madam."

I give her everything she asked for. Amelia starts by backcombing the base of my hair, then pulls the back half in a side ponytail that she transforms into a side bun, and finally, zip-zap, she pins the rest of the hair on the bun in a perfectly-messy fashion. As promised, I'm red carpet ready in five minutes.

"Wow! This is super. Thank you, Ames."

"You're gorgeous."

I put eyeliner on, a generous quantity of mascara, blush, and lip-gloss, so that when the bell rings, I'm just about ready.

I shut off the dock station. "I'm going."

"Have a great night."

"I will."

"And be home by midnight," Amelia yells jokingly after me. "Or, don't come back at all."

Outside, Richard's waiting for me next to a black cab, wearing a tux. He looks dashing. As I throw my arms around his neck to kiss him, he hands me a white rose.

"You're beautiful."

"Thank you." I take the rose and smell it. "You're not too bad yourself."

"Shall we go?"

As I step into the cab, nerves attack me. Richard has gone to a lot of trouble to organize this night and I have a feeling the surprises aren't over yet. Suddenly, a horrible thought pops into my mind. He wants to ask me to move in with him. Dylan asked Amelia a while ago and she's moving out of my apartment soon. But Richard and I are definitely not ready for such a big step; we've been dating for as long as they have, but it's been casual dating, nothing too serious. I throw a side-glance at him and he smiles.

"Where are we going?" I ask.

"Be patient, we're going to get there soon."

"Haven't I suffered enough?"

He buffets my nose with a finger. "Poor you, look at the state of you," he mocks me.

"Okay, I've definitely had worse days. But you know how curious I am."

The cab stops in front of The Dorchester.

Richard gives me his hand to help me out of the cab.

"You're joking," I say as I stare at the building. "This is the most expensive restaurant in London."

"It's a special night; it called for a special place."

"What's so special about tonight?" I ask, the nagging worry poking again at my stomach. This whole thing is screaming serious relationship, commitment, moving in together. And I'm definitely not ready for all of that. Not yet.

"I got a promotion today; I wanted to celebrate with you."

So this is it. We're celebrating his promotion. I relax at once. Oh, Richard. He has style.

The restaurant's amazing, dinner's amazing, and Richard's amazing. We eat a seven-course meal with wine pairing, and by the end of the night, I'm more than a little tipsy. My head's spinning a bit, so when Richard suddenly gets incredibly serious, I don't immediately grasp the meaning of what he's saying.

"…these have been the best six months of my life. I love you so much, Gemma, I couldn't contemplate spending a day away from you."

I nod my head in assent. This is all very nice. A bit over-dramatic, maybe. But hey, who am I to complain?

"And this is why I want to make sure I don't… have to spend a single day away from you."

I keep nodding. Where's he going with this speech? And why is he being so melodramatic? The penny drops when he gets up, rounds the table, and drops to one knee.

Oh gosh! No, this isn't happening. Panic clutches my throat and my head starts spinning, for real this time. The entire room is swaying around me. I'm going to be sick. What's Richard doing on one knee? Well, there aren't many things a guy in a tux would do down on one knee in a Michelin-starred restaurant. The other patrons gasp, and the entire room stops to watch us.

I stare at Richard in horror. Is he really doing this? I watch in slow motion as he picks a blue velvet box out of his jacket pocket and opens it. Inside, there's a ring.

"Gemma Dawson, will you marry me?"

I smile a nervous smile; tears prickle my eyes. Not because I'm overwhelmed by joy, but because now I'll have to break up with him. I can't marry him. Where did he get the idea that we're marriage-ready at this point in our relationship? We've never even glossed over the topic. Tears stream down my cheeks. I try to speak, but I'm choked with emotions and I can't.

"Look how happy she is," a woman nearby says. "She can't speak."

If only you knew why, lady.

As I try to speak again, the crowd starts clapping and cheering in support. I look at Richard, his eyes warm with love, his forehead dotted with pearly beads of sweat, and his lips parted in a hopeful smile. I can't break his heart. I just can't.

"Yes, I'll marry you," I hear my voice say.

Richard slides a beautiful solitaire onto my finger and suddenly my hand feels heavier than it has ever been before.

Seventeen

Floating Memories

♥♥♥

Friday, March 2—London

"Oh, you're home already." I greet Jake with a kiss. "And you're cooking?" The apartment smells of grilled meat.

Jake looks super cute in my pink 'all about that bake' apron. (Not that I actually bake, it was a present.)

"I'm making burgers," he says.

"What's the occasion?" I ask him, immediately afraid I've forgotten something important. I'm not the best with dates, anniversaries. Since the rise of smartphones, I manage birthdays well enough, but that's about it.

"Oh, nothing special." Jake comes over to take off my coat and guides me to the table. "Wine?"

"Sure."

He pours me a glass.

"Mmm, this is good. What is it?"

"I thought you'd recognize it."

"Should I?"

"It's Fumé Blanc."

"From Napa?"

"Meow." Lucky comes brushing at my legs.

I put the wine glass back on the table and pick Lucky up. "Oh, and you had a makeover too." He's wearing a new red collar with a red bow tied to the top. "You look handsome."

"Prrr, mrrr."

"Are you sure nothing's up?" I ask Jake.

"I'm just in the mood to celebrate. Now sit down, dinner's ready."

One bottle of Fumé Blanc and one delicious burger later, Jake seems to edge on nervous rather than full and pleasantly tipsy like myself.

"Are you going to tell me what's going on now?" I ask.

Jake gets up. "Come with me." He grabs my hands to pull me up. "I have a surprise."

He drags me to the spare bedroom and opens the door. I walk inside. The room's filled with floating red and pearl white party balloons.

"Jake, what's this?"

He smiles. "Have a look around."

I take a few tentative steps inside the room, noticing various objects dangling from most of the balloon ribbons. I grab one, and immediately, a furious blush spreads across my cheeks. I cover my face with my hands and press it against Jake's chest to hide.

"Oh, gosh. You've found the Jakebox!"

"I had a tip-off."

"I'm going to strangle that sorry excuse for a best friend. You were never supposed to find it."

"Why not? It's super cute. And I've added some things of my own."

"You did?" I peep at him from between my fingers.

"Come on, you should own the Jakebox." He spins me round and pushes me gently into the room.

I navigate the balloon maze and each one's a surprise. A million pictures of us stare back at me, some from the Jakebox and others not. They range from age fifteen up to last week. I find tickets from movie nights, concerts, vacations.

On the next balloon, I recognize a sheet of crumpled paper Jake passed me in class the first year we started dating. On top, it says, "*Prom?*" Below are two option-squares, one says, "*Yes,*" and the other says, "*Yes.*" I marked both of them and stamped a lipstick kiss underneath.

"You were already such a charmer," I say.

Next, I find a page from my diary.

"Oh, you didn't read this!"

"I *soooooo* did."

I keep moving through the balloons. I find some Post-its. I used to leave them on the bathroom mirror of his house before I left in the years we were living apart. "You kept these!"

"These were my lifeline. I hated being away from you so much, especially knowing it was my fault."

"It wasn't your fault. I know I blamed you, but I shouldn't have."

"But if I'd followed you to Boston…"

"You would've hated it. And who knows where we'd be now." I turn around. "The important thing is that we're here, now." I kiss him.

"Ouch." Jake pulls back as Lucky starts climbing on his leg to try to get to the balloon ribbons.

"Someone wants to play," I say.

"He already *helped* enough with the setting up." Jake drops Lucky to the floor where he stares intently at the ribbons, one paw stretched forward menacingly.

"I bet he did."

I scratch him behind the ears and keep walking through the hidden treasures of our past. Some of the heavier items need three of four balloons to keep them afloat. Like a heart-shaped stone we picked up at the beach, or a small bag filled with seashells, and even two golden miniatures of the Little Mermaid from McDonald's Happy Meals. And a vial filled with sand.

"Where's this from?"

"The lake. My parents' cabin."

I blush.

"Remember that day?" Jake takes hold of two pictures and shows them to me.

They're from the day we lost our virginity together. "Of course." One is my favorite pic of him. Shirtless, he has one arm raised above his head, braced on a tree branch. He's wearing a surfer necklace, which he wouldn't take off for the whole summer. The other pic is of me. I'm not staring at the camera, but at the lake. The sun's shining through my hair as if I were radiating happiness and love. Which I was.

"I don't remember this picture," I say, looking at it.

"I had this one. It's my favorite of you."

"And this is my favorite of you," I say, pointing at the other picture. "Remember that necklace I gave you? You never took it off."

"Wait, it should be here somewhere." Jake shuffles some balloons around and finds it.

"You should put it on." I take it from him and tie it around his neck. He gives me that same crooked grin, and I'm so full of love, so full of life I might explode.

Toward the end of the room, I spot a postcard of a beach in Hawaii. Where we promised we'd go for our honeymoon. My heart rate accelerates.

As I reach the very end of the room, a particularly thick cluster of balloons stands out. My heart jumps into my throat as I notice they're holding a small jewelry box. Dangling below it, there's a sheet of paper. I snatch it. It says, *Marry me?* Below are two option-squares; one says, *Yes*, and the other says, *Yes*. I look up from the sheet of paper to find Jake has detached the tiny box and is on one knee in front of me with it open. Tears fill my eyes.

"Will you…"

His words are cut off by me barreling into his arms. "Yes! Yes, yes, yes, yes!"

As I kneel on the floor in front of him, he takes the ring, a breathtaking square sapphire with a diamond halo, out of the box and slides it on my finger. An electrical tingle sparkles where his skin touches mine and my left hand feels so light it could be made of air.

We lock eyes. "I love you. I want to spend my life with you and fill the Jakebox with so many more memories."

I smile and cry at the same time. "I love you so much, I don't even know how to say it."

"Then you shouldn't talk." Jake kisses me and I melt in his arms. We make love on the floor with the same passion, the same frenzy, and the same love as our first time.

Eighteen

Lattes and Rings

♦♦♦

Saturday, March 3—London

The day after proposal-gate, I leave Richard's house as soon as I can without appearing too ungrateful, saying I want to share the good news with my friends and family and feeling like an impostor all along. I ask Amelia to meet me at a Starbucks near our house, hoping that coffee and my best friend will help me find a solution. *A way out*, my treacherous brain thinks. So here I am sharing the 'good' news over lattes.

"So what is the big announcement you had to drag me out of bed on a Saturday for?" Amelia isn't a morning person; Dylan's trying to change that.

"Richard proposed," I say flatly.

"Aw," she squeaks. "That's wonderful, amazing. I can already picture him looking dashing in a tux, and you glowing in your white gown. Let me see the ring."

She grabs my left hand, but the ring isn't there. I took it off the moment I left Richard's house.

"Why aren't you wearing it? Was it too big? You need to re-size it?"

"No, it fits me just fine. Here it is." I take it out from an inside pocket in my bag.

"This is beautiful." Amelia looks at the ring, then at my face. "Wait, if it fits, why aren't you wearing it?"

"I was afraid of losing it," I lie.

"It's not any safer in your bag. Put it on."

I do and stare at my hand questioningly.

"Why aren't you giddy with happiness?" Amelia asks. "You said yes, didn't you?"

"Mmm-mmm."

"So, what's wrong?"

"It was an ambush. I was forced to say yes."

A woman sitting next to us scoffs. We turn toward her, but she's steadily looking at her iPad and not at us, so we go back to our conversation.

"What do you mean you were forced to say yes?" Amelia is giving me a no-crap look. "Nobody held a gun to your head, I'm sure."

"Amelia, he asked me in a room full of people after the most romantic night ever. How could I have said no? I was cornered, I panicked!"

"So you said yes out of politeness?"

"At first I couldn't speak, I was too shocked. I wanted to say no. I wanted to ask him, 'What the hell? We never even discussed moving in together, what made you think I was ready for marriage?' But Richard was looking at me as if I were the most beautiful thing in the world, with his eyes full of love, and I just couldn't say no. I couldn't break his heart."

"Because you love him. You're just freaked out by the marriage thing."

"I care about Richard, he's wonderful. But I never thought about him as The One, the love of my life, Mr. Right. Call it what you like. I mean, who proposes after six months?"

The woman next to us lets out an even louder snort. I can't ignore it this time.

"Excuse me, you have a problem?"

"Actually, yes, I do." She stops pretending to be watching her iPad and turns toward us. "Do you have any idea how rare it is to have a bloke ask you to marry him these days?"

"Err, no."

"No, exactly, you don't. All guys want to do nowadays is to Tinder you one night and never see you again. And honestly, having to sit here and listen to you complain about your—according to her," she points at Amelia, "dashing boyfriend proposing after the—according to you," she points back at me, "most perfect romantic night, is boggling my mind."

"Nobody asked you to listen in to our conversation," I point out.

"Hard not to when you're babbling aloud two feet away from me. You've ruined my breakfast. Are you happy?" She gets up and storms out of the coffee shop.

I stare at Amelia at a loss for words.

"What was that about?" she asks.

"No idea. You should introduce her to Flotsam and Jetsam, they'd make a beautiful trio."

"She did have a point, though."

"What point?"

"Any woman would be happy, ecstatic, her boyfriend proposed."

"Even after only six months?"

"Yes. What's holding you back?"

I bite my lower lip.

Amelia throws me a warning stare. "If you're about to bring Jake into this, I'm going to scream and get out of here."

"Says the one who was getting married out of inertia instead of love."

Hurt appears on Amelia's face. That was a low blow.

"I'm sorry." I backtrack immediately. "I didn't mean it like that."

She nods her understanding.

"But I have a serious problem here," I add. "I thought you would've understood, seeing as how you almost married the wrong guy."

"William was the wrong man for me because we weren't in love with each other anymore, not because I was chasing after a ghost of my past. I thought you had closed that door."

"I have."

"Have you? Honey, Jake's gone. He's married to someone else."

"Do you have to keep rubbing it in my face?"

"Apparently, yes, as you seem inclined to overlook the fact."

"What fact?"

"That Jake *is* married. You think marrying Richard would put an end to any remote possibility you might have of getting back with Jake one day. But let me tell you, that train has departed."

"That's not… it's not like that. I have many other reasons to question this decision."

"What reasons?"

"That it's too soon. That Richard and I don't know each other enough. That my relationship with Richard works so well because it's on a day-to-day basis. I could go on if you like…"

"Are things going well on a day-to-day basis?"

"Yes."

"So what are you afraid would change?"

"Nothing… everything. It doesn't sit well with me that the thought of marrying Richard never crossed my mind until he was down on one knee, proposing."

"If that's what you think, why did you say yes?"

"I told you. He caught me off-guard, I didn't know what to do. I care about Richard and he was there on one knee, offering me all his heart. I said yes, it's what you do when your boyfriend proposes. But now it's giving me anxiety."

"Why don't you talk to Richard about it?"

"And say what? 'Sorry, remember the other night when I said I wanted to marry you? Well… I didn't exactly mean it one hundred percent.' I can't talk to him about it."

"Then you have to decide on your own. But promise me Jake won't feature in it."

"What are you saying?"

"I'm saying you have to decide if you want to marry Richard. I'm saying you should marry him if you love him and want to spend your life with him. And I'm saying the one thing you shouldn't do is not marry Richard because of Jake."

I scowl. "It's not that simple."

"Actually, honey, it is."

Nineteen

A Shared Moment

♥♥♥

Saturday, March 3—London

I enter Starbucks sporting a smile so radiant people ought to wear shades.

"I'm engaged," I squeak the moment I reach Amelia. She's sitting at a round table and already has two lattes in front of her.

She gets up with a smile almost as radiant as mine, hugs me for a long time, and settles back down at the table. I join her.

"And you don't seem surprised," I chide her.

"I confess Jake might've asked for some help with the setting up." Amelia smiles mischievously.

"You snitch! You broke the code. You told him about the Jakebox. But I forgive you because it made for the most perfect night of my life."

"Let me see the ring."

I proudly extend my left arm, and the little diamonds on the ring catch the light, sending rainbow sparkles in all directions.

"This is gorgeous."

"It's perfect. Did you help him with this too?"

Amelia shakes her head. "No, he chose it all on his own." She looks at me expectantly. "Tell me everything; I want to know every little detail."

I do tell her everything—well, minus the X-rated parts—and we giggle all along.

"Will you be my maid of honor?" I ask when I'm finished with my report on Jake's proposal.

"Of course I will. Have you already set a date?"

"No, not yet. It's still so new. But sometime within the next year or so. I don't want to do anything big; I'm not a huge fan of big ceremonies."

"Yeah, they're overrated." A bittersweet smile surfaces on her lips. Even if she's moved on, I can see divorcing has left scars on her.

"Definitely overrated," I say supportively. "I want something simple. Just close friends and family."

"U.S. or U.K.?"

"I've no idea! What do you think?"

"You should do it at home. It's where it all started."

"I like the idea… Jake's parents' cabin at the lake would be perfect for a summer wedding. We could set a flowery gazebo just in front of the lake and lay the beach with white chairs…"

"I thought you didn't like wedding planning."

"Well, I don't like planning in general. But the thought of becoming Jake's wife… I want our wedding day to be perfect."

"Whatever you decide, I'm sure it will be."

"But enough about me, what about you and Dylan?"

Her expression becomes bittersweet again. "What about us?"

"Well, how's the living together going?"

"Great, but it's still so new his dirty socks on the bathroom floor haven't started to annoy me yet."

"What is it that males have against laundry baskets?"

"I'm not sure, but they're probably all convinced house elves take care of their discarded underwear."

"Yeah, I bet they do. Dirty socks excluded, how's it going?"

"It's perfect, and I'm even exaggerating on the socks. He's not all that bad. Who am I kidding? Dylan's great. Gem, I'm so happy it scares me. I'm afraid everything will be taken from me when I least expect it."

"I know the feeling. At least you don't have bad karma on your side."

"Meaning?"

"I stole Jake from Sharon, so in theory, bad things should happen to me and good things to her. Whereas in your case, the bad karma should go all to William and the good things all to you. So, really, you're good."

"That's the stupidest thing you've ever said."

I giggle. "Maybe, but I hope your half is true. Do you and Dylan ever talk, uh, marriage?"

"You want to send me running for the hills?"

"Why? Is the idea of marrying Dylan so bad?"

"Gem, I'm not sure I want to get married again; I'm not even divorced yet. And before you say anything," she raises a silencing finger at me, "it's not about Dylan. I don't want to do the whole wedding thing again, like *ever*."

"Is it just the wedding you have a problem with, or is it marriage per se?"

She shrugs. "As I said—this may sound stupid—but I feel last time, getting married ruined everything with William."

"But it wasn't because you got engaged that everything crumbled between you two. You weren't right for each other."

"Mmm, I've been racking my brain, trying to decide when it all started to go wrong. I told you the year before the wedding is a bit of a fuzz. But before that, I've tried to remember when it was that I started loving him less and less and when he drifted away from me… but I can't pinpoint a moment."

"There wouldn't be a specific moment to choose from. Not when it happened so slowly."

"But was it a coincidence that Will began his affair around the time he proposed?"

"No, but it didn't start because he proposed."

"Why then?"

"Okay, I'm not an oracle here, so I don't presume to have a universal knowledge of why Will did what he did. But when he proposed, you guys were probably already having problems…"

"But that's the thing," Amelia interrupts me. "From what I remember, we were doing just fine."

"On the surface maybe, but deep down you probably both sensed something was amiss. And you ignored the thought because it was a scary one. You guys had been together for so long, neither of you could face the idea of leaving the other. So maybe—mmm, subconsciously—getting engaged was a way for you to throw your hearts over the fence. You were drifting apart, and instead of letting go, you found a way to cling to each other even more."

"So your theory is we got engaged out of fear? I remember being happy when Will proposed; I remember *him* being happy."

"As I said, I don't assume I have all the right answers, but think about it—were you *happy*-happy or more… mmm… *relieved*-happy?"

Amelia blinks at me. "Oh. I see what you're saying. When Will proposed, I felt suddenly lighthearted and took it for happiness. But according to you, I was just relieved I didn't have to break up with Will, or even begin to think about breaking up with him, because if he was proposing, surely he was the right man for me. And he probably got the same reassurance when I said, 'Yes.' So if this is what happened, why start an affair a minute later?"

"Ah, this is guesswork again. Maybe it just happened. Maybe he felt reassured on one side, but he started to feel trapped on the other. There's no way to know when he realized he wasn't in love with you, or why he didn't call off the wedding."

"Because he's a coward." Only bitterness shows in Amelia's voice now. "He didn't even have the guts to tell me; he accidentally on purpose left his computer open for me to discover everything and throw him out of the house."

"Yes, he was weak and a coward. He behaved as badly as one could. But Dylan, he's ten times the man William will ever be. And things didn't go wrong because of the engagement or the wedding, they just did. You shouldn't be afraid of being happy; you deserve to be happy more than anyone else does. If you want to marry Dylan, do it."

"It's not like he proposed, we just moved in together."

"Okay, but he might propose one day. And I don't want you to exclude the possibility because of what happened with your ex-husband."

"A marriage that lasted the whole of three weeks, can I even call him an ex-husband?"

"We can call him dung beetle if you prefer."

Amelia cracks her first smile since the wedding talk started. "He is a bit of a dung beetle. And you're right, I shouldn't be scared. I love Dylan, and this time I'm sure it's love with a capital L."

"Giant capital L," I agree.

"If he ever does ask me to be his wife, I'll keep an open mind. Thank you." She hugs me.

"For what?"

"I needed to talk about William and the divorce. And you waited long enough to tell me everything you said today for me to be ready to hear it. You're my best friend in the world; I don't know what I'd do without you."

"You'll never have to find out. Come here." I pull her into another hug, feeling a bit teary.

"Are you crying?" Amelia asks with her chin resting on my shoulder.

"A little bit."

"Me too," she sniffs.

We giggle and cry at the same time. Two friends sharing a moment.

Twenty

Significant Ex

◆◆◆

Monday, March 5—London

At the office, I close a document folder, satisfied. My first meeting of the week went well. The negotiation was smooth. Both parties got what they really wanted to begin with. No one relented too much or lost face. As everybody else leaves the room, a lawyer from the other team lingers behind. She's being extra slow in collecting her files from the glass table and she's looking at me with a keen expression I can't interpret.

"Can I help you with something?" I ask.

"I thought you were going to go a lot harder on us. I admire you for not doing it."

Why was she expecting me to hammer her team? Do I have the reputation of a shark?

"We cut a fair deal that made everyone happy, wasn't that the goal?"

"Yes, of course. But sometimes people tend to get personal..."

This conversation isn't making any sense.

"Would there have been a reason for me to get personal with your client?"

"My client, no. Me, on the other hand…"

I stare at her blankly.

"You seriously have no idea who I am."

Why is she giving me a 'you don't know who I am' speech? Who *is* she? I keep staring at her, dumbfounded.

"So you haven't googled me, not even a peek on Facebook. I'm impressed; I certainly didn't have that willpower."

This woman's giving me the creeps. "I'm sorry, but I don't usually google, or stalk on Facebook for that matter, counselors opposing me. If you don't mind, I have another meeting to go to. Have a safe trip back to California."

I turn to leave. I'm almost at the door when she speaks again.

"I'm Jake's wife."

I freeze. My heart starts racing in my chest, pounding blood to my temples. I give myself a couple of seconds to allow my face to go back to presentable as opposed to I'm-about-to-have-a-stroke, and I turn to face my nemesis. Involuntarily my gaze flies over her left hand. There, a delicate rose-gold band is resting on her ring finger. How can such a simple piece of metal cause so much pain? How did I walk into this ambush without knowing anything? I know why! It's all Amelia's fault: she's the one who made me promise never to look this woman up and let me walk into this trap. Unprepared. Unarmed. Strong willpower, my foot. *I would've looked you up the second I had a chance, lady, if it weren't for my I-butt-in-all-situations best friend.*

"You really had no idea," she states.

I shake my head, no. What does she want?

"And to think that I was so nervous about meeting you, I went to a salon to have my hair done. I thought you did the same…"

I furrow my brow questioningly.

"But you didn't. Of course, you'd look like that on a regular day."

I look down at myself and it's nothing that great. I have my lawyer uniform on—black pencil skirt and white blouse. I stare in horror at the chipped nail polish on one of my fingers, and I ask myself why I chose not to blow-dry my hair this morning. So, I'm sure I'm not that impressive.

I focus on my rival. She's a good-looking woman, with fabulous blonde hair and perfect grooming. Then again, she had the advantage of knowing she'd be standing for this revenge-on-the-ex high noon moment today and went out of her way to look her best. So really, it isn't fair.

"So is there something you wanted to say to me?" I try to smile, but I'm sure I accomplish a grimace at best.

"No, not really. I was just morbidly curious to meet you. I've heard so many stories about you."

Jake talks to her about me? I'm afraid the having-a-stroke face is making a comeback. I swallow a bitter pill as my brain runs free with the knowledge of all the embarrassing things Jake knows about me. How many has he told her? When? Were they discussing it in bed after a passionate night of lovemaking? Am I a running joke between them? Oh gosh, I can feel my teeth grinding.

"I'm sorry, but I can't say I've heard anything about you. So we're not going to be able to swap anecdotes, are we?" I wish my voice wasn't shaking so much. My fake smile has definitely collapsed into grimace territory right now.

"Well, Jake still talks about you a lot…"

"I haven't spoken to Jake in years."

"Well, you're still his significant ex. And I'm sure he's yours…"

If only you knew how much.

"Well, you're his wife. He married you, and I'm engaged." I show her my rock, feeling glad I'm wearing it for the first time since Richard proposed. The thought I nearly had to face Jake's wife unmarried and unengaged is horrific.

"Oh, that's wonderful. When are you getting married?"

"In a year, perhaps two. Anyway, it all worked out for the best in the end." *At least for you*, I add internally.

"Yes. Yes, of course, it did," she says unenthusiastically. She looks at me in a weird way, sad almost. What has she to be sad about? She's married to the love of our lives; she doesn't get to be sad. "I'm sorry if I caught you off-guard. I just wanted to meet you."

"Well, it was very nice meeting you," I lie with a straight face. Lawyer skills and all. "Now if you don't mind I really have to get to that meeting."

"Yeah, sure. Sorry again. I've already stolen too much of your time. Goodbye."

That's not the only thing you stole from me. "Bye."

I walk out of the room steadily enough until I'm sure I'm out of sight, then like a drunk person, I brace myself on the walls of the hallway for support. I pinball from left to right until I reach my office, close the door and lock myself in, lowering all the blinds. Finally, I collapse on the couch usually reserved for making clients comfortable—or avoiding them fainting when I give them my invoice, I'm not sure—and cry my heart out.

The pain of losing Jake comes back to me in waves of shock and fear. I'm sobbing so hard I'm hyperventilating. Amelia was right: seeing her face has only made things worse. He did marry lawyer Barbie. Knowing this is the woman Jake goes back to every night, the one he makes love to, the one he has pillow talks with—and about me too, apparently—racks my body with an amount of sorrow I didn't know I had in me. After missing Jake's wedding, I thought I had it bad. But things moved on so quickly with Richard I never really contemplated how Jake was building a family with someone else. I'm nothing more than a distant memory, I've been reduced to the ex he tells amusing stories about.

The thought of that woman knowing things about me stings. It feels like such a violation of my privacy and tells me how little Jake holds dear our relationship—or the memory of our relationship, more accurately. It's a betrayal. He doesn't care anymore; I've become an anecdote to amuse his friends and wife over dinner. What did she say I was? Yeah, his significant ex. She should've said *insignificant ex.* Why does he still have the power to hurt me so badly? Why can't I just stop loving him? Why can't I love Richard the way I love Jake? And what am I doing marrying Richard, anyway? This is too much for one person to bear alone. I need to talk to Amelia.

Twenty-one

Is It Too Late to Say Sorry?

Monday, March 5—London

I enter the meeting room holding the files of my next settlement case in my arms. I can't help but walk on air around the office surrounded by a halo of happiness. As I move toward my chair, I go over my notes on the terms our client's willing to offer. I glance at the opposing lawyers, who are already seated at the glass table opposite to me, and resume my quick shuffling of documents. That's until my brain registers one of the faces I just glanced at. My halo of happiness shatters as my head jerks back up. I look at the only woman sitting on the other side of the room. Oh gosh, it's *her*! And she's looking at me with a face that says, "Yes, it's me. You wedding-crashing bitch!"

Crap. What do I do now? This is Sharon. The woman I stole Jake from. The woman whose life I ruined. What's she doing in my office? Is she a lawyer? She has to be. Panic floods my body, and as I try to sit, I crash into the chair, sending all my papers flying in the air. This is like one of those forever-embarrassing high school moments. Like walking across the cafeteria, tripping, and splashing the lunch tray on yourself in front of the entire school.

I collect my papers in a dignified way and sit at the grown-ups table, trying to appear respectable. I so wish my face wasn't so hot right now. I must be redder than a chili pepper. And my boss is in the room. Sweat starts pooling under my armpits. At least I'm wearing a white blouse. I hope it doesn't show.

Thank goodness I asked my junior associate to present our proposal today as a learning experience. I wouldn't be able to talk right now. I keep my gaze low and look at my watch under the table. The meeting shouldn't last more than an hour; everything's straightforward and all the parties should be able to get what they're after easily. So no big deal.

"That is when the opposing counselor doesn't hold the biggest grudge against you," says a nasty little voice in my head. All right, Gemma, let's get ready for the longest sixty minutes of your life.

I stay silent for the entire negotiation and only nod here and there at Logan, my junior associate, who's doing a wonderful job with his presentation. I keep my gaze lowered, but I can feel her blue eyes on me most of the time. It's as if she's drilling guilt messages into my skull:

"You stole my husband."

"You ruined my wedding day."

"How does it feel to be this happy at the expense of other people?"

I could die of shame. The way she looked at me. Withering. It was as if I was clubbing a baby seal or something.

"No, you just clubbed her chances at happily ever after. No worries."

I mentally scowl at my sarcastic inner self. I can't believe there's a person in the world who could hate me that much. If ever there was a death stare, Sharon has mastered it.

"Well, when you steal the groom from the glowing bride on her special day, death wishes could easily present themselves as side effects."

"Oh, shut up."

The buzzing noise of people talking in the background suddenly dies away. Did I just say it aloud? I dare to lift my head.

Sharon's staring at me. Apparently, *she* was speaking at that moment.

"I'm sorry, did you say something?" she asks.

I wish the ground would open and swallow me up.

"No, no." If you put together all Ally McBeal's most embarrassing moments they wouldn't add up to this. "Please go on."

"Glad we have your *blessing* to move forward." Sharon gives me a shrewd, evil smile and resumes her speech.

Well, I deserve this. I deserve to be humiliated and shamed. I ruined her life; I took Jake away from her. All her hopes, her dreams of a future with him now are mine. I stole her life. I deserve all the bad shit she wants to give me. What I did to her is bad karma. I need to suck it up and apologize to her. Yes, when the meeting's over I'll own my mistakes and say I'm sorry. Then maybe I won't come back in the next life as a cockroach.

Twenty unbearably long minutes later, the meeting's over. As everyone gets up to leave the room, I linger behind. So does Sharon. It's as if we're both aware we can't just leave without talking to each other. I don't even know if we reached an agreement for our clients, I was too busy rehearsing my apology speech in my head. The last of her remaining colleagues murmurs something in her ear, they exchange a nod, and he's gone. We're alone.

"Err, Sharon. Would you mind having a word with me?" It's the best opening line I can come up with.

"You usually don't ask my permission to talk."

She delivers a jab-cross combo and sends me back to my corner.

"Right, mmm… I really need to talk to you."

"Am I allowed to scream?"

"Please, it's only going to take a minute. You don't know how many times I've thought of picking up the phone to call you."

"Why? Did you leave something out of your last speech?"

She's sharp. Everything she says is a blow to my face. Jab, cross, hook, uppercut, repeat. And since I don't intend to punch back—figuratively speaking—I'm just going to hold my arms in front of my face and parry her verbal assault. She deserves her retribution, and if being mean to me helps her, I'm letting her do it.

"About that. What I did to you was horrible. I never meant for it to happen the way it did. I never meant for it to happen at all. And if there was a way to take it all away, I would…"

"You mean you'd rather not have stolen Jake from me? It seems to have worked out pretty well for you." She jerks her chin at my hand. "Is that from him?"

I follow her gaze to my engagement ring. Oh crap, this is getting worse by the minute.

I blush. "It is. And that's not what I meant. What I wanted to say is that if I could turn back time, I wouldn't wait so long to sort myself out. What I did, the way I did it… it was wrong. But I can't turn back time and I can't take it back. All I can do is to say how sorry I am. I am deeply sorry. I never meant for anyone to get hurt and I know I did hurt you. And I'm sorry for that."

Sharon sighs, shakes her head down, and looks back up at me. "I've never hated someone the way I hated you. That day you took my life in the palm of your hand, crushed it into a ball, and threw it in the trash."

Should I say again how sorry I am? I decide to keep silent and look contrite.

"And you can stop with the beaten-up-dog act."

"It's not an act. I really feel terrible for what I did."

"And what do you expect? What do you want from me? My forgiveness, so you can keep living your life with no remorse?"

"I don't expect anything from you. I owed you an apology, and I wanted to give it to you. That's all. I'm not going to steal any more of your time. Thank you for listening."

I make to exit the room, but she calls me back.

"Wait."

I turn again.

"There's something I want you to hear as well."

"Okay."

"As I said, you're probably the person I hated the most in my entire life. Being left at the altar was the worst experience I ever had. I was lost, heartbroken, humiliated… but," she pauses, "it probably wasn't nearly as bad as going through a divorce would've been, which was probably where Jake and I would've ended up some years down the line. I was in love with him, and being dumped on my wedding day was painful, but not as painful as slowly realizing I'd married someone who could never love me the way I deserve to be loved. I never understood that until I fell for my husband."

I stare at her, stupefied. My eyes travel to her left hand where a tiny gold band is wrapped around her ring finger. Never has a little piece of metal given me more joy than the one sitting on her finger.

"You-you're married?" I stutter.

"Yeah, I eloped to Vegas last month. I couldn't stand to go through the whole ceremony-with-family-and-friends thing again. No crazy-ex-girlfriends-barging-in-to-yell-stop hazards this time."

She's married, and she's making jokes about me ruining her life, which I really didn't do. Right?

"You're married," I repeat, more to convince myself that it's actually true.

"I am, so no matter what happened, I ended up in a good place. As did you, as did Jake, as did my husband. He's your biggest fan!"

"He is?"

"Yeah, he's over there. You can check for yourself."

I stare through the glass wall of the meeting room where a tall, handsome man's smiling at me. He's the counselor who left the room last. His lips part in a warm smile and he bends forward in an obliged bow. I beam at him.

"He came to work for my firm when I was already engaged. He says he fell in love with me during our first joint trial. The day I didn't get married was the happiest day of his life, so you're his hero. Seriously. He was there to pick up the pieces when I broke apart, and a fine job he did. Now I know what real love feels like, and I can understand why you had to do what you did. So all's well that ends well."

I nod as I'm a little too choked up to speak.

"I'd better go now."

"Sure," I say. "And thank you."

She smiles and exits the room. Outside, her husband puts an arm around her waist and pulls her in for a kiss. I watch Sharon literally beam with happiness as the sunrays bounce on her blonde hair, and a huge weight lifts from my chest. My closet's empty; no more skeletons lurking in the dark.

Twenty-two

Doubts

◆◆◆

Monday, March 5—London

"At least you've warmed up to the engagement idea," Amelia teases me.

I wave to the barman to bring us another round. We're having drinks in a bar halfway between our offices and I don't care if it is only lunchtime. I'm getting wasted.

"I don't think feeling glad you had a diamond ring to show to your ex's wife qualifies as warming up to the engagement, do you?"

"But you said it was the first time you were happy Richard proposed."

"Just as a social shield. If anything, this is telling me I shouldn't marry Richard even more."

"Why? Because you're in love with a married man you can never have?"

"It's not fair to Richard. I don't love him enough to marry him."

"But you do love him?"

"I do, but it's not consuming, it's not breathtaking. It's just, well, lovely."

"Gemma, what are you going to do if you don't marry Richard? Spend the rest of your life waiting for Jake to suddenly realize he can't live without you? Be single forever? Become a crazy cat lady and die alone?"

"No, no and no."

"What then?"

"I could meet someone else…"

"Someone better than Richard?"

She has a good point there. I'm never going to meet someone better than Richard. He's good-looking, kind, charming, fun, and full of life. His only problem is he's not Jake. I so don't deserve him.

"No, you're right. I'm never going to meet someone better than Richard."

"So?"

"So, I'm screwed." I shake my head. "Richard doesn't deserve this; he deserves a woman who loves him with all her heart and soul. I'd be doing him a favor if I broke up with him now before we're too invested."

"But he loves you, not some hypothetical perfect other woman. You make him happy. You're just freaked out because he proposed."

"But doesn't that say enough about where we stand? Every other woman in my position would be ecstatic—worse even, she would've probably been pressuring her boyfriend to propose. Isn't the fact that the thought never even crossed my mind enough of a telltale?"

"You've never been particularly girly about weddings. When I was telling you the details of my wedding with William, you kept rolling your eyes at everything I said."

"You were a tad overbearing."

"I was a bride," Amelia says with pride. "You'd probably rather elope to Vegas so you don't have to organize anything."

"I would," I admit.

"So, see, you're not your typical woman when it comes to weddings."

"Listen, I'm not scared of the ceremony; I'm scared of making a life-commitment to a man when I don't really mean it."

"Let's try this way: were you thinking of breaking up with Richard before he proposed?"

"No."

"And since I told you I was moving out, did you think about Richard potentially becoming your new roommate?"

"I might have," I mumble.

"I'm sorry, what was that?"

"Okay, okay. I thought about it. But more like something that would happen in the distant, indefinite future."

"So you were basically planning a long-term future with Richard anyway, except for the married label, right?"

"I've never given it much of a thought, to be honest. I was going with the flow."

"But you still saw yourself with Richard in the future?"

"Near future, yes. I never went past the next couple of months. Isn't that weird? Shouldn't I have been doodling Mrs. Gemma Stratton way before Richard proposed?"

"Let's try out some scenarios. Let's say you were to give Richard his ring back—the thought of never seeing him again wouldn't trouble you in the least?"

"I never said I don't want to see Richard again. I said I'm not sure if I want to marry him."

"Well, darling, you don't have many options left since it's clear he wants to marry you. From where things stand, you can either move forward with Richard or part ways. You can't give him his ring back without breaking up. Is that what you want?"

"No. No! I want things to go back to the way they were last week: easy, uncomplicated. I want to never have met Jake's wife. I want to love Richard the way I still love Jake. You should've seen the way I cried today. I completely lost it. It's not normal to be that desperate about your ex."

"Listen, Gemma, if I saw the flight attendant in person, I'd cry. Even if it's been ages and I haven't been in love with William for the longest time. It's still a wound. Healed, but the scar's there and it's staying with me for the rest of my life. Please don't throw away a perfectly good man who adores you to chase after the idea of a teenage love. You need to stop trying to replicate what you had with Jake. He was your first love. But it doesn't mean you can't build something even better with Richard. Something real, not a dream."

"Maybe you're right. It's just been a crazy day."

"Imagine if the redhead walked into my office and I didn't know who she was. I'm surprised you didn't pass out when she told you."

"That's the adrenaline for you, prevents you from passing out. It was scary, Ames. She was standing there, telling me how curious she was to meet me after all the stories Jake had told her about me. I wanted to rip her head off."

"I'm sure Jake didn't tell her anything bad. When a person has been so important in your past, it's natural to talk about them."

"I didn't tell Richard stories about Jake."

Amelia raises an eyebrow at me.

"Richard might've asked questions, and I might've answered them," I admit. "But I didn't entertain him with funny anecdotes about my *significant ex*. That's what they call me: the significant ex."

"It could be worse." Amelia smirks.

"You're making fun of my misery."

"I wouldn't dare." She hugs me, still smirking, though.

"Despite the fact that you're such an insensitive best friend, I'm glad you're still living with me, even if it's just for a few more nights. I need you there tonight."

"I'm not going anywhere. Even when I move out, you can count on me whenever you need me."

"You're my rock."

"And you mine."

"Do you think I should tell Richard?"

"That you met Jake's wife?"

"Mmm-hmm."

"If you do, he's going to ask questions, and unless you're ready to answer them, you should keep quiet."

"Questions like what?"

"Like how it made you feel to meet your ex's wife."

"Yeah, you're right. I should keep quiet." I stay silent for a while. "Jake's really gone, isn't he?"

Amelia looks at me with sympathy and nods.

"What am I going to do?"

"Move on and stop looking back."

I give her a confident nod back. But inside my chest, my heart's screaming all its dissent.

***

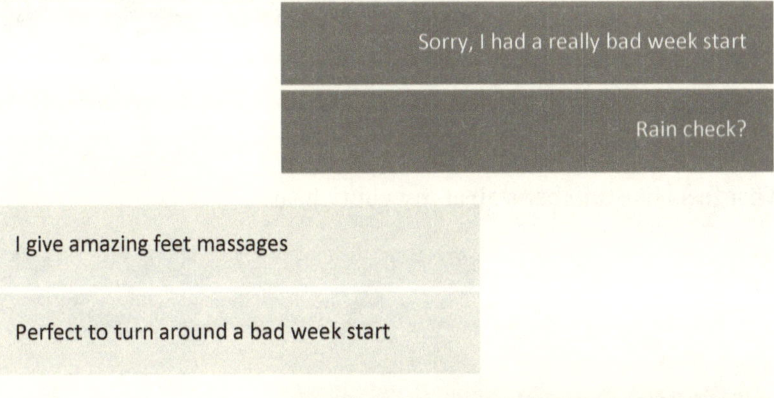

When I read Richard's text my heart shrinks.

I'm also a backstabbing, lying bitch. Because all I want to do tonight is log onto the internet and stalk my ex and his wife, who I met today and who made me cry over how much I hate and envy her. And I don't want to be with Richard because I know the moment he sees my face, he'll be able to tell something's wrong. And I don't want to talk about it, not anymore, especially not with him.

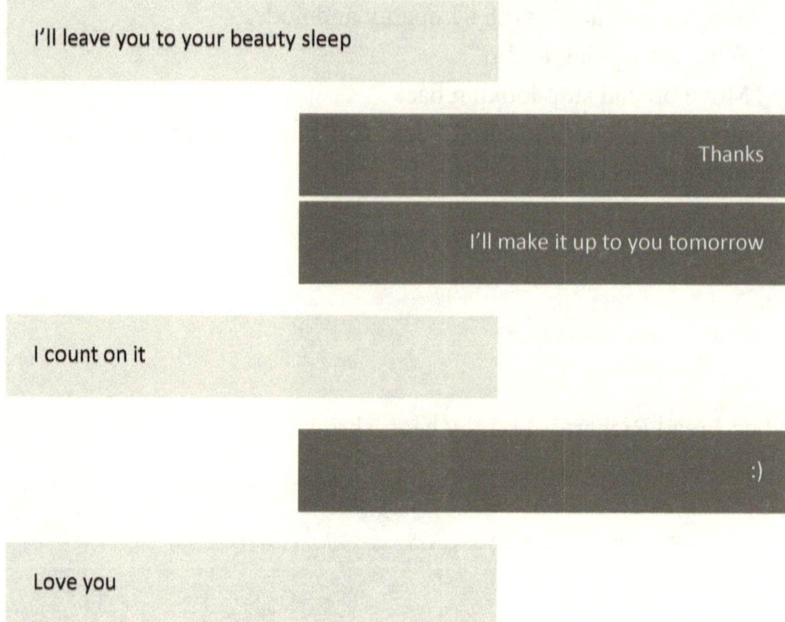

That feels like another stab at my guilty heart.

Twenty-three

Save the Date

Monday, March 5—London

The moment Sharon walks out of the building, I call Amelia and ask her to have lunch with me. We do a complete post-mortem of my meeting with Sharon and she agrees I need to tell Jake immediately. So that night I walk home a bit wary. When I get there, I find Jake already home. He's passed out on the couch and Lucky's nestling on top of his chest. My two boys. I brush the hair off Jake's forehead and kiss him there. Then I scratch Lucky's head. They both look at me from under the lid of one eye.

"Hi." Jake smiles, stretching his arms.

"Hello, sleepyhead. How was your day?" I give him another kiss.

"Exhausting, yours?"

"Mmm, interesting." Why am I so nervous about telling him I met Sharon and that she's married? I have an irrational fear he's going to get jealous or something.

"Interesting, how?"

"I saw Sharon."

"Sharon as in…?" Jake furrows his brows.

"Your ex wife-to-be? Yes." I sit on the couch next to them, level with Jake's chest. "I had a settlement case with a California-based company; she was on the opposing counseling team. I never knew she was a lawyer."

Jake sits up moving Lucky onto his lap and shifts to sit by my side.

"Did you talk?"

"Yes, I finally apologized."

"What did she say?"

"She-she sort of forgave me."

"She did?"

"You seem surprised."

"I am a little. So, was she okay?"

"Yeah, she's married. Eloped to Vegas with a colleague a month ago. She said she didn't want any more crazy-ex-girlfriends hazards."

"Sharon was making jokes about you crashing the wedding?"

"She was. She said not marrying you was the best thing that ever happened to her. No offense."

"None taken."

"She said my little stunt probably saved you two from a painful divorce. She also told me how humiliated and heartbroken she was, and how much she used to hate me. But apparently, I'm her husband's hero for breaking you two apart." I smirk a little. "He'd been secretly in love with her for a long while."

"I think I know the dude."

Is he jealous?

"So how does this make you feel?" I ask.

"Is this a trick question where I can't possibly give a right answer?"

I laugh. "No, no tricks. I swear. I just want to know how you feel about Sharon being married."

"Glad, I suppose."

"No sting?"

"No, definitely not. Sharon's a good person. I'm glad she found her happiness with someone else. I can only wish for them to be as happy as we are."

"That's such a perfect answer you should write a boyfriend manual."

"Hem-hem. Fiancé manual, if I'm not mistaken."

"You most definitely aren't." I kiss him.

He pulls me closer and Lucky protests at being disturbed during his nap.

"Speaking of weddings," Jake says when we finally pull apart, "my mom's pestering me for us to set a date."

"I should keep the mother-in-law happy." I get up to detach a calendar from the kitchen wall. "After all, I owe her a wedding. Did you have any preferences?"

"For the date? No. End of summer?"

I sit back on the couch and leaf through the calendar's pages. "The first of September's a Saturday. It's in six months so we would have enough time to sort everything. How does that sound?"

"First of September. It sounds great!"

"We have a date," I squeal, throwing my arms around his neck, much to Lucky's displeasure. He jumps off the couch, throwing us a resentful evil-kitty glare, and settles himself on the empty armchair in the corner. "Aw, don't be such a sourpuss," I call after him. "We have to celebrate."

"Let me text Mom so she can get off my back."

Jake taps away on his phone and sets it on the coffee table where it starts vibrating at once.

"Does Mrs. Wilder have any other requests?"

"Apparently she wants to know if we've any idea whether we're having the wedding here or at home."

"Okay, this is just an idea, and if you don't like it you can say no. But I was talking to Amelia the other day…"

"Is this where I should get worried?"

"No, don't worry. I'm not going Bridezilla on you. But we were talking, and she suggested we did the wedding at home where it all started, and I immediately knew where I wanted it to be…"

"Well?"

"How'd you feel if we got married at your parents' cabin?"

"I couldn't think of a better place," Jake says in a low voice. His eyes pierce deep into my soul. We're both thinking about our first night together. And in the dark of his irises, I can see the reflection of all my love for him and his for me. It's so intense I'm overwhelmed for a second.

I break the eye contact. "Do you think it'll be a problem for your parents?"

"We can find out."

He taps a reply on his phone, which again vibrates back as soon as Jake drops it on the coffee table.

"What does she say?"

"Here, read for yourself."

I couldn't be happier.

I always knew that girl had some sense in her. Please tell Gemma I can help her as much as she wants with the planning.

With her being there and me being here… but not in a pushy way, of course.

"Be careful here," Jake says. "If you give her an inch of control on the ceremony, she's going to take over completely."

"Can I confess something?"

"Sure."

"I sort of hoped she'd offer to help. I don't care that much for wedding planning. Does that make me a horrible bride-to-be?"

"It makes you the daughter-in-law of the year. She loves throwing parties."

"And she has impeccable taste."

"She does. Do you think *your* mom will get offended if we do it at our house and my mom does all the planning?"

"No. She hates planning parties but adores going to them. And she's going to be thrilled we're going to be at home. Our families are a match made in heaven."

"We're a match made in heaven." Jake lifts my chin with a finger to kiss me.

"You're totally right and impossibly cheesy."

"And you're an insolent little minx who needs a good seeing to."

He manhandles me from the couch, throwing my limp body over one of his broad shoulders, and gets both of us up. I punch him playfully in the back and scream in delight as he drags me toward the bedroom.

Twenty-four

September the First

♦♦♦

Friday, March 9—London

I help Amelia load the last of her boxes into Dylan's car, hug her close, and send her off to her new life. I watch the car disappear around a corner, comforted by the warmth of Richard's body towering behind me.

Back inside my apartment, I take a moment to mentally process all the new empty spots. A vase missing here, a book missing there, nothing big… just all the small telltales of Amelia being gone from the house.

I hug myself. "Feels a bit empty, doesn't it?"

Richard comes up behind me and massages my neck. "Are you sorry Amelia's moved out?"

"Well, yes. Of course. But I'm also happy she's moving in with Dylan. She deserves to be happy after everything that happened to her last year. I'm glad she found him."

"He's a good bloke. And now that you're one roommate short, how'd you feel about taking in another one?"

"No, the roommate I had before Amelia was a nightmare. I'd much rather be alone."

"I promise this roommate won't be a nightmare; he gives the best massages."

I turn to face him. "Oh, you mean you! You want to move in together?"

"We're engaged, so why not?"

"I thought you loved your apartment."

"Yes, I do. I hoped you'd want to move there with me?"

The walls of the apartment seem to close in on us. Call it cabin fever. "I'd love to," I lie. Too soon, way too soon. "But I just renewed the lease on this place; I've another nine months before it's up."

"Can't you sublet it?"

"No, it's in my contract," I lie again. "But when the lease expires, we can discuss it again."

"I hope a little sooner than that."

"Why?"

"Well, I'd always imagined myself actually living with my wife."

"W-wife? You mean you want to get married right away? Don't engagements last years?"

"They could, but why wait? I want you to become Mrs. Stratton as soon as possible…"

Mrs. Stratton. It sounds so grown up.

"I want to start a family with you, have children…"

"C-children?" I swear the house is shrinking. The walls are imploding.

"And I'm freaking you out big time."

"No, no." I move away from him and go sit on the couch. "It's just that it's all happening so fast. Ten days ago we'd never even discussed getting married and now we're having kids already."

"We're not having kids." Richard smiles at me and sits next to me. "I'm just saying I want them one day after we're married. You want to have children, right?"

"Yes, of course. As you said, one day. It's a huge, scary change."

"It is. So, speaking of weddings, my mum asked me if we'd set a date yet. I told her we'd pick one soon. Want to have a look at the calendar?"

"Sure," I say with the enthusiasm of a zombie.

"Would you prefer a summer or winter wedding?"

"Summer, I guess."

"Me too. What do you say to early September?"

September, next year. Eighteen months from now. A waiting time equal to two consecutive pregnancies should be enough for me to adjust to the idea. "I like September."

"The first is a Saturday; don't you think that'd be perfect?"

"Wait, isn't that this year's calendar?"

"Of course."

"You mean *this* September, as in six months?"

"Yes. Why, don't you?"

Six months from now. Not even one full pregnancy. "Does that leave us enough time to organize everything?"

"That could depend. Do you want a big wedding?"

"No, absolutely not. The simpler, the better."

"Then it shouldn't be a problem to get it running in six months."

I just scored the auto goal of the millennium. "No, I guess not."

"You want to do it here or back in the States?"

"London. Organizing it in the States would be a nightmare." I can't marry Richard in the same town where I met Jake. Definitely not.

"Do you ever miss home?"

"Of course I do."

"Ever thought of moving back?"

"Maybe. Eventually, yeah, it could be a possibility. Would you hate it?"

"Actually, no. I've always had this dream of living in New York, building a business that was mine."

"You want to start a marketing agency? You could do it here."

"I was thinking more an online magazine, a liberal place, a new voice…" He stares up at the ceiling with a dreamy expression. "Would you consider moving to New York?"

"Why New York?"

"It'd be the place to be."

"Is this a real conversation or a hypothetical one?"

"Why, you don't like the Big Apple?"

"Uh. To me, it's just a bigger, dirtier Chicago with less kind people."

We're getting married, having kids, *and* moving to New York? I wonder if Richard is planning to drop any other bombshell on this relationship anytime soon.

"Is everything okay? I'm not really being serious about New York. It's just one of those 'if-you-could-change-your-life-completely-what-would-you-do?' fantasies. You look worried."

I search my brain for something to say to justify my funereal face. "Yes, it's just that… don't take this the wrong way, but I really don't want to plan the wedding. I hate planning events, it stresses me out."

"Don't worry, we'll keep it as basic as it gets."

"You mean you're fine with not having mint-colored birdcages fly open to free a million butterflies as we cut the cake?"

"Is that a thing?"

"If you're Amelia, yeah, it is."

"Don't worry, I don't expect any volatiles. I only want you there."

He kisses me on the forehead and guilt creeps through me.

"I'm calling my parents to tell them."

"Sure, I'll do the same." I use the excuse to take up my phone and walk into my bedroom. I close the door behind me, collapse on the bed, and suppress a frustrated scream by covering my mouth with a pillow.

<u>Six Months Later</u>

Twenty-five

Home

♥♥♥
Saturday, August 25—Chicago Area

Nine days before the wedding, I fly to Chicago with Jake, Amelia, and Dylan. Amelia decided to come with us a week in advance to spend some time with her family and finally introduce Dylan to them. They're staying at an inn in our hometown. As for me, I'm staying at my parents' house in my old room, and Jake's at his parents' too. We're just a block away and it'll be fun to sneak out of the house and rediscover all our old meeting spots in the neighborhood.

We land in Chicago early on Saturday morning and I don't even have the time to take a shower before my mother and sister whisk me away to go shopping for a wedding dress. I know—with just a week to go before the wedding, it's crazy not to have a dress. I'll have to make do with whatever dresses the stores already have in stock, and a week's barely enough time for the fitting. But I'm confident I'll be able to find a wonderful dress in the whole of Chicago, and I want to choose it with both my mom and Kassandra. And given our complicated family geography, I had to do it here.

So here we are. Amelia's coming too—she put Dylan to bed, then joined us at our house in time to leave—as is Mrs. Wilder, Jake's mom. I suspect she put Jake to bed before coming too. And I could use a bit of sleep too after a sleepless night on the long flight from London, but I guess the wedding shopping adrenaline's running strong in my blood because I don't feel as exhausted as I should.

Nonetheless, when the shopping assistant at the wedding store asks me if I'd like a glass of champagne while she shows us some options, I ask her for a double shot espresso instead.

I choose six of the dresses she presents us and leave my audience comfortably settled in plush settees to go change into the first one. The assistant helps me pull it on and pins it at the back to make it fit. When she's done, she gently grabs me by the shoulders and turns me toward the mirror. I blink.

For a second I'm overwhelmed. This is it. I'm getting married. Once the initial shock wears off, I stare at the dress more closely. It's a romantic design made of tulle and Chantilly with a layered skirt. And the bateau neckline is decorated with gemstones. It looks good. But I don't feel any special bonding with it.

I go out to see what the others think.

I've barely walked out and my mom's already in tears. Everyone else seems close to joining her, and even Kassandra's usual swagger is a bit subdued. The shop assistant seems to be the only one aware of my indecision; she squeezes my hand and asks me if I'd like to try some other options. I nod and follow her back to the fitting room.

For the second dress, things go more or less the same: ooohs and aaaahs all around, tears from everyone but me, and a definitive no on my part.

But the moment the shopping assistant pulls up the zipper of the third dress, I know we've found a winner. Finally, tears well up in my eyes, and I take a minute to stare at my reflection before going out to the others. The assistant gives me a knowing nod and leaves me alone in the fitting room to have a private moment with The One Dress.

The gown's in a plain white fabric, with no decorations, beads, or ruffles. It's sleeveless with a bateau neckline and an A-line silhouette. The skirt has some volume and, I discover with delight, side pockets. I swirl to look at the back where a beautiful line of delicate buttons traces my spine. I wipe a few tears from my cheeks and walk out of the room, beaming.

***

After the dress fitting, I'm still not free to go rest as I have to drive to the lake with Mrs. Wilder to oversee the final preparations for next week. Jake's mom has kept me up to date on everything via Skype, but she wants me to approve the last details in person. She still has to give the final okay to the landscape artist for flowers and decorations, to the baker for the wedding cake, and to the guys bringing up the tent she ordered in case it should rain.

Jake's mom walks me around the property with a document holder in her hands, checking away items on her list as I give her my input.

"Flowers, cake, chairs, wedding gazebo, tent, photographer, tables map... we have everything." She looks at me. "Of course, I ordered plastic flats for the ladies in case they don't want to walk on the grass or sand in heels, and shawls should it get cold. We have a delivery of umbrellas coming in, even if the weather forecast's good. Anything else?"

She looks at me then past my shoulder. I follow her gaze and see a team of Ghostbusters approaching, complete with work jumpsuits and proton packs.

"Who are they?"

"Oh dear, I almost forgot. The disinfestation's today, we'd better go."

"Disinfestation?"

"Yes—we don't want you or the guests fending off mosquitos all night now, do we?"

My chest swells with a wave of gratitude. The last hour has made me appreciate how much pressure Jake's mom took off my plate in organizing this wedding. I launch myself forward and hug her tight.

"Mrs. Wilder, I can't begin to say how grateful I am you did all of this for us."

"Oh hush, dear, it was nothing. And it's about time you started calling me Susan."

"Well, Susan. Thank you so much; I don't know how I'll ever be able to repay you."

"Just make my son happy, and perhaps," she gives me a wicked smile, so similar to Jake's it freaks me out for a second, "grandkids?"

"I'll see what we can do."

"Now let's go before they disinfest us too."

Once I get home, I take a quick shower, ask my mom to wake me up for dinner, and collapse on my bed, finally exhausted.

Twenty-six

Stupid, Stupid Ruffles

◆◆◆

Saturday, August 25—London

A tinge of panic pinches my belly as I stare in the mirror at the millionth wedding gown of the day and feel absolutely nothing. No emotion. No tears. No this-is-The-One-Dress feelings. I'm getting increasingly frustrated with every wrong dress. And positively homicidal toward the shop assistant, who I overheard call me one of the difficult ones.

It's not my fault if she can't find the right dress for me. Okay, I've been a little generic with my requirements, but she's the one who should be able to suggest the right style for me. And the client's always right, so she can wipe that sour expression from her incompetent face.

Or it could be my fault. I shouldn't have left this so late. Finding an already-in-stock dress a week before the wedding is proving more difficult than I anticipated. But I wanted both Kassandra and my mom to be here, and they couldn't come to London too much in advance or take two trips in six months. It's an expensive flight. I should've gone to the States and chosen a dress there.

"Are you ready to go out?" the shop assistant asks.

"No, no point. I don't like this one."

I catch an eye roll in the mirror, but she doesn't say anything. She helps me out of the dress and into the next one. I examine this one in the mirror. It's in a mermaid shape, fitted to the hips with a sweetheart neckline and strapless. The tail part of the skirt's made of ruffled white and blush tulle.

"You want to show the others this one?"

"Sure," I say, unconvinced.

In the main client lounge, I'm met by an unexplainable awed reaction. Everyone seems convinced we have a winner.

"Your face's glowing," my mom says.

"You're so beautiful." Kassandra.

Amelia's speechless.

I try to let their enthusiasm soak under my skin and tentatively smile in the mirror from my pedestal. The shop assistant seizes the momentum and asks me if I want to try a veil. I tell her yes, and she scurries away, happier than I've seen her all day.

She's back in less than a minute and already pinning a short veil with a lace trim on top of my head. She steps back and looks at me expectantly, just like everybody else. I feel so much pressure on me that I don't have the strength to say I don't feel anything for this dress, or any of the other dresses I tried on. So I smile and nod.

My audience erupts in loud whooping and congratulates me. The shop assistant's keeping a neutral face, but it's as if she can read me. Her eyes seem to say, "I know you're faking, but I'm not about to complain. I've earned the commission; you were the client from hell." Okay, maybe her eyes are not that argumentative, but if I were to take a guess, this is what I'd imagine she's thinking.

Back in the fitting room, a seamstress comes to take all my measurements and fit the dress corset and skirt. When everything's pinned in place, the shop assistant helps me out of the gown one last time. She carefully places the dress back on its hanger and finally leaves me alone. I put my clothes on and stare at my wedding dress dangling from its hanger. The ruffles look stupid. I hate ruffles.

"You're hideous," I tell it.

Why did I say I liked this dress? When did I become such a pushover?

"Come on, Gemma. You're getting married, the dress isn't important; it's the groom who matters." My stomach twists. Okay, let's not go there either. I'm sure every bride's nervous before her wedding, and dresses must be the single most second-guessed item of all weddings.

"Not grooms, though."

Inner self, please shut the hell up.

I put on my I-am-so-happy face again and join the others outside to go to lunch. After we're done eating, I send everyone off doing touristy things around London and go on a maddening wedding suppliers round. I go to Fulham Palace, the wedding venue, to give my final approval to the logistics, flowers compositions, and menu. Then I bring the advance check to the photographer and meet the cake designer to make sure he has the right instructions for delivery. I hate wedding planning.

By the time I get back home, I've barely managed to shower before we go out again. Richard and I take my family to a restaurant. Unfortunately, even dinner turns out to be too much of a formal affair. Everyone is making an effort, but the conversation's stiff at best. That's when I realize my parents don't know my future husband, like, *at all*. Richard's being as charming as ever, but they lack that mutual coziness, which can only come from years of mutual interactions.

"Like it was with Jake."

Ah, Gemma, don't go there. I swat the thought away like an annoying fly.

I find it hard to enjoy the fine dining when the atmosphere's so awkward. The only person not having difficulties is Kassandra. She's stuffing her mouth full of as much food as she can take, very much resembling a chipmunk. She doesn't have a problem making conversation either, talking to Richard as if she'd known him her entire life. Then again, she does that with everyone.

To be fair, Richard's parents don't know me any better. They live up north, and we've only been to visit them a couple of times. These things take time, and we have the rest of our lives for our families to get cozy with each other.

A server finally brings the check and Richard and my dad squabble over who should take it. Dad wins in the end. So Richard insists on paying for the taxi ride home. My parents are staying in my spare bedroom and my sister's sleeping in mine. I usually stay at Richard's house, but Kassandra insisted on me staying here with them tonight.

"Are you coming back with me?" Richard asks after saying goodnight to everyone else.

"No, not tonight. Kassandra asked me to stay."

Richard purses his lips.

"You know something?" He leans in to give me a goodnight kiss. "It's your hen party tomorrow," he whispers in my ear, "but I didn't say anything." He winks at me and hops back into the cab to go home.

***

"Shouldn't you be further ahead with the packing?" Kassandra asks once we're both tucked into my queen bed.

"Nah, my lease doesn't expire for another three months. I've all the time in the world to pack."

"Okay, but shouldn't you at least have started? Aren't you moving in with Richard next week?"

"Why are you so concerned about my packing?"

"I'm not. You're a bit touchy, you know?"

"Sorry. It's all this wedding planning… I hate it. It's like having a second job on top of mine. Why couldn't I get one of those butt-in mothers-in-law who wanted to organize everything?"

"You mean Richard's mom refused to help?"

"No, no. Not at all. I never asked, and she never offered. She doesn't even live in London, so there's not much she could've done, anyway. I just wish I had a party planning mother-in-law, that's all."

Kassandra throws me a piercing stare and I know we're both thinking what we're not saying: "Like Jake's mom."

"We should sleep now," my sister says.

"Why?" I pretend not to know anything.

"Because we have an early start tomorrow."

"Why?"

She beams at me. "It's your bachelorette party. We have a full schedule so you'd better get your beauty sleep."

"What have you planned?"

Kassandra closes a phantom zipper over her mouth. "My lips are shut."

"Oh, come on. Tell me."

"Nope."

I tickle her sides. "Tell me, tell me, tell me."

She squeals like a pig but doesn't spill the beans. As the screeches increase in volume, my dad pounds a fist on the wall, yelling, "Be quiet, girls."

"Yes, Daddy," we chorus.

Just like old times.

Kassandra turns off the light and we fall asleep, holding hands like we used to do as kids when my baby sister sneaked into my room because she was afraid of the dark. Only tonight, I'm the one who's afraid. Of the dark, of where my life's going. I'm scared I'm about to make the biggest mistake of my life.

Kassandra gives my hand a gentle squeeze and I relax a bit. Everything's going to be okay. It has to be.

Twenty-seven

Remember That Time?

♥♥♥
Saturday, August 25—Chicago Area

After dinner, I'm unpacking in my bedroom when a familiar *tap-tap-tap* noise drives me to the window. I open it and lean forward on the bottom rail. Jake's standing in the shadows of my backyard, throwing pebbles at my window as he used to when we were teenagers and he wanted me to come out after-hours. Unnecessary, but utterly romantic. For a second I'm tempted to use my childhood escape route and climb out the window and down the flower trellis, but I don't want to break a leg—good luck notwithstanding—a week before the wedding. Instead, I blow Jake a kiss and ask him to wait for me on the front porch. He gives me a military salute and walks around the house.

Downstairs, I find my parents watching the news in the living room.

"I'm going out for a walk with Jake," I tell them.

"Not too keen on climbing out the window anymore?" my dad asks with a smirk.

I stop dead in my tracks. "You knew about that?"

"And many other things. You'd be surprised, sweetie pie."

"I don't want to know," I say truthfully.

"Have fun, pie."

I wave goodbye and join Jake on the porch. He wraps his arms around my waist and pulls me down to the grass while I kiss him.

"To the river?" he whispers in my neck.

"To the river."

As if no time has passed at all, we stroll toward our favorite secret spot. Even if now I'm not so sure whether it was that big a secret.

"You know how all these years we thought we were being so smart?" I ask.

"Mmm-hmm."

"Well, it appears we were so busted instead."

I tell Jake about my dad. He laughs heartedly.

"Do you think it's the same with your parents?"

"Maybe—probably."

I blush. "I hope at least they don't know about the lake cabin. That'd be so embarrassing."

We reach our favorite bend in the river and Jake spreads a blanket on the grass in a spot where we're sheltered from the road by the trees but can gaze up at the stars. We lie down next to each other and stare up at the night sky.

"Remember the first time we came here?" Jake asks, rolling over to face me.

"You mean the night you didn't kiss me for the first time? Hard to forget—I cried about it for a week. I thought you didn't like me enough to kiss me."

"I liked you too much to kiss you." He kisses the tip of my nose and electric currents shoot from where his lips touched my skin to my cheeks, making them burn red. After all these years, he can still make me blush. "I'd never kissed anyone, and I was scared you'd think I was a bad kisser."

"I hadn't kissed anyone either, so I wouldn't have been able to tell."

"Well, I didn't know that at the time. It took me a while to work out the courage to finally kiss you."

"Jake Wilder," I pull him closer by the neck of his shirt, "I'm so glad you did."

We kiss for a long time until Jake pulls back. "Did you find the dress?"

"Yes." I beam. "And it's wonderful, it's…"

He places a finger on my lips. "Shhh. Don't tell me anything, I want it to be a surprise."

"Of course I'm not telling you anything. What about you? Did you sleep all day?"

"Not all day." He pinches my nose affectionately. "When you and my mom came back, she made me drive her around town all afternoon. I didn't know a wedding required so much work."

"Oh Jake, your mom has been awesome. We couldn't have done it without her. We should do something for her."

"She just wants grandkids."

"And what do you say about that?"

"That I can't wait to start working on it." He bites my earlobe, knowing it makes me lose my mind.

I push him back. "Mr. Wilder, I'm sorry, but we're old-fashioned here. You're not getting lucky until the honeymoon. Can you believe we're finally going to Hawaii?"

"I can't wait to be on a white sand beach with you. But for old times' sake, we should take a trip to the cabin." He bites me again. "To oversee the final details, obviously."

"We're not going near that cabin before our wedding day." I stifle a yawn. "Besides, the place's under disinfestation."

"You're falling asleep on me." He gets up and offers me his hands to pull me up. "I'm taking you home."

We walk back to the street. "Tomorrow I want to sleep all day," I say.

"I'm afraid that's not going to happen."

"Why?"

"Our friends have organized our bachelor and bachelorette parties tomorrow."

"Oh, where are they taking you?"

"No idea."

"Where are they taking me?"

"I know nothing."

We stop outside my house. "Promise me you won't wake up on a hotel roof in Vegas, not remembering anything that happened to you."

Jake laughs. "That's an easy promise to make. Honestly, it's just going to be a fishing trip with beers and burgers afterward."

"Aw, you think the girls will get me burgers too?" I lift my arms in front of my face, holding an invisible burger in my hands. "I want real, fat American burgers."

"I'm positive they'll have some burgers for you at some point."

"This is good night then." I'm leaning in to kiss him when the porch lights flash on.

"Did your dad just turn on the lights on purpose?"

"Old habits die hard, I guess." I give Jake a quick peck on the lips and run inside the house.

Twenty-eight

Champagne Tea and Tarot Cards

◆◆◆

Sunday, August 26—London

I wake up with screaming in my ears. My sister yells, "Wakey, wakey. It's bachelorette party time."

I smother her with a pillow. "Go away, I want to sleep."

"Come on." She throws the blankets away from my body. "You can sleep later. The first part of the day's at a spa."

That does it for me. The only thing I can use more than sleep right now is a relaxing massage.

"You can dress casual for now; we have your other outfits planned for you."

"Yes, sir."

I abide by the dress code and join everyone else in the kitchen for breakfast. My nostrils flare with the aroma of cinnamon and sugar. Mom's cooking and Amelia's laying the table. Exactly like she used to do when she came over to my house for breakfast back in the States.

Mom hands me a plate filled with her best recipe cinnamon French toast. "My sole contribution to your bachelorette party is to make you your favorite breakfast."

"Thank you, Mom. What are you and Dad doing today?"

"Don't worry, we're sightseeing. You go have fun," she tells me, then scowls at Kassandra. "Not too much fun."

Kassandra mumbles something unintelligible as her mouth's too full of bread for her to speak.

"Who else is coming?" I ask Amelia.

"Your friends from work. And Mary and Jessica were the only ones able to make it from back home. They're going to take a trip to Paris on the Eurostar next week and come back in time for the wedding. All the others said they could make it only to the wedding."

"Wait—you didn't invite Flotsam and Jetsam?"

"I can call them if you like."

"Absolutely not." We laugh. "I'm ready for my pampering. Let's go."

We move through London in a rented black limo equipped with champagne and all sorts of spirits. The others meet us at the spa. We stay there until four in the afternoon, getting every beauty treatment ever heard of. After the spa, we go to the Waldorf for their champagne afternoon tea. Amelia and Kassie decided an afternoon tea somewhere for a British hen party was fun, and I completely agree. From the Waldorf, we move on to a boutique perfume shop where we all make customized scents.

I enter the limo, holding my little perfume bottle. "I'm hungry," I say.

"We've another stop before dinner," Amelia says.

"But I'm starving," I protest. "Where are we going for dinner?"

"It's gourmet burgers for you, but only if you're good and behave."

"You can drink champagne if you're hungry," Kassandra says, passing me a flute of bubbly.

I'm not sure it's a good idea on an empty stomach, but I take it all the same.

Two glasses of bubbly later, the limo stops in front of a nondescript building in an area of London I'm not familiar with.

"Where are we?" I ask.

"We're at the Psychic Sisters."

"To do what exactly?"

"We're going to have our fortunes told."

A round of excited giggles spreads around the back of the limo.

"Oh, you know it's nonsense," I whisper in Amelia's ear.

"It might be nonsense, but it's fun. Come on, everyone said this was an absolute bachelorette party must."

Amelia takes my hand and drags me out of the car and inside the building. We enter a sort of office worthy of Whoopi Goldberg's house in *Ghost*. The hall opens on to three different rooms, apparently each reserved for a gifted diviner sister. We split into three groups and queue in front of the different doors. Amelia and I are at the front of the middle one and we're ushered in at once.

Inside, the atmosphere's kind of dark and gloomy. The air is suffocating and impregnated with the smells of cedar wood and jasmine coming from some incenses burning in a corner.

"Welcome, dears." An old crone with black hair and yellowish eyes greets us from the farthest corner. She's so small crouching behind a wooden desk, I hadn't noticed her when we got in. "Come,

come, have your future unraveled."

We take our seats in two ancient looking armchairs. I take in the chandelier dangling from the ceiling, the baroque style of my armchair, and the ridiculous costume the hag's wearing, and I'm tempted to snort. I hope we're not spending too much on this old fraud.

"You have a specific question you'd like to ask the cards?" the crone asks us, unfazed. Apparently, she isn't getting my incredulity vibes. "You want to know about your past lives, parallel lives, or about your present life?"

"Make it about her love life," Amelia answers for me.

"The True Love spread then, very well. Take the cards, dear, mix them, and cut the deck for me, please."

I do as instructed and then pass the deck to the crone who spreads it in a semicircle of sparkling blue and gold cards.

"Now pick six cards and pass them to me one by one. Let the energy in your hands guide you to the right cards."

I pick the cards at random, not feeling any particular chakra energy flowing from my fingertips, and hand them to the crone.

The fortuneteller puts the first and second card in a row at the top, the next three cards in a row below, and the last one at the bottom, alone. She turns the first two cards.

"The Fool reversed for you—it seems you're a bit of a reckless soul. And for your other half, The Tower. Interesting." She gives a little smile.

"I-interesting how exactly?" I stutter.

"The Tower symbolizes upheaval and a sudden change."

"You mean because we're getting married?"

"Perhaps, or perhaps not. Let's see what the other cards have to say." She smiles knowingly.

So far, so *bad*. The other three cards are unveiled next.

"The Wheel of Fortune for the thread that connects you to your love. The Wheel of Fortune's a powerful card. It represents karma— you can't escape it. Next, The Devil, reversed, for your strengths. It states you're ready to take control. As for your weaknesses, Judgment. This one tells you to pay heed to your inner calling."

"Meaning?"

"In simpler words, follow your guts. Trust your instinct."

Whatever. "Great advice," I say awkwardly.

"And now the final card, the True Love card. The one that reveals if your relationship can be successful." She turns it and stares at it silently for a while before fixating her yellow eyes on me. "Death."

"Oh, that sounds promising." I snort.

"Death, my dear, is a symbol of transformation and of new beginnings."

"So what do you make of this entire… uh," I try to remember the word she used, "spread?"

"You're about to meet your fate."

"So, I'm—uh—not making a mistake getting married?"

"When the moment comes, just follow your heart, darling, and you'll be fine."

I don't pay much attention as Amelia gets her future predicted, and when we leave the room, it isn't one minute too soon for me. The old hag has unsettled me.

We wait for the others in the limo, and I hope those burgers really are gourmet because I need a cheer up after that ominous Death card.

The burgers *are* great. After two or three cocktails, any thought of a relationship's demise flies out of my head and I'm cozily beginning to feel ready for bed. Amelia seems to have read my mind when she announces the final stop of my party.

"And now, ladies, back to my house for a pajama party and a showing of all our favorite Molly Ringwald movies."

I cheer along with the others. "Thank you for making this day so special," I whisper to Amelia.

She hushes me.

"Where did you put Dylan? Is he watching Molly Ringwald with us?"

"He's staying at Richard's. They're having his stag party tonight too."

"Oh gosh, I hope they don't buy him strippers."

"I specifically forbade it."

I squeeze her arm to thank her as we walk toward the limo, holding each other. That's until Kassandra barrels into us from behind, wriggling herself in between us and wrapping one arm around our shoulders.

"I'm so glad we have the limo to go home." She slurs her words a bit. "I could never figure how to drive on the wrong side of the road."

I smile, nod, and silently add that driving on the right side of the road wouldn't make much of a difference for her tonight.

Twenty-nine

Bridesmaid Wars

♥♥♥

Sunday, August 26—Chicago Area

"You know, orange really *isn't* the new black." I eye Amelia sideways as she enters my old bedroom at my parents' house. "Why are you wearing a puffy orange meringue?"

She beams at me. "It's bachelorette party day! Almost a week before the wedding, so you'll have time to recoup."

"Recoup from what?"

"It's a surprise. Here's your outfit." She hands me a bridesmaid gown I had to wear at a cousin's wedding many years ago and that I honestly thought I'd burned. I gingerly take the dress from her.

"Are we trying to get arrested by the Fashion Police?" The thing is a cotton candy nightmare of ruffles, sheer fabric, and bows. "Do I really have to wear this?"

"Yes, it's going to be fun. Trust me!"

"I don't see how it's going to be fun unless we're doing a fashion exorcism."

"Stop complaining and get dressed!"

Kassandra bursts into the room clad in a heinous maroon tablecloth. "Is she whining about the dress?"

"Yes, she is."

"It's lucky I managed to find the headpiece then." She regards me with an evil grin, shaking the flowery tiara in her hands. "Chop, chop, sistah. We don't have all day."

I reluctantly pull on the dress, which strangely enough still fits, while Amelia secures the tiara on my head with some bobby pins.

When she's done, she pulls my zipper up and I'm ready to go wherever they're taking me.

"Ta-dah! I'm the bridesmaid from hell. You two happy?"

"Very." Kassandra nods with approval. "You're missing the shoes." She hands me a pair of white sneakers.

I look at their feet for the first time and see they're both wearing sneakers as well. What the hell have they planned for the bachelorette party? I put on a pair of socks and lace up the shoes as further complaints would be useless.

"Everybody else is already here," Kassandra frets. "Let's go before we're late."

We shout our goodbyes to my parents and stream onto the front porch where I halt, shocked. Parked in front of my house is a white limo, and lined up in front of it are all my closest friends from high school, college, and even a couple who made the trip from London. They're all dressed in heinous bridesmaid gowns and sneakers—they make the final lineup from *27 Dresses* look like a classy display in comparison. It's a vengeance of ruffles, of flowered curtain-style prints, of pajama dresses, foil fabrics, and frilly frocks. It looks so horrible I'm starting to believe it's brilliant.

I jump the few steps down the porch and run across the garden to greet everyone. It takes a few minutes before Kassandra herds us into the car where I keep going with the catching up—with the added perk of champagne and the soundtrack from *Sixteen Candles* playing in the background. The eighties songs actually go really well with our dresses.

The journey to our destination takes about half an hour, and when the car stops my friends and I swoop out in a rush of colored tulle. We're standing on dry grass in front of a massive barn. The building's standing on the side of what looks like a larger roving amusement park. When we exit the limo, the driver leaves to go park somewhere, and I spot a guy dressed in military gear and boots heading our way.

"Ladies, welcome," he greets us with a slight Southern lilt. "Please follow me."

He beckons us into the barn. Inside, we form an orderly line. We're surrounded by racks of military green rifles—plastic I assume, or hope at least—white working jumpsuits, and plastic goggles.

"Good morning, ladies, and welcome to Paintball Wars Game Center. Rules are simple," military guy tells us without preambles. "On the field, you must wear your goggles at all times, no exception."

He hands us each a plastic mask.

"Paintball Wars?" I mouth to Amelia.

This is brilliant, and finally, the dresses make sense. We're going to take revenge on the bridesmaid dresses from hell and splatter them in paint.

"These are your weapons," military guy continues. "You unlock them like this." He shows us how to remove the barrel plug. "You aim and pull the trigger to shoot. No blind shooting's allowed at any time. You have a bag of ammo each. You load them here." He shows us where to insert the paint balls. "If you're hit, you're dead. Plug your barrel and move off the field. All right, that's all, ladies. Go have fun."

The game starts, and it's hilarious. Right from the beginning, it's obvious most of us—myself included—have never played paintball before, but we're all good sports and it makes for the most comical hour and a half of my life. Watching my friends trip on their floor-length satin dresses as they try to pull off sneak attacks, or seeing them dive behind a barricade, dress trains flowing in the air as they go down, is priceless. Amelia also hired a photographer to document the battle. We take silly shot after silly shot in our frilly dresses and plastic rifles.

When the game's over—I'm not even sure who won or if I'm still "alive"—my friends lead me to the other side of the barn where I'm hit by a cloud of grill smoke. A table laid with pretty colored cocktails and a hamburger extravaganza awaits us. My mouth waters at the sight—after an hour of running this is like a dream come true. We sit at the table, all of us still wearing our bridesmaid dresses—some looking more worse for wear than others after the paint riddle—and sporting thirty-two-teeth smiles.

After stuffing my mouth with as many burgers as my body can handle—I know, bad for my bride-to-be diet—we stroll through the rest of the amusement park, playing different games and going on the various rides. It's fun to see the disbelieving looks our colorful attire wins us. We're shuffling around the various stands—I'm contemplating getting real cotton candy to match my dress—when Amelia stops in front of a blue and yellow pointy tent with a red silk door.

"You should get your fortune read," Amelia suggests.

"Oh, no. It's just a bunch of crap."

"Crap or not, it's fun. Come on, I'll do it with you."

We go inside, and it's as if we've entered a different world. The noise from the circus outside is dimmed in here, and the atmosphere's dark. The tent smells like cedar wood and jasmine, and the mixed scent seems inexplicably familiar. There are incense sticks burning in a corner. That must be it: I must have been in some other place with the same incenses at some point if my life, even if I can't remember where. Gosh, the air's suffocating.

"Welcome, dears," an old crone greets us from the farthest corner. As I look at her and take in her black hair and yellow eyes, a powerful sense of déjà vu attacks me. "Oh, it's you," the crone says. "I've been waiting for you for a while now."

"You have?"

"Oh, yes. I wondered how you'd turn up in this life."

It's probably all an act to set the divination atmosphere right, but she gives me goosebumps all the same.

"Maybe this wasn't a good idea," I whisper to Amelia.

"Come on, don't be a chicken!" She grabs my hand and drags me forward in front of the diviner. Amelia and I each pick one of two short stools waiting empty in front of the tiny card table.

"My friend would like to have her fortune told," Amelia says.

"I know, dear," the hag says. "The True Love spread then, right? Do you remember what to do?"

"Err… no?"

"Pity. Take the cards, mix them, and cut the deck for me, please."

I gingerly do as I'm told. Once the crone has her deck back, she spreads it in a semicircle of sparkling blue and gold cards.

"Pick six cards from me and pass them to me one by one. Remember, let your interior energy guide your fingers."

I pick the cards randomly, not feeling any particular force guiding me as I do, and hand them to her.

The fortuneteller puts the first and second card in a row at the top, three cards in a row below, and one at the bottom, alone. She turns the first two cards.

"The Star for you and The Magician for your other half. He's a powerful, resourceful man and you're a pool of serenity and confidence surrounding your love. Much better this time around, aren't we?"

What does she mean this time around? As if I were having my fortune told every other day. But so far, so good, so I nod and smile.

She turns the second row of cards.

"The Wheel of Fortune for the connection between you—we already knew that. You have a powerful destiny awaiting you. The High Priestess for your strengths. Interesting how things change." She gives a little smile.

"C-change?" I stutter.

"Yes, dear. Change. The Priestess is a symbol of steadiness and calm."

"Good, I guess."

"Good indeed. As for your weaknesses," she looks at the last card of the row. "But of course, The Emperor, reversed."

"What does the Emperor mean?"

"Upright, it is a symbol of structure. Reversed, it shows a desire for domination, excessive control, rigidity, and inflexibility. Which was what got you into trouble in the first place, wasn't it?"

I swallow at the accuracy of her statement. It was pride and my unchecked need to feel in control that ruined things with Jake last time. I'm never letting my pride or the necessity to affirm myself through my job get in the way of my relationship ever again.

Amelia smirks beside me, and I kick her sideways in the shins.

"And now the final card, the True Love card. The one that reveals if your relationship can be successful." She turns it and stares at it silently for a while before fixating her yellow eyes on me. "The Lovers."

I blink at her.

"Well, it doesn't get any better than this now, does it?"

"I-I suppose?"

"Oh, darling, of course, you do."

"So what do you make of this entire... uh," I try to remember the word she used, "spread?"

"You're right where you should be, nothing to worry about." She winks.

I don't know what to make of this assessment. It seems just like a ball of nonsense to me.

Once Amelia has had her future predicted as well, we exit the tent and rally the others for the final stop of my party.

"Where are we headed next?" I ask my sister as she tackles me from behind. She's definitely had many more drinks since lunch.

"Oh, you're going to love this! We rented the old drive-in, and they're doing a special showing of *Sixteen Candles* just for us!"

I squeak and giggle with joy while jumping and clapping my hands. "Thank you, both of you…" I brace one arm over Amelia's shoulders and one over Kassandra's. "This has been the best day of my life."

"Eeeeee." My sister winks at me. "Wait until you see Jake in a tux waiting for you at the altar before giving away the best day prize."

I giggle again and we head toward the limo where the driver's patiently waiting for us in the parking lot. Watching my favorite movie in an old drive-in is the perfect ending to a perfect day.

"Wait, how are we going to watch the movie from the limo?"

"They're giving us the Cadillacs in the front row," Amelia says. "Real fifties style."

"The limo's just for driving us home after the movie," Kassandra explains.

I smile and silently add that she'll probably need a lift home more than anyone else will.

Thirty

Cold Feet

◆◆◆

Saturday, September 1—London

On my wedding day, I wake up at the crack of dawn with the alarm clock drilling a hole into my skull. It takes a long while for everything to get started. Even if I have planned every last detail, somehow it still seems I have a great deal left to do. Mom's so nervous she burns breakfast and I spend a good ten minutes telling her it's okay and send Dad to grab some muffins from the next-door bakery. Kassandra appears in the living room already dressed in her bridesmaid gown and I send her back to my room to change. I don't want a coffee-stained bridesmaid.

The makeup artist is late, and she squabbles with the hair stylist. But they manage to get Kassandra, Amelia—who arrived at my house at some point during the morning—my mom, and I ready in time. At noon, we eat cold sandwiches, and half an hour later, a car's here to pick us up. I clamber in the back with my mom and Kassandra, and Amelia hands us my wedding gown that we lay across our laps to minimize wrinkles. Dylan should come to pick up Amelia shortly and bring along the hair stylist and makeup artist for on-site retouches. My dad climbs in the front seat and, at last, we're ready to go. The driver starts the engine and the car flings forward into London's traffic. I barely have time to wonder how long the journey will take when we're back. Kassandra forgot her clutch. We're not exactly late, but I'm getting anxious. Luckily, we reach Fulham Palace with time to spare before the ceremony, and all I have left to do is slip into my white dress and wait for the guests to arrive.

My mom pulls up the zipper of my wedding gown and flashes me a proud smile in the mirror. Her eyes glistening with unshed tears, she makes me emotional too.

"You look perfect." She squeezes my shoulders gently. "I'm going to give you a minute."

"Thanks, Mom." I squeeze her hand in return before she exits the dressing room I've been given to get changed in.

I stare at my reflection in the mirror, trying to decide how I feel. I feel like the last six months have rolled me over. Since Richard proposed, it's as if my life's slipped out of my hands. Decisions have been made, venues, dresses, meal courses have been chosen, and I let it all flow past me. As if it wasn't my life that was being decided; as if it wasn't my wedding. But I can't escape the fact that this *is* my wedding day. That today I'm pledging to love one man, and one man only, for the rest of my life. Looking at myself in my white dress, I think of a man other than my fiancé.

I moved across the world to forget him. I burned all memories of him. I've refused to even voice his name for months now. But he always finds his way back into my heart. Is this how Jake felt on his wedding day? As if he was saying his final goodbye to me at that moment? I doubt he spared me a thought.

Amelia bursts into the dressing room and stops as she spots me. "You look… oh gosh, I don't have the words. I'm going to cry."

"That makes two of us," I sob.

"Gemma, what's going on?" Amelia shuts the door behind her before rushing to my side. "Are you overwhelmed by emotions? Nerves?"

"No, I'm just being stupid. I couldn't help thinking about him just now. How this is goodbye, for good."

"*Him*? Are you… you mean Jake?" Amelia asks in a shaking voice.

I nod.

Amelia looks at me aghast. "But you haven't spoken about him in forever, not since…" She searches in her memory for the last time his name came up. "Not since you met Sharon, ages ago."

"Well, you chided me every time I tried to talk about him. But you were right: he's married and I've no business thinking about him on my wedding day."

Amelia grimaces and blushes tomato red.

"What?"

"Nothing."

"Ames, don't say, 'Nothing.' You couldn't look any less *nothing*."

"Okay, but promise me you won't freak out… this is the worst time, really… I probably shouldn't…"

"Freak out about what? What is it? You're making me freak out by not telling me whatever the hell it is you're not telling me."

"Why don't we sit down?"

"I can't. Whenever I try to sit I'm stabbed by the boning—. I hate this dress; I don't know why I bought it, and if you don't start speaking soon, I'm going to scream."

"Okay, okay. But *I'm* sitting down." She also takes a flute of champagne and downs it in one sip. "Now, try not to get mad. But I thought it was better not to tell you…"

I narrow my eyes at her. "Not to tell me *what*?"

"You seemed finally happy, so I didn't want to stir up useless doubts. You'd finally stopped talking about Jake, and I had no idea you'd just stopped *talking* about him, but not thinking about him…"

"So what? If you're about to give me a lecture, I'm not in the mood."

"No, no lecture. Gem, I'm so sorry I didn't tell you…"

I watch her wring her fingers in agony. "Out with it," I hiss.

"It was some time ago, I bumped into Jake…"

"You what? I don't understand. When did you go to San Francisco?"

She shakes her head. "I didn't. It was here in London."

"What was Jake doing in London?"

"He-he sort of m-moved here."

"I need to sit down."

"But the boning."

"I'll take the stabbing, and a glass of that too." I point at the champagne and Amelia pours me a glass. "So he's moved here with *her*?"

London's *my* city.

"Without," Amelia whispers.

"So she lives in San Francisco and Jake lives in London. I'm not following you."

"Oh, Gem. Jake got… Jake got d-divorced!"

I shoot out of the chair as if I've been given an electric shock. Actually, my body did give me an electric shock, like when you're sleeping and your body thinks you're dying so it electrocutes you. I pace in circles around the room.

"Tell me everything you said to him and everything he said back."

"Gemma, this isn't a good idea."

"Not telling me Jake got divorced was the bad idea. How could you?"

"I'm sorry, but you seemed finally happy."

"Do I look happy now?"

"Not so much."

"I need you to tell me everything. When did he get divorced?"

"He told me they started discussing a separation in early April this year,"

"But that's just after I met his wife in my office. When was it? Right after Richard proposed, so first days of March. That explains the melancholy expression she had. Did he say why they got divorced?" My brain and my heart are in a race to decide which one's frying faster. And adrenaline's fueling them both.

"Something about understanding they weren't right for each other."

"So when did he move here?"

"Two months ago, early July."

Jake. Wifeless. Living in my city for two months. And I didn't know. What if I passed him on the street and did not see him?

"Did he say why London?" I'm not letting myself hope yet.

"He said The London Clinic offered him a research position here a year ago, around the time he got married. He refused it at the time, but they kept insisting… offering him bigger and bigger salaries and more and more research independence every time. So when they renewed the offer just after he'd signed the divorce papers, he finally took it."

Uh, not what I expected. What did I expect?

"Did he… hem… ask about me?"

"Yes, he asked how you were and told me he knew you were engaged and asked when the wedding was."

"I told Sharon that day in my office and she must've told him. What next?"

"I told him you were getting married the first of September at Fulham Palace, so he told me to give you his felicitations."

My heart seems to be winning the race for the more stressed organ. "Did he… did he say anything else?"

"No, he told me to take care and went on his way."

I collapse back on the chair and my sides pay for it as I receive a vicious stab from the corset.

"How did he look when he asked about my wedding? Sad? Genuinely happy? Indifferent?"

"He didn't have any particular look. Listen, Gemma, it was a five-minute conversation on the street, nothing more."

"Nothing more? How can you say that? Jake living here, in my city, single! And you say, 'Nothing more.' How could you not tell me? I could've… I could've…"

"What? Canceled the wedding?"

I don't need to tell her that's exactly what I'd been thinking because she knows.

"This is exactly why I didn't tell you," she says fiercely.

"You don't get to decide how I should live my life. You should've told me."

"And what? Watch you throw away a wonderful man who simply adores you to chase after a memory?"

"Don't you think it's destiny Jake ending up here, of all places? And after all this time, just when he got divorced. He married the wrong person. You almost married the wrong person. Maybe I'm about to marry the wrong person too."

"So tell me. In the two months Jake's been here, how many times did he call you?"

"He doesn't have my number."

"You've been working at the same firm since you moved here. If he wanted to contact you, all he had to do was call your office."

"Maybe he thinks I don't want him to call me. I left him. I never answered any of his calls. I never told him I still loved him… and if I did…"

"What? You'd get back together with him? Do you even know Jake? When was the last time you spoke to him?"

I blink at her, get up again, and move toward the door, giving Amelia my shoulders. *I need to think.*

"Listen, I'm not saying you should marry Richard at all costs," Amelia says. "Tell me you don't love Richard and you don't have to say another word. I'll get you out of here and take care of everything. The guests, the minister, your parents…"

At that instant, the door bursts open again and I see a brief image of Richard looking dashing and full of life in his tuxedo before he closes the door again.

"Sorry, wrong room!" he shouts from the other side. "I know it's bad luck to see the bride before the ceremony, but I'm glad I got a peek. You're breathtaking. I love you."

I hear steps moving down the hall and assume Richard's gone.

Staring at the door, transfixed, I can feel Amelia's eyes piercing two holes between my shoulders.

She's right. I know Richard. I know where I stand with him. Jake? I don't know him anymore. It hits me like a punch in the stomach. It's been too long. The Jake I knew wouldn't have married a woman to divorce her only months later. Maybe he's a different man, altered beyond all recognition. He won't be the same Jake I once knew. The boy I lost my virginity to one summer afternoon at his parents' lake cabin. Amelia's right—I'm not going to throw everything away for the memory of something that's long gone.

Thirty-one

Vows

♥♥♥

Saturday, September 1—Chicago Area

On my wedding day, I wake up when it's still dark outside. It takes me a couple of blinks to remember why my heart's beating so fast and why my entire body seems to be sparking with electricity. *I'm marrying Jake today.* I savor the thought, snuggling under the warm blankets in a cocoon of sheer happiness.

My solitary bliss is short-lived. A few minutes later, alarm clocks come to life around the house and everything seems to explode in a bustling mayhem. Neighbors and friends scamper in and out of the house like little ants along with makeup and hair professionals. It's as if the entire block's celebrating. I glide through everything with a smile on my lips until it's time to drive to the lake.

The inside of the lake cabin has been reserved for my entourage. When Mom pulls up the zipper of my gown, I twirl in little jumps, hands tucked in the delicious pockets of my skirt. And Kassandra and Amelia both clap and hug me.

There's a knock on the door and Jake's mom pokes her head in. "You look radiant," she says. "Jake has arrived; we're ready whenever you are."

I smile and nod. "I'm ready. Can you send my dad in?"

"Sure." Susan winks and she's gone.

"You." I point at the others. "Go."

"We'll see you outside." Amelia hugs me again before exiting.

My dad comes in next. "All right, pie. Let's do this."

He offers me his arm and I take it. Outside, it takes a minute for my eyes to adjust to the bright, mid-afternoon sun, and a little longer for my heart to recover from the sight of Jake in a tux, waiting for me under an arch of white roses. We make our way down the beach along the pretend aisle delineated by two rows of white flowers and green leaves. Until we're there. My dad gives my hand to Jake, and the ceremony begins.

I have trouble following what the minister's saying, as I'm lost in the sea of mountain mist and snowstorm of Jake's gray eyes. I notice we've reached the vows part when Jake gently relieves me of the bouquet, passing it to Amelia, to take my hands into his.

"Gemma, I love you. There isn't a time when I can remember not loving you. As someone once said at another wedding, you are my life."

Edward, Jake's brother, cheers at his quote from my wedding-crashing speech and the crowd gives a chuckle or two. Heads turn as those who know what the quote is about, tell the ones who don't.

I fight back the tears as I listen to the rest of Jake's vow.

"Today's the best day of my life because you're here with me. All I want to do is to protect you and make you as happy as I am today for all the days ahead of us. I vow to love you and stand by your side through everything life will throw at us. I promise to laugh with you, and cry with you, to love and honor you. To never let you go again and always find my way back to you, to us. I vow to love you even when it takes you an hour to order a pizza because you read the entire menu then just order a Margherita."

I chuckle and the first tears roll down my cheeks.

"Gemma, you're the person I want to grow old with, the person I want to see every morning when I wake up and the one I want to kiss goodnight. I promise to give you all of me and to love you, from this day forward, always."

"Jake." I pause to steady my trembling voice. "Today's the happiest day of my life too. It took us a long time to get here, and some crazy moments…"

The crowd chuckles again. This time everyone knows what I'm referring to.

"I love you because you're the best person I know. The kind of person who even a dying animal would trust with the most important thing she had." I wave toward an iPad set on a pedestal. On the screen is our cat sitter in London, who's following the ceremony via Skype with Lucky. She waves Lucky's paw back.

"Today I give myself to you, completely. I vow to love you even when you make me cry with your incredibly romantic words, completely ruining my makeup on our wedding day."

He brushes the tears away from my cheeks with his thumbs.

"Jake, from the night you kissed me for the first time my heart started to ache with how much I love you. It felt like my chest could no longer contain it as if it didn't belong to me anymore. And it didn't; it doesn't because my heart belongs to you. It always has. Even when we were apart, you were always with me. You were my first love and I want you to be my last. You're the only man I've ever loved, and I promise to love and cherish you from this day forward, always."

Ten minutes later, we're husband and wife.

Thirty-two

At the Altar

◆◆◆

Saturday, September 1—London

After I've made my decision to go through with the wedding, it all spirals out of my control. The hair stylist inserts fresh pink roses in my hair, the makeup artist gives my cheeks a last minute brush of color, and before I know it, the wedding march is playing and I'm at my father's side, walking down the long, long aisle. I hold on to him, hoping this walk will be over soon and willing it to last forever at the same time. So I'm not marrying my first love; almost no one does. Nothing wrong with that. I focus my attention on Richard's adoring face. *I don't deserve you.* The treacherous thought slips out of my head.

I'm such a fraud. Richard's face is glowing with love, and not two minutes ago, I was contemplating leaving him at the altar to chase after another man.

We reach the front of the chapel and my dad gives my hand to Richard. I hold tightly onto Richard's strong arm, trying to stop mine from shaking. I try to plaster a confident smile on my face. Richard leads me to our spots in the center of the aisle and the minister opens the ceremony.

"Dearly beloved, we're gathered here on this beautiful day to celebrate the union of Gemma and Richard in matrimony…"

Right, there's no turning back at this point.

As the ceremony progresses, increasingly frequent shivers of panic spider walk down my spine. My palms begin pooling with sweat and I try to inconspicuously dry them on the skirt of my dress. I hope no one notices.

"…In the time that Gemma and Richard have spent together, they've built the sturdy foundation for a lifelong relationship…"

Now, seriously. We've been together barely a year. It hardly qualifies as a sturdy foundation. Lifelong relationship. It gives me pause; I'm committing myself to Richard for life. It's not on a day-by-day basis anymore; it's forever. *Forever!* Tiny beads of sweat make their appearance on my forehead. Why are those huge yellow lights pointing right in our faces? Are they trying to melt us?

"…May you all remember and cherish this ceremony, for on this day, with love, we will forever bind Gemma and Richard together…"

This forever thing again. Why does he keep repeating it? Isn't once enough?

A noise behind us distracts me. It sounds like the chapel's front door opening. Some late guest maybe. I'm tempted to look back, but I'm afraid that if I see an open escape route, I'll take it.

My corset's too tight. I can't breathe. Oh gosh, I'm going to pass out. I can't breathe. I need to get out of this dress; I need out. Out, I need out.

"If there is anyone in attendance who has cause to believe that this couple should not be joined in marriage, you may speak now or forever hold your peace…"

"STOP," I yell at the top of my lungs, surprising even myself. "I can't do this," I whisper. Aw, it feels good to say it aloud. "I'm sorry, I can't."

The minister stares at me in shock and there's a collective intake of breath from the guests. I look at Richard, petrified. I can already see the sad drop of his brows and read the resigned pain in those beautiful eyes. I can't stand that I'm the one who's doing this to him, so I look away. The door, I need to get to the main door. I want to run away and never stop running. I gather my skirts in my hands ready to make a run for it, turn toward the chapel's front door, and my heart positively stops as I spot Jake standing in the middle of the aisle, looking at me as if seeing me for the first time.

Just like that, the rest of the world disappears, and it's just the two of us, staring at each other. I take in all the details of the face I know so well. I see the boy who stole my heart so many years ago standing before me. My first love, my first everything. The only man I ever truly loved. And I do know him, and he does know me. It doesn't matter how much time has passed, I can read it in his eyes. In a moment, everything changes. My heart swells in my chest, suddenly too big, too full of love to be contained. I look Jake in the eyes and a million unspoken words fly between us, the whispers of our past and the promises of a future together.

Jake's lips curl up in an uncertain smile, hopeful maybe, before he says, "You sort of stole my opening line there."

Something half-way between a sob and a chuckle escapes my lips. Out of the corner of my eye, I catch Richard moving a step backward. I dare to look at him again and find his features set, resigned.

"Is this the bloke you told me about the first night we met?" he asks.

"Yes, Richard. I-I'm so, so truly very sorry…"

"It's not your fault. I knew you weren't ready to marry me. I could tell from the moment I asked." His shoulders sag. "I just hoped that if I made it perfect for you, you'd eventually want it as much I do. But you don't. You never have."

"Oh, Richard." I hug him tightly. "One day you'll make one woman really lucky," I whisper in his ear. "I'm just not that woman."

"I know. I've known for a long time. Go, be happy," he whispers back.

I let him go, gather up my skirts again, and sprint down the aisle toward Jake. I take his outstretched hand and together we run out of the chapel into the sunset.

***

Outside, Jake stops behind me and pulls me backward. "If I have to wait another second to do this…" He cups my face and leans his forehead against mine. "I've missed you so much, I love you so much." He presses his lips to mine in a passionate kiss before I can say anything. My knees buckle underneath me and I grip his arms to stay upright. If one could die of happiness, I'd be heading to heaven.

Jake pulls back. "When I found out you were getting married, I got so scared. I told myself I'd leave you alone, that I wouldn't come here today, and before I knew it, I was in the car driving here."

"Jake, I know. I wanted to crash your wedding when I found out, but I couldn't. I-I love you. I love you. I love you." He kisses me again.

"You really wanted to crash my wedding? How? What happened?"

"Later," I tell him, looking over his shoulders at the chapel door as the first stunned guests flood out. "Let's get the car and get the hell out of here, *now*."

He takes my hand again and drags me forward to his car. We're almost there when someone screams my name. I turn around and see Amelia running toward us holding her long skirt in one hand and dragging my honeymoon suitcase behind with the other. She catches up with us in the parking lot and throws her arms around my neck.

"I'm sorry I didn't tell you," she whispers in my ear. "I was wrong."

"It doesn't matter, it's all good now." I beam at her.

"I can see that." She smiles back at me then at Jake. "You stole the bride."

He gives her his best mischievous grin.

"Make her happy," Amelia says.

"Will do." Jake nods. "I'll get the car," he says. "Give you ladies a minute."

Amelia seems about to cry. She hands me the suitcase and takes from her shoulder my purse with my phone, wallet, and passport inside. "After being a runaway bride myself, I thought you might need these."

"Thanks. Tell my parents I'll call them soon. And please say sorry to everyone."

"You don't worry about a thing, I'll take care of everything here. Now go and be happy."

Jake backs the car next to us and I climb in the front seat, waving goodbye one last time as we screech out of the yard, sending gravel flying behind us.

"Any idea where we're going?" I ask.

Jake looks at me then back at the road. "There's a flight leaving for Hawaii in two hours. If we hurry, we can catch it."

"Are you sure you didn't plan this?"

He gives me that wicked, lopsided grin I love so much and winks at me.

I take Jake's hand and look at the road ahead, unable to wipe a huge smile off my face. "Woo-hoo. Hawaii, here we come."

Thirty-three

Two Become One

♥♥♥

Sunday, September 2—Honolulu

After the beach ceremony, we party all of Saturday night and leave for our honeymoon in Hawaii early on Sunday Morning. We arrive in Honolulu in the evening, the day after the wedding. At the arrivals gate, a guy's waiting for us with a piece of paper saying, Mr. and Mrs. Wilder. The writing sends a thrill down my spine.

Our hotel is in Kapalua Bay and the drive there takes a little less than an hour. Most of the road runs along the coast; we pass several beautiful beaches, and in more than one, wedding ceremonies are taking place in the sunset.

"Do many people come to Hawaii to get married?" I ask the driver.

"Yes, many. One of the easiest places to tie the knot, as easy as in Vegas. You just need to take your license and find a minister."

Cool.

At the hotel, Jake takes care of the check-in while I stare at the ocean from the hotel's lobby. Its waves seem to pull at me, the wind to whisper in my ears as if this moment is somehow a significant one.

We follow a clerk who shows us to our room, the honeymoon suite. While the clerk shows Jake the perks of the room to earn his tip, I feel the pull of the ocean again. I spring the French doors open and walk outside onto the patio. A gentle ocean breeze caresses my skin. I look up at the stars and they seem to wink back at me as if they know something I don't; as if my destiny is written in their constellations. My husband comes up behind me and wraps his arms around my waist.

"Beautiful, aren't they?" he asks, looking up with me.

"You think we were destined to be together?"

"I don't know if it was destiny, fate, sheer luck or whatever. I'm just glad we found each other once and then again."

"It was destiny. I believe that if things had gone any other way, we'd still be here, under these same stars, married, happy."

Feeling as one with the universe, I kiss Jake. He lifts me up, never breaking the kiss, and walks me back into the room, wedding night style. I rest my head on the nook between Jake's shoulders and neck, breathing in his scent. My heart's pulsing with life—a new life I'm going to live with Jake by my side.

♦♦♦

Sunday, September 2—Honolulu

A thirty-hour flight, a visit to the Honolulu Marriage License Office, and a $95 Beach Wedding booking later, Jake and I are standing on a beautiful beach in Maui at sundown, holding hands before a minister. Jake proposed to me in the middle of Heathrow Airport, and on the journey to Hawaii, we talked and talked and talked about everything that has happened to us over the years. We had so many things to say, but it still felt as if we'd only said bye to each other the day before.

"Gemma and Jake," the minister says, bringing me back to present.

I stare into Jake's eyes.

"Congratulations to both of you today," the minister continues. "You should enjoy this special moment in your lives. Today's an exceptional day. Today your memories and hopes merge together. Today they become one. Today the word marriage has a special meaning. It means the end of the search for that special love. Today it brings fulfillment, it brings completion to your lives... Now to the proceedings. Jake, do you today, sir, take Gemma to become your lawfully wedded wife?"

Jake squeezes my hands. "I do."

"And do you today, Gemma, take Jake to become your lawfully wedded husband?"

I squeeze back. "I do."

"Would you please repeat these words after me: to love and to cherish..."

"To love and to cherish..." we echo.

"To have and to hold..."

"To have and to hold..."

"To honor and respect..."

"To honor and respect..."

"From this day forward."

"From this day forward."

"Now the rings exchange."

Jake takes out of his jacket pocket two wedding bands we bought at a cheap jewelry shop at the airport.

"You are about to present rings to one another," the minister goes on. "As you can see, rings are round. This circle will remind you that your love shall always be with no end. As you walk together through life, protect your love, always speak from your heart, and listen closely to one another. Cherish every moment you're given together. And you'll strive together with your love for each other. Now, on to the final words. Please repeat after me: with this ring, I marry you..."

"With this ring, I marry you..."

We both put a band on the other's finger.

"I join my life to yours..."

"I join my life to yours..."

"All that I am, all that I have..."

"All that I am, all that I have..."

"All of my love, I gift to you."

"All of my love, I gift to you."

"And now, for the power invested in me by the state of Hawaii, it's my privilege to pronounce you husband and wife. You may kiss the bride."

***

We end up staying in a hotel in Kapalua Bay. The minister suggested this part of the island, and we were lucky enough to find a hotel without an advance booking. Jake takes care of the check-in while I stare at the ocean from the hotel's lobby. Its waves seem to pull at me, the wind to whisper in my ears as if this moment was somehow a significant one.

We follow a clerk who shows us to our room, they gave us the honeymoon suite. While the clerk shows Jake the perks of the room to earn his tip, I feel the pull of the ocean again. I spring the French doors open and walk outside on the patio. A gentle ocean breeze caresses my skin. I look up at the stars and they seem to wink back at me as if they know something I don't; as if my destiny is written in their constellations. My husband comes up behind me and wraps his arms around my waist.

"Beautiful aren't they?" he asks, looking up with me.

"You think we were destined to be together?"

"I don't know if it was destiny, fate, sheer luck or whatever. I'm just glad we found each other once and then again."

"It was destiny. I believe that if things had gone any other way, we'd still be here, under these same stars, married, happy."

Feeling as one with the universe, I kiss Jake. He lifts me up, never breaking the kiss, and walks me back into the room, wedding night style. I rest my head on the nook between Jake's shoulders and neck, breathing in his scent. My heart's pulsing with life—a new life I'm going to live with Jake by my side.

♥♦♥♦♥♦♥

Two weeks later, the last day of our honeymoon, Jake wakes me by nuzzling my neck.

"How's my beautiful bride?"

I want to say, "Wonderful," or "Crazily happy," but the truth is I'm feeling groggy at best.

"I'm sleepy. Do we have to start packing already?"

"What's wrong?" Jake's immediately up and alert. He turns on the lights and checks my temperature, placing the back of his hand on my forehead. "You're pale."

"Nothing's wrong. I'm just a bit queasy. Maybe the Lao-Lao from last night was a bit heavy."

"Are you sure?"

I'm about to say yes when I gag. And before I know it, I'm running for the toilet.

Jake's at my side in a matter of seconds and he holds my hair back as I puke. Not the most romantic ending to our blissful honeymoon, but a good insight into that 'in sickness and health' promise.

When there's nothing left in my stomach, I wash my mouth in the sink and sit on the closed toilet to recover.

Jake hands me a damp towel to place on my forehead. "Better?" he asks.

"I just wish I didn't have to fly thirty hours with food poisoning. But I'm fine."

From under my towel, I can see Jake's gone doctor on me. He grabs my wrist and stares at his watch.

"What are you doing?"

"Taking your pulse."

"Why?"

"It's a good indication of body temperature."

"I don't have a fever."

"You feel lightheaded?"

"Slightly."

"Does your back ache?"

"A little."

"Are your nipples more sensitive than usual?"

"Are you being dirty with me right now?" I attempt to make a joke, but he gives me a serious scold. "They are, a little. I should get my period soon. It's normal."

"When was your last period?"

"I have the date on my phone."

He retrieves it from my bedside table and I check the notes. "August 17."

Jake gives me a dreamy smile.

"What?"

"Are you still regular?"

"Yeah, like a clock. Why?"

"You're two days late." His smile widens.

Both anxiety and excitement grip me. "You think I'm... you mean..." My dizziness worsens. "Are you sure?" A honeymoon baby, it'd be too good to be true—nausea aside.

"You'll have to take a test. I'll run to the resort's pharmacy and see if they have one."

He literally runs out of the room. When he comes back, he's sweaty and a little out of breath. "Here." He hands me the test and gives me some privacy.

We wait for the result on the bed. I'm nestling in between his legs and lying back against his chest, the little plastic stick in my hands. Almost immediately, a vertical line makes its appearance across the horizontal one.

"It's positive!" The strongest, weirdest feeling of joy wraps around me as I lean back to look at my husband. "We're going home as a trio."

Jake's whole face lights up now. "You know what they say? First comes love, then comes marriage and then..."

I don't let him finish as I pull his face down in a kiss. Our first as parents...

End of Book One

I HAVE NEVER

A laugh out loud offfice romance

BY CAMILLA ISLEY

One

Never Make a Scene

The day it all goes wrong starts as a more or less ordinary one. My fit watch startles me awake at dawn and, forty minutes later, notifies me I've run five miles through Central Park. A perfect six-minute-per-mile time.

Back at Gerard's apartment, he's still asleep. I peel off my sweaty clothes, take a quick shower, and wake Sleeping Boyfriend with a kiss and the aroma of French-pressed mocha.

"Morning, sleepy head," I say affectionately.

"What time is it?" he asks, still groggy.

"Six-thirty, time to go."

Gerard groans and shuffles out of bed. We eat breakfast in the kitchen listening to the morning news. Me wearing a towel, him in boxer shorts.

Fifteen minutes later, I brush crumbs off my lips and get up. "I'd better get going, big day ahead!"

"Oh, right. The announcement for the new junior editor is today."

"Yes, this morning."

"Nervous?"

"Positive," I say, showing more confidence than I feel.

"Listen, babe," Gerard says, jaw twitching. A sign he's worried. "Why don't we go out tonight to… mmm… celebrate?" He's being awkward. *Why is he so tense?* "I want to talk to you about something important."

Something important? Is Gerard finally going to propose? After three years together, it's about time.

I smile slyly. "Sure, dinner out sounds amazing."

P&P. Promotion and proposal all in one day. This is going to be the best day of my life.

"Now I really have to get ready for the office." I kiss Gerard's forehead. "Text me when you've made a reservation, yeah?"

He nods, and I waltz into his room to change. Many people hate their jobs, but I love mine. Well, not exactly the job I have—

advertising—but the job I *could* have starting today. Junior Fashion Editor of Évoque Magazine, the top female media brand in the world. Marketing was just my way in—an editorial position has always been the end goal.

Unfortunately, almost everyone else working at Évoque shares this dream. But I still hope to beat the odds. Annabelle Visser, our Editor-in-Chief—yeah, the mean devil wearing Prada—more than hinted that sales numbers will have a weight in the decision. Since joining Évoque five years ago, I've worked like a slave to become the star of my department. So if not written in stone, my promotion has at least been stitched in silk.

On all fours, I retrieve my sleepover bag from under Gerard's bed. One of my chief rules in relationships is *don't move in without a ring*. So whenever I spend the night at Gerard's house, I bring the essentials and leave nothing behind. This duffle bag is like an extra limb.

I shove my dirty running gear in a separate tote bag, then change into the working clothes I brought over: a black leather pencil skirt and emerald blouse that makes my green eyes pop. To intensify the effect, I shadow my eyelids to get that smoky look. At the office, exceptionally prim grooming comes with the territory and is expected of every employee.

Makeup done, I pull my natural strawberry red hair up in an intentionally messy bun, put on a bold shade of red lipstick, and wink at my image.

I'm the picture of a young, successful woman ready to conquer the fashion world.

From Gerard's Park Avenue condo, I can walk to work. The weather's perfect, and the late spring breeze only adds to my good mood. I wear foldable flats up to the edge of Central Park and then switch gears: plastic ballerinas for gel-cushioned pumps. I never show myself in public without heels. Not since that time when I went to Six Flags in my twenties wearing sneakers, and an attendant asked to check my height before he allowed me on a ride. For the record, I was a good six inches above the minimum.

In front of my office's skyscraper, I pause for a second to admire the building. Working at Northwestern, the publishing powerhouse of Manhattan, always gives me a thrill of pride. This is the place everyone wants to be. The building itself screams luxury and power from every glass panel and metal joint.

Ahead of me, the automatic doors sweep open, a strong, cool draft tightening my pencil skirt against my legs. Even the air feels expensive. As usual, I'm the first one in. *Good.* I always enjoy working in the quiet hours of the morning.

I stuff my duffle bag out of sight under my desk and turn on my laptop.

Will HR call me? Or will it be my new boss? This is the first time I've been promoted to a different department, so I'm not sure if the procedure is similar to same-department promotions. In the past, my current boss always delivered the news, but since I'll no longer work for her…

My landline trills, jolting me out of my thoughts.

I inhale, exhale, and then answer. "Blair Walker, Évoque Magazine."

"Miss Walker, this is Emilia Peterson from Human Resources. Please come up to my office right away."

"Absolutely, I'll be there in two minutes."

Emilia is our Talent Manager Coordinator—and she wants to see *me*. With a cheek-aching smile on my face, I rush to the elevators.

One floor up, I knock on Emilia's door, my stomach knotting in anticipation.

A muffled voice comes from behind the panel wall. "Come in."

If voices could be described as lipstick shades, Emilia's would be a Chanel Rouge. Suave. Confident.

I step into the office. Emilia—tall, platinum blonde, and lethally thin—lifts her icy gaze from some papers and says, "Ah, Blair. Please close the door and sit down." She gestures at the white chair in front of her white desk. Cold blue eyes settle on me. "Would you like some water?"

More some champagne. "No, thanks. I'm good."

"Very well, let's get straight to it." She folds her hands and sighs. "As you know, the position of Junior Fashion Editor was extremely coveted…"

Was? Is it mine now? I can't wait for her to say it, but I politely let her continue with her perfunctory speech. I can wait a few more minutes before I ask about the pay rise and extra benefits.

"...the race was tight, and you were an honorable runner-up..."

I nod my approval before my thoughts screech to a halt. *Wait, what?* Isn't this the part where she congratulates me and assigns me a new corporate phone? I was really hoping to get the new iPhone.

"What do you mean runner-up?"

"I mean you were an outstanding candidate."

"But not the winner?" My voice isn't nearly as steady as I'd like it to be—it projects a 99cents lip balm at best, regardless of the actual shade I'm wearing.

"Unfortunately, no. You didn't get the position," Emilia confirms, never taking her eyes off me.

"Who?"

"It doesn't really matter—"

"It does matter. Annabelle herself said sales figures would count toward the final decision. My numbers are better than everybody else's!"

"Your numbers are good, but not the best."

"No other sales manager signed as many contracts as I did this past year. I've put in more overtime and weekends to make sure of that. No one beats my numbers."

"Someone did," Emilia insists, her tone severe.

"Who?" I ask again.

For the first time, the corporate witch lowers her gaze, a shadow of guilt crossing her face. "Aurora."

"Aurora?" I repeat. "But her figures are awful!"

Emilia looks at me again, impassible. "One of her long-standing clients increased their expenditure considerably... it tipped the balance in her favor." Again, I sense she's holding something back.

Comprehension hits me. "You mean her mother bought the editor position for her!"

Aurora's mother, Rebecca Vanderbilt, is an iconic fashion designer with the power of old and new money combined. I never stood a chance against that kind of firepower.

"I know it might seem unfair..."

Are my ears functioning? Is our dear Talent Manager Coordinator trying to deny the injustice?

"Because *it is* unfair," I say. "You're ignoring the best employee to promote the one with a pedigree."

Emilia's nostrils flare. "We're promoting the employee who brought the magazine the most business, regardless of how they got it."

No point in arguing further. It's clear the decision is irrevocable. Emilia's immaculate white desk blinds me as I fight the tears threatening to shed. I take a few moments to steady myself before asking, "Is that all, am I free to go?"

"I understand you want to get this over with. You'll see we've put together an extremely generous severance package..." Emilia switches to a brisk, down-to-business tone so quickly it dizzies me.

"Severance?" I repeat.

"Yes. This might seem like a setback at first, but I'm really doing you a favor here."

"A favor?" I sound like a talking parrot, only able to repeat the words I'm hearing.

"Yes. Advertising is not your field. You don't like marketing, and I don't know when there'll be another editorial position available."

"Why are you firing me?" I ask, still in disbelief.

"Motivation is an important aspect of your job, and you wouldn't be able to bring your best effort to the table after today."

"Is it just me, or are all the other applicants being fired as well?

"Some other senior advertisers are being let go. Of course, I can't disclose their names," she says without batting an eyelid. "As I said, motivation is key—"

"Meaning you can no longer dangle the carrot of an editor position in our faces to have us slave for you day after day. What's next? Are you hiring college grads to string them along instead?"

"Your replacement does not concern you."

"Oh gosh, that's exactly what you're doing!" I nearly shriek. "Are you trying to run for worst employer of the year?" The words leave my mouth before I can swallow them back.

"No, Blair, we run a business. I thought you were sensible enough to know that. And honestly, I expected you to behave like a professional. If anything, this behavior just wiped away any regrets we might have had about not promoting you. Really, Blair. There's no need to make a scene."

Those last words slap me harder than if she'd actually hit me. Making petty scenes goes against my creed, against my list of dos and don'ts. The list that's helped to keep me focused on my life goals and out of trouble since I was a teenager. I carry it wherever I go; it's the secret to my success. Until now, anyway. With Emilia's words still ringing in my ears, I picture the number one item on the list: *never make a scene.*

That thought is enough to bring me back from blind rage to controlled fury. Emilia's right, I don't need to humiliate myself any further. I'm going to leave in a dignified way and my head held high.

I school my expression into one of neutrality as Emilia slides a brown envelope over her stupidly white desk and taps it. "In here you'll find all the info about our offer. Please review it. I'll be happy to answer any questions you might have."

I take the manila envelope without opening it.

"I'm sure you did the best you could," I say. No point in trying to negotiate a better deal. When you get the ax, Évoque Magazine gives you what they deem fair and not a cent more. "Is that all?"

"Yes. It's understandable if you want to leave before everyone else gets in. A security officer will escort you back to your desk to collect your belongings and will take your security pass on the way out."

Security, seriously? Are they afraid I'll steal a Birkin on my way out?

"Very well. Goodbye, Emilia," I say in the most civil tone I can muster.

Outside the office, a guard is already waiting for me. With a deep breath, I prepare myself for the most humiliating fifteen minutes of my life.

***

"You didn't get the promotion." Gerard's mouth hangs open. "I really wanted you to get it."

Oh? When did he start caring so much about my *career?* Being a corporate lawyer, he always seems so focused on *his* job. But the concern in his eyes is genuine and so sweet.

"Me, too, honey." I take his hand across the restaurant table. "But I don't want to ruin our night brooding over my lost job." I spent the entire day crying, curled in a ball on my couch, and only the prospect of tonight kept me sane.

Gerard looks aghast. "I thought this would be the best day to tell you… that you'd be happy…"

He's worried my job's demise is going to ruin his proposal. "You can tell me anything," I reassure him. "It doesn't matter what happened at work. We can talk about whatever it is you wanted to discuss." *Or you could just give me the diamond ring and be done with it.* "I won't be sad, I promise."

Gerard frowns. "I'm afraid you will be."

"Be what?"

"Sad."

"Sad?" He has it all wrong. Wedding planning is exactly the kind of distraction I need from the pile of CVs I'll have to send to find a new job. Right, let's focus on the half of my life still going according to plan. "Why would I be sad?"

"Blair." Gerard sighs. "I think we should take a break."

"A break?"

The talking parrot is making a comeback.

"Yeah, we should see other people."

"Other people?"

"Yes, I'm not sure we're compatible."

I blink. "After *three years?*"

He nods. "Yes, you'll agree w—"

I narrow my eyes at him. "Who is she?"

"S-she? There's no one else," Gerard stutters defensively.

"Is it Laura?"

After endless arguments about my "unwarranted" jealousy for his secretary, I'm not going to pull any punches.

Gerard shakes his head frantically. "No."

Still, he dares to deny it.

"You're lying," I hiss. "How long have you been screwing her?"

"It's not like that." His entire face turns red. "We're…"

"What? In love?" I scoff. "An affair with your secretary— *seriously?* You're such a cliché."

"Blair, lower your voice. People are staring."

I sweep the room with my eyes and, indeed, more than a couple of heads have turned our way.

"Am I embarrassing you, Gerard? Is that why you brought me to this nice restaurant to talk, so we'd be in a public space?"

"Blair, we can discuss our problems like the two civil adults we are. There's no need to make a scene."

No. Need. To. Make. A. Scene.

My head begins spinning, filled with a whirlwind of memories. My mother admonishing me whenever I threw a tantrum: "Blair, a well-educated young woman should always behave properly. We don't make public scenes. That's not what we do."

I remember the speech my ballet instructor gave me when I didn't get the lead role in *The Swan Lake:* "Blair, real ballerinas take setbacks with their heads held high. They don't make scenes."

Emilia this morning. Gerard now.

The vortex stops on a clear image of the list's number one item: *never make a scene.*

It's all been for nothing. All the sacrifices I made. All the times I said, "No," to anything even remotely fun. All the lost opportunities… *to live* rather than just behave. The list, my secret recipe for success, is worthless. At twenty-nine, what do I have to show for it? Nothing. No job. No boyfriend. Everyone thinks they can walk all over good old Blair because she's too polite to say anything. *No more.*

Rage takes over. My fury bubbles up and I vomit years of repressed feelings and self-imposed restraints on Gerard. "*A scene? You don't want me to make a scene?*" I get up and throw my napkin on the table. "Well, guess what! You're out of luck."

"Blair, don't—"

"Why?" I scream. "So you can run to your office's side dish with a clean conscience?"

"Don't talk about Laura that way. I won't allow it!"

"Do you prefer boyfriend-stealing bitch?"

Everyone in the room is staring at us now.

Gerard's ears turn a deeper shade of red. "Blair, please sit down, you're embarrassing yourself."

"I've nothing to be embarrassed about," I yell. "I'm not a cheating, lying bastard! Ladies and gentlemen, please give a round of applause for Gerard Wakefield and his mistress, the secretary, Laura."

A server arrives at our table and stares at us, perplexed. "Spaghetti marinara?"

In a crazy impulse, I say, "Mine." I grab the plate and before I know what I'm doing, I tip it over Gerard's head. "How's this for a scene, Gerry dear?"

Gerard shoots to his feet, his head, face, and suit dripping marinara. "You crazy bitch!" he shouts, dabbing the sauce off his face with his napkin. "It's hot sauce! You could've blinded me. I'll sue you for this."

"Please do," I shout back. "But be prepared to fight me in court. I'm sure the managing partners at your firm will be thrilled to learn of your extracurricular activities with their employee. They'll fire you on the spot!"

That shuts him up. Gerard opens and closes his mouth like a gaping fish. To stare at his spaghetti marinara-covered head would almost be funny, if the situation wasn't so tragic.

With one last glare, I storm out of the restaurant. Utterly lost and with no idea where I'm going, I run outside into the night. Oh, it felt so good to let it all out. Gerard's spaghetti-splattered head flashes before my eyes again and I can't help but laugh. A crazy, hysterical, uncontrollable laugh. Not being in control is great. Not holding back is fantastic. I should've done it a long time ago. I should've done so many things. All my life, I've had it backward. I've spent years caged behind the bars of the list, never allowing myself a moment of fun. That's over. The list's regime ends now.

I fish the page out of its honorific pocket in my bag and do a quick scan of all the taboos there.

"You're a fraud," I accuse it. "You're a useless piece of nonsense."

Years spent always being good, always being in control, always working hard—and for what? I have nothing.

My first instinct is to tear the sorry piece of paper into a million pieces, but a more powerful, self-destructive impulse takes over. Tearing the list is not enough; I need to completely overthrow it! Each line, each forbiddance, each bit of life I've denied myself will be experienced, starting tonight!

I scan all the don'ts in search of something stupid and reckless. My eyes stop on a vicious-looking set of words. I nod. It's as good a start as any, and I can tackle it right away.

Two

Never Get Drunk

My entire body aches. Even the tips of my hair are in pain. Instead of blood, it feels like acid is pumping through my veins, and my lids have been replaced by sandpaper. *What's happening to me?*

I try to move. Easier thought than done. My muscles feel like Jell-O. I'm stuck lying on something soft, something that smells like a cold winter day: pine cones and rain. Slowly, I open my eyes. Daylight stabs my pupils, sending tendrils of pain through my brain. *Where am I?* In a bedroom, it seems. *Whose bedroom?* Ah, that's the question.

Panic gnaws at my stomach, followed by a flood of nausea. I turn to one side and spot a glass of water and a blister of Aleve on a nightstand. *A lifeline.* I pop two pills and drain the water before collapsing back on the bed.

Whose bed? Oh, crap… I'm in someone's bed, in my underwear, and I've absolutely no idea how I got here.

The last thing I remember is walking into a bar determined to tackle the next item on the list: *never get drunk.*

Ding-dong. Mr. Hangover, we meet at last… Not sure I like you. I close my eyes, hoping the Aleve will act quickly.

When I open them again, I've no clue how much time has passed—a minute or an hour—but at least I'm slightly better. Well enough to roll over and retrieve my discarded clothes from the floor. There's my bag, too, and I always carry a compact mirror. *Face damage assessment time.* Gingerly, I flip the little metallic lid open. I've got panda eyes, but it's nothing some makeup remover wipes can't fix. The cool touch of the damp cotton is heavenly on my heated skin as I scrub myself clean. The soothing moisture helps also with the headache, so much so that I don't stop until I've used up the entire packet of wipes.

With my head a little clearer, I search for my phone and unlock the screen. Eight fifteen in the morning. There's an unhealthy number of missed calls and messages waiting to be answered. *Later.* My temples are still pounding. I open the map app to check where in the world I am exactly. The little blue dot stops on Brooklyn Heights.

What the hell am I doing in Brooklyn? How did I get here? Whose house is this?

Time to find out.

Still sitting on the bed, I put on the silky turquoise dress I was wearing last night—perfect for a proposal, not so much for a morning-after commute from Brooklyn. There's nothing I can do about the hair, so I scrunch the red tangles in a messy-for-real bun and stand up.

The room spins. I blink several times to fight the dizziness and shake my legs until the dress's skirt slithers into place, reaching my knees. Shoes in one hand, bag in the other, I drag my feet to the door and tentatively exit the bedroom to enter… a cool loft. One of those with brick walls and modern furniture.

Feeling like a burglar, I slip my pumps on and shuffle into an open-space living room with floor-to-ceiling windows.

"Hello?" My voice sounds thick.

"Morning," someone says. A *male* someone. "I was starting to worry you were dead."

"I thought I was d—" My throat catches as a guy in jeans and a light blue shirt comes out from behind a pillar. He's so good-looking I literally can't talk. Rumpled dark hair on the longish side. Dark brown—almost black—eyes, a strong jaw covered in five o'clock shadow, and he's smiling at me. A little sexy dimple on each cheek. My stomach flips.

Is it the smile or the hangover?

But the real question is, did I have sex with this hunk? Well, I woke up in his bed wearing only underwear. I hope we did it. And I hope he wants to do it again because I can't remember a thing and the guy is too handsome for me to leave, not remembering having sex with him.

Eeeeee, somebody please censor my brain. Never in my life would I have had sex with someone I just met—but that was the whole point of throwing out the list and getting crazy drunk. If this man is the first outcome of my new lifestyle, high five to me. But how embarrassing not to remember if we slept together. What do I do? Do I ask him? I don't even know his name!

"Er, Blair?" he says. "Are you all right?"

Mr. Hot knows my name. "Yeah, super… mmm… uh…"

"Richard." He smiles again. "The name's Richard Stratton. I made coffee, you want some?"

If he wasn't already hot enough, the dude has an impossibly sexy British accent that's making my knees wobble. Either the accent or serious dehydration.

"Richard, sure." I pretend like he needn't have told me his name. "Coffee would be great, thanks." I stroll to the kitchen bar, sit on a stool, and drop my bag to the floor.

"Black? Sugar? Milk?"

"Sugar equals poison," I declare. "Do you happen to have almond milk?"

Richard's eyes widen.

"Black's fine," I hurry to say.

Mr. Hot hands me a mug. "You didn't seem to have a problem with the sugar rim of your cocktails last night."

"About that…" I take a sip of coffee, hoping caffeine will help my synapses connect. "I'm not exactly sure what… er. To be honest, last night's a bit—uh—foggy. How did we meet?"

"I called you."

"You called me?"

I have to kill the parrot possessing me and stop repeating whatever people say.

"Mm-hmm."

"How? Did I give you my number?" I think I'd remember giving my number to someone as hot as him.

"No, I got it through a friend of mine."

I frown. "A friend?"

The parrot lives.

"Yes, I'm the Editor-in-Chief of an up and coming web-based magazine. We're looking for a Fashion Editor—"

I hear magazine, I hear fashion, and the other shoe drops. *He's gay.* Ninety-five percent of Évoque male employees are gay. "Oh, you're gay," I interrupt him, a bit crestfallen. "Of course you're gay.

That face is too handsome for you to be straight. I mean between the hair, the eyes, and the smile you'd have to go around with an I'm-too-hot warning sticker on your chest..." I'm babbling and Richard's eyebrows have shot up. *Blair, shut up.* But I'm possessed, and can't stop talking. "And that accent! Imagine what it would do to women. You sound like Prince William. Well, at least now I don't have to ask you if we slept together last night..." I brush my hand over my forehead in a gesture of relief and laugh nervously. "Phew."

Richard stares at me dumbfounded for a few seconds before saying, "I thought I made it clear last night I wasn't gay." His tone is dead serious.

Something in my guts twists. "You mean we"—I point at my chest and then at his—"slept together?"

"No, we didn't. I was mocking you."

"But I woke up in your bed in my underwear."

"I left you in my room with your clothes *on.* You must've done the undressing."

"Oh, so you *are* gay."

"No, I'm not gay." He scoffs. "It's just that so-drunk-she-can't-remember-her-name doesn't do it for me."

I'm too mortified to speak, so I hide my red-beyond-control cheeks by staring at the floor.

"Last night," Richard continues, "I called you to talk about a job opportunity, and you told me to join you in a bar in downtown Manhattan. When I got there, you were already drunk and delirious about a list, spaghetti marinara, and someone's secretary..."

I'm feeling smaller and smaller. From under my lids, I dare a peek at Richard.

"When we left the bar, I tried to put you in a cab to get you home, but you weren't able to supply an address. So it was either leave you on the street or bring you back here."

"Oh, okay." I drop the empty coffee mug on the bar and get up. "Sorry for all the trouble I caused and thank you for... mmm..." *Giving me a bed to sleep in instead of the curb? Saving my life? Making me believe for five seconds that we had sex?* I go with, "For hosting me last night. I'll get out of your way now." I pick up my bag from the floor and... I've no idea where the exit is. "Where's the door?"

"This way." Richard leads me to the opposite side of the room and stops in front of a metal door striped with faux rust, or real rust, I'm not sure. Cool, design rust in any case. "About that job interview," he adds. "You want to reschedule?"

"You still want to interview me?"

"You look suspicious."

Not look, am. "I don't mean to be rude, but if you're still considering me for a job after last night's stunt and this morning's conversation, you must be desperate."

His jaw tightens. "I'm not desperate."

"So what's your magazine's circulation?" I challenge.

"It's an online-only editorial hub; we hardly have any circulation."

"You've no printed edition?"

"No."

"Alexa rank?"

Richard holds my gaze for a couple of seconds before answering, "In the lower thousands. But most of our traffic comes from in-app views, with no ad blocking, and we want it to stay that way."

"As I said, you're desperate."

"Well, from what I gathered last night, so are you."

Ouch. Below the belt, Richard. Way below the belt. What else did I tell him while I was drunk as a skunk? Probably better I don't remember.

"Listen." He rolls up the sleeves of his shirt, and I get distracted looking at his forearms. *He has really pretty forearms. Correction: he has really pretty everything.* "I don't claim to be Évoque Magazine, but I'm working on making something fresh. *Something better.* I've put together a great team, so before you snub us, why don't you hear me out?" Richard takes a business card out of his pocket and hands it over.

As he comes closer, I get a whiff of that same pine cones and rain scent I smelled in the bedroom. *His scent.* So, Richard was my cold winter day. The combination of shower gel or aftershave plus male skin is intoxicating. I bite the inside of my cheek to keep focused and take the card. "Thank you."

"Go home, take a shower, and come back to check us out at the address on the card. This afternoon, tomorrow morning. Whenever works." Before I can politely decline, he adds, "If nothing else, stop by so you can see my too-handsome face one more time," and winks.

My mouth hangs open, and my face sizzles in shame for the millionth time since I woke up. "You know you can't use anything I said while I thought you were gay against me."

"Nice try." Richard gives me a wicked smile and opens the door. "See you later?"

I scold him on the way out. "Maybe."

"This way."

He guides me down the hall in silence until we reach the elevators. There, I push the down arrow and wait. When the doors sweep open, I briskly step inside, push the lobby button, and say, "Goodbye."

Richard braces both arms against the doorframe. "I'll see you soon," he says, stepping backward, and, as the doors begin to move adds, "And I'll work on finding that sticker."

The doors close so that I'm left staring at my shocked, beet-red face reflected in the metal.

Three

Always Move Up the Ladder, Never Down

Phone in hand, I search for the nearest subway station to get back to my apartment in lower Manhattan. A cab would be much better, especially considering my pounding headache, but my recent unemployment status demands immediate cutbacks. I don't even have my foldable flats, so my walk of shame is painfully done on five-inch heels.

The ride on the crowded train, besides killing my feet, does nothing to improve my queasiness. I need to drink a gallon of water and run an hour to sweat out all the toxins in my body. But most of all, I need another coffee and a cool shower.

As I unlock the door to my apartment, the only positive thought I can muster is that, if nothing else, the list did produce one good outcome. Item number four, *don't move in without a ring*, saved me from having to sneak back to Gerard's place to retrieve any personal effects. The thought of him and his secretary doing it in his office makes my skin crawl.

Did he bring her home too? Did they do it in our bed?

Technically, his bed… but still. I suppress a gagging reflex and step into the living room.

"You're alive!" Nikki, my roommate and best friend, barrels into me as soon as I enter the apartment. "I was so worried." She hugs me. "And you're in one piece," Nikki whispers before pushing back. "You're alive and in one piece and now I can *kill you!*"

"Nikki, please," I plead. "I've had a horrible two days. Let me take a shower and then I'll explain everything."

"You didn't come home last night. You didn't answer any of my calls. No text to say you were staying over at Gerard's either. So finally, I tried his number, and he yelled at me, saying you two were over. Then this morning I called Évoque, and some woman told me you were let go yesterday. I thought you'd jumped off the Brooklyn Bridge!"

"I didn't jump off, but apparently I crossed over. And, in my defense, I was unconscious most of the time I spent there."

"Unconscious? Were you mugged? Kidnapped?"

"No, relax. Nothing like that, I was only drunk."

Nikki crosses her arms over her chest, skeptical. "You're never drunk."

"I was last night. What are you doing home, anyway?"

Ten in the morning is too late even for Nikki to still be at home and not at least on her way to work.

"I have to catch a plane for New Orleans in a few hours, so no point in dropping by the office."

"How long will you be gone?" I have the scary feeling I'll need someone here to babysit me.

"Two days. We have to shoot a commercial." Nikki works in a digital media agency specialized in video commercials. "And I leave in an hour, so you have to spill the beans *now*."

"If you want to hear the whole story before I shower, I need coffee. Want some?"

"Sure."

We move into the kitchenette. Nikki watches me expectantly as I put the water on to boil, but I wait until after grinding the coffee to launch into my tale.

Nikki asks me a million concerned questions when I explain the circumstances of my breakup with Gerard.

"A plate of spaghetti over the head was the least he deserved," she says. "But are you sure you're okay?"

"Nikki, I don't know. It's only been twelve hours, of which I can remember only three, four tops."

"So where did you spend the night? Did you get drunk and hook up with a random guy?"

"I wish. It's so much worse than that."

I tell her the rest of my misadventures as we wait for the coffee to steep in the French press.

By the time I reach my morning encounter with Mr. Hot, Nikki is laughing her head off. "You seriously told this Richard guy he should wear an I'm-too-hot sticker?"

"Unfortunately for my dignity, I did."

"So when are you seeing him again?"

I stop pouring the coffee. "Never!"

"Didn't Mr. Hot offer you a job?"

"Yeah, he did, at an 'online editorial hub.' Code for startup news digest with no traffic."

"What's the name of the website?"

"The dude gave me a business card." I fish it out of my bag. "Inceptor Magazine."

Nikki grabs her laptop and we look at the homepage.

"The graphics are cool, stylish even." Nikki scrolls through a few articles. "The writing doesn't seem too bad, either."

"'Not too bad' isn't good enough."

"What's the guy's full name?"

"Richard Stratton," I say.

Nikki types it in the browser's search box and Richard's LinkedIn profile pops up first.

"Well, he's definitely *not bad*. And you woke up in his bedroom! You should work for him; if it were me, I'd work under him anytime…" She waggles her eyebrows.

"Oh, stop it." I cover my face with my hands. "You've no idea how humiliating this morning was."

"Richard didn't seem to care."

"The guy's desperate. Nikki, my curriculum is here"—I place my right hand level with my nose—"and his online whatever is here." I move the hand to my navel.

"Didn't you say you wanted to overthrow the list completely?"

"I did. But what has this to do—"

"Can I see it?" Nikki interrupts.

She's one of the few friends ever to be trusted with knowledge of the list's existence.

"Why?"

"I want to check something."

I search for the slip of paper inside its honorary pocket in my bag, but it's not there. I rummage through the main compartment and find it crumpled at the bottom.

"Here." I hand it over.

Nikki snatches the list from me, gets hold of a pen, and searches the various items with her eyes. "So, we can cross out never make a scene and never get drunk." She draws two lines on the respective entries. "And here, number fifteen, always move up the ladder, never down." Nikki pins me with a satisfied stare. "You're so taking the job."

***

I wait until the next morning to crawl back to Brooklyn, buying myself some time to become human again. As awakenings go, today couldn't be any more different from yesterday. The fit watch goes off at five thirty a.m., and on autopilot I shuffle out bed, dress in sporty clothes, and go for a run. From my apartment, I jog up Canal St. to the Hudson River waterfront and then up to 57th Street and back. It takes me longer than my usual time, but the ten-mile run does wonders to detox my entire system and puts me in a positive mood. *Thank you, endorphins.* After a long shower and a healthy breakfast, I get ready to make the trip to hell—*er*, Brooklyn.

I walk to Canal St. subway station in my foldable flats and I'm about to automatically jump on the uptown train when I remember my real destination. My chest contracts in pain as I break out of auto-pilot and steer away from the uptown train at the last moment. I already miss Évoque so much, and not just for its geography and wardrobe perks. I miss the halo of power.

On edge before even starting the trip, I study the map to figure out the most convenient route to Richard's office. Irony of ironies, I still have to take the blue line. Only instead of heading up to Columbus Circle, I'm literally moving down and out of Manhattan to High Street, Brooklyn.

The address on the card brings me to one of those historic factory loft buildings. There's no reception so I walk straight to the elevators—not even proper ones, freight. Richard's card says third floor. I push three and wait for the freight machine to make its slow, slow way up. As I pass the second floor, voices drift down from above—raised voices.

"I'm having your license revoked," a woman is shouting. "According to New York MHY 33.21 in providing outpatient mental health services to a minor, the important role of the parents or guardians shall be recognized. That's me."

"Instead of worrying about having my license revoked," a man replies, "you should ask yourself why your daughter came to seek my help. And while you're at it, have a good look in the mirror."

"You've no idea the amount of trouble you'll find yourself if you don't stop meddling in my daughter's affairs."

"Well, someone has to deal with her problems since you clearly don't! All Tegan needs is for someone to listen to her."

Just as I reach the third floor, a door slams shut followed by a twin sound a few seconds later. Wary, I step on the landing. It's empty except for a woman braced against a set of industrial metal and glass doors. She's an Archie Panjabi lookalike in her mid-twenties.

"Don't mind our neighbors," she tells me. "They bicker all the time. Personally, I think it's only foreplay. Are you here to see one of them or one of us?"

There's a plate next to the metal doors saying Inceptor Magazine. I swallow; I've walked into a madhouse. "Hi, I'm Blair Walker," I say, extending a hand. "I sort of have an appointment with Richard Stratton for a job interview."

"Ah, Blair, I'm Indira." She shakes my hand. "The boss told me you might stop by. He's on a call right now, but I'm to give you the tour. Come in."

As I close the five-step distance between us, we give each other the ultimate once over. I take in her Brooklyn Soccer League pullover, skinny jeans, and black-and-white All Stars. Indira does the same with my below the knee dress and beaded sandals and it's as if we mutually acknowledge that we come from two different planets. Except her expression tells me I'm the alien in this zip code.

She guides me into an open-space office with oversized sunlit windows, exposed walls and beams, and wood flooring—straight from the twenties by the look of it. Someone would call it cool and modern; to me, it screams hipster.

"So." Indira points at a room with glass walls. "That's the boss's office."

Richard is sprawled out on a chair behind a giant black desk, talking on the phone. Seeing him is enough to make my throat clench.

Strangled, I only manage to hum an acknowledgment.

"Richard is our Editor-in-Chief, of course," Indira continues. "All other editors are based here in this lovely open space, coexisting as one big, happy family."

I can't tell if she's being sarcastic or not.

"That's Hugo, the News Editor."

A guy with ginger hair and a short beard lifts his head and waves.

"Then there's Saffron. She's our social media and digital guru."

Indira points at a cute woman with long dark hair no older than twenty-two or twenty-three. Even their names are hipster-y, though Saffron's style is more grunge than bohemian.

"Zane is our Communications, Partnerships, and Distribution Manager."

Another bearded hippie waves.

"Ada is at entertainment."

A blonde woman out of a commercial from the fifties smiles and pushes her Cat-Eye glasses up her nose. I guess going vintage is equally accepted over here.

"And Nico is in charge of business and politics." Indira lowers her voice, "Never pick an ideological argument with him. Even if you're right, he'll bore you to death before you can prove your point."

I nod. A glance at Nico's bow-tied neck is enough to send off pompous alarm bells in my brain. The guy is frowning so hard at his screen he doesn't even notice we're talking about him.

"Over there in the corner are our techies and I'm in charge of everything non-content related. I guess this leaves you with all the fun stuff. Ah, and yes, that's our meeting room." She points at another glass-walled room next to Richard's office where he's still on the phone.

"You can either pick this station." Indira knocks on the desk to her left. "Or the one beside mine. I'm the best neighbor you could wish for."

"Well," I stall. "I'm not even sure if I got the job yet." *Or if I want it.*

"If you want it, the job's yours." Indira smiles knowingly. "Best piece of advice I can give you to survive around here is"—once again, she looks me over—"dress more casually and don't fall for the boss." Her eyes throw a wistful glance at the office behind me. "He's damaged goods."

I give her a questioning look, and she leans in with a conspiratorial air. "Rumor has it someone pulled a real number on him a few years ago. The boss hasn't been in a serious relationship ever since. Real commitment-phobe."

"You mean he's single?" I blab before I can stop myself.

Indira raises an eyebrow at me, and I blush.

Smooth, Blair.

"I'd hardly call it being single." She's looking at me with too-perceptive eyes. "Richard dates a lot, but no gal sticks around for long."

"You know what happened to him?"

"The gossip is he was about to—" She halts mid-sentence.

"Blair." Richard's voice, coming from behind me, sends a chill down my spine. "You've made it. Did Indira give you the tour already?"

"Hi." I turn around and am once again hit by Richard's unchecked good looks. "Yeah, we just finished."

"Perfect. Want to come into my office to discuss the gory details?"

"Sure."

I follow him and blush as the first thought that pops into my head is that we won't be able to have sex on his desk—as per the glass walls. *Stop it, Blair. Even if he wasn't about to become your boss, Indira says he's damaged goods and commitment phobic. Huge no-nos.*

Unfortunately, following Richard means I have a good view of his rear in a pair of nicely fitting jeans. The sight erases any rational argument the sensible half of my brain tries to make. So I stare at the floor instead and try to think of gruesome, unsexy stuff. *Fanny packs, ugly Christmas sweaters, spiders, Gerard and his secretary doing it.*

I suppress a gagging reflex. The fact that Gerard's affair is causing me more disgust than heartbreak is another clear sign my priorities have been all wrong. As the perfect boyfriend on paper, Gerard ticked all the right boxes in another stupid list of requirements. Good upbringing, check. Good job, check. Good looks, check.

Pity none of the important ones checked out. Faithful, nope. Committed, nope. In love, nope. This last one goes both ways, to be fair. Was I really ready to marry a guy only because he met my stereotype of a *"good"* catch? To be stark honest, I was. Not once I questioned my love for him, because he was too perfect, too sensibly right for me to debate loving him. Oh, no… I was turning into my mother without realizing it.

I wince.

"Everything all right?" Richard asks.

I try to compose my features. "Yeah."

He keeps the door open for me and shows me inside the office.

Once we're both seated on opposite sides of his desk, he asks, "So, what do you think?"

I try to come up with a diplomatic answer. "I shuffled through your newsfeed yesterday. You have some cool pieces and a fresh perspective."

Richard leans back in his chair. "You have any questions?"

I brace myself. Before any shop talk, I need to clear the air and make sure he's going to take me seriously. "Actually, I think we should address a personal issue first."

He seems surprised, but waits patiently for me to elaborate.

"I wanted to apologize for what happened at your house yesterday and for the night before… it wasn't… I wasn't…"

Richard's lips twitch, but he keeps a straight face as he says, "Like it never happened. You had a rough day, and I shouldn't have called for an interview at ten in the evening. From now on, we can have a one-hundred percent professional relationship."

The speech is meant to be reassuring, but the girl within me—the one crushing on him—can't help being disappointed. Anyway, he's right. If I come to work here, I can't have a thing with the boss. Also, for the first time, I spot a hardness behind Richard's gaze I hadn't noticed before. A coldness that says, I'm not into any other kind of relationship.

"Good." I nod. "Now down to business, can you share your advertising and traffic data?"

"No. Unless you work here, those are confidential. But I can tell you traffic had a year-over-year growth of two hundred percent and advertising went up by one-hundred and fifty percent."

"Okay." Those numbers aren't too bad. "What would my editorial budget be?"

"Ah." Richard rolls his sleeves up, a habit, it seems, and rests his elbows on the desk. For a moment I'm distracted by prime forearms display. I never thought it was possible to have a thing for forearms, but Richard's are proving me wrong. I miss the first part of his speech. "…it's basically on a contribution base."

Those last two words are enough to leave me horror-stricken and to force my eyes away from Richard's arms. "Come again?"

Richard takes a deep breath; we both know this is a hard sell. "In a nutshell, each editor's budget depends on how much advertising he or she can bring in."

I swallow. "Mhm, but since I'm starting a brand new section, you must have something set aside for me to build on."

"Unfortunately, no." Richard shakes his handsome head.

"Hold on. You seriously mean you want me to start from scratch? How am I supposed to attract advertisers with no published articles?"

"That's why I needed someone with the creative, editorial potential, but also with the marketing experience. I'm sure you made plenty of contacts while working at Évoque. There must be some fashion influencer or big beauty blogger you can get on board."

I wrinkle my nose; this last part stinks even more. "Wait, are you offering me a position as Fashion Editor or Beauty Editor?"

Richard blinks. "Isn't it the same thing?"

I sag in my chair, a tiny pain starting in my chest. "You expect me to run an entire women's magazine on my own, and with no budget?"

Richard's mouth twitches at the corners again. "You would have complete creative independence."

I grimace. "How wonderful."

He fixes those impossibly gorgeous mocha-brown eyes on me. "And you get to keep a five percent commission on all advertisements sold as part of your compensation package."

The tightening in my chest worsens. Am I having a panic attack? *Pay on commission* are ugly enough words to unleash a panicked reaction. "Which translates into you offering me an intern-base salary, am I right?"

"I'm afraid we won't be able to match your previous compensation." Richard takes out a bundle of papers from a drawer and inches it toward me. "This is our standard contract."

I stare at the small—in all senses—numbers printed on the white paper. Yep, exactly the amount of my first paycheck after college. The pressure in my chest increases and I begin to feel lightheaded.

"But as I said," Richard resumes his pitch, "you'd get complete freedom on what to publish and state-of-the-art tech support." The handsome bastard smiles at me, giving me time to digest the news.

What choice do I have? A college graduate's pay that just about covers my half of the rent and food is better than no salary at all. At least until I can find another job.

Or maybe I should wait and see what else is out there on the job market. After all, I was let go only two days ago. If I'm careful on what I spend, I could survive on my severance check for a couple of months. That's when two nasty little words invade my brain: *student loans*.

No, I can't afford a single day with no income. And I'd rather be homeless than ask my parents for help.

Feeling like a trapped animal, I stare at Richard and ask, "Where do I sign?"

Four

Never Believe Gossip

Offices have a distinct and constant background noise. Especially open-space offices. The clacking of other people's keyboards, the clicking, the shuffling of paper, and the hum of whispered conversations. The background clatter is there, *always*. So much so, that a sudden silence is deafening.

I jerk my head up from the computer screen. I was right—everyone has stopped working. All my colleagues' heads are turned in one direction. Their expressions range from shell-shocked to mildly interested to unadulterated worship—this last one seems to befall the male population in particular. I follow the stares to the main entrance where silhouetted against the threshold is none else than Saskia Landon.

I join the staring contest. *Saskia Landon?* She is *the* model of the moment. Fashion editors all over the globe would claw each other's eyes out to have her in a photo shoot. Designers have to book her two years in advance for a catwalk. And she topped Forbes World's Highest-paid Models list, bypassing the runner-up by over thirty million. Saskia is the top one percent of A-list celebrities. *What is she doing here?*

"Is that Saskia Landon?" I hiss at Indira. "Am I seeing right?"

"In the flesh."

"Do we have a photo shoot with her? How did we manage that? Why wasn't I informed? I'm the Fashion Editor!"

"Relax." Indira rolls her eyes. "The lady is not here to work."

"Why then?"

"I suspect she's the boss's date for the night."

"Saskia Landon going out with Richard? *Impossible!*"

"You'd be surprised how well-connected Richard is. How else do you think he managed to pull together this"—she uses her pen to point around the office—"in less than six months? And then make it cash positive after only one year in business."

I want to reply, *by underpaying over-qualified employees like myself*, but I refrain. Instead, I say, "Okay, Richard knows people. But

Saskia is supposed to be dating actors, NFL stars, or billionaires. What is she doing with Richard?"

Indira sighs. "They don't make for a bad couple."

I follow Indira's hinting stare toward the door where Richard has appeared next to Saskia.

Unfortunately, Indira is right. Saskia is tall, but Richard is taller. Side by side, both wearing jeans and plain T-shirts, they look like a Calvin Klein ad. Sleek, glamorous, sexy. Worst of all, they do belong. Richard with his dashing smile, one-day stubble, and effortlessly cool vibe. Saskia with her long limbs, out-of-this-world face, and hair to die for.

As if hypnotized, I watch Richard guide Saskia out with a hand on her lower back. I wonder how that would feel.

Would Richard's hand be warm on my back? Would I feel it through the fabric of my shirt? Would it send electricity up my spine?

The answer is probably yes to all three.

"Does that mean the receptionist is gone?" I ask.

Richard was dating a hotel receptionist when I accepted the job three weeks ago.

"They never last," Indira replies. "I told you the boss is damaged goods."

"Yes, but you didn't tell me why."

Indira leans in closer, speaking in a hushed tone. "It's just gossip, but..." She looks around for a second as if to check if someone is eavesdropping.

I make a "give it to me" gesture. Sometimes Indira is a bit of a drama queen.

"Well, legend has it the boss was about to get married, and the bride did a runner on him."

I gasp. "No!"

"Mm-hmm."

"You mean he was engaged, and his fiancée broke it off before the wedding?"

"No, I mean he was at the altar *literally* getting married and the bride panicked or something and ran out mid-ceremony. I don't know the details."

I purse my lips, unconvinced. "Who told you this story?"

"Oh, you know how urban legends start. One knows the story, but somehow can't remember how, when, or who told it. It's just something everyone knows."

"You think it's true?"

"I've never met someone as commitment-phobic as Richard. True, it could be innate. But somehow, I don't think it is. It's like the boss is trying too hard to pretend he doesn't care. All that cynicism has to come from a scar somewhere in his past. One that runs deep. Plus, all his friends from London say he was a completely different person before he moved here."

"Different, how?"

"Just the opposite of how he is now. The perfect boyfriend who would plan the perfect date for his girlfriend. Romantic, ready to commit, to start a family. But now… I mean he's a great friend, boss, and businessman. But he would make a dreadful boyfriend."

"Don't you think he would change if he met the right woman?"

"Why?" Indira gives me her signature I-see-everything stare. "Are you nominating yourself for the role?"

My cheeks heat up and I break eye contact. "No, not at all. I was just speculating."

"Maybe one day, who knows? But I'm sure whoever that woman will be, she'll have to sweat blood and tears before pinning Richard down. And as much of a piece of eye candy as the boss is, that's just too much work for me."

"Yeah, definitely," I say awkwardly. "Who would want that?"

***

I spend the night staring at the ceiling torn between two opposite instincts. The first, my growing forbidden crush for my boss; the other, my unchecked work ambition. Having Saskia Landon do a photo shoot for Inceptor Magazine would skyrocket my style page to fashion heaven. But the mere thought of asking Richard to intercede with his supermodel girlfriend-of-the-week makes my skin crawl. Would he ask her as they cuddled in bed?

Yuck!

Unable to sleep, I grab my tablet from the nightstand to indulge in my new favorite hobby: reading Richard's weekly column. As Editor-in-Chief, he spends most of his time supervising other people's work. But the boss has cut a small literary space for himself where every Monday he writes an editorial. Sometimes it's humorous, other times it's more serious. But every single time his writing is brilliant.

Each week, the first thing I do over breakfast is read the newest column. Forget the Monday Blues, it always puts me in a good mood. And on nights like this, when I don't have a book or something else to read, I like to go over older pieces and get lost in his musings. Can you fall in love with someone by reading their words?

Yes.

No.

Maybe?

Anyway, Richard couldn't just be a piece of eye candy. Oh, no. He had to be smart, witty, and inventive, too. The more time I spend with him, the harder it is not to fall under his spell. And the more I read his words, the more I feel this connection with him. As do all the other women who read the column, I'm sure. I scroll down to the comments, penned, as suspected, mainly by female users. Male readers appreciate his writing, too, but I bet women are prompted to leave a comment by the author headshot posted at the top of the page. Could a man this intelligent really be afraid of serious relationships?

This is stupid. Richard is my boss. He'd be off limits even without his baggage. Richard, left at the altar. Could it be true? How could any woman about to marry Richard leave him? The gal must've been crazy.

I get a mental picture of his handsome, chiseled face staring at the bride as she runs down the aisle away from him. The intelligent spark of his chestnut irises subdued as he lowers his gaze to the church's floor in defeat. The lovely crinkles he gets around the eyes when he smiles banished by sorrow. Forehead creased. Jaw tense.

Then he raises his face again, and the gentle, trusting man is gone. Features hardened, cheeks gaunt, and lips parted in that cynic, uncaring grin Richard uses to scorn the world. He's a man wearing a mask. He's the Richard I know.

***

In the end, ambition wins out over my silly crush for the boss. The next morning I find myself knocking on Richard's door as soon as he gets into the office.

He looks up and smiles. "Blair, come in."

"Hi," I stutter nervously, taking the chair in front of his desk.

"How can I help my star employee?"

"S-star employee?"

Richard frowns. "Nobody showed you the numbers?"

"Uh, no."

His entire face lights up, and my stupid belly flutters in response. I need to swallow mothballs and kill the love bug infestation. Richard shuffles some stacks of paper on his desk until he finds the folder he was looking for. "These are the first analytics from your pages; it's amazing what you were able to do in only three weeks."

To build some one-hundred backlist articles, I had to call in every favor anyone in the industry owed me, and now I'm all spent. That's why a big, Saskia-Landon break is what I need.

"These looks great." I grimace, staring at numbers that are a teensy fraction of what I used to pull at Évoque. "But we need something truly spectacular if we're hoping for a real breakthrough."

Richard shakes his head. "Even with numbers as good as these, I can't allot any extras to your section."

"Okay." I flash him a mischievous smile. "But you can intercede with your connections."

Richard frowns questioningly.

"Was that Saskia Landon you left with yesterday?" I cut to the chase.

Richard's eyes widen. "Yeah, Saskia is a good friend."

A good friend? As in *only* a friend?! *Please be specific, Richard, these things matter.* Friend or *girl*friend? I ignore the ramming questions in my head and ask, "As your *good friend*, would Saskia agree to do a photo shoot for us?"

"We can't afford her."

"Don't you worry about that. Deliver Saskia for two hours, and I can get any brand on the planet to pay her fee, the photographer's fee, and book a year's worth of advertisement with us as well. Fashion houses will fight each other to jump at the opportunity."

"And you can guarantee this?"

"One-hundred percent."

"All right," Richard finally agrees. "Saskia leaves New York in three days; can you pull it off with such short notice?"

"You tell me which two hours she has and I'll sort the rest." I stand up. "Do you think you can get her to agree?"

"I can try." Richard smiles dashingly and with a sinking heart, I realize he might not have to try too hard. "Anything else?"

"If she says yes, get me her manager's contact information. Before making a proposal I need to be sure she doesn't have any feud going on with a designer or a photographer."

"Feud?"

"A Kanye West vs. Taylor Swift sort of thing, know what I mean?"

Richard stares at me blankly. "No."

"It's probably better that way. Anyway, as soon as you have news, please let me know."

"Will do."

I walk back to my station and sit at my desk, not at all triumphant. As I pull names for potential sponsors and photographers, I try to shake off the image of Richard asking Saskia as they lie on rumpled sheets after hours of mind-blowing sex.

***

Saskia agrees to the shoot. Was it because Richard gave her the best seeing-to of her life? Or are they genuinely friends? I don't let myself care. Instead, I wire my brain to professional mode and, in record time, I whip together the photo shoot of the season.

Photographer: Adam Bell
Sponsor, clothes, and accessories: Angelika Black. In-house stylist (Mandy)
Location: Grunge rooftop in Brooklyn
View: Manhattan Skyline
Makeup artist: Hire two just in case. All unexpected events must be covered.

So it is that the following Saturday morning by six o'clock, I've already been working for three hours. The set had to be ready early to shoot Saskia in the flattering light of dawn.

Our star arrived at five. We went through the racks of clothes, together with the stylist from Angelika Black, and Saskia agreed to every single outfit. She's so irritably nice. Honestly, I'd hoped she'd turn out to be a diva to compensate for her perfect genetics. But no, Saskia Landon is professional to a T.

More than that, she's super kind to everyone and even cracks jokes with the staff. Why would Richard ever look at anyone else?

The boss didn't come to the shoot. The only other person from Inceptor Magazine here is Saffron, our social media expert. She wanted to take some edgy backstage pics to build our Instagram feed.

As I watch the photographer take one perfect shot after the other of the most beautiful woman on earth, my emotions swing wildly between editorial lust and primal female jealousy. The stylist, Mandy, has no reservations. She can't stop clapping and squealing as she watches the shots appear on the screen after every click of the camera.

By seven thirty, we have enough frames to build two editorials: one for spring and one for the fall. To get the most out of this opportunity, I asked Mandy to bring some items from next year's collection as well.

Adam clicks his camera one last time and looks at me with an interrogative frown.

I clap my hands and call, "It's a wrap, everyone."

The staff claps along. Saskia hugs Adam, Mandy, and me. *Bah, she even smells good.* Saskia would probably hug everyone else on set, but her PA herds her downstairs to get changed before moving on to their next commitment.

Saffron comes to stand next to me. "Cool stuff," she says, sliding pictures on her phone with a finger. "Exactly the edgy, young vibe we needed."

I bend my head closer to hers to peek at the screen. "These are amazing."

If Saffron managed to snap pictures like that with an iPhone, I can't wait to see Adam's final product. He and his assistants have already dismantled the set and are carrying away the last bits of equipment. Before Adam leaves, we agree he'll send me as much as he can by Monday.

When everyone else is gone, I do a check of both the makeshift dressing room downstairs and the rooftop to make sure we left nothing behind. Alone on the terrace, I rest my arms against the railing to look at my old office building across the East River. My eyes travel all the way up to the thirty-eighth floor, to Évoque's windows. Manhattan might've chewed me up and spit me out in Brooklyn, but I'll be damned before I renounce my dream.

"You'll see," I promise the sunlit building. "I'll be back."

Five

Never Make Impulse Decisions

Monday at the office, I'm happily shuffling through all the amazing photos Adam sent me when my personal inbox flashes on the computer screen.

Transfixed, I stare at the sender's name and subject for a few seconds.

```
Date: Mon, May 1 at 9:18 AM
From: gerard.wakefield@aol.com
To: blair.walker@yahoo.com
Subject: Our Breakup
```

I haven't heard from the ex since spaghetti night. What does he want? Despite myself, my pulse quickens. I let the mouse hover over the subject line without actually opening the email. What will the text say? What do I want it to say? Do I want it to be a groveling apology and desperate plea for me to take him back? *Sure.* But why? Is it only pride or am I kidding myself thinking I could get over a three-year story in less than a month?

After some serious soul-searching, I'm ready to read what Gerard has to say. Yes, I want him to apologize for cheating on me with his secretary. But, no, I don't want Gerard back. Our breakup, however un-classy it was on both our parts, was the right call.

One click and the full message appears on the screen. With every passing line I read, bile swells in my throat, and by the end, I'm full of acid and anger. To think that for a second I even considered taking him back!

When I hit reply and start playing whack-a-mole with my keyboard, Indira stops her work and turns to stare at me.

"What's the matter?" she asks. "If you keep batting the keys like that your fingertips will bruise."

"The matter," I hiss, whacking along, "is that I wasted the last three years of my life dating an imbecile—"

"Imbecile?" Indira arches her brows. "Are you classy even when you swear?"

I finish my reply and hit the send button with satisfied ferocity.

Indira studies me a little longer and says, "Repeat after me. My ex-boyfriend is a dickhead."

"Is that the best insult *you* can muster?"

"I agree, we can do better. How about—"

My phone rings, interrupting her.

"It's him," I say.

I press a button to silence the ringtone.

"Care to tell me what happened?"

"The *imbecile* sent me an email offering not to sue me for throwing a plate of spaghetti on his *dick-head* if I sign a confidentiality agreement about his affair. He basically wants me to sign a document that says it's okay for him to keep screwing his secretary."

"Mmm." Indira purses her lips. "And what did you reply?"

"I thanked him for providing written proof of his misconduct at work in case the senior partners at his firm needed it on paper. And I told him he can expect news from my lawyer as I'm the one suing him for emotional damages."

Indira makes a fist and swirls her arm in the air in circles. "Go, girl. Finally, the redhead in you comes out!"

When the phone rings again, I'm about to put it permanently to silent but Indira stops me.

"Let me handle him." She picks up the phone, frowning at the caller ID. "Edward Cullen? What's his real name?"

I have this little habit of naming my contacts after book or movie characters, and I still haven't updated Gerard's to a more appropriate one.

"Right, I need to change that. Real name's Gerard."

"What a sorry-ass name. Surname?"

"Wakefield."

Indira makes a gagging face and answers. "Blair Walker's phone."

I can hear Gerard's voice even if the phone's not on speaker. "Hello, who is this?"

"Hello, Mr. Wakefield. This is Indira Singh, Miss Walker's attorney."

"She hired an attorney? What's the name of your firm? Is this for real?"

"Given the considerable amount of emotional distress you caused my client, Miss Walker intends to pursue legal action against you. We should probably thank you for sending a written confession of your immoral conduct, Mr. Wakefield. It couldn't have come at a better time."

"*Blair* is pressing charges against *me?* After what *she* did?" Gerard is yelling now. I imagine his face red and contorted with rage as he spits into the phone, "Should I remind you she's the one who threw a bowl of scorching pasta over my head? Are you out of your mind? What kind of lawyer are y—"

"As I'm sure you're aware, I can't discuss any details of the proceedings with the counterpart. You can expect to hear from us soon. Have a good day." Indira ends the call and gives me the phone back. "Let the vermin squirm in fear for a little longer."

Our eyes meet, and we collapse in a fit of laughter. We stop, try to remain serious, only to burst out worse than before. It takes Richard passing by and asking us what's so funny for me to sober up. I give Indira a warning stare. I'd rather the boss didn't know I'm so lame my ex sent me a confidentiality agreement about his affair.

Indira shrugs. "Girl stuff."

I shrug as well, making an innocent face.

Richard shakes his head and moves along. "I suppose I don't want to know."

"Sage, boss," Indira calls after him.

We share another secretive smile and get back to our respective jobs.

Since my center of gravity shifted to Brooklyn, this is the first time I'm glad for the forced change of scenery.

I can't help but think my old colleagues would've been more snickering than supportive about my breakup with Gerard. Everything at Évoque was so competitive. All people thought about was who had the best job, clothes, boyfriend, house, vacations. No one would've had my back the way Indira did today. The bitches would've probably been happy my perfect lawyer boyfriend had ditched me. At Inceptor, I feel part of a family.

***

When the first editorial photo shoot of Saskia goes live, it's an instant hit. In its first week, it gathers so many page views that I'm sure I'll be able to pay rent this month. That five-percent commission didn't turn out to be so bad after all. Anyway, one success—however big—doesn't mean I can rest on my laurels.

"Do we have the budget to rent a car?" I ask Indira.

"Honey"—she detaches her gaze from her screen to fix me with a look—"after your Saskia Landon stunt, you can ask for a Ferrari."

"Thanks, but a compact for the day is plenty."

"That will do, too. Where are you going?"

"Cherry Hill, New Jersey."

"What for?"

"I want to convince a big makeup house to sponsor a regular feature. I convinced Adam's wife—the photographer for Saskia's shoot—to video blog for us. She's a YouTube tutorials star, and she's agreed to work with me. Now we're only missing some cool products for her to vlog about."

"When do you need the car?"

"Tomorrow. Please make the pickup time as early as possible and in Manhattan, near my house. The drive to New Jersey will take at least two hours."

"All right." Indira taps her keyboard. "You have a Hyundai Elantra booked for tomorrow morning at seven-thirty. Return time is the same the next day." She prints a page and gives it to me.

The rental office address is just a block from my house. "What time do they close in the evening?"

She checks the screen. "Six."

"Hopefully I'll be able to return it the same day. It would cost more to park the car overnight than to rent it."

"The joys of living in Manhattan," Indira replies.

***

As expected, the drive out of New York is a nightmare. But having left early, I manage to get to my before-lunch appointment in time. Brenda, my contact from my old job, welcomes me into her office with a tight smile.

Still, coming off from my Saskia Landon success, I'm confident. I finally have the validation my fashion pages needed. Now I need to secure the same big-brand recognition for the beauty section.

The meeting doesn't last long. Skeptical as Brenda might have been, I came with my marketing guns loaded. Having Tracy Bell as the beauty vlogger and mentioning Saskia is enough to lock in a weekly supply of products for Tracy to test, review, and give away. Brenda doesn't agree on any extra paid advertisement, but that was only a long shot I had to try. All in all, I get to go home satisfied.

When I stop to fill the tank two hours later, my body is a muscle-cramping mess. I just crossed over into Manhattan, and I can't wait to give this metal box back. I use every movement getting out of the car to stretch a needy muscle, anticipating the yoga workout I've been planning in my head for the entire return drive.

It takes me a minute to locate the button to release the gasoline cover. Why would they hide it almost under the driver seat? As I round the car, I catch the eye of a guy refueling his bike at the next pump. He's clearly giving me a sexist woman-at-the-wheel stare. Chin up, I ignore him and move along with my business.

As I'm struggling to lock the hose, something cold and moist touches my naked calf. I jerk back and yell in surprise. Unfortunately, I yank the hose away from the tank as well, spilling gasoline all over the station and my legs. I release the handle and try to assess the damage. My skirt is soaked and I've spilled gasoline on the side of the car and… on the dog at my feet.

"Hello. Who are you?"

The small animal yelps pityingly and sniffs my calf again. I put the hose back into the tank and kneel down. The dog, more of a puppy actually, tries to jump in my lap. "Oh, look at you. Are you alone?"

I get another cry for an answer. My heart breaks. The pup looks like a golden retriever with more of a dirty brown fur and a longer snout. He must be a mutt. Apparently an abandoned mutt.

"You smell awful." He must have even before my gasoline shower seeing how dirty he is. I pat his head all the same and he waggles his tail happily in response. "Oh, I see what you're trying to do. Forget it; I can't have a pet." As if in protest, the dog sits on my feet. Is he trying to prevent me from leaving? Maybe the puppy isn't as abandoned as he looks. What if it the gasoline alone got him dirty? He might be lost. But he has no collar or tag.

Let's finish with the gas, and then I'll see.

When the tank is full, I go inside the convenience store to pay. Someone there may know whose dog he is. But as soon as I step a foot inside, the clerk says, "Hey, miss, you can't bring your dog in here."

Startled by the remark, I lower my gaze. The pup has followed me inside.

"This is not my dog. Actually, I wanted to ask you if you knew who he belonged to."

"Are you sure it ain't yours?" The man looks suspiciously at my feet where the puppy has stopped next to me, sitting down as if trained to do so.

"Yes. I was filling the tank, and he came out of nowhere."

"Well, if it ain't yours, I'll have to call pest control."

"Pest control? He's no pest he's just an abandoned puppy."

"Sorry, but I can't have no stray dogs in my station."

"I'm sure there's a better way to solve the problem."

"If you're so worried about the fur ball, why don't you take it?"

"I can't keep a dog."

This statement earns me a desperate, pleading howl from the little mutt.

"What?" I lower my gaze to him again. "You speak English?"

I get a subdued bark as a reply.

"Listen, miss, if you ain't taking the dog, I'm calling pest control or animal control or whatever you like to call it."

"All right, all right," I say impulsively. "Tell me how much it is for the gas, and I'll deal with the puppy."

"Thirty-nine dollars."

I give him my card. "Wait. Do you sell garbage bags?"

"Third aisle behind you."

I grab an eighty pack of perfumed ones, pay, and exit. Mr. Mutt walks at my heel again.

Back to the car, I kneel down next to the puppy.

"Just to be clear, this is a temporary arrangement," I tell him. I swear the dog smiles at me. "There's no way I can keep you in my tiny Manhattan apartment. Understood?"

I get two enthusiastic barks back.

I open the trunk, remove the security shade cover, and line the inside and the rear of the backseats with garbage bags.

"All right." I pat the bumper twice. "Up."

Mr. Mutt gives me another excited bark and jumps in.

"Please be good while I figure out where to take you."

He starts whining again.

Since my skirt is still soaked in gasoline, I line the driver seat with another garbage bag and search for a dog shelter on my phone. There's one not too far from my apartment. I copy the address in the map app and pull out of the gas station.

Less than a mile from the shelter, blue and red lights appear in the rearview mirror. The police must be trying to pull someone over. I keep driving, being extra careful to avoid any infraction, but the flashing lights stay with me. I check the left lane for suspicious-looking cars, but it's empty.

Those flashing lights are making me irrationally nervous, so I turn right even if the navigator is telling me to go straight. But I'm out of luck, the police car turns right after me, and not just that, they flash their headlights twice and turn on the siren.

Crap, they were following *me*. I pull over and watch the side view mirror as a police officer ominously approaches.

Six

Never Break the Law/Get Arrested

"Good evening, officer," I say, using my most polite, law-abiding-citizen tone.

The cop looks serious in his dark uniform, bulletproof vest, and heavy boots.

"Evening, ma'am. Where are you coming from?"

"Cherry Hill, New Jersey. I was there for a business meeting."

"And where are you headed?"

"To Animal Heaven. I found a stray dog."

Mr. Mutt barks on cue.

The officer leans in closer to the window and his nostrils flare.

"What's this smell?" he asks.

"Oh, I had an accident at the gas station. Spilled gas all over myself."

"Isn't Animal Haven in the opposite direction?"

That's when the map app rats me out. "Please make a U-turn and proceed to the route."

"I suppose you're right."

"Why did you turn this way?"

"Er… mmm…" *To lose your tail* doesn't seem like a great answer. "I got confused."

"Is this vehicle yours, ma'am?"

"No, no. It's rented."

"I'll need to see your license and the rental agreement."

"Sure."

I take my driver's license out of my wallet and search in my bag for the rental contract. It's not there.

"Is there a problem?" the cop asks.

"I can't find the contract."

"Is that so?"

"I'm sure I had it in here somewhere."

"Ma'am, please step out of the car."

"What? No. I have it. It's here somewhere, I swear."

I drop the bag on the passenger seat and make a quick dash for the glove compartment. *Maybe I put it in there without realizing.*

That's when everything goes south. The officer jumps back and grabs the handle of the gun strapped to his belt.

"Stop!" he yells.

Hand still on the compartment handle, I freeze.

"Place both hands on the wheel," the policeman instructs me. "Slowly, and where I can see them."

What the hell? What does he think, that I have a gun hidden in my glove compartment? *Oh! That must be exactly what he's thinking.*

I comply and place both hands on the wheel. "You people are unbelievable. I was just searching for the rental agreement, and I don't have a gun. For your information, I'm against firearms."

"Ma'am, please step out of the car. And from now on, only *slow* movements."

"This is ridiculous. What are you going to do? *Arrest me?* I've done nothing wrong!"

The officer not-so-patiently sighs. "Ma'am, your car plate is registered to a blue Toyota Corolla, whereas you're driving a gray Hyundai Elantra. The plate recognition camera picked up the discrepancy as we drove behind you. And you're transporting an unrestrained animal apparently soaked in gasoline. Once again, please step out of the vehicle."

"I've told you the damn car is rented. It's not my fault if the rental company put the wrong plate on. And I've told you I just found the dog at a gas station and that I was bringing him to a shelter."

"But then we flash you and instead of pulling over you turn in the opposite direction. Don't make me ask again, please step out of the car."

The brute is only missing an "or else" at the end of the sentence. "Or what? What are you going to do?"

"Ma'am, step out of the car or you'll force me to call reinforcements." The officer taps the walkie-talkie strapped to his vest, close to his shoulder. "As of right now, you're resisting arrest."

"You're seriously arresting me? For what?" I open the door adding, "You're a big, uniformed bully." I get out of the car. "You can't do this. I'm an honest, tax-paying American citizen."

"Then you've nothing to fear."

"This is still a free country. You can't arrest me for no reason, it's an abuse of power."

"No, it's not. Please turn around, ma'am."

"Why?"

"Turn around."

I do as he says.

"Now place your hands on the back of your head."

"Are you handcuffing me? Is it really necessary?"

"Yes, ma'am. And I suggest you fully cooperate."

"Are you going to tell me I have the right to remain silent next?"

"You most definitely have that right, ma'am."

***

After a short journey spent handcuffed in the backseat of a police car with Mr. Mutt by my side, the cops bring me to a police station. Another officer asks me questions to fill out a personal information sheet and confiscates my watch and bag. A third policeman makes me sign a property log for my personal effects. No one takes my fingerprints or a mug shot, leaving me to wonder if I've really been arrested or if I'm only being held in custody.

Will I have a criminal record after today? For what? Renting a car? For saving a dog's life?

No one answers my questions. A female officer escorts me down a depressing cellblock and shows me into a cell. Mr. Mutt follows me around and nobody seems to mind so we're locked up together. Luckily, we're alone. No crazy cellmates.

I sit on a small cot bed—the only piece of furniture in this dump. Mr. Mutt lies next to me, resting his head on my thighs. Without my watch, it's hard to tell how much time is passing. How long will they keep us here? Will I get to make the famous phone call? Who should I call? I really don't wish for anyone to see me behind bars, especially not when I'm so dirty and smelly. I can't call my parents, they'd get a heart attack. *Nikki.* I'll call Nikki and ask her to find me a lawyer. It's my civil right to see a lawyer! The police can't keep me here indefinitely.

The rental company is so screwed. I'm so going to sue them. This mess is *their* fault! They mix up license plates and I end up in jail. *Jail,* more a tiny concrete hellhole with bars and no air. I'm getting cabin fever. I get up and pace around. Not that it helps. I can only take three steps wall-to-wall. How do people spend years caged like this? I've only been here a few hours and I'm already panicking. I need to know how long they'll keep me here.

Against my better judgment, I grab the bars and place my face as close between two as I can without actually touching skin to metal. I peek down the hall to see if I can yell for someone to come explain my position.

That's when Richard appears on the hall threshold holding a folder.

"Well, well, well," the boss says, walking toward me.

It takes me a minute to believe he's not a hallucination. Of all the people I didn't want to see me at rock bottom, my impossibly sexy boss definitely tops the list.

"What are you doing here?" I ask.

"They finally tracked down the rental agreement, which was in the company's name." Richard stops in front of my cell. "So NYPD called the office to verify your story. Honestly, when the police called to say one of my employees had been arrested, I never imagined it'd be the office's Miss Goody Two-shoes."

Is that how Richard sees me? Like a prissy princess? To be fair, I spent years trying to cultivate exactly that image. Still, his words hurt.

"I'm a victim of the system," I complain.

"Let's see." Richard opens the folder. "Unruly conduct, resisting arrest, disorderly person's offense under animal cruelty laws," he reads the charges against me. "And driving with the wrong license plate!"

"The car is rented. And I was rescuing the dog from a guy who wanted to send him to pest control." Mr. Mutt barks his support. "Also, I haven't resisted arrest, as unjust and unnecessary as it was."

"It says in here you called the police officer trying to take you in 'a big, uniformed bully' and that you accused him of abuse of power."

"Can you please wipe that stupid"—*lips-magnet*—"grin from your face?"

"I'm sorry, but this is just too fun. Of all the dumb things you had on that list of yours, I never thought you'd tackle the getting-arrested one."

"You know about the list?" I ask in horror, releasing the bars and taking a step back.

Richard nods, still grinning.

I slap my forehead. "The night we met. So I didn't just talk about a list in general, I showed you the actual thing?"

"That you did."

"But you didn't tell anyone else about it, did you?"

"No, I promise. But me knowing is the least of your problems." He taps the folder. "I believe the city of New York now has it on record."

"Not funny."

"Not joking. It was in your bag." Richard searches the file with his eyes. "Item twenty-one, a crumpled sheet of paper."

I scowl at him. The sheer humiliation doesn't matter now. I'll worry about never being able to look the boss in the eye ever again later. First, let's get out of prison.

"Has everything been cleared with the plate?" I ask again.

"Yes, the rental company admitted it was their mistake."

"So they know I'm innocent! Why am I still in here?"

Richard can't help his lips from curling up as he speaks. "There's still the matter of the other misdemeanors."

"So what?" I collapse on the cot bed. "Are they keeping me here overnight?"

"The officer who took you in *kindly* agreed to let you off with a warning if… you apologize."

I shoot off the bed and grab the bars again. "Apologize? *Apologize?* They mistreat me. Arrest me for no good reason without reading me my rights. Then they keep me locked in here for hours without letting me speak to a lawyer or make a phone call… and *I* should apologize?"

"The officer had probable cause; a Miranda warning wasn't necessary. And since you haven't really been charged with anything yet, you didn't need a lawyer."

"Since when did you become such a legal expert? You're not even American."

"I came to the rescue with a lawyer friend. She's waiting for me outside."

She? I get a mental picture of a sleek, attractive femme fatale in stiletto heels. Like Kim Basinger in *LA Confidential.* Another *friend.*

"So what are my options?"

Richard shrugs. "If I were you, I'd suck it up, apologize, and go home to shower." He flares his nostrils for emphasis. "But if you want to spend the night in here with your furry inmate and face real charges, be my guest."

"Easy for you to say. You weren't mistreated."

"Now, you'd better decide," Richard says, turning his head toward the main entrance. "The officer in question is coming. Want me to wait and give you a lift home?"

Hell, no. The less time the boss spends with me while I'm this messed up the better. And I can't stand to meet his lawyer "friend" in this state either. "No, thank you. I'll call my roommate."

"See you tomorrow at the office, then."

Richard winks and walks away.

Mr. Mutt barks.

"I know," I say, patting the dog. "I like him, too."

***

By the time I get out of jail, it's already dark outside and the animal shelter is closed. The rental company has retrieved the car from the location of my arrest, and there's no cab or Uber in the world who'd take me for a ride while I'm this dirty. Not to mention the gasoline-soaked pup. Unfortunately, Nikki doesn't have a car—I only used that excuse to get rid of Richard. So I—we—have to walk home. Luckily, this morning I picked shoes comfortable enough to drive in so they're not too bad to walk in either, and my house is only a few blocks away.

On the way there, I stop at a Petsmart and buy all the dog-grooming products they carry. At home, I give Mr. Mutt a very long bath. Then I give the bath a thorough cleaning before finally showering myself, hoping to wash away not only the dirt, but today's humiliation as well. I'm dry and wearing PJs before Nikki comes home.

"Is that a dog on our couch?" my roommate asks as she comes into the apartment.

She's not wrong. I spent the last twenty minutes losing another battle of wills. It started with me saying Mr. Mutt wasn't allowed on the couch and ended with the puppy nestled in my lap.

"Yes."

"I thought you weren't an animal person. I've been begging you to get a cat for ages, you always said the house was too small for a pet, and now you bring home a dog?" Nikki sits on the coffee table, staring at us accusingly. "Does he have a name? Where did you find him?"

"I call him Mr. Mutt."

"That's a horrible name."

"And I found him at a Chevron…"

Mr. Mutt barks.

"…gas station. What's up with you?" I ask the dog.

Nikki studies him. "He barked when you said Chevron."

The pup barks again.

"Chevron?" I repeat.

And again.

"I think we settled that horrible Mr. Mutt name, right, Chevron?" Nikki asks.

"*Ar-rooff!*"

Nikki finally pats him. "So are we keeping him?"

"No."

An excruciating howl rips through the room.

"Oh, I forgot," I say. "The pup speaks English."

"Right," Nikki says skeptically. "So what is he doing here if he isn't staying?"

"The plan was to drop him at Animal Heaven, but by the time I got out of jail the shelter was closed. I couldn't leave him on the street."

Nikki is about to pet Chevron again when she stops, hand in midair. "Wait, reverse. *Jail?*"

"Yeah, jail…" I tell her of my afternoon of misery.

"Aw, so now Mr. Hot Sticker even saved you from prison."

"Richard didn't save me from prison. He just had to be there as a witness, and used it as an excuse to hook up with a lady lawyer."

Nikki scrunches her face. "Ouch."

"I don't care."

"Of course you don't. Just as much as we aren't keeping the puppy."

"*Woof!*"

Seven

Always Be Responsible

There's something bulgy on my bed that's preventing me from stretching my legs. *So annoying.* I ignore the nuisance for as long as I can until finally I blink my eyes open and find a set of big brown eyes fixated on me.

When Chevron notices I'm awake, he starts wagging his tail like mad. *Oh, right! I still need to take him to a shelter.* At five thirty in the morning, shelters must be closed, but it's not too early to take Chevron for a run.

"Let's see what you're made of," I tell him, getting up.

After putting on my running clothes and sneakers, I secure Chevron with the brand new leash I bought yesterday. The pup pants hah-hah-hah happily the entire time, his tail never sitting still. I reward him with a dog cookie and we exit the apartment.

As soon as we're outside, Chevron stops near a streetlight to relieve himself. Oh, crap! What if he has to go number two? I've nothing to pick it up with. Luckily, Chevron lowers his leg and looks up at me expectantly.

"Let's go."

"*Woof!*"

We make our way to the Hudson River. I start with a slow jog to see how Chevron copes as I'm not sure how malnourished he is. From the way he devoured his dinner yesterday, I'm guessing very.

Still, he seems able to keep up. I quicken my pace and he follows suit. Having this little ball of fur run at my feet makes me strangely blissful. Weird… running alone has always been my thing. Whenever a boyfriend or a friend asks to join me, I can't help but resent them. Feels like an intrusion on my special me-time. Running is a moment of self-reflection and liberation I usually want to spend alone. But today, having Chevron track alongside, I'm one-hundred percent glad for the company. And the puppy seems to enjoy the exertion just as much.

All the same, I cut the run short. I don't want to overwhelm this little guy.

Back home, I shower and search for shelters' hours as I eat breakfast. Most don't open until noon. I guess I could work from home in the morning and go to the office in the afternoon. Richard seems the kind of boss who'd be flexible about office hours. But I'd better make sure, so I text him to ask if it's okay, explaining the dog situation. My phone pings back at once with his reply.

Why don't you bring the little guy with you?

As per my contacts renaming kink, Richard ended up as Jerry Maguire. The sexiest boss in chick flick history seemed like a good match for him.

Yeah

A friend of mine runs a vet clinic here
Brooklyn

I can take you both there when it opens

Another *friend*, huh? Someone with long legs and batting lashes, I'm sure.

I type, "Okay, thanks," and end the text with a double paw emoji.

"Good news," I tell Chevron. "You're coming to the office with me."

"*Woof.*"

"All right, let's do this."

Before we leave, I check the subway website for regulations on dog transportation… And we're out of luck again. Apparently, all animals need to be inside a pet carrier to be allowed on trains.

"You know what? We're going to walk today. It's only two miles."

"Ar rooff."

Nikki, clad in cat-print PJs, shuffles out of her room like a zombie and joins us at the kitchen bar.

"Is there coffee?" she asks.

I pour her a mug while an overexcited Chevron waggles his tail in welcome.

Nikki ignores him. "You're wasting your charms, little guy. I'm a cat person."

With a single cry, Chevron lays at her feet, subdued.

"She's joking," I console him.

"I'm not," Nikki insists.

Chevron wails again and nuzzles her bare feet with his wet nose.

Nikki tries to remain aloof, but her resolve breaks. "All right." She leans down to pat Chevron's head, and the good pup tries to jump into her lap. Nikki pets him a little longer and then asks, "So what's the deal with the dog?"

When I tell her of my plans with Richard, she raises an eyebrow at me. I wish I knew how to do that skeptical expression. If I tried to raise just one brow in a sassy way, I'd end up looking ridiculous.

"No comment," Nikki says.

"Why? What's wrong?"

"Nothing, just saving the 'I told you so' for later."

"What exactly did you tell me?"

"That the dog is staying… Hmm, what else?" Nikki gives me a shrewd look to clue me into the fact that she's really talking about Richard. I play dumb, so she adds, "Anyway, I'll be gone tonight."

"Where to this time?" Video marketing is the best job; she gets to travel so much.

"Just upstate for the night; gotta get ready. The crew is picking me up in"—she looks at her watch—"twenty minutes."

Nikki turns around the bar and hugs me goodbye then bends down to scratch Chevron behind the ears. The puppy is so ecstatic that he follows her to her room.

I go after them and turn right instead of left to reach my bedroom. Since I have to walk, I change into a pair of pants and a blouse so that

I can wear gym shoes for the crossing to Brooklyn without appearing too weird. Foldable flats do the trick only for short trips. I grab my duffel bag from under the bed where it's been since my breakup with Gerard, and put together a basic dog-at-the-office survival kit. A bag of dog cookies, a bowl for food, another bowl for water, and, for me, a pair of high-wedged pink All Stars. No matter if I'm in sportswear, no one can see me without heels. At the last minute, I add a bundle of plastic bags.

There. Now I'm ready for any doggy situation.

***

As soon as Chevron steps a paw into the office, he becomes the center of attention. I leave him with grungy Saffron and vintage Ada to go drop the duffel bag at my workstation.

There's a big bowl of oranges placed on the desk. *How odd.* I'm about to take out Chevron's water bowl and fill it when Hugo, the ginger News Editor, comes near my desk with two weird metallic mugs.

"Want some coffee?" he asks, offering me one.

"Oh, wow. Thanks." Hugo never makes me coffee. Where does the extra-nice attitude come from?

As I bring the mug to my lips, it feels like everyone is watching me. Like one of those slow motion moments in sitcoms where all the actors are holding their breath, waiting for something to happen. My eyes finally focus on the black writing on the side of the mug: USP ALCATRAZ. I lower the cup, aghast, and everyone starts laughing. They *were* watching me. That's also when Indira spins in her chair, showing the front of her bright orange T-shirt. It spells, "I want to be your prison wife."

My entire body heats. Not just my face, but my neck and shoulders all flare bright red. Everything makes sense now. The oranges, the mug, the suspense… they know I've been in jail. Damn Richard, I'm going to strangle him!

"Very funny," I say. And the laughter doubles.

I have to endure half an hour of prison jokes before Richard appears. "How are our two inmates doing today?" he greets Chevron and me.

I scowl at him.

"Still ruffled, are we?"

"I'd like to see how happy you'd be after being unjustly arrested and made to apologize for it," I reply pettily.

"You should write an article about police brutality," Indira suggests, unable to hide the amusement in her voice.

"Nice shirt," Richard tells her.

She winks. "Thanks, boss."

I roll my eyes and hide under my desk to pat Chevron, who promptly nudges my calves in support.

"So." Richard squats down next to us, eyes level with mine.

For a moment, all the air leaves my lungs. Finding myself almost nose-to-nose with Richard is giving me heart palpitations. When will he stop having this effect on me?

"Want to check out the clinic?" the boss asks, scratching Chevron behind the ears.

The treacherous dog forgets all about me and goes to nuzzle Richard's face. And for the first time in my life, I'm jealous of a quadruped.

***

The veterinary clinic is only a ten-minute walk from the office, but as our trio strolls down the streets of Brooklyn, I can't help noticing the seething looks of envy New Yorker women send my way. Walking with Richard and a happy puppy, I must look like I'm living the dream. If only the ladies knew how far from picture-perfect my life really is.

Needless to say, the vet is female. Not only that, she greets us with a perfect smile worthy of a toothpaste commercial. Actually, her general wholesomeness would play well in a family friendly advert. With big blue eyes, chestnut hair, and rosy cheeks, she's an image of friendly beauty—particularly friendly toward Richard.

As she comes out from behind the admission desk, her cheeks become rosier, her smile broadens—*how is that even possible? How many teeth does she have?*—and her eyes sparkle with something that could only be described as utter adoration. So the vet, too, has a crush on the boss. Have they dated in the past? Is everything Indira said true? Has Richard literally left a trail of broken hearts sprinkled all over New York?

After greeting us and introducing herself as Michelle, the vet shifts her entire attention to Chevron. Not even Richard's Bambi-like eyes can compete with real puppy eyes.

Michelle picks Chevron up and cuddles him. "And who do we have here?" The puppy loves the attention and yaps and nuzzles in response. "Good boy, oh, you're such a good boy."

As Michelle walks away with my dog, an explicable pang of something makes my throat tighten. Okay, no need to get territorial. Not over Richard and not over the dog—*who's not your dog, by the way, as there's no way you can keep him.* Begrudgingly, I follow the vet into an examination room.

With Chevron placed on a metal table, Michelle asks me an infinite series of questions—most of which I have no clue how to answer—and then she tells us she needs to do a full checkup. The clinic closes at six in the evening and Chevron will be ready for pickup after four.

Even if I know I'm going to see him in just a few hours, I get withdrawal syndrome symptoms as early as my first step away from the room. His desperate cries following us as we leave don't help either.

Richard must notice because he tries to distract me with conversation. "You actually named the dog after the gas station?" he asks as we walk back to the office.

"Every time someone said Chevron he barked, what was I supposed to do?"

"That fur ball is so adorable, he makes me want to go to a shelter and adopt a little guy just like him."

"No need for a shelter, you can adopt exactly *him*."

Richard stops dead in the street and turns toward me. "You're not keeping him?"

"Even if I wanted to, there's no way I can."

"Why not?"

"My apartment is too small, I'm out all day, and I don't have a car."

"You could bring him to the office. He could become our mascot.

And since when is a car essential to having a dog?"

"For one, he's not allowed on the subway."

"How did you come to work today?"

"We walked."

"All the way from Manhattan?" Richard seems impressed, and we start walking again. "You could've told me. I would've picked you up."

I wave him off. "It's no big deal."

"So what are you going to do with the puppy?"

"I'm bringing him to a shelter… unless you want him."

"He's not going to a bloody shelter."

This time I stop. "What else am I supposed to do? I'm only being responsible here."

"That's your problem. Maybe you should put more heart into what you do!"

I gasp. "That's rich coming from you."

"Me, why?"

"Because you should take your own advice."

"Meaning?"

"Put your heart in what you do."

"And where did you get the notion that my heart is not in what I do?"

"Maybe from the fact that in the short time I've worked for you, you've dated—what? Three, four different women? And the vet seems like another old flame."

Richard doesn't deny it. A dark shadow crosses his face, and he flashes me a hard, reproachful glare. "How I spend my time outside the office is none of your business. You've no place passing judgment on my personal life."

"Neither is it any of your business if I want to adopt a dog or not, and you shouldn't judge me if I say I can't. Again, take your own advice." With that, I march away, quickening my pace without waiting for my stupid boss.

***

Even if we don't say another word to each other for the rest of the day, the moment I get up to leave the office, Richard joins me.

He stops next to me as I wait for the elevator. "I'm coming with you," he threatens, and I don't dare retort.

Wrapped in a heavy silence, we walk back toward the clinic.

Until Richard breaks. "I should apologize for earlier; it wasn't my place to talk to you the way I did."

"I'm sorry, too. Same as you said."

"So we're good?" Richard asks, staring dead ahead.

"Yeah, we're good."

Tension lingers. We were both out of line earlier. Still, I appreciate Richard apologizing first.

At the clinic, I bear witness once again to Michelle's love-struck attitude toward the boss. And it's a good ten minutes before she notices I'm even there and brings us to see Chevron.

"So how's he doing?"

"Our puppy is actually a she," Michelle informs us.

"You're a girl?" I ask Chevron, who's back on the table chasing her tail in circles and yapping. I focus on Michelle. "Anything else?"

"She's slightly underweight for her age and she was malnourished and a bit dehydrated. Anyway, we gave her fluids, and a good diet with plenty of love should cure the rest."

I bite my lower lip. "Right."

"You don't seem convinced?"

Tears already prickle my eyes. "It's just that I don't think I can keep her."

Chevron stops running and lays flat on the table, resting her head on her front paws while whining.

I explain my situation to Michelle and in response, she informs me of all the programs New York City offers to pet owners in need. Reduced routine veterinary care, reduced pet boarding fee, free supplies, and she even gives me a few names of trusted dog-sitting services.

"But ultimately it's your decision," Michelle concedes.

"What if I helped you?" Richard blurts out.

An unwise ecstasy grips me as I listen to Richard trying to convince me to keep Chevron, advertising all the things he could do to help. The more my mood brightens, the more Michelle's face darkens. She seems annoyed with us. The Most-friendly-woman-on-Earth starts getting snippy, and unceremoniously ushers us out of the clinic claiming she has to close. Even if it's still twenty to six.

Just outside, there's a small park. Seems like a good place to reflect on what to do. We sit down on a bench. Chevron jumps up and sits quietly, resting her snout on my thigh. Her big, scared eyes stare into mine.

Richard looks at her and asks, "How can you think of abandoning her?"

I shake my head, close to tears. "I can't. But how can I keep her? I could walk to work every day now that the weather is warm. But what about winter? I can't walk two miles in the freezing rain or snow across a bridge. She'd get too wet and cold; it wouldn't be good for her."

"I could drive you home when the weather is too bad to walk."

I stare into Richard's brown eyes, not daring to let my hopes rise too high. "You'd pick me up and drive me home every time it rains or snows? This is New York, Richard. Awful weather is pretty much a given in winter. And traffic is just awful."

"For a cutie like this one"—he pokes Chevron's nose—"in a heartbeat."

As though conscious of her fate being discussed, Chevron nuzzles my hand with her moist muzzle and whines. How did I get so attached to her in less than a day? Yesterday, I didn't know she existed, and now, the thought of living without her is too heartbreaking to even consider. But I have to think of Chevron's best interest. Be responsible.

"So why don't you keep her full time?" I ask.

"I'm often away for the weekend, and I go back to England at least twice a year. I wouldn't be able to manage a dog full time."

"Mmm…"

"Come on, the solution is right here. I can cover for you when you're away and drive you home if the weather is awful… or you could borrow my car. Or she could stay at my place sometimes. Or, even better, you could move to Brooklyn."

Over my dead body. Sorry Chevron, but I can't leave Manhattan, not even for you. *"Yeah, right!"*

"Why not?"

"I don't know, Richard. What if I change jobs? What would happen then?"

The boss smiles a bitter smile. "Already sending out CVs?"

"That's not what I meant. A dog is a ten-year commitment at the very minimum. And it's not as if we can decide to keep her now and change our minds in five, ten, or maybe even fifteen years. What if you move back to England? What if one or both of us moves away from New York?"

"We'll figure something out. You really want to bring Chevron to a shelter?"

I shake my head. "No, but the responsible thing would be to find her a forever family that will adopt her."

"Then don't be responsible. Live a little. What if no one adopts her? You want her to stay caged up forever?"

The same cabin fever from the few hours I spent in jail makes my pulse race. I can't send Chevron to live in a cage. Not even for a day.

"No!"

"So let's keep her. If we join forces, we can."

"Are you really ready for this kind of responsibility?"

"I am, if you are."

I stare into two pairs of puppy-dog eyes and there's no way I can say no. "Okay then." I could be going crazy, but Richard's enthusiasm is infectious.

Richard smiles, too. "So you want to leave her with me tonight?"

"No!" Instinctively, I put a hand on Chevron's head as if to protect her. "I mean, it's only May. The weather's great. She can stay with me for now."

"So you're going to walk to work every day?"

"Or bike. I'll do it instead of running."

Richard smiles again and shakes his head.

"What?"

"You're never letting go of that dog, you know that, right?" I start to protest, but he cuts me short. "Come on," he says, jumping up from the bench and offering me his hands. "Let's go."

As I walk home over the Manhattan Bridge, I can't help the little smile pulling at my lips. I know Richard offered to help only for Chevron's sake, but still, he was ready to commit to us—okay, to her—for an undisclosed number of years. All Indira's theories about his phobia must be exaggerated. All the boss needs is a little push…

Eight

Always Dress Properly

The need to walk to work forces me to tone down my wardrobe and sort of embrace the athleisure movement. So today my outfit—a pale pink scuba-jersey sweatshirt, shiny paneled leggings, and the irreplaceable pink wedge All Stars—gains me a wink of approval from Indira as soon as I round my desk.

"Cool outfit, girl," she greets me. "The boss wants to see you."

After setting down Chevron's food and water bowls, I knock on Richard's door.

"Come in," he says, voice muffled by the glass.

I poke my head in. "You wanted to see me?"

"Ah, Blair, yes." Richard beckons me, and I sit in the chair opposite to his desk.

Today he's wearing a deep blue shirt that's begging to be ripped off him. I swallow.

"This is a bit last minute, but are you free this weekend?" Richard asks.

My heart skips a beat.

Is he asking me on a date? What do I say?

"This weekend?" I repeat trying to buy time to think.

"Yep. How would you feel about flying with me to LA?"

A weekend in California? *That sounds so romantic.* Is this really happening?

"We would have to fly economy as the company budget is low…"

Company budget? *Oh.* My heart plummets. So it's a work thing. Stupid me for thinking otherwise.

"Sorry, I'm not following," I say. "Why LA?"

"A good friend of mine is hosting a charity ball in Los Angeles… You know Christian Slade?"

"Christian Slade?" My eyes bulge out. "As in the mega Hollywood star?"

"Yes, him."

"He's your friend?"

"Yes, we go way back. We met at boarding school in England."

"Wow!" Richard really is connected, Indira was right. "Why do you want me to come?"

"The event will be A-list celebrities only, with a red carpet and everything. I thought as Fashion Editor you could piece together a few nice articles…"

"Something like best and worst dressed…"

"To be honest, I'd like to give Christian's charity better exposure through a more commercial approach."

"Make the ladies lust over the Hollywood glam to spread the word about the cause?"

"Exactly."

I lean forward in my chair and switch from deluded-employee-helplessly-in-love-with-her-too-handsome-boss to professional magazine editor. "What's the name of the charity?"

"Teachers without Postcodes."

Opening my notepad, I scribble the name down to research later. "Interesting name. What's the cause?"

"A program to bring better school systems to kids in neighborhoods with underfunded education. The charity supports a network of charter schools."

"That's a great mission. Do you have a list of the attendees?"

"Yeah, I'll email it to you."

"What about interviews? Am I allowed to ask the guests questions, like when they reach the end of the red carpet, or something?"

"Let me double check with Chris, but I'm sure it won't be an issue."

I put a checkmark next to interviews. "And for photos?"

"How good is your phone's camera?"

I stare up from the pad. "Seriously?"

"You can buy freelance shots with the budget you have, no extras. The plane ticket and hotel will already be expensive enough."

"I can't do a spread without professional photos."

"Isn't Saskia's page still bringing in loads of ad revenue?"

"Yeah, but I've allocated the profits to other projects. What am I supposed to do?"

"Be creative. I don't like to micromanage my staff."

I suppress a scream of frustration.

"What about the fundraising?" I ask. Attending a black tie event like this can't be cheap. "Who pays for that?"

"The fee comes out of my pockets. I believe in the cause and I'm happy to support it."

Oh, so Richard has a Good-Samaritan side, too. *Not fair.* "That's very generous of you. When do we leave?"

"Friday, mid-afternoon. With the time change, we should get to California in time for dinner."

Dinner? You and me alone? *My palms get sweaty.*

"Is Chevron going to be okay?" Richard asks. "Can you leave her with someone? Or I could ask Michelle if she can board her."

"No, no. It's fine. My roommate will take care of her."

"Great. You can go home Friday at lunch, get Chevron settled, and meet me at the airport."

"Sure."

"Please ask Indira to sort the tickets and hotel. The gala is Saturday night; we can fly back Sunday on whatever flight costs less."

"Perfect. I'll sort everything with Indira." I get up to exit his office.

"Ah, Blair…"

"Mmm?"

"Not that I need to say it, but the dress code is formal. Bring a gown."

"And here I was thinking of borrowing one of Saffron's T-shirts."

Richard smiles and waves me out of his office.

I sit at my desk, unable to wipe a little satisfied smile from my lips. An entire weekend alone with Richard. A two-night stay in the same hotel, dinner, and a gala. *It means nothing.* No, but still. We could walk along the Santa Monica pier at sunset, and we're going to a Hollywood ball together. Anything could happen…

"What are you daydreaming about?" Indira says from beside me.

"Nothing." Despite myself, I blush. *Busted.*

"So what did the boss want?"

"Oh, right. There's a charity event this Saturday in LA, with celebrities and everything. Richard wants me to do a fashion-slash-gossip report and asked if you could book our tickets and hotel."

Indira scrutinizes me for a long moment. "What did I tell you on your first day here?"

I stare at my sweatshirt and grab the hem. "I thought you liked this outfit, isn't it casual enough?"

"Wrong one. You've nailed the 'dress more casually.' It's the 'don't fall for the boss' you're having issues with."

"I-I haven't… you don't know what you're t-talking about," I stutter.

"Yeah, right. Should I book adjoining rooms?" She flashes me an evil grin.

I crumple up a sheet of paper and throw it at her. "You're wicked."

The ball rolls off Indira's desk, and Chevron promptly chases after it.

Indira shakes her head. "And you're in so much trouble, girl."

***

When I get home that night, Nikki is already back from her trip upstate.

"Oh, see… the dog is still living here," Nikki says and makes jazz hands. "Surprise."

When Chevron hears her voice, she yaps and jumps onto the couch, nuzzling Nikki's face. Good girl, buttering Nikki up. She doesn't know about my agreement with Richard to share custody, and she'll have plenty to say about our new canine roommate. But right now, she's too busy making cute voices at Chevron.

"Good boy," Nikki coos. "You're such a good boy."

"Actually," I say, sitting on the coffee table in front of them. "Chevron's a girl."

"A girl? We need a pink leash, then."

"Yeah, when she gets a little bigger, I'll get her a new one."

"When she gets bigger, huh?" Nikki gives me a smug *told you so* smirk. "So we're keeping her?"

"Well…" I explain my custody agreement with Richard and her face becomes more smug by the second. "Can you please wipe that self-satisfied expression from your face?"

"No, honey. Honestly, I didn't think you had it in you."

"Had what in me?"

"The cold blood to use this cutie"—she ruffles Chevron's ears, making them fly up and down—"to reel in a man."

"I'm not using Chevron to wheel anyone anywhere. Richard just offered to help me take care of her so she wouldn't have to go to a shelter or be put up for adoption."

"Oh, so you haven't fantasized about romantic walks down Central Park hand-in-hand with the boss?"

"No, I haven't," I lie through my teeth.

Nikki flashes me a skeptical smirk but doesn't call me out. "Besides adopting a dog together, how's it going with Mr. Hot?"

"He's bringing me to LA for the weekend."

"No! I mean, how?"

"Promise you won't freak out…"

She does the Girl Scout salute.

"Richard's taking me to a charity gala and wants me to cover the red carpet."

"And why should I freak out?"

"It's Christian Slade's charity ball."

Nikki sags against the couch backrest. "You lucky biatch!"

"I know."

"Can I hide in your luggage, please?"

"Eh, here's the thing…" I'm glad she hasn't stopped cuddling Chevron for one second since we came home. "Would you take care of our new roomie this weekend?"

"Oh, so you get to go to California with your hot boss to a party hosted by the sexiest man alive and I'm stuck here with this fur ball?"

"*Woof,*" Chevron yaps, and licks her cheek.

It works, Nikki's already a goner.

"I'll do it."

"You're the be—"

The buzzer interrupts me.

"I didn't order take out," Nikki says.

"No, it's for me."

"Who is it?"

"Mandy, from Angelika Black. They're lending me the dress for the gala."

"How come a major designer is giving you a dress?"

"They love me after I picked them for the Saskia Landon shoot."

"Life's unfair."

I buzz Mandy in and help her carry the wheeled garment rack from the elevator into our apartment, along with the six black garment bags it's carrying. Fashion lust makes my fingers prickle. I can't wait to pull down the zippers and discover the designer treasures inside.

As we drag the rack into the living room, Chevron jumps off the couch and barks to welcome the newcomer.

Mandy's reaction to our puppy isn't exactly warm. "These gowns are extremely delicate." She wrinkles her nose. "I'm not sure having a dog around as you try them on is a good idea."

Chevron stops yapping and goes to sit quietly on the rug in the faraway corner of the living room. She's the image of a well-behaved puppy.

Mandy raises her brows.

"Chevron understands English," I explain.

"Well." Mandy's face illuminates in a big smile. "The dog can watch from over there. So"—she turns toward me—"want to have a look at what I brought?"

I attack the zippers and reveal six stunning gowns. Yet the one furthest to the right catches my eye at once. It's a flowy dress in the exact pale jade shade of my eyes. The textile plays with tulle and lace in an illusion of transparencies and is covered in lace flower appliqués. The V of the neck plunges deep, making the gown slightly scandalous. And the long skirt flows to the floor, ethereal and lovely.

Registering my expression, Mandy says, "And who said love at first sight isn't a thing? Want to try it on?"

I nod.

She carefully takes it off the hanger and hands it over.

The fabric is soft in my hands, like the consistency of a cloud. I walk into my room feeling as if I, too, were as light as air. At the speed of light, I peel off my clothes and then carefully pull the gown on, cautious not to pinch the delicate tulle anywhere. After some contortions, I manage to pull up the zipper on my own. I complete the look with a pair of heels and stare transfixed at the results in the mirror. A-mazing. A dream translated into fabric. But on my short frame, the neckline drops so deep it reaches almost below my ribcage. I swallow. It's indecent.

As perfect as the dress is, it can't be worn in public. At least not by me. I'm tempted to strip it off right away, but pulling down the zipper proves more complicated than pulling it up. And I don't want to risk tearing the tulle anywhere. I've no idea what this gown costs, but I'm sure I can't afford it.

Shyly, I step back into the living room.

Nikki gasps. "You look amazing."

Mandy's assessment is more professional. "Fits you like a glove. We only need to shorten the skirt by three or four inches."

"Well, yeah. Except for the fact that all this dress says about me is, 'hello, meet my breasts.'"

"Seriously, sweetheart?" Mandy arches an eyebrow. "You're going to Hollywood. You'll still look like a nun."

"I doubt this is nun-wear, even in LA. This is the kind of dress you have to double tape to keep everything in place."

"So it's a bit more revealing than what you're used to," Nikki says. "What's the big deal?"

"I can't show up at work like this."

"Come on," Nikki insists. "It's not work."

"But Richard will be there!"

"The more reason to wear the dress."

Mandy injects herself into the conversation. "Is there a gentleman involved?"

"No," I reply, just as Nikki says, "Yes."

"Then you must definitely choose this one," Mandy concludes, taking Nikki's word over mine.

"Definitely," my nasty roommates agrees.

"Or maybe I should try on one of the other dresses…" I take a more conservative-looking black gown off the rack. "This looks much more—"

"Safe," Nikki ends the phrase for me.

"I was going to say appropriate. Come on, Nikki," I protest one last time. "This is not me."

"That's exactly my point."

"What do you mean?"

"This dress was totally made for the new you. If you can go to jail, you can wear the dress."

Mandy is looking at us as if we're crazy. "You went to jail?"

I jump to reassure her. "It was a bureaucratic misunderstanding. I wasn't really arrested."

Her expression relaxes.

Nikki pushes her point, "There must be something on your not-to-do list of things you have to do that forces you to wear this beauty."

I mentally scroll through the items and smile devilishly. "Always dress appropriately…?"

"Then it's decided!" Nikki's smile is almost as wicked as mine.

Mandy nods her approval, but it's Chevron's bark of endorsement that seals the deal.

Nine

Never Confide in Strangers

I shouldn't be so early. Simple as that. There are a million reasons to keep a decent buffer when traveling, but I should've kept it practical. Three hours for a domestic flight is an eternity. Even the monstrous departures board of JFK informs me I'm definitely too early. No gate info yet.

I need to find somewhere cozy to wait. The only place with seats in sight of the board is an airport bar, so I drag my suitcase along and sit on a stool at the counter.

"Hi," the bartender—a friendly looking blonde-hair-blue-eye type with a warm expression—greets me. "What can I get you?"

"Something to drink, please," I say.

"Cocktail, beer, a soda?"

"No thanks. Do you have any organic juices or a relaxing tea?"

The bartender's blue eyes twinkle. "Let's see." He squats behind the counter to open a fridge, I assume. "On the organic shelf, there's OJ, Honeycrisp apple juice, carrot beet ginger juice, or mango tea."

"The carrot ginger, please."

Mr. Friendly & Cute shakes the bottle and pours the juice into a tall glass. "Here you go."

"Thanks." I take a sip and check my watch.

"Waiting for someone?" the bartender asks.

"Yeah."

"Are they late?"

"No, I'm early."

"Better safe than sorry. When does your plane leave?"

"In three hours."

He raises an eyebrow. "International?"

I shake my head.

The bartender lets out a low whistle. "That's a big buffer for a national flight," he says, and then pours me some tortilla chips.

The poor guy hasn't asked why I'm so early, and Mr. Cute here probably doesn't care, but I don't know why I start spilling out all the details of my personal life. "Truth is, I have to go on a business trip with my boss. We're going to LA for the weekend and I was nervous about this whole away-with-the-boss thing. So I came to the airport super early. Just in case. One never knows when traffic will go crazy in this city."

"Is your boss the fastidious type?"

"No, no. Nothing like that. I'm probably more fastidious than him."

The bartender chuckles. "So what is it?"

Totally against my will, my cheeks heat up, and I try to hide the blushing by taking another sip of juice.

"Ah." The bartender smiles knowingly. "I see. You have a crush on your boss?"

No point in denying it. Mr. Cute knows.

"Can I at least ask your name before I tell you all my darkest secrets?"

"Mark Cooper, pleased to meet you."

Mark offers me a hand and I shake it. "Blair Walker. Nice to meet you, too."

"So, this boss…" Mark lets the phrase hang.

"Do you ask all your patrons about their private lives?"

"Occupational hazard, I guess."

Again, his kind expression compels me to talk. "Yes, I sort of have a crush on my boss."

"Mmm…"

"And we're going to LA for the weekend," I continue.

"For?"

"A charity gala."

"Oh, black tie event?"

"Mm-hmm."

"What do you do for a living?"

"I run the women's section of an online magazine." I hand him a business card. Never miss an opportunity to market. "You should check us out."

Mark takes it. "Inceptor Magazine. Cool name."

"Yeah, Richard picked it."

"Richard the forbidden boss?"

"The one and only."

"So tell me." Mark leans his elbows on the counter. "What are the obstacles for this impossible love story? Is the boss-man already taken?"

We chat a little and I explain the situation, even including the sordid details of the first time I talked to Richard—at least the one time I remember.

"So you're hoping something will happen this weekend?" Mark asks when I'm finished.

I shrug. I don't know what I do or should hope. From the moment the boss asked me on this trip, I've spent countless hours daydreaming about what *could* happen. Dinner *à deux* by the ocean, dancing at the ball—very *Beauty and the Beast* in my head—bookended by Richard whisking me off my feet at the end of the night. In reality, I'm pretty sure nothing is going to happen. This is just business for him. I wouldn't be surprised if he brought a Californian date along for the evening. *Oh, the horror… what if he does?*

"Are you still here?" Mark interrupts my mental rant.

"Yeah, sorry." I'm about to explain my inner turmoil when my phone beeps, startling me. "It's Richard, he's here."

"Please tell him to join you," Mark begs. "I have to meet this guy."

"You can't say anything," I warn.

He does a zipper-over-the-mouth gesture. "My lips are sealed."

"Do you mind if I change shoes?"

Mark seems surprised by the question. "Please, go ahead."

I climb down from the stool and swap flats for spiky black pumps.

"Whoa." Mark's eyes widen when my head comes back level with his. "You shot up… like… five inches!"

"That's the whole point." I store my ballerinas inside the hand luggage, close the zipper, and sit back on the stool.

I wring my hands together until Mark places a warm, dry hand on top of mine and says, "Relax. You don't want to spook the boss." He smiles encouragingly.

When he lets go, I force my hands apart and dry my sweaty palms on my skirt. "Do I look okay?"

"You look perfect. The guy's a fool if he doesn't notice."

"Blair." Richard's voice makes me jolt. "There you are. I thought I was early, but you beat me."

"Hi, Richard." Even if I see him every day, my pulse starts racing and I suspect my cheeks are once again matching my red hair.

Mark winks and buys me some time to recover. "Hello there, can I get you something to drink?"

Richard scratches his head. "What are you having?" he asks me.

"Organic carrot beet ginger juice."

"Erm, sounds delicious." The boss tries not to make a too-disgusted face and turns toward Mark. "A pint of lager please."

Mark's lips twitch. "I only have American-sized pints if that's okay?"

"You shoddy Americans." Richard laughs and Mark chuckles along. At once, it's like they're old friends who've been running the I-am-American-you-are-British joke between them for years. This Mark guy really has a way with people.

Right at this moment, my mind's whizzing with unspeakable thoughts so I let Mark entertain Richard while I enjoy the view. The boss didn't shave before coming here. His jaw is already sporting a five o'clock shadow, making him even sexier than usual. From the way he casually places his sunglasses on top of his head, to the way he now rolls up the sleeves of his shirt—making me stare like the little pervert I am—everything about Richard exudes sex appeal. The only flaw being that lingering sadness behind his eyes. The one he works so hard to hide.

When he's halfway through his beer, Richard's phone rings. He looks at the screen and smiles apologetically. "I've got to take this," he says, walking away.

"Well." Mark smirks scratching his short beard. "I'm not an expert on guys, but the dude has charm. So what's your plan for the weekend?"

I shrug. "Survive without embarrassing myself too much?"

"That sounds like an awful plan."

"You have a better suggestion?"

"Live and embarrass yourself the most you can."

"Meaning?"

"Tell him how you feel."

A speaker in the background announces our flight.

"No way!" My stomach drops at the mere idea. "Shh, he's coming back."

"They announced our flight," Richard says, and chugs the remaining half of his beer. "How much for everything?" he asks Mark.

Mark gives him the bill, and Richard pays for my juice as well. We both say goodbye to Mark, and I catch a furtive wink from my new bartender bestie as I stroll after Richard.

The boss frowns at me. "Collecting admirers?" he asks, as we walk toward our gate.

"What?"

"That bloke was all over you."

"Who?"

"Blue eyes, standing behind the bar."

"I seriously doubt that."

"He winked at you."

Oh, so the boss caught that. *Panic! He knows.* But then I remind myself that there's no way Richard could know Mark and I were talking about him. Let him assume Mark's wink was about how much the bartender liked me and not how much I like my boss.

I shrug and stop in front of our gate. "Mark is a friendly guy."

"Mark? Is that why you were holding hands when I arrived?"

Richard stops next to me and gives me a once-over, his eyes

lingering long enough to give me goose bumps.

"We… I mean, what?"

Is the boss annoyed because he thinks I'm behaving unprofessionally? No, Richard isn't prissy like that.

So what then? Could he be acting… *jealous?* No. No way. *Blair, repeat after me: "You are on a business trip."* But I'm not the one getting all worked up over a stupid wink. And he's ogling my shoes.

Richard's eyes travel back up my body, stopping when they meet mine. "Do you always fly dressed like this?"

Okay, I admit I made a bit of an effort. In my defense, it wasn't to seduce the boss. After only a few days, I was so fed up with the athleisure style, I couldn't wait to put on an elegant dress. And this little black midi dress is nothing too provocative. Maybe it's the shoes. The super narrow, super high stiletto heels must be eye-catching. Richard was openly staring at my feet just a moment ago.

"Well, since I didn't have to walk for once," I finally reply.

Richard's gaze flickers to the ground again, and I suppress a tiny smile. Are shoes his weak spot?

Ten

Never Make Exceptions

By the time we land, I'm so over the shoes. As gorgeous as my pumps are, I can't wait to kick them off. No matter that I've been sitting the entire time; these shoes were not made for pressure-bloated feet. Outside LAX, we hop in a cab to reach our hotel, and I have to muster all my willpower not to kick the stilettos off during the ride and reach for the flats in my suitcase. No pain, no height.

Indira chose a nice hotel in Santa Monica, near the ocean and with a stunning view of the pier. We check in and agree to meet in the lobby in an hour for dinner. The room is cozy if a little nondescript—a typical hotel chain with standardized furniture. But the view is everything.

A quick shower, and it's already time to get ready for the night. To pack light, I've picked out all my outfits in advance. The designated one for tonight is a sheath bandage dress in a shimmering metallic gold-bronze. The bandage's horizontal stripes and thick fabric are body-sculpting and make sure everything hangs just right.

But the real stars of this outfit are the shoes. As I take them out of their travel bag, I smirk. If Richard liked my pumps, wait until he sees these beauties. Knee-high metallic sandals with eight narrow straps, toes-to-knee, of which I have to individually buckle the last six. Not a quick job, but worth the trouble.

The soles are cushioned enough for me not to need gel inserts. Since the shoes are already such a statement, I keep the makeup light and natural.

In the lobby, I'm rewarded for my efforts with a long stare at my lower legs and two raised brows as I walk down the hall to meet Richard.

I smile. "Hey."

"Hey, yourself," Richard says. "Fancy dinner near the beach?"

"Couldn't think of a better place."

If May in New York is mild, in California it's already summer. I don't have much time to enjoy the warm evening breeze, however, as we hop in a cab right outside the hotel.

Richard gives the driver the name of a restaurant and we zip off into traffic.

"You know why Indira picked a hotel in Santa Monica when the gala is downtown?" he asks.

I suspect it was her idea of a joke. The beach being more romantic than skyscrapers.

I pretend to be clueless. "She said no one comes to LA to sleep downtown."

Richard doesn't ask me any other questions, and I'm too on edge to spark a conversation. The protracted silence makes the journey seem even longer. By the time the driver pulls over, we could've traveled from New York to Philadelphia for all I know. But I guess LA has a different spread than Manhattan. Everything seems broader here.

The driver kills the engine. "Sorry, but you'll have to walk from here. The boardwalk is pedestrians-only."

I step out of the cab, breathing in the sea air. Our destination looks a lot like the pan shots they do of Venice Beach in movies, even if I'm sure we're in Some-Other-Name Beach. Wooden buildings litter the concrete promenade on one side. On the other, it's tall palms, then sand, and finally the ocean where the last sunlight is sinking below the horizon.

Richard leads the way to… *oh, no. No!* A steakhouse. Story of my life. Guys love meat, and I'm a vegetarian. Maybe we'll skip the whole   why-don't-you-eat-meat-oh-I-could-never-live-without-bacon drill. I'll order the one pasta dish on the menu, politely decline Richard's suggestion of bone-in filet or New York strip, saying I'm not in the mood for a steak, and I might get away with it.

That chance shatters five minutes after we're seated when a server arrives at our table parading a tray of bloody cuts and starts explaining the various merits of the differently sliced cadavers.

The sight of raw meat makes me slightly nauseous, so I sip some water to stop my stomach from heaving.

Richard notices. "Are you okay?"

"Mm-hmm," I mutter, staring away from the tray of death. "Could we skip the visual presentation, though?"

The server gives me the I-know-what-you-are-you'll-order-the-cheap-pasta-and-cut-my-tip-in-half evil eye, but he takes the hint and shuffles away.

Richard blinks. "What's the matter?"

"I sort of… don't eat meat."

"Like ever?"

No point in circling around it. "I'm vegetarian."

Richard scoffs. "You should've said something. We could've switched places. I thought vegetarians were supposed to tell you."

Now I get touchy. "Why? Did you introduce yourself saying, 'Hi, I'm Richard. I'm carnivorous'?"

"I was talking about the joke."

"What joke?"

"How do you know if someone is a vegetarian?"

I stare at him blankly.

"Don't worry, they'll tell you. And… you aren't laughing."

His discomfort is so genuine that I crack a smile. "Don't worry. I'll have the pasta. Steakhouses keep it on the menu to save dudes like you from first date fiascos… N-not t-that I think we're on a date."

"Imagine that." Richard chuckles. "I'd be sweating cold right now. So why the meat aversion?"

"Do you really care?"

"Is it a sensitive subject?"

"Not for me, but sometimes people get defensive-aggressive about their right to eat meat."

"I won't bite, I promise."

He meant it as a joke, but the phrase only makes me imagine the touch of Richard's lips on my neck as his teeth graze my skin. *Brrrrrrrrrrrrrrr.* I forcibly pull my degenerate brain away from neck-biting scenarios and back to meat-avoiding diets.

"Well, there's the animal cruelty, of course," I say. "The fact that meat is actually bad for our health. And the staggering amount of pollution and water consumption it takes to feed, grow, and slaughter a cow."

Richard is looking at me with a weird expression, his lips contracted and eyebrows drawn together. I'm not sure if he's embarrassed, or if he's trying too hard not to laugh. The latter, I suspect.

He clears his throat before speaking. "Is it just meat or everything coming from animals you don't eat?"

"I'm vegetarian, not vegan. Otherwise, you'd be totally screwed as I wouldn't eat a thing in this place. Anyway, I try to steer clear of dairy, but I eat eggs if they come from happy chickens."

Richard's lips twitch. "And how do you assess the happiness of chickens?"

"If they're free-range chickens that eat real grass and are not stuck in a cage all their lives, they're happy chickens."

The boss roars with laughter. "I'm sorry," he says between chuckles. "But before today, the welfare of chickens was a foreign concept." Still smirking, he adds, "And I don't mean it in an insensitive way."

The server arrives with our salads.

Richard takes a forkful of his bacon-covered lettuce wedge and asks, "So you're never having a bite of meat ever again in your life?"

I take a second before answering. *Never eat meat* is part of the list, but so is *never make exceptions.* I'll make the exception to stay a vegetarian and cross out the two.

"Nope."

After the potentially rocky introduction, the conversation flows between us for the entire evening. Our food arrives—T-bone for him, mushroom fettuccini for me—and we eat, drink wine, and chat happily.

"So how was it growing up in England?" I ask at one point. "Did you do all that cool Harry Potter stuff?"

Richard stops cutting his steak. "You mean battling the most powerful dark wizard of all time and destroying his soul bit by bit?"

"No." I giggle. "I meant going to a fancy boarding school in a castle somewhere with houses and everything…"

"Ah, that part. Then, yes. I told you boarding school is where I met Chris."

"Was it as cool as Hogwarts?"

"If you can compare math to charms and chemistry to potions…"

"I guess being away from your parents was a plus too."

The boss frowns. "Not really. Okay, being away from home was an adventure at thirteen, but I missed the old folks."

"I would've given everything to leave home at thirteen instead of having to wait five extra years."

"Why?"

I hesitate. "Well, my parents' marriage wasn't exactly a happy one…"

"They argued a lot?"

"No, more… politely ignored each other. And they were so strict with me. Don't do this, don't do that…"

Richard smiles. "Now I'm beginning to understand that list of yours."

I drop my fork and cover my face with both hands. "I still can't believe you read the list. I try to forget about it."

"Besides getting drunk and arrested, how's the conquering going?"

Liquid courage, help me. In one gulp, I finish the wine in my glass and Richard pours me another one. "I bet I could still win at Never Have I Ever."

He throws me an interrogative stare.

"The drinking game?"

The boss shakes his head. "How does it work?"

"All participants take turns in saying something embarrassing or daring they've never done. All others who've done that particular deed have to drink a shot. I never took a shot."

"So your new life's goal is to get wasted at a drinking game?"

No, apparently it's digging my own conversational grave. "Of course not. I'm just saying that if I were to play, I'd still end up sober because I've done nothing that interesting."

"Besides getting arrested."

"I wouldn't call that interesting." I need to change the subject, *fast.* "But enough about me, tell me more about England."

That gets him started on boarding school, his college years, and eventually the move to the big city. Richard is in the middle of telling me how much he loves London when I ask the wrong question.

"So why base Inceptor in New York?"

The boss shakes his head and looks far away into another life, mouth tense, lips pressed in a sad line. The easy-going atmosphere drains away from the table, only to be replaced by a thick emotional wall between us.

Richard stares at his plate and takes a sip of wine. "Something happened, and I needed a change of scenery."

He doesn't look at me as he speaks, and I don't know what to do. I'd like to ask more, but I sense it'd be an awful idea. Especially with him sending me mind-your-own-business vibes so strong I'm tempted to run to the restroom and hide there. *Hello, brain? Please provide something to say.* But I was never good at improvising.

Richard proves better. "How was your pasta?" he asks.

"The fettuccini were delicious," I say, glad he came up with a conversational decoy.

"Good."

There's a weird, too-intense look in his eyes. Surely, fettuccini— tasty as they are—can't make the boss this emotional.

"What?" I ask.

"I'm just glad you don't eat burgers."

That's a weird thing to say. "Why?"

He shakes his head again in that resigned way. "It's a long story."

Uh-oh. Was the ex a meat-eater? A burgers-lover? She must've been.

"It's getting late," Richard says, shifting the topic completely. "We should probably ask for the bill."

No sooner has the word bill left Richard's lips that our server magically appears next to us. *Is the table bugged?*

"Would you care to have that boxed, sir?"

Richard and I reply at the same time.

Him: "No, thank you."

Me: "Yes, please."

The server stares at us, confused.

"We'll take everything," I say. "Please box the bread as well."

The server boxes our leftovers and hands me the bag. "Can I get you anything else? Coffee? A dessert?"

"Just the bill," Richard says.

The server takes it out of his apron and drops it on the table. "Please take as much time as you like."

Richard slips some dollar bills into the leather folder and gets up. I follow.

"I thought you didn't eat meat," he says, jerking his chin toward the doggy bag in my hands.

"No, but since the poor beast has already been slaughtered, I'd like to put the sacrifice to good use."

Near the low wall separating the beach from the promenade, a homeless man is sitting on the floor with his back against the barrier. Balancing my tight dress and spiky heels, I crouch in front of him, feeling Richard's gaze burning a hole in my back.

I give the food to the poor man and try to ignore the filth on his hands as he shakes mine to thank me. Trying not to fall on my butt, I straighten up and turn around ready to be taunted.

"Go ahead," I say. "Call me goody two-shoes all you like." The remark has stayed with me since he bailed me out of prison.

Richard gives me a long stare. "I wasn't going to."

Something in his gaze makes it impossible for me to keep eye contact, so I walk away.

Richard falls into step next to me. "That was very generous. Such a simple way to help, but the thought never even crossed my mind."

I look at him, searching his eyes for any trace of mockery. There's none.

"These people… it's so easy for them to disappear. We become so used to seeing them on the streets that they become invisible, but they each have their stories. You'd be surprised by some."

"You know many homeless?"

"In a way. I volunteer at my neighborhood canteen for the poor once a month. When I have time, I sit down for a chat."

"That's remarkable. You're putting me to shame."

"A day a month is nothing. I bet you did more good with your donation for tomorrow night."

"Maybe, but that's just money. Devoting your time to a good cause is different. Come here, Walker"—Richard slips an arm around my shoulders—"let's go get some sleep."

Together? I don't think he meant it like that. *Pity.* Anyway, it's the first time he's called me by my last name—I like it—or touched me beyond a handshake. I'm not sure if it's a gesture of camaraderie or… something else. I let my shoulders enjoy the weight of Richard's arm and try not to read too much into it.

At the hotel, we stand awkwardly in front of my door to say good night. I-had-two-glasses-of-wine me wants to haul Richard into my room and onto the bed by the collar of his shirt, but it would probably require I-had-two-bottles-of-wine me to do something like that. So I politely say good night and agree to meet him in the morning for a day of sightseeing. I slip under the covers, alone, feeling a disproportionate euphoria at the idea of touring LA with the boss.

Indira was right; I'm in so much trouble.

Eleven

Never Skinny Dip

Thanks to the three-hour jet lag, I'm up earlier than usual at four thirty. Even if it's seven thirty in New York, I doubt Nikki will be up, unless Chevron—tuned to my hours—dragged her off the bed. Either way, better if I wait a couple more hours before I call. It's silly how quickly I've turned into such an anxious pet parent, but I literally feel like I've left my child behind.

I change into running gear—leggings, tank top, iPod strap, fit watch—and wander down to the lobby.

"Hi," I say, startling a half-asleep receptionist.

"Hello, ma'am." He jerks himself awake and sits straighter in his chair. "How may I help you?"

"Is there a good running trail around here?"

The clerk blinks at me, still shocked someone would be this chirpy at such an ungodly hour. But he recovers fast. "Er, the best option would be to turn left as soon as you exit the hotel and run along the beach. If you head south, you'll find yourself on the Strand, a paved bike path that will bring you to the Venice boardwalk. Or you could go north and loop Palisades Park."

"Is the park open this early?"

"Yeah, it's twenty-four hours."

"Great, thanks."

I press play on the iPod and jog outside where it's still entirely dark. There's only a hint of light glimmering behind the hills on my right, which means the temperature is still manageable. I doubt I'd be able to run with the Californian sun shining high in the sky.

I turn left, follow the road to the beach trail, and head north toward the park. If the Hudson waterfront is one my favorite trails in New York, it has nothing on the ocean. I'm only missing Chevron.

After the first loop, I check my watch. *Eight minutes per mile.* Way below my average. Lately, I've only had time to run on the weekends, and my lack of constant training is showing. I should start over, but I'm too lazy, so from the park, I cross over a bridge to the beach to go exploring. The shore is deserted, too dark even for surfers.

As I stare at the water, a terrible idea strikes me. Faster than I can stop myself, I remove all my clothes and run into the ocean stark naked. *Never skinny dip—I can cross you off the list!*

I don't linger in the cool water more than thirty seconds. Not just because I'm butt naked in a public space, but also because the Pacific is freezing. I re-dress faster than ever and with fresh adrenaline pumping in my bloodstream, I run back to the hotel, breaking every personal speed record ever made.

By seven, I'm showered, dressed, and ready to rock LA. I'm finishing applying makeup when a knock distracts me.

"Who is it?" I call.

"Richard."

My stomach does a triple axel. I slip on my cord wedges—a good compromise between the necessity to wear heels and a long day of walking—and open the door.

"Whoa." Richard's eyes widen. "And I thought I was up early," he says, eyeing my already-prim attire.

He's still wearing gray sweatpants and a black T-shirt. Soft, damp curls are clinging to his forehead as if he just came out of the shower, which he must have. *Someone, please shoot me now!* Sweat-panted Richard is too good a sight, and showering Richard too good a fantasy, for me to preserve my brain cells.

"I'm a morning person," I say apologetically. "And there's the jet lag."

"Yeah, so would it be okay to meet downstairs in fifteen?"

"Super, see yah there."

***

Richard jerks his chin toward my shoes, unimpressed. "Are you sure you want to walk in those all day?"

So wedges aren't his thing. Mmm, I'll see if I can do better tonight.

"Yeah, I always wear heels."

"Why?"

We are not all blessed with Saskia Landon's legs.

"I just love heels."

"But we'll be walking a lot."

"I'm used to it, no big deal."

He shrugs. "I was thinking we should turn today into something different." *Thu-thump, thu-thump, thu-thump. Can anyone else hear my heart beating?* "Would your readers be interested in an 'LA in One Day' feature?"

Good thing I removed the fit watch. Otherwise, it'd be sending off all kinds of alarms at my heart stopping to beat due to mortification. When will my brain finally grasp that this is only work for Richard? Strictly business. No romantic agenda.

"You might've just dug your own grave." I smirk vindictively.

"Why?"

"Because my readership would prefer something titled 'One Day Shopping Spree in LA.'"

"Ah. You're killing me." Richard mockingly brings a hand to his chest. "Where should we start?"

"A walk towards the unique finds of Venice Beach, and then we'll work our way up to Rodeo Drive."

***

Richard bears the window-shopping like a man. From Venice to Beverly Hills to the Fashion District, he follows me around town not once complaining. I select a bunch of indie stores and interview the owners and designers. Richard is a good sport even when we try out a few male boutiques, going so far as to offer himself up as a human guinea pig—er, *male model.*

As we walk out of the umpteenth shop, Richard asks, "How much time do you need to get ready for tonight?"

"An hour, an hour and a half tops. Why? Should we already head back?"

Richard looks at his watch and sighs. "No, we're good for another two hours or so."

"Then what do you say we do something non-shopping related?"

The relief on his face is humorous.

"What did you have in mind?"

"A quick trip to Griffith Observatory. Everyone agrees it's the one view in LA you can't miss."

"Will we have time? With traffic and everything."

I check my phone. "The map app authority says it's half an hour to get there and half an hour to get back to Santa Monica, even in traffic."

"And how long from Santa Monica to downtown?"

I swap addresses. "Half an hour."

Everything seems to be spaced half an hour away in LA.

"Then we're good."

Richard calls an Uber, and we ask the driver to wait for us as we do a quick tour of the observatory.

After taking a couple—okay, an unhealthy number—of pictures of the Hollywood sign, we make our way along the promenade that wraps around the main dome. We stop under an arch to admire the Los Angeles skyline. The day is clear, and the view stretches far into the distance.

"This city is ginormous," I say. "I could never live here."

"Because of the long drives?"

"No, the weather. Too hot."

"I thought you'd enjoy the warmth."

"Why?"

"You're like fire."

I stare up at him and find him gazing intensely at me.

"Let me guess, the hair? I get that a lot."

"Yeah." He nods, looking almost relieved. "The hair."

Being this close to Richard, his scent fills my nostrils. *Pine cones and rain.* Even in sunny California, the boss still manages to smell like a cold winter day.

"Anyway, I prefer winter..." and before I can shut my stupid mouth, I blab the next thought that pops into my head, "Your aftershave smells like a snowy forest, you know?"

No time to add anything to justify my silly, and totally inappropriate comment before his jaw tightens and his eyes harden.

"We should probably go," Richard says, looking away. "The meter is running."

"Sure."

I follow him around the dome and back to the car with a large, inexplicable lump in my throat.

***

The wistfulness of the observatory visit dissipates as I take advantage of every minute I have to get ready. I scrub and pamper myself until I'm the best beauty products can make me. Tablet connected to the hotel Wi-Fi, I experiment with two of Tracy's tutorials to style my hair in a loose hairdo, and contour my cheekbones so they'd make Katharine Hepburn burn with shame.

At the designated hour, I make my way down to the lobby and, for once, Richard's eyes don't wander straight to my shoes but linger on my plunging neckline. I take a deep breath and try not to blush.

"Wow." Richard's eyes widen. "You're stunning."

"Don't sound so surprised," I say.

"No, it's just... I didn't expect your dress to be so..." Flattering? Revealing? Sexy? I'm right there with you, Richard, I would've never expected to wear a dress like this, not in a million years. *"...colorful."*

"Colorful?" That's not the adjective I was expecting.

"Yeah, somehow I had myself convinced you'd come out in a black dress."

Which I totally would have if it weren't for the stupid list and stupid friends. "Why black?"

"It's safe."

"Are you calling me boring?" I say, more flirtatious than reproachful.

My coquettishness earns me a smile, a real one, not Richard's usual guarded smirk. And as the boss lets himself go, his entire face changes. Crinkly lines appear at the corners of his eyes, and for once, warmth radiates from his gaze instead of mistrust. His sexy dimples make an appearance too. If I thought he was handsome before, I knew nothing. When Richard smiles, really smiles, he is sensational. It sucks the air out of my lungs and sends my heart into a pounding frenzy.

"I wouldn't dare," he says.

"You clean up well yourself," I manage to say.

"Shall we go?"

He offers me his arm and I take it. Outside, we hop in a cab and spend the obligatory half-hour journey mostly in silence. I am too self-conscious of my spiraling crush to make small talk. Like an inexperienced teenager, I jolt in my seat every time our legs bump due to a sharp turn.

After stepping out of the cab, we're admitted to the red carpet by security. I'm blinded by the photographers' flashes and their reflections on the metallic walls of the Disney Concert Hall. The paps, however, soon realize we're nobodies, and the clicking craze stops.

At the end of the carpet, there's a small press area with other correspondents from magazines and TV. We're early. The big celebrities will start arriving a bit later. Presumably in a slow trickle that will carry on for at least an hour. Events managers time the arrivals so that all the guests will get their dedicated moment in front of the photographers and with the press.

"I should wait here," I tell Richard. "See who gets in, do some interviews…"

"I'll get started on the champagne." He winks at me and disappears inside.

Alone and with work to do, I regain some presence of mind—meaning only half of my brain cells are being fried by the memory of Richard's smile.

Plus, red carpets are fun! All the celebrities I meet are incredibly down-to-earth and exciting to talk to. They make jokes, tell me wardrobe malfunction anecdotes, and I record more than a few good quotes to publish in a bubbly article on the evening. Even if I'm from a relatively unknown magazine, no one snubs me. And the first part of the night flies by in a series of incredible conversations, swooshing gowns, and some fan-girl moments on my part. When no one new arrives for twenty minutes, I move inside to finally join the real party.

I queue with some other guests at the wardrobe. Nothing can be brought upstairs. Phones, bags, jackets… everything has to be checked in.

I've just dropped my clutch when I find myself face to face—more face to chin—with my nemesis: Aurora Vanderbilt.

Aurora's lips part in an evil smirk as she says, "Blair, good to see you. I didn't know amateurs were invited."

We haven't seen each other since she stole my promotion, so my reply is pure vitriol. "You mean you thought it was a party reserved for toddlers still attached to their mother's skirts?"

As if on cue, Rebecca Vanderbilt appears at her daughter's side. "Who's your friend, dear?" she asks.

Aurora gives me a look of death. "No one," she says, steering her mother away.

Blood pulsing, I let them go and wait at a distance for the next elevator. Aurora being here isn't the only reason I'm edgy. Richard is waiting for me upstairs. In the last hour, I've met and spoken to a good chunk of the sexiest men alive top-ten chart, but no one gave me goose bumps the way only thinking about Richard does.

If my Belle-goes-to-the-ball dreamy filters weren't set high enough already, the event being hosted at Disney Hall's rooftop garden doesn't help. Talk about enchanting venues. Up here, it's all blooming trees and winding pathways around a magical rose fountain, all enclosed by sweeping metallic walls. As romantic settings go, it doesn't get any more suggestive than this space.

I step out of the elevator and walk into this wonderland of fairy lights and whimsical alleys accompanied by Disney-esque classical music playing in the background. To ease the anxiety gnawing at my stomach, I grab a few canapés and wash them down with champagne.

"There you are."

Richard's voice makes me jump so high that if my glass were still full, I would've splashed us both with bubbly.

"Richard." I turn, steadying myself.

In the semi-darkness, his sharp features appear even more attractive, aided by flickering shadows and contrast. Maybe it's just the tux. That must be it. You can *so* judge a book by its cover. I'm judging right now. More than judging, I'm thinking of ripping the cover off the book entirely.

"Did you have a good time downstairs?"

"Yeah, wonderful. I collected loads of material." I smile tensely. "Don't worry, I'll be able to put together a few amazing editorials."

"I'm not worried. I've complete confidence in your work."

Someone bumps into him from behind, and Richard stumbles forward, landing with both hands on my bare collarbones. Whoa! I'm being electrocuted. Tingling electric currents spread from my shoulders down my arms and up my neck to my brain where the last few surviving cells are being short-circuited for good.

Richard steadies himself but doesn't pull away immediately. We stand there, under a tree blossoming with ridiculously pretty red flowers, staring into each other's eyes. Finally, Richard frowns and takes a step back. Neither of us speaks, and the silence becomes awkward quickly. A server breaks it by offering us a tray of hors d'oeuvre. Richard declines, but I take one and stuff my mouth full before I say something stupid.

Panic swells as I'm about to swallow the last bite. Richard hasn't taken his eyes off me and still isn't speaking. What am I going to say when I've finished chewing and have no more excuses to keep quiet?

Will we just stay here all evening, staring at each other in utter silence?

My dilemma is solved by some six-foot-four hulking human careening into Richard and pulling him into a bear hug. "Mate, you're here."

Richard and the newcomer start a primordial dance of friendly grunts and shoulders slaps. When the ritual is over, the stranger turns, and I'm blinded by Hollywood's most wanted million-dollar smile.

"Blair, this is my good friend Christian," Richard makes the introductions. "Chris meet Blair."

"Hi," I say, and shake Christian Slade's hand as if I was used to meeting out-of-this-world-gorgeous men all the time.

A tiny part of me wants to take a selfie with him and post it on my Instagram feed right away. So I'm equally disappointed and relieved that only the official event photographer is admitted up here. At least I'm forced not to embarrass myself with the request, but I want the selfie so badly.

Richard and "Chris" do some catching up, and I'm content to just ogle the pair. It's like staring at a box of bonbons, trying to decide which one you want to eat first. These two are the yin and yang of masculine sex appeal. Christian: tall, blonde, green-eyed. Richard: equally tall, dark hair, dark eyes. Both impossibly sexy. Both with knee-wobble-inducing British accents. And both bachelors. *Yum!*

"So, how's the evening going?" Richard asks Christian after a while.

"Ah, too much public relations. I need a break." That's when the mega-Hollywood star surprises me bending his head toward me in a small bow. "May I steal the lady for a dance?"

Twelve

Never Make the First Move

Aaaaaaaah! Christian Slade, asking me to dance?!

"Sure," I say, taking his hand.

There's a small square in the garden serving as a dance floor, and some other couples are already swaying in the middle. Christian escorts me to the center, and we start swirling in time with the music. With a hand on my lower back and the other holding mine, he leads me like a professional.

"You're an impressive dancer," I say.

"You seem surprised."

"Not many men can waltz this gracefully, not in this century at least."

He chuckles. "Comes with the job, I guess."

"Of being an actor?"

"Yeah, sooner or later we all have to star in a costume movie with a ball, and the dance-like-a-gentleman training becomes mandatory."

"What movie?"

Christian raises a brow. "Not a fan, I take it?"

I blush. "No, it's not that. But I'm not a stalker either. You've been in so many movies… I don't remember them all."

"Which ones have you seen, then?"

"Ah, well. Last year's sci-fi flick… mmm… *Dancing in the Rain,* of course. See, that's another one you had to waltz in."

"Indeed. That's my excuse for being a good dancer—what's yours?"

"Several years of ballet with some ballroom dancing on the side."

"Brilliant."

"Your real-life British accent sounds weird."

Christian flashes me another of his million-dollar smiles. "You don't like it?"

"No, I do. It's just that on TV, you usually speak American. It's fascinating how you can sound totally natural with both accents."

Christian chuckles. "That's diction training for you. And having an American mum helped too." He winks.

Is he flirting? Wow, it's so weird to dance with a man I've only seen on TV who's so incredibly gorgeous. Mr. Slade here looks like a marble statue, and I'm pretty sure his skin is smoother than mine. Not to mention, Christian has been named "Sexiest Man Alive" three years in a row, as well as Hollywood's most wanted bachelor. This whole experience is surreal.

But for all his good looks and A-list status, I'm still at ease talking to him. And, weirdly enough, I don't want to rip his clothes off and haul him off to my hotel room. Chatting with him feels more like talking to an old friend.

"You have an odd expression," Christian says, interrupting my musings.

"It's just that you're so normal." That came out wrong. He raises his brows and I hurry to explain better. "I thought I'd be completely star-struck by you. But you're just a regular human being."

Christian is silent for a split second, making me worry I might've offended him. But then he throws back his head, roaring with laughter.

My cheeks heat up. "Did I say something wrong?"

"No," Christian says, still chuckling. "I wish I met more people like you."

The song changes and we pause for a second.

"Another round?" Christian asks.

"Sure," I say, and let him pirouette me around.

After some more dancing, I ask, "Do people treat you very differently?"

"You've no idea. Feeling normal is a welcome novelty."

"Aren't actors supposed to have these huge egos? You know, always needing to be the center of attention."

"Not *all* the time, makes me wish I had a switch. Of course, it's cool to meet fans and have people ask for autographs and pictures, but sometimes it's exhausting to catch the awe in people's eyes. It makes building real relationships hard."

"Is that why you're still single?"

Christian frowns, and his movements become more rigid. "Am I off the record?"

"Completely, t-totally off the record," I stutter. "I'm so sorry. Did I give you the impression I was interviewing you?"

"My fault." He shakes his head, and his hand relaxes again in mine. "But it has happened before. I say something in a friendly conversation and the next day my words get printed on page one."

"That must suck."

"It does. It's made me suspicious of even the most innocent questions. And yes, it makes it almost impossible to date."

"Why?"

"Every time I meet someone who's not *Hollywood,*" he rolls his eyes as if to air-quote the word Hollywood. "I wonder if the woman likes me only for the fame, money, or worse if she's in love with one of my characters…"

I smirk. "I'm sure uncanny good looks are a factor too."

Christian chuckles again. "See, no one ever gives me cheek."

"So why don't you date fellow celebrities? Actresses must be immune to the fame thing."

"Ah, see, but they're not. In a way, it's even worse."

Another song goes by, and we only nod to each other and keep dancing.

"Why are actresses worse than fans?"

"The movie industry is weird, complicated and… layered. It sort of has hierarchies."

"I'm sure you can date out of your caste, though."

Before replying, Christian spins me in an inside-outside turn. "Sure I can. But when I date someone less famous, I can't help wondering if she likes *me* or the career boost and extra publicity in gossip magazines. It's a feeling I can't shake. And if I were to date someone more famous, then she'd probably have the same doubts. Not to mention that dating actresses is a nightmare. Schedules are the worst. Most of my past breakups happened due to scheduling conflicts."

"You sound as wretched as Julia Roberts in *Notting Hill* when she tries to get the last brownie."

As another song ends, Christian lifts me up and smiles as he lowers me down. "I'm just saying it's not all bling."

I squeeze his hand and motion him to pick up the quicker rhythm of the new song.

"So basically," I say. "You need to meet a woman who's never watched a day of TV in her life, fall in love with her, and make her fall for you."

"And how many women like that do you know?"

Countless nights spent binge-watching TV shows with Nikki flash before my eyes. "Not many, I agree."

"Blair, you're an amusing little thing. Where has Richard been hiding you?"

I turn rigid in his arms.

Christian immediately notices my discomfort. "What did I say wrong?"

"I'm self-conscious about my height, or lack of thereof," I say, which isn't a lie, but also isn't the truth. Just hearing Richard's name turns me into a bundle of nerves.

"Really? Don't be. Men love tiny women."

"And of the many adjectives women enjoy, 'tiny' and 'little' are not on the list."

"Petite?"

"Nope."

"Mmm, delicate?"

I raise my eyebrows.

"Okay, I'll drop it."

"Sage man."

"What about you?" Christian goes back to our original conversation. "Any man in your life?"

I shake my head.

"I know I'm not supposed to ask, but how come?"

"Well, I spent my life giving too much importance to stupid things and wasted the last three years on a cheating bastard. So right now I'm focusing on myself and on straightening my priorities."

And on the side, I have this ridiculous crush on my boss, you know, your friend Richard—the one who doesn't do relationships.

"How's that going?" Christian asks.

"So far, I changed jobs, my ex threatened to sue me on multiple occasions… mmm… I experienced my first hangover, got arrested, and adopted a stray dog."

Christian laughs wholeheartedly, then lets out a low whistle. "And I thought my life was interesting. What did you do to get arrested?"

The music slows to an end again. How many songs have we danced together? I've lost count. I'm about to answer Christian's question and launch into another dance when a towering presence appears next to us.

Richard has a weird expression on his face. Hard to say what's going on inside his head, but he seems annoyed.

"If you dance another song together," the boss says, looking at me, "you'll end up on all the gossip magazine covers as Christian Slade's mysterious new flame."

"Richard, mate." Christian lets me go and takes a step back. "I've been selfish; I completely stole your date."

"Blair isn't my date, she's here to report."

Since Richard asked me to join him on this Californian weekend, a tiny hope has been burning inside me. Hope that these few days together away from the office mean more than a business trip. Hope that something will happen between us, that if something in New York is impossible... you know, what happens in Hollywood stays in Hollywood.

Richard's words extinguish that hope completely. They chill my heart and fill my mouth with the taste of ashes.

Christian smiles, shaking his head. "Mate, you're such a slave worker." He pats Richard on the shoulder and then looks at me. "Group projects back in school were the same. Richard kept us all in line."

I try to smile, and I hope the tight-lipped grimace I'm producing doesn't look as ashen as my heart feels.

"I've got to mingle with the other guests anyway," Christian adds. "Blair, it's been a pleasure." He takes my hand and kisses it. "You'll tell me all about your adventures next time."

I manage to nod. Christian pats Richard on the shoulder one more time and is gone.

Refusing to meet Richard's eye, I say, "I was tired of dancing, anyway." I make to shuffle away from the dance floor.

"Not so quickly."

Richard grabs me by the waist and pulls our bodies together while imprisoning my left hand in his. Without another word, he leads me back to the center of the square to dance.

The boss's style is more basic, a steady one, two, three... one, two, three... But honestly, I couldn't care less about Richard's dancing skills, not when he's looking at me as he is now.

I'm confused. He just spelled out for everyone that this isn't a date. I mean, if this is the way Richard stares at his non-dates, how much neuro-damage can he inflict on his date-dates?

As we dance, neither of us talks. We just move, staring into each other eyes. It's some sort of non-verbal conversation that is making my head spin like no pirouette ever did. I get lost in the brown of Richard's eyes, and the world around us disappears. Only our bodies exist. The heat of his right hand on my lower back, the pressure of his hand on mine as he holds it, and his hypnotizing gaze.

I don't know how long we dance, or for how many songs, or to what rhythm and steps. I notice only when the music stops. Someone, somewhere, is making a speech, probably Christian. I don't care. I only care that Richard has let go of my hand and I've been suddenly deprived of his body heat.

The boss takes a step back, looking at me as if I was a murder scene.

Still looking horrified, Richard shakes his head once and backs further away. Before I can say or do anything, he's making a run for it.

What the hell was that?

I try to chase after him, but my gown isn't exactly conducive to running. The full skirt certainly doesn't help me navigate the crowd converging toward the center of the garden to listen to Christian's speech.

Slowly, elbowing my way through Hollywood's best, I manage to reach the edge of the group. Richard is nowhere to be seen. I frantically turn my head left and right, but he's not here. Not caring that it's rude to leave without saying goodbye to the host, I take the elevators down and walk to the wardrobe to retrieve my shawl and clutch.

My phone is in my hands as soon as the clerk hands me the clutch. I try Richard's number… straight to voicemail. From upstairs comes a boom of applause and, slowly, all the guests start spilling out of the elevators and walking through the reception hall toward me. Well, toward their coats more accurately. Before the horde can trap me, I hurry outside. On the steps of Disney Hall, I try his number again and… get his voicemail again. *Awesome.* Richard has fried my brain with his insane eyes and made every fiber of my body want him even more, and now he's disappeared.

Something boils in my veins. I'm not sure if it's fury or lust, but I'm certain I'm not ready to let this go. He can't dance with me like that and then leave me here to fend for myself. *Sorry, Richard, but I know where you're sleeping tonight.* I hail a cab and give the driver the hotel address.

***

In the lobby, I pause at the reception desk. There's a line, so I wait my turn impatiently tapping a shoe on the marble floor. The receptionist is a statuesque blonde who must go around LA carrying headshots. Around here, it seems every other person is in their job only temporarily, waiting to make their big break as actors.

"How can I help you, ma'am?" the receptionist finally asks me.

"I'm traveling with Mr. Richard Stratton. He's staying in room 354. We got separated at a charity gala and his phone must've died." The receptionist keeps on a kind expression, but she's probably wondering why I'm telling her the story of my life. *TMI, Blair.* "Anyway, I just wanted to check if Mr. Stratton came back."

"Very well, I can call his room for you." The receptionist focuses on the screen in front of her, clicks the mouse twice, and then looks back at me. "I'm sorry, ma'am, but Mr. Stratton has activated the 'do not disturb' function. We cannot contact him at this time."

"Oh. Does that mean he's back?"

"The option can only be activated from within the room. So, yes, Mr. Stratton must be in his room."

"Thanks so much."

Dread and elation play a boxing match in my guts as I backtrack to the elevator. The fight continues all the way up to the eleventh floor, and by the time I get there dread wins, so I decide to stop in my room first to rally.

Down the hall, a red light next to Richard's door catches my attention. The words 'do not disturb' are spelled clearly underneath the glowing light. Is he sending me a message?

In my room, I pace, trying to decide my next move. Should I really go knock on Richard's door? *To say what?* Should I go to bed instead? *I wouldn't sleep.* The memory of dancing with Richard is too intoxicating. The feel of his hand clasping mine, his arm around my waist, our bodies pressed together… and his eyes. Oh gosh, even thinking about his stare makes me flush.

I open the window to let some air in, but it's not the cooling breeze one could expect in New York. *Stupid LA heat.* This isn't me. I'm losing my sanity, and I'm not one to lose her head over a guy—especially arrogant, meat-eating, playboy types. I'm also not one to get arrested, adopt a pet, or wear a scandalous dress. This line of thinking suited the old, list abiding me. The new me doesn't play by the rules.

On impulse, I walk toward the luggage rack, open my suitcase and fish inside for the list. The sorry sheet of paper has never been more crumpled. I lay it out on the desk, trying to flatten the edges with my palms. Pen in hand, I sit at the room's desk and scan the list. After crossing out *never make exceptions* and *never skinny dip,* I search for something that will give me an excuse to ignore Richard's 'do not disturb' sign.

There. *Never make the first move.* If ever there was a time to ignore that rule, tonight is it.

I kiss the list and get up, trying to smooth the wrinkles in my skirt. Should I change into something less dramatic? A mental vision of Richard undoing my zipper flashes through my head. His hand slowly pulling it down as he stands behind me, his breath hot on my neck. I can almost feel Richard's hands pulling down the straps of the dress over my shoulders and this once-in-a-lifetime gown falling to the floor, pooling at my feet in silky waves. *The dress stays.*

Mirror check: makeup still good, but the hair would be sexier loose. I remove all the clips and fluff it, letting the locks cascade down my back. The bobby pins have left it wavy and voluminous and the curls add a bit of wildness to my look. I give myself a wink in the mirror, and go.

Richard's room is only three doors down from mine. Standing here, I suddenly don't feel so brave. The gold metal plate with the number 354 engraved in black seems to get bigger as I stare at it. This was stupid. *Blair, go back to your room.* I take a step back; then stop. No, I'm not going back.

Inhale, exhale, and knock.

With a pounding heart, I wait for the door to open.

Thirteen

Never Lie

It takes me a few seconds to focus on the person standing in front of me. A tall woman who's looking back into the room, showing me only a mane of black hair. "Don't worry, I'm sure it's room service," she says, then turns to face me. Her mouth forms an "O" of surprise before her lips spread in a vicious smile.

"Blair, what an unexpected visit," Aurora Vanderbilt says.

Not her.

Everything within me breaks. I blink back tears of rage and frustration, but there's no fighting the angry blush that spreads across my face. The shock and misery must show along with the rash because Aurora's smile widens.

"Did you need something?" she asks in a honeyed tone.

"N-no... just work stuff... n-nothing important..."

I'm still blabbing nonsense when Richard appears on the threshold. Jacket off. Bow tie gone. Shirt invitingly open at the neck. *Sexy as hell.* Our eyes meet and a bolt of shame strikes me.

"Blair!" His eyebrows raise. "What are you doing here?"

I can't hide my disappointment, so I look away. Either he's a better actor than Christian Slade, or the electricity of the night was all inside my head. *It wasn't all inside my head.*

"N-nothing." I flutter my hands in the air. "It can wait until tomorrow."

"Are you sure?" Now his expression is closer to pity.

Mercifully, at that moment a server pushing a cart stops next to me and asks, "Is the champagne for this room?"

"Yes," Aurora says, opening the door wider.

The waiter pushes the cart inside and I seize the opportunity to escape. "I'll leave you to your... uh... thing." *Why can't I stop my hands from fluttering?* "Good night."

I don't wait for a reply. All I can say for myself is that I manage not to run. I retrace my steps to my room, insert the card in its slot with trembling hands, and rush inside. Resting my back against the door, I take a few deep breaths that quickly turn into heavy sobs.

How could I be so stupid? How could I misread the signals so badly?

I thought Richard and I had shared a moment, but clearly, all the boss cares about is sharing a bed with Aurora Vanderbilt. But I'm not crazy. Sparks happened, and it must've scared the boss so much he wanted to kill this new connection in cold blood.

Maybe.

No matter how much I try to rationalize Richard's behavior, it still sucks. And no justification will change the fact that he's spending the night in a hotel room with Aurora Vanderbilt. True, I'm not his girlfriend so it's not like he's cheating on me.

Feels that way all the same.

A glob of bile rises to my throat. I might throw up. In the bathroom, I splash my face with fresh water, not caring that it'll send the makeup streaming down my cheeks. I dry my hands and unzip the dress on my own. So much for the sexy fantasies. When the gown reaches the ground, I kick it away from my legs, abandoning it in a puddle on the bathroom floor. Back in the main room, I fling myself onto the bed and cry into a pillow until I fall asleep.

***

I wake up early after a restless night spent tossing and turning over nightmares of Aurora and Richard rolling in bed. A mix of all the fantasies I've had about Richard played before my eyes. Only the woman in the dream—*nightmare*—wasn't me.

I throw the blankets away, and after carefully washing my face, I launch myself into my running ritual. Energizing playlist, on. Fit watch, on. I-can-run-my-sorrow-to-death plan, so on.

This time I choose the running path heading south, and it doesn't take me long to reach the Venice boardwalk. With only surfers braving the waters, the beach is almost deserted this early in the morning. The quietness helps calm my nerves. So do the exercise endorphins.

I kick my shoes off and abandon the concrete trail. The sand is cool under my feet, a nice sensation after a long run. I choose a spot on a small dune to sit and stare at the ocean and the surfers paddling on the water. They seem so free and careless as they ride the waves.

When the sun starts burning my skin, I head back to the hotel. Unfortunately, the jog hasn't cleared my head as much as I'd hoped.

And nothing can change the fact that I have to spend six hours stuck on a plane next to Richard.

The boss doesn't know why you knocked on his door last night.

Maybe not. Aurora might've guessed, but no one knows for sure. What if Richard asks me point-blank? A resolution forms in my heart. If asked, I'll lie through my teeth.

Hoping to work my body to exhaustion so that I'll sleep on the plane and avoid unpleasant conversation, I take the stairs up to the eleventh floor. When I get there, I'm positively puffing.

To my horror, as soon as I push the stairs door open, I spot Aurora and Richard embracing in the hallway. I freeze. My room is past theirs. I consider running away, but Aurora catches me out of the corner of her eye and presses herself even closer to Richard in a goodbye kiss.

The kiss seems to last forever, but eventually, the leech releases her sucker. Aurora walks toward the elevator, waving at me with a nasty grin on her face. That's when Richard spots me.

No escape, then. The only way is forward.

"Morning," Richard says, as I pass him.

I ignore him and carry on along the corridor, walking on tiptoes. Richard has never seen me at my real, non-heeled shortness.

He follows me. "Hey, I'm talking to you."

"Morning."

"Would you please stop for a second?"

"Why?"

"Did you want to discuss something last night?"

"I wanted to pick your brain on some creative ideas…" I say, not looking at him and trying to fit the key in its slot. My hands are shaking so badly it's difficult.

"What ideas?"

I give up the fighting and spin around to face the boss. "It doesn't matter. I sorted everything out on my own."

"I'd like to hear those ideas all the same."

"I thought you didn't micromanage."

"Why are you being so snippy?"

The nerve of him to ask.

"I'm not. I'm sweaty and what I'd like to do is go take a shower.

Last night, I wanted to discuss ideas, but you seemed more interested in trolloping. And I don't want to talk about it now."

Richard scowls. "Aurora isn't a whore."

"I wasn't talking about dear *Aurora*."

As soon as the words leave my mouth, I regret them. He'll catch me now, see right through me. The boss will know this is all my jealousy talking.

"Judging again, are we?" Richard's voice rises. "I'm an adult and single. I can do whatever I please."

Thank you, boss, for showing all the limitations of your male brain.

"Of course you can."

"And you can stop your self-righteous tantrum and bring that prissy ass of yours back to earth."

I narrow my eyes. "If you think this is me judging your lifestyle then you're such a brazen idiot, I feel sorry for you." And then I add what I've really been burning to say. "Or you're playing dumb, which is even worse!"

Working behind my back, I give the key another try and finally manage to slide it into the slot. In a swift move, I free the lock, enter the room, and slam the door right in his idiotic, arrogant—stupidly handsome—face.

Richard pounds his fists on the wood almost immediately. "What's that supposed to mean? Hey, open this door."

I unstrap my iPod from the belt on my arm and plug it into the dock station sitting on the nightstand. "Sorry, I can't hear you," I shout. And to make sure my statement is true, I blast the speakers until I can't actually hear the pounding anymore.

With a nod of satisfaction, I shed my sweaty clothes to the floor and hop into the shower.

***

"If you keep staring at that window like that, it'll melt," Richard says.

I scoff, shrug, and do not turn my head. I keep my arms crossed over my chest and my gaze focused on the clouds out of the plane's window.

"So you're going to pretend I don't exist for the next six hours?"

Finally, I turn. "How could you sleep with Aurora?" I hiss.

Richard raises both eyebrows. "Excuse me?"

"Of all people, why *her?*"

"Why not? Aurora is very attractive… a lot of fun."

Which I'm not, I suppose. Oh, why did I ask? His words are like daggers to the heart. Richard wants to keep pretending I've no reason to be upset?

Let's pretend along.

"She also stands for everything you hate," I point out, trying to move the conversation away from my obvious, blinding jealousy.

"What do you mean?"

"Aurora never had to work a day in her life for what she has. Mommy fed it all to her with a silver spoon."

"Oh, so that's where the drama comes from. You're jealous because she beat you for the editor position at Évoque."

Oh, Richard, if only you knew work is not an envy trigger here. Still, better than you knowing the truth.

"Aurora didn't beat me, she cheated. Her mother bought the position for her."

"So she's from a rich, privileged family and she takes advantage. Wouldn't you do the same?"

"Not if my family actually stole money by not paying taxes. How dare they show their faces at a fund-raising? They must enjoy pretending to be generous to the community while they're ripping everyone off instead. All that extra cash has to go somewhere… right?"

Richard chastises me with a reproachful expression. "That's a very serious accusation to make."

"Not an accusation, *a fact.*"

"You've proof?"

"There were rumors at Évoque about a story on Rebecca Vanderbilt that got killed before publication."

"Are we talking office gossip or real facts?"

"A rumor like that wouldn't spread for no reason."

"Why would the magazine kill the story?"

"Too serious for our type of publication and Maison Vanderbilt is a big cross-magazine advertiser at Northwestern. Even more now after they had to shop for Aurora's promotion."

"Is the reporter who had the lead interested in selling it elsewhere?"

"She can't freelance while working at Évoque. Why? I don't see you running a story about dear Aurora's mommy."

"If Rebecca Vanderbilt is cooking her books, you're damn right I want to run the story."

I finally relax my pout. "Are you serious?"

"Bring me proof and I'll publish the article."

"How am I supposed to prove anything? I'm not a reporter. I never did investigative journalism, I wouldn't know where to start. And finance isn't my strong suit."

"But you're smart, bet you can figure a way."

"For real? You're not just saying this?"

"If you can get the evidence, the story is a go."

"Deal."

We shake hands, and I regret the physical contact immediately. Richard holds my hand, and my gaze, a second longer than necessary, and I can't help but enjoy the sensation.

Arrrgh, this man will be the death of me.

✳✳✳

That night I'm brooding in solitude on the couch when the apartment door opens and Nikki walks in with Chevron in tow.

"Hey, you're back." My roomie smiles. "How was Hollywood?"

"A disaster."

"That good, huh?"

"Imagine the worst thing that ever happened to you. It was worse."

Nikki releases Chevron's leash and they sit down and jump, respectively, onto the cushions next to me. "Better or worse than Bridget Jones going to the house party in the bunny costume?"

"Worse: I was humiliated."

"Better or worse than when Ross said 'we were on a break'?"

"Worse."

"Better or worse than when Jon Snow died on *Game of Thrones?*"

"Nothing could ever be worse than Jon Snow dying," I hiss.

"See? Then there's hope." She pats my knee. "Tell me what

happened."

I do.

"Ah, well." Nikki sighs. "I'd still swap lives."

I make big eyes at her. "Why?"

"At least you went out and met Christian Slade. I'm married to my job and in love with my sister's boyfriend… So…"

"What a pair!"

Pale as hell and with blue bags under her eyes, Nikki does look even more downcast than me.

"What happened to you?" I ask.

Nikki stares ahead, unfocused. "I bumped into Paul."

"Was he alone?"

"Yeah."

"And?"

"We had coffee."

"And?"

"He was nice and polite as you should be with your girlfriend's sister. Every time I see him, *them*… I die a little inside."

"And Julia still has no idea?"

Nikki massages her temples and shrugs. "Sometimes I think it was obvious something was happening with Paul when she swept in and stole him. Other times I think I'm so damn introverted that maybe it was obvious only to me, and neither Julia nor Paul have any idea how I felt."

"So the 'time cures all ills' motto doesn't really work?"

"I'm afraid not. I've spent the last two years hoping my sister's love life will crumble to pieces. What does that say about me?"

"That we can be spinsters together, all three of us."

"*Woof.*"

Nikki shakes her head. "At least someone's excited at the prospective." She pats Chevron. "No, seriously, there's no hope for me, but what's your next move?"

I stare out the window at Manhattan's lights. "Grind Aurora into the ground and bring the whole Vanderbilt fashion empire down with her and her witch of a mother."

"You know Aurora Vanderbilt isn't the real problem, right?"

"What do you mean?"

"It could've been anyone else in Richard's room. It would've hurt just as much."

"No, it wouldn't."

"Okay, you hate Aurora so it stung more. Fact remains, the real issue is that you have a crush on your boss and he doesn't reciprocate."

"That's not it."

"What then?"

Hours spent analyzing the weekend showed a clear pattern in Richard's behavior. Whenever we got closer or personal, Richard had a Dr. Jekyll/Mr. Hyde change of personality. Face changing from open and warm to that tough mask he always wears. The boss works hard at keeping his distance… Aurora Vanderbilt being the ultimate space-keeper.

"I'm almost sure Richard reciprocates on some level…" I tell Nikki about the dinner, our day in LA, and the way he danced with me. "But he's doing everything he can to fight his feelings."

"Why?"

"Because he's scared it could get serious."

"He's your boss. It's natural he'd have reservations."

"That's not it. Richard's scared of commitment after his incident at the altar."

"And you want a guy like that… why, exactly?"

"Look at it this way: Gerard ticked off all the right boyfriend boxes, and he was a disaster. A perfect match on paper, a cheating scum in real life. Richard may seem like the wrong guy for so many reasons, but he's not for the most important one."

"Which is?"

"The way my pulse quickens whenever I'm next to him, or the drop in my stomach I get just thinking about him."

"So you have a crush, it won't last forever. The beating heart, the stomach dives… they all disappear, eventually. You'll get used to him and get over it."

I look away, afraid to meet Nikki's eye.

"What is it?" she asks.

"This is more than a silly crush."

"What? You're in love with him now?"

I shake my head. "In love is too much. But it's something more than a crush."

"But you've never even kissed him."

I stare my roommate down. "Have you ever kissed Paul?"

Nikki blushes. "Fair enough. So, what are you going to do?"

"If Richard wants to play games, I'll play right along with him."

Fourteen

Never Play Games

On Monday morning, I kick off a new game called the shoe game. Richard likes heels, so I'm going to give him a run for his money. Even if buying new shoes is financially verboten, I've hoarded for years, and Carrie Bradshaw's closet has nothing on mine.

First, I shed the athleisure once and for all. If I can't walk to Brooklyn in stiletto heels and a pencil skirt, I can surely change before getting to the office. As for grooming, I do my makeup with the same chirurgical care I used to adopt at Évoque and pin my hair in a bun with a stick. The bun is only temporary; at the right moment, the stick will come out and the hair will cascade over my shoulders in voluminous waves.

Shoes. I go with nude patent leather pumps with a cute bow to accentuate the peep toe.

Clothes. A military green halter-top over a taupe satin maxi skirt with a vertiginous slit.

I carefully fold the top and skirt, place them in a garment bag, and fit them in my ever-present duffel bag that now has been compartmentalized. One side for me and one for Chevron. I pull on an old pair of black sweatpants, a matching sweatshirt, and my running shoes.

"Are you experiencing multiple personalities?" Nikki asks as I join her in the kitchenette.

I catch a glimpse of myself in the hall mirror and smirk. From the neck up, I'm Upper East Side, from the neck down, I'm sick-day-at-home.

"I'll change at the office. Did you make coffee?"

She nods.

I pour some into a thermos, kiss Nikki goodbye, and leave for my morning walking commute with Chevron.

When I get to the office, no one's there so I use the restroom to get changed. Besides the need for privacy, the early hour will help with the ridiculous amount of work I have to do: write two or three pieces on Saturday night, buy and match pictures to each article, investigate Maison Vanderbilt, and maintain all my other regular features. *Whoa.*

An hour later, it takes two steps through the door before Indira wolf whistles at me and asks, "Where are you going dressed up like that?"

"Flash news: I dress posh. Love me or love me." I'm tired of all this hipster, grunge, athleisure nonsense.

Indira drops in her chair and spins toward me smiling. "Hell, girl. Love the attitude. How was LA?"

I give her an upbeat version, leaving out Richard's escapades and our argument, and focusing on my dance with Christian Slade instead.

When Richard arrives, I oh-so-casually send a document to the printer and get up, removing the pin from my hair. The path from my desk to the print station and the one from the entrance door to Richard's office are on two parallel lines in opposite directions. The boss hasn't spotted me yet as he's reading a text. When he finally looks up and we lock eyes, I silently count… one… two…

On three, Richard's gaze flicks down to my shoes.

A second before we meet in the middle I say, "Morning, boss."

Let's pretend nothing ever happened.

Richard's eyes—somewhat wide—snap back to my face.

"Morning." The boss gives me a curt nod and continues on his way.

I get to the printer, retrieve my copy, and walk back. From behind his desk, Richard watches me like a hawk the entire time. He's not the only one. Indira scrutinizes me with the slyness of a fox.

In fact, as soon as I sit back at my desk, a chat window pops up on the computer screen.

Mon, May 22 at 8:56 AM

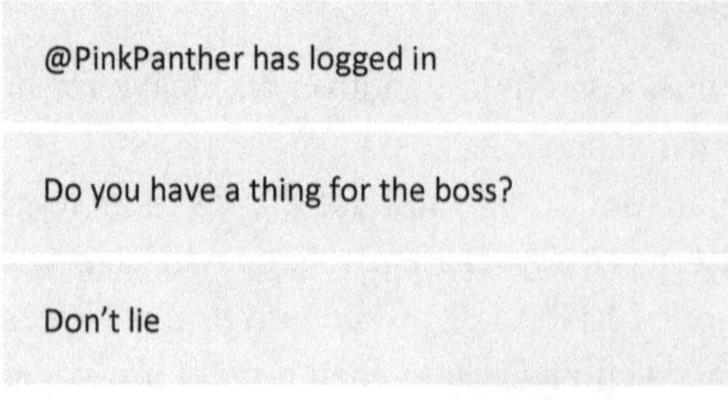

It's easier to tell the truth via instant messaging. Full disclosure: I didn't pick my chat nickname.

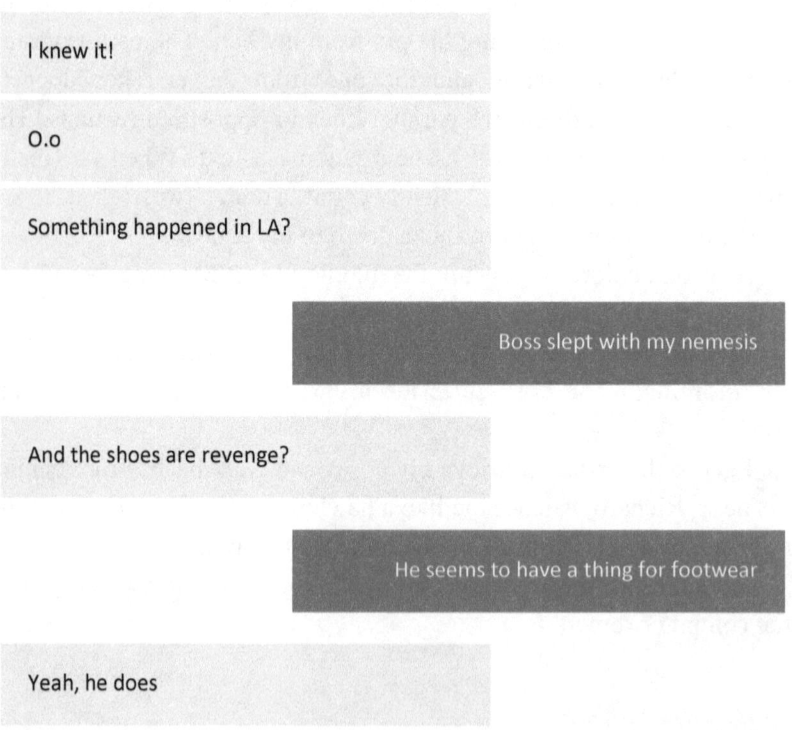

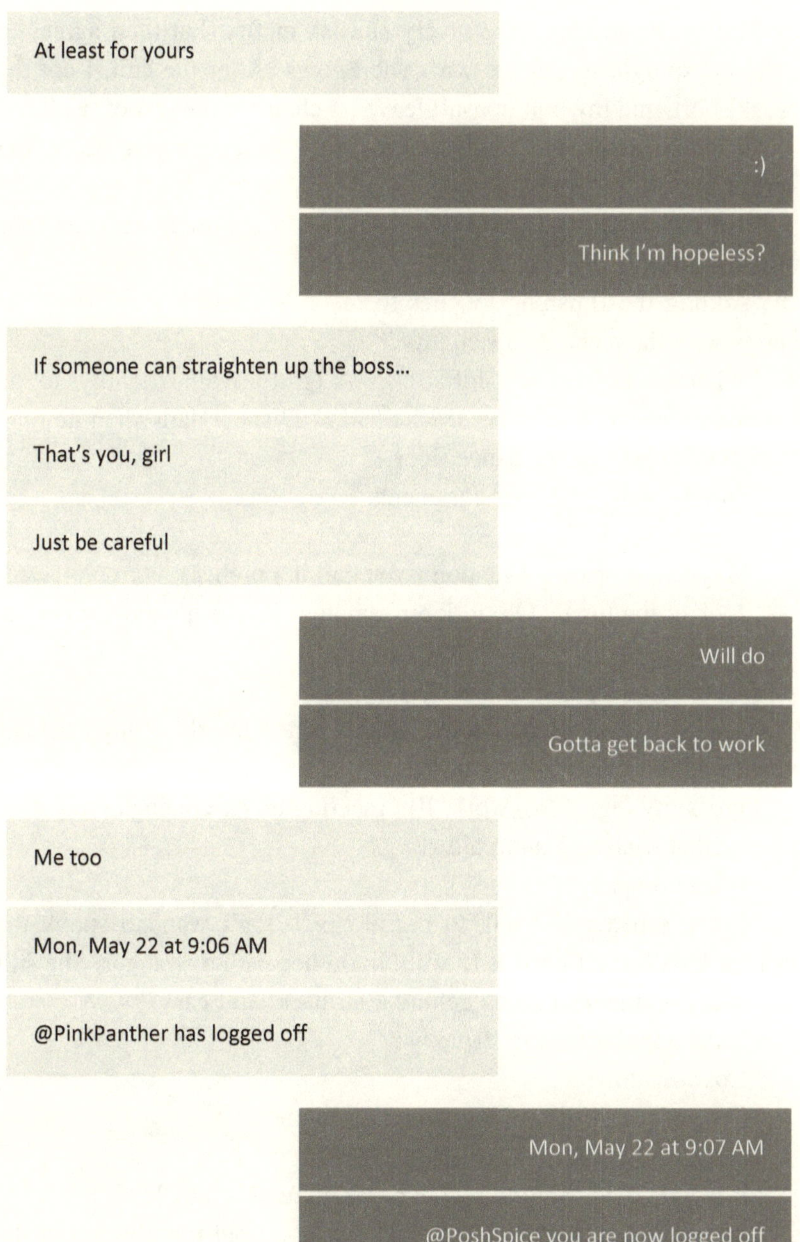

We exchange a got-your-back stare and resume our respective tasks.

I spend the rest of the morning threading interviews with pieces of gossip and shuffling professional shots of the gala. At lunch, I take my break alone to call the ex-colleague, Melanie, who had the story on Maison Vanderbilt. She's very skittish at first but then agrees to meet me tonight to tell me what she knows. After the call, I cut the break short, and my butt doesn't leave its chair for the rest of the day.

"Walker." Richard's voice startles me. "What are you still doing here?"

I lift my gaze from the screen. Outside, it's already dark, and the office is empty.

"Adding the finishing touches to my LA posts. Christian will be happy with the piece on his charity."

Richard's expression shifts oh-so-slightly from friendly to an enigmatic frown. The same one he had at Disney Hall when he took Christian's place on the dance floor.

"Sure he will," the boss comments.

"Want to see it?"

"Maybe tomorrow. Why don't you call it a night?"

I look at the time. "Oh, it doesn't matter. I have an appointment at nine-thirty."

The frown deepens. "A date?"

Richard's gaze wanders to my thighs where the slit of my skirt has opened a bit too much.

I cross my legs. "No, work. I'm meeting an ex-colleague to gather info on that Maison Vanderbilt story."

"Want company?"

"No, it's better if I talk to her alone. I don't want to spook the source. Last thing I need is to walk in on her with a stranger. She still works at Évoque, and going behind their back isn't easy."

"Is the appointment in Brooklyn?"

"No, downtown."

"Get your stuff, I'm giving you a lift home."

"Why?"

"It's dark. You shouldn't walk home alone this late."

I'm tempted to say I'm a big girl and point out that this is not the same New York of the eighties. But I'm so tired I'd gladly skip all the fuss of changing and walking home.

"Come on, Chevron," I call. "We're going home."

"*Woof.*"

I haven't attached her leash yet so that as soon as we exit the office, Chevron launches herself into the hall.

"*Ouch!*" someone screams.

There's a teenage girl sitting on the floor of our landing who's trying to fend off Chevron's overenthusiastic reception.

I dash after the pup, trying to grab her by the collar while apologizing to the girl. "I'm so sorry. I didn't expect someone to be out here. But she doesn't bite, I promise."

"It's okay," the girl says, cuddling Chevron. "She's the cutest thing."

I manage to drag my overexcited puppy off the girl, who looks a bit too sad for her age.

"Hey, are you all right?" I ask.

The girl rolls her eyes. "Yeah, just waiting for my mom to finish work." She points at the door to her left.

I follow her finger to a plaque on the wall.

Vivian Hessington
Attorney at Law
Family Law — Divorce Attorney

The only other door on our floor opens, and a tall guy with a mop of curly dark hair comes out.

We all exchange a polite greeting and then his blue eyes widen when he spots the girl on the floor. "Tegan."

"Hi, Luke," the girl says.

The girl and the newcomer seem familiar with each other. Suddenly, I remember the shouted conversation I overheard the first day I came here. The woman was screaming for the man to keep out of her daughter's life. And the man was yelling back how someone ought to intervene since her mother didn't seem up to the task. So this Luke is Mr. Meddling. I read the plaque next to his door.

Lucas Keller
Psychologist
Marriage Counseling, Couples Therapy, Family Specialist

Mmm, interesting pairing.

I never noticed we were sharing the floor with a divorce attorney and a couple therapist.

"What is she doing?" Luke asks, sounding mad.

"She's working late," the girl says. "Big surprise…"

"Up," Luke offers her a hand. "Come wait inside my office."

They disappear behind the door just as the elevator arrives. I attach Chevron's leash and follow the boss inside.

Richard scoffs. "What's the point of having kids and then acting like they don't exist?"

"That seems a little harsh. You don't know that girl's mother. The woman is probably doing the best she can."

"It's not the first time our neighbors have argued about the girl."

"Still not your place to judge."

Richard gives me a hard stare. "You seemed pretty quick on passing judgments yesterday."

Ah well, Richard, gut-wrenching jealousy does turn me into an ugly person.

I can't really say what I'm thinking, so I keep quiet, already regretting taking the boss up on his offer for a lift home.

***

Richard drives some sort of vintage sports car. I'm not sure what the make is, but I gather at first glance what the car isn't: cheap, ordinary, American. The wheel is on the wrong side so I have to mount from the left. Richard hops in next to me, starts the engine, and drives away at an alarming speed.

After only two turns, I'm already convinced I'm going to die. Sitting on the left side of a car in a right-driving country is no fun. It gives me the impression we'll slam into the opposing traffic at any second. I turn to Richard to protest but find I can't.

The boss is looking straight ahead with a fierce, assured expression. One hand on the wheel, the other on the gear stick. His feet work the pedals, and our speed increases once again.

Then it hits me. That's how James Bond gets all his women. It's the sporty British car. Or the speed. The adrenaline? *Oh, who am I kidding! It's the pilot—and his stupidly sexy forearms!*

"Enjoying the ride?" said pilot asks.

"More wondering if I'm going to make it home in one piece." I sulk. "You always drive like this?"

"I can slow down if it bothers you."

Please don't. "Yeah, thank you."

"*Oooooooooooooooooowhoo,*" Chevron howls her remonstrations at the reduction in speed.

Richard laughs. "At least one of my girls knows how driving should be done."

His girls? How am I one of his girls? Does he mean one of the girls in *his* car?

I spend the rest of the ride overanalyzing Richard's choice of possessive pronoun and don't even realize when he pulls onto my street.

"Sure you don't want company?" Richard asks.

"No, thanks. As I said, my source is skittish."

"Look at you, already protecting your sources. Next thing I know, you'll go for a Pulitzer."

I roll my eyes and exit the car, whistling for Chevron to follow me. When she jumps off, I secure her leash and lean my head back inside. "Thank you for the ride." Richard is struggling to look me in the eye, and in the eye only, given how deep the neckline of my top is in this position. "See you in the morning."

"Morning. Good night, I mean," he says, choked.

With a smile, I close the door. Richard waits for me to get inside before he burns rubber.

I barely have time to let Chevron in, say, "Hi," to Nikki, and dash out again. I ignore my self-imposed austerity regime and take a cab uptown. The nude heels are too high to walk comfortably in, and I'm too lazy to take the subway.

My phone pings halfway through the ride. It's a series of messages from Melanie, the ex-colleague who supposedly had the dirt on the Vanderbilts. I hope the office gossip is reliable. If after all my boasting to Richard I show up empty-handed, I'll die of shame. And I can't stand the thought of Aurora beating me once again, even if she isn't aware that we've engaged in a new fight.

> I won't be there tonight

> The person you need to talk to is waiting at table 18

> Please do not contact me again

I almost expect to receive a follow-up, "your phone will self-destruct in ten seconds" message, but that's it. Good thing I didn't accept Richard's offer to come along. I don't even know who I'm meeting.

The bar Melanie—or this other person—picked is not very spy movie. The vibe is more standard Manhattan post-work drink: low lights, lounge music, expensive cocktails. I follow the table numbering to eighteen where a woman in her middle/late thirties is sitting, a dry martini in front of her. Brown hair, blue eyes, dark suit—I lower my gaze—*cool shoes*. We'll get along just fine.

"Hello." I stop next to the table. "I'm Blair Walker, Melanie's friend."

"Oh, hi." The woman gets up to shake my hand. "I'm Alison."

I sit opposite her and order a diet Coke, wanting to keep a clear head. To break the ice, we do a small round of get-to-know-you chitchat until she seems relaxed enough, and I move on to the real reason for this meeting.

"So, Maison Vanderbilt. Mind if I take notes?" I ask, fishing in my bag for a notepad and a pen. How old-fashioned of me. I almost went and bought a tape recorder but it seemed a bit much, and I wasn't sure a bar with music would've been the best place to use one.

"Please, go ahead," Alison says.

"Okay, ready to get started?"

She nods and takes a sip of her cocktail.

"First, I need to know if you'd rather have your name on the record or if you want to remain an anonymous source."

"Anonymous."

"Good." *It's not good.* Anonymous sources pose an issue of credibility, and Richard is already all over me with this investigation. I hope at least Alison has some definitive proof. "So, Melanie didn't tell me much over the phone. She only said you're the one who came to her with a potential story two years ago and that she'd arrange this meeting."

"Yeah, Melanie and I were roommates in college and I knew she worked at a magazine. Even if Mel wasn't a reporter or anything, I thought she could be interested in a fashion house scandal or at least pass the info on to a real journalist." Alison keeps fidgeting with the stem of her glass. "But she didn't. She told me her Editor-in-Chief had killed the story and forbidden her to pass it on. I was surprised when she called me. I was sure no one at Northwestern would touch the info with a ten-foot pole."

"Oh, I'm not with Northwestern. Not anymore."

Alison lets out a nervous laugh. "That explains the call then. Where do you work?"

"At an online-only outlet. Here, let me show you." I use my tablet to show her the homepage.

"And how come you're interested in this story?"

"If the Vanderbilts are committing tax fraud the public has… a right to know."

Alison gives me a long, piercing stare. "Care to share the real reason now?"

If I want her to trust me, I should return the courtesy.

I sigh. "Rebecca and Aurora Vanderbilt cost me my job."

"How?"

"I was in a race for a promotion with Aurora and her mother thwarted me with money. It got Aurora promoted, and yours truly fired."

Alison nods and leans back in her chair. "That makes two of us."

"You were fired?"

She nods.

"So what was your relationship with Maison Vanderbilt?"

"I used to work there as an accountant."

"Can we cite our source as a former company accountant?"

"Yes." *Oh, finally a welcome surprise.* "Just don't specify male or female and how much time I worked there."

"Just for my personal record, how long was that?"

"Nine years."

"Then what happened?"

"I asked the wrong question and three months later I got the ax."

"And you're sure the two are related."

"Positive."

"Were you the only employee let go?"

"Oh, no. They're not that stupid. HR called it a functional restructuring and fired eight other people alongside me, all accountants. Perfect cover up, really. That way I couldn't sue them for wrongful termination."

"Which is also why you're allowing us to disclose that you were an accountant there. With nine people fired at the same time, they can't point the finger at anyone in particular."

"Exactly. I'm using their smarts against them."

"Great, so tell me what happened. Start at the beginning and don't leave out anything, however small the detail may seem to you."

"It all started when I noticed repeated monthly payments going to an off-shore company that didn't seem to provide Maison Vanderbilt with any real service…"

I lean back in my chair and listen to Alison's tale.

Fifteen

Never Dwell on the Past

"So you've no *actual* proof," Richard says, after listening to my account of the chat with Alison—whose name and gender I've kept private.

For the past half hour, I've been watching his frown get deeper. We're facing each other on opposite sides of his desk, and the outright enthusiasm I felt this morning is bleeding out, stabbed in the chest by every new crease that appears on Richard's forehead.

"Define *actual* proof," I say. "I have an ex-accountant on record—"

"You have an anonymous source."

"So what? We can say they were an accountant at Maison Vanderbilt and they're sure the company had a false billing scheme in place."

Richard rolls up his sleeves. "Had or *has?*"

Oh, no. I won't be distracted by his forearms today. *Eye on the prize, Blair.* "My source can only testify to what was going on while under… their employment." This conversation is draining. How long until I accidentally slip and mention Alison's gender?

"Meaning the scheme might not be in place anymore. Or that it could be under completely different names and shell companies."

"It doesn't matter. The scheme did exist and we have everything we need to expose Maison Vanderbilt."

"Except hard evidence."

"We don't need hard evidence. The IRS can get them after we tip them off with the exposé, and once the tax police start looking, they'll find something. Because the fraud *did* happen."

"So says you."

"So says their ex-accountant."

"Oh, please. Your source is just some sour ex-employee who was fired and who has a big, fat chip on their shoulder. Same as you."

That last comment strikes where it hurts. Nostrils flaring, I say, "Chip or not, the facts remain. Neither of us is lying."

"I can't publish a story based on hearsay."

I clench my fists and try not to grind my teeth. "So you're pulling the plug?"

Richard massages his temples. "Not yet. We're going to get a second opinion."

***

Two days later, we head to the-middle-of-nowhere, upstate New York, to meet with an "expert" financial reporter.

The drive is no less an aphrodisiac than the other night, only this time much longer. My hormones are all over the place. Chevron is going crazy in the backseat, too, only she's crazy happy, not randy. My dog enjoys her speed and luxury cars.

Richard's contact, Michael, welcomes us at the gates of his house—a mansion in the middle of a forest.

Very scenic, only mildly unpractical.

Our host is in his late forties, but fit for his age, with salt-and-pepper hair, and intelligent blue eyes. After Richard parks the car and lets Chevron loose in the fenced backyard, Michael shows us inside to his study.

The walls are lined with bookshelves, and everything—desk, shelves, chairs—is in dark walnut. The floor is covered in rugs, and there's a big, oval table in the center of the room. *Very English country quarters.*

Michael's wife appears five minutes later with tea and cookies. "Hi, I'm Susan," she greets us, dropping the tray on the table.

"Blair. Nice to meet you."

"Richard."

"Oh, the pleasure is all mine. I just wanted to bring you some treats before the meeting started."

"Thank you," Richard and I both say.

"The cookies are homemade," Susan explains, "dairy-free, and the eggs come straight from our hens, so don't worry, they're happy chickens."

Where do I sign to have Michael and Susan adopt me?

Next to me, Richard almost chokes on a bite of cookie. I smile and give the boss a stare that says, "See, everyone is concerned with chicken welfare."

Susan leaves and Michael turns to us. "Richard, why don't you tell me what this story we couldn't discuss over the phone is? I'm intrigued."

Richard doesn't reply.

I raise my gaze from the table and catch them both looking at me. Oh, the boss expects *me* to do the talking. And here I was, too busy deciding how many cookies I could eat without appearing like a total pig.

"So." I swallow the last bit of crunchy deliciousness and give Michael the same report I gave Richard two days ago.

The journalist listens patiently and doesn't interrupt once so that when I'm done talking, I have to ask for his opinion. "What's your take?"

Michael strokes the back of his head. "Your story does add up, but you don't have definitive proof."

Richard speaks before I can. "Would you run an article based only on what you've heard today?"

"I would"—Michael gives him a piercing stare—"if my editor backed me."

I love you, Michael!

Richard frowns. "And would any *sane* editor back you?"

"You have a source and a credible one. I'd say it'd be fifty-fifty…"

Michael's implied meaning is all too clear. *Depending on the attributes of said editor.*

Richard shakes his head.

"Whatever you do," Michael continues, "you need to ask Maison Vanderbilt for a statement. They can refuse, and you put in your piece they weren't available for comment. But you're required to contact a representative beforehand and give them the chance to refute your case."

A mean idea is taking form in my head. "What if we asked Rebecca Vanderbilt point-blank?"

Richard shakes his head. "She'd just deny it."

"What if she couldn't?" I insist.

"You want to base your strategy on the hope that Rebecca Vanderbilt doesn't lie?" Richard snaps. "Think again."

"That's not what I meant. We'd have to trap her with our line of questioning."

Richard crosses his arms. "Give me an example."

"We ask her if she's ever heard of Heron LLC. If she lies and says no, then we ask how come Maison Vanderbilt paid millions in management fees to that very company for at least three consecutive fiscal years."

"All that would achieve is perhaps for you to make Rebecca Vanderbilt blush, at best." Richard isn't budging. "No one would see her reaction, and she'd then work to cover her tracks even more thoroughly. If she hasn't already."

I expected this argument. "What if everyone *did* see it?"

"And how would you make that happen?"

"We could tape her."

"Walker," Richard scoffs. "This isn't a spy movie. You can't go around taping people. She'd sue the second the video aired."

"What if she'd given us permission to tape her?"

"And why would she do that?"

"I know this might sound far-fetched, but hear me out." I push both of my hands forward, palms up, to prevent objections. "What if we contacted her saying Inceptor Magazine wants to do an interview? Something about how Rebecca Vanderbilt built her fashion empire. Or how good Maison Vanderbilt is to the community with all the charities it supports. Or how Rebecca is a role model for so many young women. Then mid-interview, *bam!*" I slam my hand on the table. "We drop the bomb and ask her all the questions we want about tax evasion."

Richard doesn't reject the idea outright, and Michael is staring at me with an appreciative "holy s—, lady" expression, so I press on. "At that point, the cameras would be rolling and Rebecca couldn't possibly refuse to answer or she might as well admit she's guilty. All we have to do is come up with the right questions…"

"I can help with that," Michael offers.

I turn to him. "Thank you." Then back to Richard. "And even if she left in a rage at some point, we would have everything on the record."

"What makes you think Rebecca Vanderbilt would even agree to an interview with you? You're not exactly friendly with her daughter."

I blush, and then punch below the belt. "But you are."

"Not that much," Richard says, and my heart leaps. At least their little gathering in LA was a bona fide one-night stand. "Anyway," Richard continues, "even if I were close to her, what would you have me do? Trick Aurora into ruining her mother's life?"

"Would you do it?"

A girl can hope.

"It's out of the question."

And have her hopes crushed. Anyway, I wouldn't have respected Richard if he'd said yes.

"And what if I got the interview all by myself?" I ask.

"If you can do it without dropping my name."

"I'll have to use the magazine name, and you're the Editor-in-Chief."

"As long as you leave me out of it personally, it'd be fine."

"Perfect! Are you giving me the green light to try?"

"Not yet." Richard drums his fingers on the table. "What if

Rebecca Vanderbilt were to sue?"

"For what? We'd make her sign a disclaimer beforehand granting us permission to air the interview."

"What if she sues for slander?"

"They can win a lawsuit for slander only if the accusation is false," Michael says. "And if they do sue you, it'd give you the right to access their books to prove your innocence. I doubt any lawyer in his right mind would initiate that kind of lawsuit with a guilty client."

"So we don't risk anything?" Richard asks.

"The way I see it," Michael scratches his chin. "Worst-case scenario, the interview is a YouTube flop and you've made an enemy for life. Best-case scenario, it goes viral, and the IRS picks up the investigation where you left off."

"You think that could really happen?" I ask.

Michael nods. "Half the government's investigations start from anonymous or public tips."

"Then why don't we just tip off the IRS and let them do all the work?" Richard asks.

"Ah." Michael sighs. "In that case, there's no guarantee they'd follow up on the tip, but if you make a big public splash…"

Richard sighs. "I really have no choice here, do I?"

"Sorry, buddy," Michael shrugs. "The lady has you cornered."

Michael winks at me and I beam back. I can hardly sit in my chair.

"So the interview is a go?" I ask.

Richard looks at me and gives a resigned nod.

***

A week later, my phone starts vibrating on my desk. The caller ID— recently changed—shows, Billy Loomis. Okay, my ex-boyfriend isn't exactly a serial killer, and he didn't try to murder me and all my friends while wearing a stupid white mask. But still, I couldn't keep Gerard as Edward Cullen.

I let the call go unanswered. Two minutes later the phone rings again, and again a third time. At the fourth call, I press ignore, letting Gerard know I'm willfully ignoring his calls. The phone goes silent after that.

Yay, he's given up.

A mail banner flashes on the screen.

Nope.

```
Date: Thu, June 1 at 10:22 AM
From: gerard.wakefield@aol.com
To: blair.walker@yahoo.com
Subject: I'm sorry, please don't ruin my life
```

Blair, please. I know you're mad at me and that I behaved like a total bastard with you. There are no excuses for what I did and I'm so very sorry I threatened to sue you and for everything else. But I got scared and didn't know what else to do. You can't talk to the partners at my firm. It would destroy me. Annihilate me. Please, I'm willing to negotiate a settlement with your lawyer. Whatever you want, you can have. But please not a word to anyone at my firm. If you can find even the smallest shred of compassion in you, please try to forgive me.

Sincerely,

Gerard

Wow, talk about a groveling apology! I know Gerard doesn't really regret what he did and that he's just scared I'll use the affair against him. Still, a crappy apology is better than no apology. I had completely forgotten about my threats to expose him. Does he really think I'd do something so mean and spiteful? *Yes, probably because he's the kind of person who would.* I realize then that I never really knew Gerard, and he must've not known me. Anyway, despite him behaving like vermin, the bastard has suffered enough. I don't want to ruin anyone's life. I quickly tap a reply.

```
Date: Thu, June 1 at 10:25 AM
From: blair.walker@yahoo.com
To: gerard.wakefield@aol.com
Subject: Re: I'm sorry, please don't ruin my life
```

Gerard, do us both a favor and relax. I was never going to sue you. I'm not that kind of person. Please stop calling me.

```
Blair
```

I'm about to press send when I change my mind. If Gerard was a shitty boyfriend, something he is not is a shitty lawyer. I press delete and type a different message.

```
Date: Thu, June 1 at 10:27 AM
From: blair.walker@yahoo.com
To: gerard.wakefield@aol.com
Subject: Re: I'm sorry, please don't ruin my life

I need a legal favor. Can you write a bulletproof
disclaimer for an interview? Do this for me and
you're off the hook.

Blair
```

Rebecca Vanderbilt's PA has agreed to do the interview. Even better, she insisted on having it in Maison Vanderbilt's flagship store in Manhattan. With the interview date approaching fast, I need to make sure the magazine is covered from any legal action against us. And what better advisor than my shark-lawyer ex who's willing to do about anything for me?

Gerard's reply arrives immediately.

```
Date: Thu, June 1 at 10:28 AM
From: gerard.wakefield@aol.com
To: blair.walker@yahoo.com
Subject: Re: Re: I'm sorry, please don't ruin my
life

Thank you, Blair. Anything. Anything you need. Just
let me know the details, and it'll be ready for you
by tomorrow morning.

Thank you.
Gerard
```

Now we're talking.

***

I could have asked Gerard to FedEx me the finished document, but there's a part of me that wants closure. After three years of my life spent with that man, our story ended in a restaurant in less than half an hour. I need to see Gerard and be sure I'm not harboring unrequited feelings for him. The only way to know if I'm over him is if he makes me feel nothing. Total indifference is the opposite of love, not hate.

We agree to meet super early the next morning, and I make him come down to my side of Manhattan. Something he never did while we dated. I leave a moping Chevron home and go to the meeting alone.

When I get to the café, Gerard is already there sipping coffee while seated at an outside table. He hasn't spotted me yet, so I assess my reactions from the safety of my side of the street. I study him. Still good-looking, but also pompous looking—expensive suit, shoes, and tie, confident smirk, and a five-hundred-dollar haircut. In short, a handsome prick. But definitely not someone I'm in love with. My breath isn't in my throat, I have no accelerated pulse, and my stomach remains level. Well, actually, it churns a little. If I can't have total indifference, I'll settle for total revulsion.

I cross the road. "Hi."

"Blair." Gerard stands up.

There's an awkward moment when it seems he's about to kiss me on the cheek, but my glare must be enough to dissuade him.

"Would you like a coffee?" he asks.

"No, thanks. I'd like to get this over with as quickly as possible."

"Sure." He reaches down into a briefcase and hands me a folder. "Here's everything you need. Get Rebecca Vanderbilt's signature on the dotted line and you're covered. Can I ask what this is about?"

"No," I reply sharply. "You'll find out by the end of next week, anyway." I tap the folder. "Is this the real deal? Bulletproof like I asked?"

"Blair, you make Rebecca Vanderbilt sign that document and you're not wearing a bulletproof jacket"—he knocks on the wooden table—"you're standing in a nuclear bunker."

"Great. I guess I owe you a thank you."

Gerard smiles in a way I used to find endearing, but now only seems sleazy.

"Not at all," he says, then takes another folder out of the briefcase.

"If you could just sign this, we're done."

I eye the folder suspiciously. "What's that?"

"The confidentiality agreement I sent you," Gerard replies, nonplussed.

"I'm not signing a confidentiality agreement."

He turns red from neck to ears. "Was this a trap? Your petty way to get revenge? You make me work for you and then you ruin me?"

"No, I'm not evil. Just because I'm not signing a piece of paper, it doesn't mean I'll go tell on you and Laura the second I leave here. Don't worry, it was never my intention."

"Why won't you sign the confidentiality agreement, then?"

"Gerard, forget it. You'll have to take me at my word." I get up. "But you can relax, as, contrary to you, I *am* trustworthy." I swing my bag over my shoulder and without waiting for a reply, I wave and say, "Have a nice life."

Always wanted to say that to somebody.

***

That same morning I go over the details of the interview with Richard.

"The equipment, plus video and audio technicians, are booked," I say. "The date is set, and here's the disclaimer for Rebecca Vanderbilt to sign." I hand Richard the document Gerard drafted. "It should be ironclad."

Richard skim-reads the pages. "Wonderful." His eyes pause on the legal stamp at the end of the document. "How were you able to afford Goldstein, Smidch, and Vander? They're a very expensive firm."

I shrug. "My ex works there."

A shadow crosses Richard's face. "You're still in contact with him?"

"No, not really. Let's just say he owed me a favor."

"He did this for you after you threw a plate of spaghetti over his head?"

"Gerard deserved the spaghetti, and he knows it."

"But why would you even ask him after everything he did?"

"What's the big deal?" *Why is Richard getting so worked up?* "We needed legal advice, and Gerard is a kickass lawyer. Plus, I wanted to see him again to see how it'd make me feel."

Richard purses his lips. Seems like he's dying to ask what my findings were, but knows he can't without being inappropriate. *Aha!* The boss *is* British after all.

"So, when's the interview?" Richard asks instead.

"Monday."

"And you plan to make it go live on…?"

"The following Friday. I don't want to give Rebecca Vanderbilt time to pull tricks out of her sleeve. No matter if we have the best disclaimer ever written."

Richard sighs. "Then by next weekend, we'll know if we still have a magazine or not."

"About that. I wanted you to know how much I appreciate the trust you're placing in me. I know this interview is causing you more than a headache and a few sleepless nights. And I can't say enough how thankful I am you're letting me run the story anyway. Even if it means facing a potential lawsuit…"

"Hey." Richard finally cracks a smile. "We wouldn't be a serious newspaper if we didn't get a lawsuit every now and then. Walker, you have my complete trust."

"Thank you, boss. I won't let you down."

Sixteen

Never Pick a Fight

Monday morning, at eight sharp, I'm shaking hands with the very woman I'm about to ruin. I've rehearsed every question several times with both Richard and Michael. Our financial expert has also agreed to write a complementary article to go with the interview. After a weekend spent obsessing over every little detail that could go wrong, I'm ready.

When the introductions are over, I inhale deeply and hand Rebecca Vanderbilt the disclaimer.

"If you could sign here, we can get started right away."

"What's this?" she snaps.

"Oh, only a disclaimer that allows us to air the interview. It's standard procedure."

I hold my breath as she scans the fine print. If she doesn't sign this, I'm toast. I can't ask her any of the burning questions.

Rebecca hands the document to her PA. "What do you think?"

The woman turns the pages with hawk-like eyes, and for the first time, I'm worried. Miss PA doesn't look like a fool.

"Seems pretty standard, but I don't think you should sign any document without a lawyer checking it first." Then she stares up at me. "We can have our in-house attorney go over the disclaimer and send it back signed after the interview."

Sweat pools under my armpits and on my upper lip. "I'm sorry, but that won't be possible. Without your explicit permission, we can't so much as record Mrs. Vanderbilt saying hello, let alone record footage of the inside of the store. If she doesn't sign, we can't proceed with the interview at all." The sweating worsens. I try to inconspicuously wipe away the cold droplets on my forehead.

The mean PA woman doesn't buy my stream of BS. "Then I suggest we postpone until our lawyers have had time to review these papers."

"Nonsense," Rebecca interjects. "Give me the document."

"Mrs. Vanderbilt," the PA insists. "I strongly suggest you reconsider."

Luckily, Aurora's mother is not very good at taking advice.

With a wave of her hand, she says, "Oh, please. I wouldn't be where I am today if I hadn't taken a risk or two down the road. Pen!"

The reluctant PA hands her a Montblanc and Rebecca happily signs her own death warrant. *Gotcha!*

After three makeup retouches, The Madame is finally ready to go on screen. We sit on the apricot couches outside the fitting rooms, wait a few seconds for the lighting technician to adjust the lamps, and then we're rolling…

After a few introductory questions, I start laying my trap. "Mrs. Vanderbilt, I don't know if you remember, but the last time I saw you, we were in LA at Christian's Slade charity ball for his Teachers without Postcodes fair education project. Given how busy you are as CEO of Maison Vanderbilt, do you often find time to attend charitable events like that one?"

"Coming from a family of entrepreneurs and being an entrepreneur myself, one of the key aspects of my work ethic is giving back to the community. That's why I always make time for public service, no matter how busy my schedule is. At Maison Vanderbilt, we constantly strain to give more than our due, contributing to various charities on top of our legal obligations."

"As it happens, Maison Vanderbilt is one of the most generous companies when it comes to charity." I shuffle my papers to check the numbers. "My records show that last year alone, you contributed over five million dollars to different projects. With a specific focus on youth and education."

"Yes, exactly. We focus in particular on nurturing the next generation of talent. It's extremely important to foster tomorrow's leaders as they represent our future."

"Public education in our country is mainly funded through taxes—property taxes for the most part, but also state and federal taxes. So what do you think of companies that use tax havens to hide assets and pay fewer taxes than what they really owe?"

"Well, they're obviously cheating society and robbing communities blind. Everyone has to do their part."

"Those are sage words, Mrs. Vanderbilt, and it's interesting hearing them coming from you. What about yourself? Have you ever had any connection to an offshore company?"

"Maison Vanderbilt has many international branches." Rebecca grimaces. "Some of them are located in countries with taxation incentives. It's common practice for multinational companies to-to... anyway, I don't see what the point of this question is... It feels almost as if you were accusing me of something."

"Are you at all familiar with a company called Heron LLC?"

She pales. "No, why should I?"

"So you've never heard the name Heron LLC. It's a company based in the Cayman Islands, a notorious tax haven."

"Never," she says haughtily, moving her chin up. "Can we return to the original scope of this interview? Why are we talking about the Cayman Islands? Unless of course it's to discuss our newest resort collection." Rebecca lets out a high-pitched laugh.

"In a moment." *Oh, you're not wiggling out of this one.* "But you see, I find it weird the name Heron LLC is unfamiliar to you. According to a former employee of Maison Vanderbilt, your company used to pay millions in management fees to Heron every year.”

“This is nonsense.” Rebecca searches with her eyes for help, looking very much like a trapped animal. No one comes to her aid.

Luck is on my side as her PA seems to have vanished after she made sure the interview was going smoothly, leaving her boss completely at my mercy.

“Mrs. Vanderbilt, isn’t paying management fees to an offshore company one of the easiest means of tax evasion?”

“I don’t know what you’re talking about.”

“Just to be clear, as CEO of Maison Vanderbilt, you’re denying ever committing tax fraud.”

“You’ve no proof of these absurd allegations you’re making.”

“I have the word of a former accountant at your company. Anyway, are you claiming I’ve no proof or that the fact never subsisted?”

Now she stands up. “This interview is over. *Over!* You silly girl. Dare make public a second of this reckless ambush and you’ll never be able to show your face in Manhattan ever again. I’ll make sure no one ever hires you.”

I stand up as well. “I already have a job, thank you.”

“Not when I sue your little magazine for every cent it has.”

“I’m sure any judge will recognize the truth of our statements, or the IRS will. Mrs. Vanderbilt, I’m afraid it will be you hiding your face around Manhattan when this interview goes live. Because rest assured, it *will* go live…”

That’s when a composed, supposedly classy, if not very honest woman completely loses it and turns into a bratty child. Screaming and destroying everything in her path.

***

A few days later, everyone in the office has gathered behind my desk to watch the video of the interview on my computer. Well, everyone except for Richard, who, for some reason, has not shown up to work yet. I hate the disappointment I feel at him not being here to witness my success.

Where the hell is the boss?

"Uuuuuhh-uuuuh," my colleagues cheer as they watch Rebecca Vanderbilt hit the camera.

I've uploaded the final footage to YouTube this morning and Hugo, our News Editor, has posted Michael's supplementary article on our homepage.

"This is my favorite part," Hugo says. "When she grabs the camera and sends it crashing down."

"No, no," Indira says. "You have to wait until the very end."

We all keep our eyes glued to the screen. Now we can only see the marble floor of the Maison Vanderbilt flagship store through the cracked camera glass. And, of course, hear Rebecca Vanderbilt's threats to sue us. She screamed a lot, and we had to add several censoring "beeps" to the audio file.

"Wait for it," Indira mutters, "wait for it… There it goes."

Rebecca Vanderbilt stomps her expensive stiletto on the camera and the video goes black.

Indira clicks her tongue. "Best finale ever."

"Yeah, pretty cool!" Hugo agrees.

"I'm posting a screenshot of the stiletto of death on Instagram," Saffron says.

"Refresh the page," Ada asks.

I do as she says.

"How many views?"

"Fifty thousand," I say.

"How long ago did you upload this?" Hugo asks.

I check the clock window on the screen. "About an hour. Are fifty thousand views any good?"

"Are you kidding me?" Saffron asks. "You're on the road to get batshit crazy viral, girl."

I smile. "I hope everyone sees this, and that the IRS indicts them."

Zane's landline rings, and he walks back to his desk to answer. As soon as he picks up the receiver, he signals for us to quiet down. We do, while also taking the opportunity to eavesdrop on the conversation. Zane is in charge of distribution and it sounds like he's negotiating with some other news outlet who wants to air the interview. And I don't want to be too optimistic, but it seems like he's talking to a TV network.

TV or not, I don't finish listening in on the conversation because, at that moment, Richard walks through the front doors. Too happy to see him, I get up and almost run toward him. I catch myself just in time and stop a few feet away. Was I really about to launch myself at him and throw my arms around his neck?

"Hi," I say. "Where were you? The interview went live an hour ago!"

Richard gives me an awkward smile. "I hit a bit of a road bump."

"Oh, what happened?"

"I had to see Aurora."

Ice spreads through my veins. "Vanderbilt?"

"The one and only."

"Why?"

Richard sighs. "I wanted to give her fair warning. I didn't want her to go to work today and get blindsided by the story breaking." He shrugs. "I owed her that much."

"I'm sure her mother must've told her by now," I say a bit too aggressively.

"No, apparently she hadn't. And anyway, nobody knew we were going live today, so…"

That's very decent of him. I still wish he hadn't done it. The thought of him and Aurora together, no matter the circumstances, makes me see red.

"How did she take it?"

"At first she wouldn't believe me. I don't think she was involved in the fraud. Her mother must've kept all their shady dealings from her."

"And after you explained, did she believe you?"

"Oh, no." Richard shakes his head. "Once the shock was over, she got mental! She tried to convince me not to publish the interview and once I refused, she… ah… threw her coffee at me."

I cover my mouth with one hand. "Did you get burned?"

"No, it was iced. But I still had to go home and change."

Right, his curls still seem a bit damp. Mmm, I have to fight hard with my limbs not to run a hand up the back of his neck.

"Anyway." Richard moves toward the group assembled at my

desk. "How are the first responses?"

Ada clicks the mouse. "Sixty thousand views already."

"Social media is going crazy," Saffron says.

"CNN wants to run the story on *CNN Today!*" Zane puffs his chest out.

"CNN," I screech. "Are you kidding me?"

"I kid you not!" He smiles.

Richard pats my shoulder. "Well done!"

I beam at him, trying not to melt under his touch.

"Now," the boss adds in a more practical tone. "Can we manage the extra traffic to our website?" he asks, looking at the techies.

"I'll make sure we get some extra server capacity," one says.

The entire tech team scurries back to their computers.

"All right," Richard says, addressing the whole office. "Let's make sure we run a tight ship today and then we can all go out to celebrate tonight!"

Everyone shouts their approval and even Chevron contributes to the general enthusiasm with a loud howl.

***

By the end of the day, I have a better understanding of what "going viral" means. The hashtag #MaisonVanderFraud is trending on Twitter, we've reached over a million views on YouTube, and the story is all over the media. Both traditional and social.

At six thirty, Richard walks to the center of the open space and claps his hands to get everyone's attention.

"All right, people." The office quiets down. "This week has been incredible, and today has been an unprecedented success. It couldn't have happened without your combined effort. Blair, thank you for bringing in the story and pulling off a magnificent piece of investigative journalism. Zane, thanks for handling the TV rights." Each announcement is followed by thunderous applause. "Saffron, for fueling the Social Media craze. Our techies, for making sure our website didn't crash. Everyone else, for your support." Richard lets the applause die before speaking again. "Now it's Friday night, and I don't know about you, but I can't wait for the weekend to get started. So what do you say we all go out for a drink to celebrate?"

Richard's proposal is approved by a standing ovation.

He lingers by my desk. "Walker, are you coming?"

"I'm not sure." The boss seems disappointed, so I add, "It's just that I don't know if a bar is a good place for Chevron."

"Right, I hadn't thought of that. What if I take Chevron to my house and join you guys later?"

"Are you sure it's not a problem?" I ask.

He kneels down to pet her with both hands, and I swear I've never seen a dog so ecstatic. "Nah, I'm sure this beauty won't wreck the place, and anyway, I can give you a lift home afterward. You can't walk home alone in the middle of the night."

"Okay." I surrender the leash and the duffel bag.

As we queue in front of the elevators, Indira leans in and whispers in my ear, "Smooth."

I scowl at her without replying.

Outside the building, I pat Chevron goodbye and say to Richard, "See you at the bar."

As I watch the two of them go, a million scenarios start playing in my head at once. Richard kissing me goodnight in his damned sexy car, or even better, him inviting me in before he takes me home…

My happy stream of fantasies is interrupted by my phone ringing, screen flashing with the ominous caller ID, Dolores Umbridge.

I sigh and pick up. "Hello, Mom."

The others are still waiting, so I gesture for them to keep going and that I'll meet them at the bar.

"Blair." My mother's voice rattles out of the phone's speakers. Already, from the single pronunciation tone of my name, I understand that she isn't happy with me. "What is this I've heard about you being on your tube? Is it proper for a future mother? My friends at the country club say it's a website with a questionable reputation."

"Mom, it's YouTube, and I did an interview. There's nothing questionable about it."

"An interview? So you got the editor position at Évoque? Why didn't you tell me? I can't wait to tell all my friends."

"No, Mom, I didn't." I stare at the sky, unsure what to say next. I've avoided talking to her since, well, since I was fired. My fuse for my mother has become shorter than ever and I don't care whether she approves or disapproves how I live my life anymore. So I rat myself out. "Actually, Évoque fired me."

"Fired? You? And what do you do for money?"

"I work at a different magazine."

"Which one? Is it better than Évoque?"

I think for a second. "Yeah, ten thousand times better."

"Well, what's it called?"

"Inceptor Magazine."

"I've never heard of it."

"Because it's a new online publication."

"Online? Have you gone mad? What's the publishing house, is it still Northwestern?"

"No. There's no publishing house, it's just the magazine."

"But… but… I mean, what does Gerard think about it?"

"I don't know, and I don't care. We broke up."

"Oh. Oh, goodness. What did you do?"

"*I* did nothing." *Somebody help, please.* I'm about to lose my temper big time. "*He* cheated on me."

"Ah, well, a man like him with an important job… I'm sure you can work through this crisis…"

The fuse reaches the end and I explode. "Mom, are you even listening to me? Gerard was having an affair with his secretary. There's nothing left to work on."

"So what? You'd rather be single? At your age?"

"Yeah, definitely. Single is not a dirty word, and it's better to be alone than to stay in a relationship because it looks better from the outside. I'm not you!"

Without waiting for a reply, I hang up on the momster and turn my phone off.

Arrrgh, that woman!

She still has the power to drive me crazy. Well, at least after our cozy chat she won't call me for another couple of months. Fine by me. I'm ready for a drink and to forget all about parental harassment.

Seventeen

Never Have I Ever

The atmosphere inside the bar has the peculiar cheerfulness only Friday nights can bring along. The guys are outside, seated at a large table in the prettiest back patio ever. Enclosed between brick buildings, covered in green ivy, and with string lights dangling side-to-side, it's modern and quaint at the same time.

Indira waves me over and points at the chair next to her. When I sit down she says, "I've ordered you a margarita and some veggie tacos." She pushes a glass and a plate my way.

"Thanks." I smile and take my reserved spot. "Mmm, these are delicious." I devour a full taco before touching any alcohol. "I'm ordering another round."

As I turn to attract the attention of a server, I catch Richard's eye instead. He's standing on the threshold of the garden, looking at me. Actually, seems like he's been standing there a while. Was he watching me the whole time? The hair on my nape immediately stands up. As he smiles and starts walking toward us, goose bumps rise all over my arms.

Richard sits at the head of the table, one seat away from me. "What did I miss?"

Indira replies, "Tacos and tequila."

The server who I tried to call before arrives to take the table's final orders. I ask for a salad and some other vegetarian tacos. Richard gets a beer and tacos as do most of the others.

The few nights out with my old colleagues from Évoque don't compare. Not with their calorie-counting remarks, bitchy competitiveness, and overpriced cocktails. Here, everyone's mood is relaxed and cheerful. Hugo is being a clown, telling Tinder dates horror stories. Indira is giving everyone sass. And whenever Nico tries to start a serious political debate, we all boo him. The quietest is Saffron, who spends most of the night glued to her phone, giving the group sporadic updates on the number of likes, shares, and views the interview is getting.

When it reaches two million views on YouTube, Richard bangs a fist on the table. "Who's in for celebratory shots?" he shouts.

There's a general cheer of approval, and the boss leaves to fetch a server who reappears minutes later with three bottles of tequila and shot glasses.

I'm trying not to get completely wasted, so I grab the least full glass and drink only for the main toast. Richard also goes back to beer after one shot. Zane and Hugo are not so shy and peruse the bottle multiple times.

As the night progresses, my colleagues start to leave one by one, until there's only Saffron, Indira, and the boss left. We move to a smaller table. Richard carrying his beer and Saffron salvaging the only remaining half-full bottle of tequila along with the shot glasses.

The adrenaline of the day, the tequila, and Richard's proximity make it too hard for me to talk. I let Indira and Saffron lead the conversation. As we listen to the other two, I occasionally catch the boss giving me furtive looks, and smiling. *Is he eye-flirting?*

"Yo, guys," Saffron says after a while, stretching in her chair like a cat. "I'm calling it a night."

"Me too," Indira echoes.

They both get up and look at us as if to say, "You coming?"

Richard lifts his half-full glass. "Mind if I finish the beer before we go get Chevron?"

"No, sure." I get up to hug Saffron and Indira goodnight.

The former pulls me into a tight embrace. "The boss likes you," she whispers in my ear, and then she adds aloud, "See you Monday."

Richard nods, and we both watch Indira and Saffron slalom through the tables and disappear inside the main bar. And then we're alone.

There's a moment of awkward silence until Richard asks, "Want something else to drink?"

"No, I'm good. Thanks."

"Pity, there's half a bottle of good tequila left." He chugs the last of his beer and takes the bottle in his hands. Then he turns toward me with a mischievous grin. "Still convinced you'd lose at that drinking game?"

"Never have I ever? One-hundred percent."

Richard flashes me a challenging smile. "Want to give it a try?"

The smile I give back is equally wicked. "Game on."

"What were the rules again?"

"You say something daring you've never done, and if I have, I drink a shot and vice versa."

Richard grabs two clean shot glasses. "And how do we decide who loses?"

"Whoever drinks the most shots?"

His eyes sparkle as he fills the glasses. "Ladies first."

"Okay." I wrinkle my nose. "Never have I ever... cheated on someone."

Richard doesn't move. "Sorry to disappoint."

"Actually, that's no disappointment." I smile. "Your turn."

"I have never..."

"Say it properly. Never have I ever..."

"That's just a waste of words. I have never... thrown a bowl of spaghetti on somebody's head."

"You're using inside information. Not sure that's fair." I begrudgingly drink my shot.

The boss refills the glass. "Your turn."

I realize Richard knows more about me than I do about him. It'll take some guesswork to hit the right spots. "Never have I ever... gotten a tattoo."

He drinks. Mmm, interesting. Now I can't stop wondering where the tattoo is. I scan his chest for a moment before catching his gaze. Richard gives me a knowing stare as if he knew I was hoping to X-ray through his shirt and see the ink.

"I have never..." Richard pauses, "been arrested."

"You're not playing fair." The tequila burns my throat. This time I do the refill, keeping the shot glasses more than half empty. I've learned how to pace myself with alcohol.

"Never have I ever"—I think for a second—"had someone slap me across the face."

Richard gives me a wicked smile and lifts the glass to his lips.

"Ow. Deserved?"

"Some of them." He shrugs. "I have never... worn a jade dress."

"That's not even something daring."

Richard raises a mischievous brow. "I wouldn't call the dress you wore in LA *not* daring."

I blush and drink. "Never have I ever... attended boarding school."

"What's daring about boarding school?"

"You tell me."

With a naughty grin, he drinks. "I have never... woken up not knowing where I was."

I scowl and drink. This is too easy for him. "Never have I ever... punched someone."

The boss drinks.

"Did *they* deserve it?"

"Oh, yes. I have never..."

Richard and I both guess the next three until the tequila in my system makes me bold enough to step up the game a notch. "Never have I ever... been left at the altar."

Heart pounding, I wait for his reaction. Richard gives me a long stare and lifts the glass to his lips.

"So it's true," I say.

"Wouldn't have drunk otherwise."

"How did it happen?"

"Easily, she changed her mind mid-ceremony. My turn." Richard makes it clear that's all I'm going to get of his backstory. "I have never..."

After a few more rounds of the game, I'm about to reach the point of no return, so before I'm irredeemably drunk I surrender. "Okay, okay. You've made your point. I've become bad enough to lose at this stupid game. But if I drink another shot, we both know where it ends, and it's not pretty. We should play a different game."

Richard flashes me a molten stare, and for a second I'm left breathless. "Truth or dare?"

I don't know why, but the truth part seems scarier than the dare. So I say, "Dare."

"Don't move."

I sit rigidly in my chair as Richard bends his head towards my neck until his mouth is barely an inch from my collarbone. He inhales. There's no touching. Only the faint caress of Richard's breath on my skin. But it's enough to send a shiver down my spine.

"Nice perfume," he says, standing back up.

Mouth dry, I ask, "Truth or dare?"

"Dare."

"Show me your tattoo."

Richard undoes the top three buttons of his shirt, moving the fabric aside to expose his left collarbone where a small, black infinity symbol is tattooed on his skin. The little symbol stands out on his marble-like skin and it's made of words. I lean in to read, getting a peek of his toned chest as an extra perk. I swallow, concentrating hard on the tiny words and not his pectorals. Depending on where one starts reading the writing says, "Love the life you live," or "Live the life you love."

"Cool," I say, leaning back, although not before inhaling Richard's green forest scent.

Richard buttons up his shirt and I'm left mourning the wonderful sight of his almost bare chest.

"Truth or dare?" he asks.

"Truth."

"Are you still in love with your ex?"

"No," I say, shaking my head. "Not sure I ever was, really. Truth or dare?"

"Truth."

"What about you? Carrying a torch for someone?"

"Nope."

"Not even her?"

Richard's features harden. "I had enough time to move on." I'm about to ask more when he cuts me short. "Truth or dare?"

"Truth."

"Tell me something true you've never told anyone."

Let's see… "I don't fold my bedsheets. I just crumple them up in a ball and store them at the back of a drawer."

Richard laughs. "Guess I should've been more specific and asked for something embarrassing."

"Poor linen management is embarrassing." I smile. "Your pick."

"Truth."

I tilt my head to the side. "Do you have a thing for my shoes?"

"Ah." He lowers his gaze to my feet and nods. "So you've noticed. Your turn."

"Truth."

"Ever thought of sleeping with your boss?"

In vino veritas and all that jazz, I tell the truth, "Yes. Truth or dare?"

"Truth."

"Why did you sleep with Aurora Vanderbilt in LA?"

"She was a safe choice."

I put a question mark on my face.

"She's the kind of person I could never fall for," Richard explains.

"And were you worried about… falling for someone else?"

Richard ignores the question. "Isn't it my turn to ask?"

Still avoiding the topic, are we?

I nod.

"Truth or dare?" he demands.

"Truth."

"Why did you come to my room that night?"

I consider my answer for a few seconds, then I stare at him boldly and say, "I wanted to hit on you. Or have you hit on me." To stop him from asking more, I press the game forward. "Truth or dare?"

"Truth."

"Why choose someone you don't really like?"

"No risk of getting hurt."

"Also no risk of getting happy. Is that why you always pretend you don't care about anything or anyone? Because the last time you cared, it ended badly?"

Richard looks down. "I guess, sometimes it just feels easier that way. Truth or dare?"

"Truth."

"The morning after, when you shut me out of your room, you were jealous."

It's more of a statement than a question.

I nod. "Truth or dare?"

His eyes darken. "Dare."

I swallow and, never breaking eye contact, I speak two simple life-changing words. "Kiss me."

Slowly, deliberately, Richard closes the space between us. He cups my face and looks at me a moment longer before his lips are on mine and the world tilts upside-down. I lose myself in the kiss. It's gentle at first, tentative, exploring. Then needier, hungry. I want it to never stop, but it does all too quickly.

Richard nuzzles my neck, whispering, "Truth or dare?"

"Dare."

"Stay at my place tonight."

Eighteen

Never Sleep With Someone On The First Date

Outside the bar, I feel dizzy. And it has nothing to do with the alcohol and everything to do with the man walking by my side.

"Want to take the short or long way home?" Richard asks. "Long one has a view."

"Long way it is, I could use some fresh air."

Richard takes my hand and leads the way. The simple gesture makes me ridiculously giddy, especially when his thumb brushes against my palm, making me shiver with the uncontrollable desire to feel those hands all over me.

Halfway between the Brooklyn and Manhattan bridges, we stop and lean against the railing to admire the view. *Breathtaking.*

A pang of jealousy stabs me in the chest. "Is this where you take all your women?"

Oh, why did I open my stupid mouth? Blair Walker, shut up and don't ruin the moment.

"Actually, no. I usually come here alone."

"Do you?"

"I enjoy the view."

"Yep." I focus on the glittering lights reflected on the water. "Manhattan is irresistible when she's wearing lights."

"I know someone else who's irresistible." Suddenly Richard's voice is behind me, his lips brushing my ear.

I turn to look at him and find myself imprisoned between the railing and his strong chest. The scent of his aftershave is intoxicating, and my hands move of their own accord up the crisp cotton of his shirt. After tracing his thumb around my earlobe with one hand, he moves the other under my chin and tilts my head up. Then we're kissing again, his mouth on mine, gently parting my lips. My hands become frantic, my entire body prickling with anticipation.

I pull away and say, "I think we should go home."

Richard leaves a trail of soft kisses down my neck. "Sorry for making us take the long road." He grabs my hand, and we speed-walk through Brooklyn, leaving Manhattan and her lights behind.

For the entire elevator ride to his loft, we make out like a pair of teenagers: bodies wrapped together, oblivious to anything else in the world. Completely lost in each other.

When the doors ping open, we tumble out and laugh our way to Richard's door. He gets the keys out of his pocket and lets us in.

"Welcome back," Richard whispers.

"Why are we whispering?" I ask in an equally low voice.

"Chevron might be asleep."

"Oh, right. Where is she?"

I tiptoe into the living room to find Chevron sprawled on the couch—belly up, legs in the air. I brace my hands on the backrest, staring at her, but soon get distracted by Richard hugging me from behind and kissing my neck. Shivers spread down my shoulders and along my spine, making my toes curl. I turn around and press my lips onto Richard's.

My body is taking over in a way I've never experienced. This man has melted my brain. My heart is beating so fast I'm afraid I might pass out. But what if this is a huge mistake? Richard is still my boss.

"Are you sure you want this?" I breathe, my ribcage bobbing up and down convulsively.

"Walker"—his teeth find my earlobe—"we reached the point of no return a while ago."

Yeah, agreed.

Richard bends slightly and swings an arm behind my knees, lifting me up and carrying me to the bedroom.

There, on his bed, we make love. I'm confident we're not just having sex. Yes, it's sensual, and heated… but if he does not say so in words, the way Richard looks at me tells me everything. I've never made love keeping my eyes open, but with Richard, it seems impossible to close them.

***

Joy. Indecent bliss. Never have I ever felt so good in my life. I roll over the bed, only to crash-land on hard muscle.

I blink. "Mmm, I remember this room…"

Richard brushes a strand of hair off my face. "Hope this time you remember why you're here."

Oh, I *so* do. Flashes of last night make me blush.

"I see that you do." Richard grabs my hand and kisses the tips of my fingers.

"I might need a little reminder."

"Careful what you wish for…"

I giggle as Richard throws the blankets away and his lips start their magic again…

In a fog of passion and burning emotions, the rest of the day is spent in bed. We only leave to take Chevron for a *very short* walk. I can't stop smiling and feeling all dreamy and happy and, well… sated.

Saturday night, we attempt to leave Richard's apartment to get some dinner. But it's a stupid mistake. We get seated and we order like two normal people would. But then we start this flirtatious eye game, which evolves in us casually touching each other's arms or legs, until we're kissing—*ahem*, making out in the restaurant like two teenagers. By the time the food arrives, Richard asks for everything to be boxed. He pays the bill and we're back at his house and in bed less than an hour after we left.

***

Sunday evening is when the bubble of happiness bursts. The pin comes in the form of an ominous suggestion from Richard. It happens in the late afternoon while we're drinking tea on the couch, my bare legs in his lap and Chevron lying quietly on the living room rug.

I'm admiring Richard's naked chest—he's wearing only sweatpants—when my fit watch sends me a pulsing notification I've been lying down for too long. A pretty common occurrence in the past two days. Out of habit, I check the time. *Already so late.* I wish I could stay in Richard's apartment wearing only one of his T-shirts forever. But I can't. I drop my empty mug on the coffee table and sigh. "Chevron," I say, patting her head. "Time to go."

"Already?" Richard protests. "It's only five!"

"Yeah, but by the time we get to Manhattan it'll be late, and tomorrow is going to be busy. If you haven't noticed, we made quite a splash Friday."

"Stay longer, I can give you a ride…"

As tempting as the offer is…

"We've been in bed for two days," I say, blushing. "I could use the walk. And you'll see us both tomorrow morning at the office, anyway."

"Speaking of the office." Richard's expression switches from a relaxed smile to a slight frown. "It'd be better if we kept this quiet, at least for now."

A chill runs down my spine. Sure, I'd had the same thought. Not wanting to have everyone else at work involved in my private life and gossiping seems like a good idea on the surface. But hearing Richard voice the same concern sets off a million alarm bells in my head. Why does he want to keep it quiet? To protect our privacy? To give us time to figure out our feelings before anyone else gets involved? Or would keeping the relationship hidden only make it easier to break off?

I want to reply that it's okay. Tell him I understand. I want to, but find I can't. After almost forty-eight hours spent naked, I'm less lost in a whirlwind of lust and able to pause long enough to question what's happening.

"Why keep it quiet?" I ask.

"It'd be awkward if the others knew about us."

Us. What does that even mean? I know I'm supposed to play cool, not make demands after such a short time. To let things evolve on their own, so as not to scare him away. It's acknowledged dating wisdom. Yet, there's a new fire burning within me that simply won't let me play by the rules.

I fold my legs and sit straighter. "For them, or for you?"

Clinginess taints my voice and I hate myself for it.

"For everyone, including you."

"Come on, Richard. We don't work in that kind of place. Everyone would just be happy for us."

The afterglow vaporizes from his face, replaced by a tense grimace. "Maybe, but what if I'm not ready to share my private life with all my employees?"

"Indira seems to always know who you're dating."

"Yes, but this is different."

"I would certainly hope so."

"What's that supposed to mean?"

"That if you're only looking for another two-week relationship, I'm not interested."

"So what are you interested in?"

"I don't know, why don't you tell me?"

"Calm down. Why are you getting so worked up?"

The answer comes from my twisting guts before I can even form a rational thought. And since I've no gut-to-mouth filters, I yell, "Because I'm in love with you!"

The silence that follows this impromptu declaration is so tense that even Chevron lifts her head to check on us. Richard is staring at me with that deer-in-the-headlights expression. Well, "terrorized to death" wasn't exactly the reaction I was hoping for. Tears prick my eyes and I have to blink fast to hold them back. Still, Richard isn't speaking.

"Don't worry," I say, getting up. "You don't have to say it back."

Coward, *I add in my head.* I know you feel the same.

I can't stand to look at his terrified expression for a second longer, so I dart for the bedroom. I manage to throw on the essentials before Richard comes in. Admittedly, having this argument wearing only a lacy bra and panties is hardly any better.

"What do you want from me?" he asks.

"Guess."

"What, love?" He scoffs. "A wedding proposal? You want the house with the white fence, the three kids, and a dog in the yard?"

"I already have a dog!" I scream. "And what's wrong with wanting any of that? What if my dream is to get married and have a family?"

"Well, that's not my dream."

"Isn't it? Or are you too afraid to admit it is, even to yourself, because your dream already got shattered once."

"This has nothing to do with that... don't throw my past in my face as an excuse for me not agreeing with your cloud nine attitude."

"Are you sure? Seems to me you hide a lot behind that past."

"You've no idea what you're talking about."

"No, I do. You're the clueless one."

"Oh, really?"

"Yeah, really."

"Why?"

"Because I told you I'm in love with you and you lost the ability to speak."

Richard stands there, gaping. Again, not a word.

I grab my pants and slide them on. "There you go again."

"Blair." He takes a few steps toward me and places one hand on each of my shoulders. "You're overreacting."

"No, Richard." I shove his hands away and grab my blouse. "You're underreacting!"

"Underreacting? What does that even mean?"

Finally dressed, I do a frantic scan of the room to locate all my scattered possessions. I toss everything in the duffel bag and put on my gym shoes. Ready to leave, I turn toward him. "It means that I just told you 'I love you' and I deserve to hear more back than a never ending silence."

Again, silence is all he gives me.

I push past him and storm out of the bedroom. In the living room, I hook Chevron to her leash. Richard hasn't followed me. Oh, no, he prefers to stay hidden. Easier that way. *Bastard. Asshole. Coward.* Tears blur my vision at last. I wait a few more seconds for him to come out. He doesn't. With my heart shattering, I dash out of the apartment, banging the door behind me as hard as I can.

For the entire walk home, I keep looking over my shoulder hoping to see a silver car following us. Every time a car passes us, my heart jolts in my chest. But it's never Richard. I make my way toward Manhattan, sobbing uncontrollably. So much so that a few people stop me to ask if I need help. I turn away the kind strangers, explaining it's only a problem of the heart. *Only.* Why is it that I'm more heartbroken after a two-night stand than I was over a three-year relationship? Is this what love does to you? If that's it, I hope I can fall out of it as quickly as I fell in.

Nineteen

Never Stress Eat

A few hours later, Nikki arrives home to find me in a state of utter misery. I'm on the couch, in my PJs, surrounded by used Kleenex, and eating ice cream.

My best friend takes in the scene and is at my side at once. "What happened to you?" She takes the bowl of ice cream from me to sniff it, and her nostrils flare. "Is this real ice cream?"

I nod.

"Industrial, processed ice cream?"

I nod again.

"No soy?"

I shake my head.

"Dairy?"

Nod.

"Saturated fats?"

I make a wimpy sound.

"Ah." Nikki places the bowl out of reach and drops onto the couch next to me. "I thought you'd spent the weekend with the boss…"

I stare at her with big eyes, trying to transmit telepathically what happened because saying it aloud is too painful.

She catches my vibes at once. "And before the day was over, you asked him where you stood…"

Nod.

"He freaked out."

Nod.

"You went on the defensive and lashed out."

Whimper.

"Richard got mad, too, the argument escalated, you both became petty, hurt each other as much as you could until you stormed out of his house, banging the door behind you. How am I doing?"

I drop my face into my hands and shake my head.

"*Awhooo,*" Chevron comments.

Nikki sighs. "And all this in front of the dog?"

Face still hidden, I nod.

"The poor thing is traumatized."

I give her a look of desperation.

"Come on," Nikki pulls me into a hug. "Everything will be all right."

"How?"

"You two just have to talk."

I snort. "Yeah, because Richard is so good at expressing his feelings."

"Give him time. You ambushed him when he wasn't ready. You should've let him get more used to you."

"I know I was supposed to wait. But what if I don't want to? What if I want to tell him how I feel when I feel it? Why is that so wrong?"

"Nothing's wrong. But it's wrong to expect Richard to be on the same page right away. Give him some time."

"Oh, he has all the time in the world."

"Meaning?"

"I'm not taking another step toward him. Not one."

"So you're just going to pretend the past forty-eight hours didn't happen?"

"Exactly. If Richard changes his mind, he knows where to find me."

***

Monday morning, I put on a brave face and go to the office. I wear a simple blouse, black capris, and sneakers to be switched with wedges in Brooklyn. *Because Richard doesn't like wedges.* I don't want to spark any extra tension, sexual or otherwise. I just want to get through the day, ignore him, and be ignored back.

I sit at my desk, bend my head low, and will myself to stare at my screen and just my screen. I don't even blink when Richard walks in. He supplies a generic, "Hello," that leaves me free enough not to reply, and then moves on to his office without a second glance in my direction. At least from what I can tell using only my peripheral vision.

So he's going for an avoidance strategy, too. *Very well!* I am the queen of avoidance, I can keep my silent treatment going for weeks if I want to.

Mon, June 12 at 8:37 AM

@PinkPanther has logged in

R u mad at the boss?

I guess not everyone is willing to ignore me though.

Mon, June 12 at 8:38 AM

@PoshSpice you are now logged in

I don't want to talk about it

We're not talking

Okay

I don't want to talk

Write

Or even think about it

???

Leave it alone

No can do

Please let it go

I might start crying

And I'd really rather not

Oh!

Yeah, oh!

You slept together

I'm logging off

I was wrong

And she's successfully baited me into asking…

About what?

The boss being a lost cause

No, you weren't

Yes, I was

It's clear from the way he keeps looking at you

(every five seconds)

A dart hits my heart. *Hope? Fear? Love?* All three? I don't know. But I don't have the luxury of indulging in false expectations. Richard has made it clear where he stands. His fear comes before his feelings and that's not going to change no matter what I do.

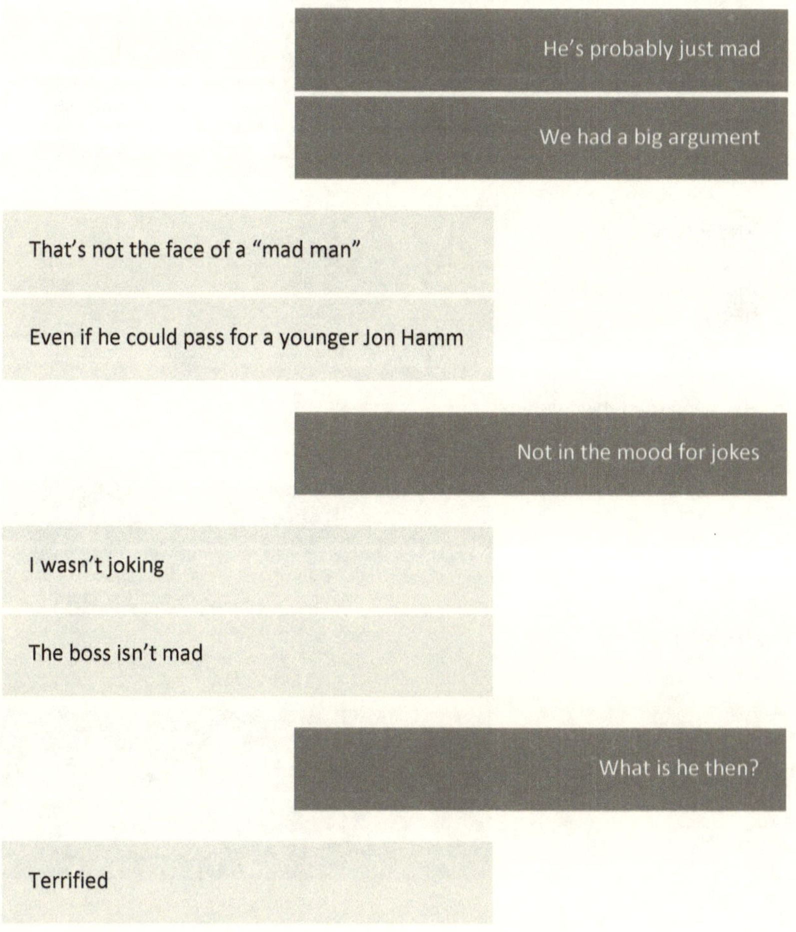

That he is for sure.

And how's that better?

He's terrified because he cares

Doesn't matter if he doesn't care

Or if he's terrified he does care

The bottom line stays the same

We aren't happening

Give it time

He'll come around

Have you read the column?

No

Read the column

Whatever

Don't you have any work to do?

All right Miss Crabby McCranky…

Talk to you later

Mon, June 12 at 9:26 AM

@PinkPanther has logged off

I log off for real this time. It took all my willpower not to open that damn column over breakfast this morning, and now Indira is making my resolve crumble. *I can read a column.* It wouldn't be like talking to him. It's only words on the screen. I mean, what harm could come from it? Before I second-guess myself, I click on the magazine's homepage and open the column.

Someone Once Told Me
by Richard Stratton

> Last night I couldn't rest. Unable to sit still in my apartment with only my thoughts as companions, I went for a walk... and I met Sally.

Sally? Another woman? A sharp pain in my chest makes me swallow as my mouth goes dry with fear. I grab my water bottle and chug a good half before I can bring my eyes back to the screen.

> No, my name is not Harry, and this isn't a romantic story.

Utter relief.

> Sally is a woman in her late fifties, who has been living on the streets of Brooklyn for the better part of ten years, and who could easily pass for a seventy–year–old with her white hair and weathered features.

> On a regular day, I would've passed Sally without even noticing her.

> Not last night.

Someone once told me how easily homeless people disappear in the eyes of passers–by, almost becoming invisible. And how surprised I'd be if I stopped for a minute to hear the stories these people have to share.

So I stopped.

I asked Sally what her favorite sandwich was and what she wanted to drink. I bought a meal for both of us and we ate it together sitting on a bench in the park.

And Sally told me her story...

Not one of drugs or alcohol abuse, abandonment, or delinquency. Simply the story of a business investment gone terribly wrong, and Sally's inability to get back on her feet after she lost everything.

I keep reading the details of how Sally invested all her money in a business that ran profitably for fifteen years before she had to file for bankruptcy, losing not only the business but everything else she had, too. But it is the conclusion of the article that gives me pause.

Sally told me all this, not with an air of bitter regret, but with sweet nostalgia in her voice. And when I asked her if she'd change any of her past choices, she told me that no, she wouldn't. She had followed her dream. Sally had bet everything she had and lost. But she'd do it all again, as those years had been the best of her life...

Richard ends the article with a question.

Would you risk everything you have for a dream?

I don't know, Richard, *would you?* Seems clear the answer is still no. Is he comparing me to Sally's business? Saying love will give temporary ecstasy followed by an inevitable hard crash? Why did Indira make me read this? I'm the "someone who once told him," but she can't know that. So what's the message here? My brain and heart are too exhausted for guesswork. Sorry, Richard. If you want to tell me something, you'll have to say it to my face.

After reading the enigmatic column, I spend the rest of the day battling my instincts. All I want to do is look Richard's way, but instead, I force my gaze ahead, not straying once.

***

There's an art in avoiding people. In the next few days, I perfect mine. I time everything so I'll never risk crossing paths with Richard. Step one, arrive at the office before him and never leave last. Step two, wait for him to come back from his lunch break before I take mine. Step three, whatever else Richard does, make sure I'm always one step ahead or behind so we never bump into one another.

Wednesday night, dead tired after three days of sitting on needles, I'm slouched on the couch when my phone rings, "Umbrella Corporation HR" appearing on the screen. *Yeah, I've renamed Évoque after the zombie-apocalypse-causing corporation in Resident Evil!* What do they want? *Aha!* They realized their mistake and want me back.

My exile in Brooklyn is over!

"Are you going to pick that up or you're just going to let it ring?" Nikki asks from the other end of the couch.

Oh, I'm so picking up. *"Blair Walker."*

"Blair, good evening, this is Natalie Rivers speaking. I'm Emilia Peterson's executive assistant."

"Of course, Natalie. How are you?"

"I'm well, thanks. You?"

"Same here." Pleasantries over, I cut to the chase. "What can I do for you?"

"We recently had an opening for the position of Junior Fashion Editor and we wanted to see if you'd be interested in coming in for an interview."

"Oh, I thought there weren't going to be new openings for a while…"

"Yeah, um…" Natalie sounds embarrassed. "We had a person resign and so the position is open now."

"Is this 'someone' Aurora Vanderbilt?"

"Yes, she quit after… well, I'm sure you know."

I wonder if Aurora really quit or if they gave her a choice between resigning and being fired. Now the tax evasion scandal is out in the open, Évoque will do everything they can to distance the magazine from Maison Vanderbilt. Guess their money is no longer good now that everyone knows where it comes from.

What a bunch of hypocrites.

"Anyway," Natalie continues. "Emilia has an opening in her calendar Friday morning at eight, would that work for you?"

"I'd need to take time off work. Would it be possible to have an appointment in the late evening?"

"I'm sorry, Emilia's very busy. This is her only opening."

That presumptuous bitch. She's asking me to come in for an interview, but of course, I have to adjust my schedule to hers. She knows I want the job more than she wants to give it to me. As much as I can't stand her, this is a real job, at a top magazine. My dream. No matter if I can't stand the HR Manager, it's not like I'll have to work with her. I only need to survive the interview. *Yeah, and go back to work at bitchland, leaving all the nice colleagues, work independence, and the boss you're in love with behind.*

Stop it, Richard won't factor in this decision. Period.

"Okay, Natalie. I'll adjust my schedule. See you on Friday."

Twenty

Never Mix Business and Pleasure

On Thursday night, I don't have the guts to ask Richard in person for a free morning. Not only because we're not on speaking terms, but also because if he were to ask *why,* what would I say? I was never good at lying, and telling the boss about the interview would only be pouring gasoline on the fire. Plus, I don't even know if I'll have anything to tell. This is a preliminary chat. No need to cause a storm yet. I text him at the last minute Friday morning, saying I have a personal matter to attend to, and that I'll be coming in later in the day.

The second hard part is leaving Chevron behind. She's at my feet wagging her tail, ready for our morning walk, but I can't bring a dog to the interview. Still unaware, said pup sits in the hallway, waiting for me to hook her leash.

"Not today, honey."

Chevron's tail slows down.

I open the door. "I'll be back in a couple of hours."

She drops to the floor, tail static, eyes wide. My heart breaks a little as I lock the apartment, leaving her all alone.

What will I do if I accept the new job? I'm sure Évoque doesn't have a bring-your-pet-to-the-office policy. Imagine Chevron running loose in the fashion closet. That would be something. *With a better paycheck, you'll be able to afford the best dog-sitter in the city.* Yeah, Northwestern must know they have to offer me a salary bump for me to even consider going back.

Foldable flats on, I reach Canal Street Station. As I push my way through the ticket barrier, the aboveground spring breeze turns into stale, deep-fried air. Okay, maybe Manhattan's air isn't exactly wholesome. But the underground air is ten times worse. Warm and clingy.

Someone stomps on my foot—not fun when my only protection is foldable flats.

"Hey," I call after the brute.

But the suit ignores me and hurries toward his track. *You sorry excuse for a commuter.* I forgot how rude, pushy, and inconsiderate of other people's existence subway-takers can be. So much better to walk to work. *Easy to say in summer. Wait until it rains, snows, and blizzards, then see how fun it is to walk on a bridge exposed to the elements.*

I squish myself onto the first uptown train and, oh, the stench. Exposed to the elements sounds more promising than squeezed to within an inch of my life by smelly strangers. I'm walled in by three people. If there's one place where being short is a clear disadvantage, it's inside a subway car. Behind me stands an overweight gentleman whose bulging belly is warmly pressed against my back. On my left, a tall woman—I hate genetics right now—has a bony elbow dangerously close to my jaw. And I can count the pills on the tie of the guy standing directly in front of me, who, besides having a dreadful fashion sense, is also drinking coffee from a paper cup.

I watch in horror as Mr. Old Tie removes the plastic lid. Is he *crazy?* The last thing I need is a hot-coffee shower. I try to edge back. But bulgy-guy's belly stops me. I search left and right for an escape route. Nothing. My head is level with my fellow riders' shoulders at best; I can't see anything. I can't breathe. Please, New York fairies, let this ride be a short one.

I spend the next thirty minutes watching that paper cup like a hawk. When I finally emerge on Columbus Circle, unharmed, if not a bit traumatized, I take a few deep breaths of air, even relishing the smog. If I come back to work at Northwestern, I'll walk. I'll get Chevron a dog-sitter nearby. *What about winter?* She'll get a doggy rainbreaker, I don't care. I'm never taking that line at seven in the morning ever again. If my relationship with Gerard had one merit, it was his Park Avenue address.

I swap flats for stiletto heels and cross the threshold of Northwestern's evil tower of power. The glass and steel are overwhelmingly cold around me. *Oh, so now you even miss brick walls and decrepit wooden floors?* What if I do? *Just saying, you used to love the power of glass and stainless steel.* Right, used to. Before they kicked me to the curb. *So what are you doing here?* It's business. A publishing house wants to make me an offer and I want to hear it. Mini-mental-me snickers at that.

As I did the first time I ever set foot in the building, I have to register as a guest at the reception desk. It feels weird not to bypass security. The receptionist hands me a visitor pass and starts giving me directions to Emilia's office. Great, my least favorite place in the building.

"I know where Ms. Peterson's office is, thanks." I cut the woman short and make my way upstairs.

Emilia's office is the same: white everything and minimalist. Emilia also appears the same paper thin and groomed within an inch of her life. She invites me to sit with the warmth of a popsicle. I take my place on the white chair opposite her white desk and fold my hands on the immaculate surface.

Emilia's icy blue eyes follow the gesture with an air of disgust. Is she worried I'll taint her space? Is she a germ freak? Her eyes focus an extra second on the tip of my fingers and her nose creases in the slightest wrinkle.

I quickly pull my hands down and check my nails. My index is missing a microscopic speckle of nail polish. So, yeah. I stopped doing my nails every night and started doing them every other night—or two. *Big deal!*

Emilia's displeased scrutiny continues. This time, I follow her razor-sharp gaze to my blouse where, just over my left breast, there's a tiny—again, almost-invisible-to-the-naked-eye—brown circle. So a droplet of that man's coffee *did* land on me. Oh, well. *Shoot me.* It's not like I'm wearing a T-shirt that says Cece Chanol.

How could I forget how much pressure they put on appearances here? A few months in Brooklyn have relaxed my standards to unacceptable levels of shabbiness it seems, given the sour expression on Emilia's face. What a wonderful way to start the interview. Was Emilia forced to offer me the job despite her—almost certain—recommendation against it?

"So, Blair. How have you been?"

"Great, thank you." *But no thanks to you.* "You?"

"Busy, as always."

I think she meant, "Bitchy, as always."

Emilia continues. "Tell me about your experience at this"—she stares at my CV and raises an eyebrow—"online *hub* you've been working at."

I launch into a professional presentation of my achievements over the last few months. The regular beauty features I've established. The team of influencers I've put together. The sponsorships. The celebrity photoshoots and interviews… The more I talk, the more I surprise even myself at the amount of work I accomplished in such a short time. I basically built an entire fashion magazine from scratch. An awesome one.

Emilia lets me talk, her face a studiously unimpressed one. "That all sounds marvelous," she comments when I'm finished. "Now, as I'm sure you remember, here at Évoque we operate on a high-end profile. As a Junior Editor, you'll only be in charge of assisting more competent and experienced professionals."

"So I wouldn't be responsible for any project? Not even smaller features?"

"Never say never. We're very open minded and it's our desire to groom the next generation of leaders. So we encourage all employees to bring forward new ideas…"

Her rehearsed speech is dribbling with so much condescension, I can't listen. I'm finally back on the thirty-eighth floor of this shiny Manhattan skyscraper, and I can't seem to find a single good reason to be here and work with these people. *It's your dream, always has been.* Yeah, but why? Why was it ever my dream to work at Évoque? Why come back? This company used me for years and then discarded me without a second thought. And all they're offering now is another junior position with no real independence. *One you would've killed for a short while ago.* Only because I didn't know better.

"So you encourage the people who work here to bring forward new ideas?" I challenge her.

"Of course, we do."

"You mean like when the story about Maison Vanderbilt committing tax fraud was brought forward."

Emilia's nostrils flare. "Blair, in case you've forgotten we're a fashion magazine, we don't do investigative journalism. Now, I'm sure at this"—she waves one hand in the air dismissively—"online-whatever you've been working for, lines and roles were more… let's say blurred, but—"

"Of the fifty-or-so papers under the umbrella of Northwestern Publishing, not a single one could've picked up the story?"

"I honestly don't see what you're trying to accomplish with this sterile polemic."

"I'm trying to say that this company doesn't encourage people to bring forward ideas, it forces them to kill stories to keep easy advertising money flowing in."

"Blair, let me be perfectly clear. This is a unique opportunity. You blew your first chance at a serious career and were lucky enough to get a second, which doesn't happen very often and wasn't the wisest idea in the first place if you ask me… You won't get a third."

Oh, she's just confirmed my worst fears. Someone higher up forced Emilia's hand, but she never wanted to offer me the job. The Talent Manager Coordinator hates me. Which means she'd try to make my head roll every chance she got. Another good reason *not to* come back.

I stand up. "No, Emilia. *I'd* like to be perfectly clear. *You* screwed up *your* first chance by promoting the wrong person for the wrong reasons. This was your second chance, and *you* blew it. Sorry, you won't get a third. Goodbye."

I don't wait for a reply, I simply show myself out of the witch's office. *Humph, goodbye.* There should be a better word. I don't want to wish her *good*bye, I want to say *bad*-bye. In the long elevator ride down, I envision a whole article on the topic.

Title: The Power of Bad-Bye
Subtitle: When Enough Is Enough

In the lobby, I give back my pass, hardly paying attention, already typing the first paragraph of the article in my head. With no regrets, I walk out of Évoque for the last time.

***

That afternoon I knock on Richard's door as soon as I get into the office.

Richard lifts his eyes from a document, and a deep frown appears as he spots me standing behind the glass. He waves me in with a dismissive flick of his fingers.

Uh-oh.

This is the first time I've approached him since our fight on Sunday and he gives me attitude? I thought we could defuse the situation and at least try to be civil to each other. After this morning, I have a deeper appreciation of the trust Richard has put in me. Sadly, only professionally. I've also realized I love the work I'm doing here and that I want to keep doing it regardless of my personal feelings for the boss. But if he wants to give me attitude, I can give attitude right back.

"What do you want?" Richard fires at me.

"Hello, good afternoon to you, too," I snap back.

"Yeah, exactly. *After*noon. Glad you finally decided to show up."

"I texted you to say I needed the morning off."

He pierces me with an angry look. "And why was that?"

I stare at him, frozen.

Does he know about the job interview? How could he?

I'm still not talking, so Richard scoffs. "That's what I thought."

We glare at each other for a few more seconds before he adds, "Are you handing in your notice?"

He knows. "No, I'm not. Yeah, I went to an interview, but I didn't accept the offer." That seems to throw him a little. "So you can take your self-righteousness and stick it... well, I'm sure I don't need to tell you where."

"The great Blair Walker will be staying with us another day. How exciting."

"What's that supposed to mean? I just told you I didn't take the job. Why do you have to be a dick about it?"

"Because since the first day you signed your contract, you've been waiting for the moment you could get out."

"That's not true. I've busted my ass off to create something from nothing for this magazine and I've given it one-hundred percent. You can't deny that. And, yes, Northwestern offered me a job at a magazine with a better name, better pay, and better benefits. So I went and listened to what they had to say. Shoot me." I raise my hands in surrender. "But I turned the offer down because I believe in what we're building."

My volume has gone up a notch and I'm uncomfortably aware that everyone outside must be able to hear us. If our body language wasn't already clear enough. *Stupid glass walls!*

"If you say so."

Richard's dismissive attitude sparks more anger and frustration. He wants to pretend nothing has happened between us? He wants to ignore his feelings? I've let him so far, but now he's pushed all the wrong buttons and I'm furious enough to tackle the real problem between us.

"Are you mad at me for the job offer, or are you mad at yourself because you can't admit what's really bothering you?"

"And what would that be?" Richard sneers.

"That you got scared you'd lose me for good, and you're too afraid to admit you have feelings for me."

"That's a bit presumptuous on your part."

"Then tell me it isn't true! Tell me I'm wrong. I mean, if you're not too afraid."

"Careful, Walker. You're taking it too far."

"You can puff out your chest all you like, the fact remains you're too much of a coward to admit the truth."

Richard jumps up from his chair. "Who are you calling a coward?"

"You, it's what you are!"

"It's better if we end this conversation now before either of us says something we can't take back. You want the truth: I can't stand to look at you right now."

"Oh, the coward wants to run away. How surprising."

"I'm out of here." Richard rounds his desk and is out of the door and leaving the main office before I can say anything.

Nuh-uh. He's so not getting out of this one.

I follow him. "You want to run?" I yell. "*Fine.* Run! But remember I can run faster."

I don't care if everyone in the office is blatantly staring at us. It's time Richard and I had this discussion and if he wants to have it in full public… *his choice.*

He stops in his track and turns toward me, eyes glaring. "What's that even supposed to mean?"

"That I don't quit. That I don't run away from the things that scare me. I run *after* what I want."

"No, you live in a world of unicorns and rainbows. Real life is not like that."

"Real life is what you make of it."

"Walker, I'm sorry. I don't live in a pink cloud of optimism."

"No, right. You prefer a black hole of fear." *Ah, gotcha.* He gapes at me but doesn't reply so I go ahead and announce it to the world, "I love you, Richard Stratton, and I'm not afraid of saying it."

"Love isn't enough."

"Love is everything."

"It's not."

"It is for me. Tell me you don't love me and you're free to go. This is the last you'll hear of it. Come on, say it. SAY IT!"

Frown deeper than ever, jaw clenched, Richard shakes his head.

With a seething look, he turns on his heel and walks out of the office.

Bang! The doors slam shut, and I'm left standing in the middle of the room like an idiot. Chest heaving, breath ragged, the same as if I had just run a marathon.

I lost.

People around me seem intent on their screens. They must think I'm a t-Rex. That if they don't move, I won't know they exist. Even Indira is avoiding my gaze. *Figures.* What could they possibly say to a colleague who just embarrassed herself in the worst possible way and was publicly turned down by her boss, *their* boss?

The only soul who shows any sympathy is Chevron. She nuzzles my calves in a comforting gesture, whining understandingly.

What now? Should I crawl back to Manhattan and beg Évoque for the job? It's clear I can't keep working here. I knew having a relationship with the boss was wrong. I knew commitment-phobic men don't turn into commitment-happy boyfriends overnight. Despite all that, I gave it my best try, and now I'm back where I started. No job. No love life. Well, at least I have a loyal companion. I pat Chevron's head, pick my dignity up off the floor, and turn back toward my desk. I need to collect my things and get ready to leave. For the day? Forever? I don't know.

That's when the office door bursts open again and there's a collective gasp. Indira lifts her eyes from the screen, her expression changing from I'm-so-busy-pretending-you-don't-exist to well-well-well-let's-see-what-happens-now.

Very slowly, I turn and watch Richard storm back into the room.

Twenty-one

Never Wash Dirty Laundry in Public

"I can't tell you that," Richard says without preamble.

Storm and thunder are dancing in his brown irises, now almost black. The face I love so much is set in a look of determined anger, ferociously handsome and just plain fierce at the same time. Something lurches inside me and my throat constricts.

Richard shakes his head as if trying to sort conflicting thoughts. "I promised I wouldn't be here, ever again."

I drop the duffel bag and take a step forward. "Where's here?"

Richard looks up again, his eyes wide, vulnerable, without a trace of cynicism—and as they meet mine, the world stops. That one look tells me more than a thousand words could; Richard's expression tells me he loves me. But I can't be the only one acknowledging her feelings. So I ask again, "Where's here?"

"Here is where I'm about to make a fool of myself, *again*."

"Why?"

"Because I do love you."

Tears of relief spring to my eyes.

"There's nothing foolish about that."

"No?" He lets out a hysterical laugh. "Love has only ever brought me pain and humiliation. I tried to avoid it, suppress it, deny it." Richard rubs his forehead and I wait patiently in silence. "But the burning just won't go away. And I've never been more scared in my life. For years, I've managed just fine on my own. But then, no, you had to come along and ruin everything. So *here* is where my heart is again in the hands of a woman who can do whatever the hell she wants with it."

"Richard, I'm not your ex."

"No, you're not."

"You say that as if it's a bad thing."

"Because it is."

"Why?"

A painful grimace twists his features. "Because I never loved her the way I love you!" The heart that was hammering in my chest until a few seconds ago stops. "Since you left on Sunday, I haven't been able to sleep, eat, work, think. You're everywhere. I can't stop thinking about you. Even if you refused to talk to me, I couldn't wait to get to the office every day to see you, and I dread the time of day when I have to go home alone. Then when you didn't show up today, I thought you were leaving, for good."

"But I wasn't."

"This time or ever?"

"Are we talking about a job here or something else?"

"We're not talking about a bloody job."

"Richard." I take another step forward. "I can't promise everything will be perfect, that we'll never argue or break up. And I don't know if we'll have a happily ever after. But I'm willing to risk my heart on that possibility. I'm in… one hundred percent."

"What if I don't want to get married?"

"I don't want to marry you." Okay, I might've doodled Blair Stratton more than once, but that doesn't mean anything. "You haven't even taken me on a real date yet."

Someone in the background cheers. It could be Indira. Or Saffron. Or even Chevron for all I know.

"What if I don't want to get married, *ever?*" Richard insists.

I sigh. "Do I want to get married at some point in my life? *Yes.* Would I consider not doing it for the right man? Seems so. I always thought I wanted a wedding. But I also wanted many other things that I've discovered were insignificant. So is a piece of paper more important than the real love of a real man? No. I watched my mother spend years in a marriage with no love. She stood by a man she didn't love, but wouldn't leave only to be proper. And that's not what I want. If marriage is the one thing you can't give me, I'd rather not have it and have everything else."

"You say that now, but you'll change your mind."

"Maybe I will, maybe I won't. Maybe you'll change your mind." He's about to protest, but I anticipate him. "Let me finish. I spent my whole life mapping out every single step I should take. Engaged by twenty-nine, married by thirty, and two point five kids by thirty-five. Same goes for my career. Then my perfect plan crumbled in a single day. I lost the perfect job and the perfect-on-paper boyfriend and I've never been happier. I don't want to plan anymore, I want to live."

"What if it doesn't work?"

"What if it does? Can you walk away without trying? 'Cause I sure can't."

"If we do this…" This time, it's Richard taking a step toward me. "What is the single thing you'd never give me?"

I take a moment to think. "My career," I say. "I'll never be a stay-at-home mom."

Richard's features relax for the first time since our conversation started, and he closes the distance between us. I inhale his scent and

I'm a goner as soon as he cups my face in his hands. "So we're having kids now?" he asks with a playful smile.

I blush and luckily don't have the time to stutter an embarrassing reply as Richard's lips silence mine. His strong arms wrap around me and he almost crushes me against his chest.

I'm pretty sure kissing the boss in the middle of the office is against every workplace protocol ever written. But right now, I'm too busy trying to stand on my own two legs to care. That thing they say about buckling knees? *Totally true.*

We finally let go, and Richard seems to become aware of the gaping faces staring at us from all around the office. Ada is clapping and crying, too, I think. I can't tell under her giant cat-eye glasses. Indira is sporting a shrewd smile. Saffron is taking a pic. Surely she doesn't plan to post it on the magazine's socials, right? And the boys are trying to project a look of composed appreciation.

"Come on, kids," Indira yells, breaking the tension of the moment. "Cheer up for mommy and daddy, they made up."

Everyone laughs and claps and cheers. And I'm so stupidly happy I can't talk. I can only keep smiling at the man I love, whose eyes now reflect the same love he must see in mine.

"What happens now?" I whisper.

My anger has burned out and I'm becoming very self-conscious. Shouting my feelings in front of all my colleagues and forcing a love admission out of Richard were not part of the plan when I woke up this morning.

"We can start with a first date," Richard says. "Dinner?"

"It's two-thirty, I'm not hungry."

Richard leans in and whispers, "Oh, you will be. Because we're stopping at my place first."

I blush a furious red and hide my face in Richard's chest.

"Everyone," Richard says aloud. "It's been a long week. Let's take the rest of the day off."

The cheers that follow this announcement are even more widespread and enthusiastic.

Richard takes my hand and whistles for Chevron to follow us out of the office. As we reach the door and exit, an echo of Indira's comment reaches me. "... if they'd told me all it took to have the afternoon off was to get the boss laid, I would've pimped him more."

"Indira." Ada's voice is barely audible through the door. "You've missed the whole point. It's not about getting laid, it's about love."

"Please don't tell me we have another hopeless romantic in the house…"

Mercifully, the elevator arrives and I can't hear any more of Indira's pretend-cynic comments.

The three of us step in, and as soon as the doors swipe closed, Richard pushes me into a corner. One hand on my lower back, the other buried in my hair.

"I love you." He nibbles my earlobe. "It's so good to say it. I love you."

"I love you, too," I whisper, trying not to combust.

"*Woof, woof.*" Chevron joins the party at our feet, yapping happily.

We pull apart and scratch her behind both ears.

"Yes, we love you, too," I say.

Richard squeezes my hand and I stare into his eyes, realizing I don't care if he's never going to propose. Our trio feels more like a family than anything I've ever had before.

Twenty-two

Don't Move In Without a Ring

Six months later...

Stretching in bed has become difficult. With Chevron—now grown into a medium-sized dog—sprawled over my feet and Richard on my right side, even my tiny figure is experiencing space rationing. Regardless of Richard's California King Bed. But the cozy warmth of two bodies pressed against mine is particularly delicious on a cold winter day.

Outside Richard's window, a rainstorm is attacking New York. It's been pouring since Monday, meaning I've spent three nights in a row at Richard's place. The boyfriend doesn't seem upset about it, but sometimes I suspect that even if he were, he'd be too British to tell me.

Rain or no rain, I have to give him a night's respite and I need a change of clothes, anyway. At five thirty, a vibrating wrist tells me it's time to get out of bed. Richard's building has a gym in the basement, meaning I can run despite the weather. But also that, even stuffing my duffel bag to the brim, between training gear, PJs, bathroom stuff, and day clothes, three days is the max autonomy I have without going back home.

Once training is over, I take Chevron out to relieve herself. When I get back into the apartment, I'm soaked, muddy, and miserable. *I hate the rain.* Before it started, the city was covered in a coat of fluffy white snow; it was a winter wonderland. But now it has all melted into a gloomy puddle.

After a very long shower, I change into my last spare outfit and kiss Richard awake, kick-starting our morning ritual. Richard prepares the oatmeal while I set a pot of water to warm for the French press. Considering the world outside is the saddest gray, Richard surprises me by staring at the storm with a contented smile.

I measure the coffee beans and put them in the grinder. When the noise is over I say, "You seem awfully happy about the bad weather."

Richard shrugs, adding a delicious mix of nuts and fresh fruit to our oatmeal. The boyfriend still eats meat, but he's being surprisingly open-minded about my dietary habits.

"At least one of us is excited about the rain." I pour the heated water and ground coffee into the press, stir, and set the microwave timer to five minutes. "Can you drive us to Manhattan tonight?"

"Tired of Brooklyn?"

"No, but it's been raining for three days... I've run out of clean clothes." I sit at the kitchen bar opposite Richard. "I need to go home and pick up some fresh outfits."

Richard smiles a goofy smile. "I'll let you in on a secret. There's a mystical object with the magical power of turning dirty clothes into clean ones. It's called a washing machine."

I chuckle. "Most of my things are dry-clean."

"There are dry cleaners in Brooklyn."

"Yeah, I'm aware. I'd still prefer to go home and get a fresh change. Come on, I can't show up at work with the same outfit two times in a week."

"Why don't you bring some of your stuff here?"

"Nah, I wouldn't want my wardrobe spread around two places. I'd get confused about where everything is."

Richard seems disappointed by my answer, but the timer interrupts him before he can express his mind. I plunge the press, pour the coffee, and we eat in silence. The mood has shifted from cozy-homey to awkward, and I don't know what I did wrong.

Surely, Richard isn't touchy over my choice of dry cleaners, and I was positive he'd be eager for an evening on his own.

Two spoonfuls of oatmeal, and Richard stops midway through the third to not-so-casually say, "So move everything here."

I choke on a sip of coffee. "Move in with you?"

Whoa! I thought I'd have to rope the boyfriend into this new commitment *very slowly.* And now he's just asking me out of the blue over breakfast on a Thursday in December.

"I mean." His lips twitch. "If you can stomach the idea of living in Brooklyn."

"It's not that. It's just… are you sure?"

"I am, but you don't seem too excited."

"No, I am. But I don't want you to rush into a commitment that might be too quick and backfire on us."

"Think this is rushed? I'll give you rushed." Richard sits taller on his stool. "With my ex, I proposed after six months and pushed her to set the wedding date in another six months without having spent a single day under the same roof."

Richard never talks about his past so I listen without interrupting.

"I sensed she wasn't ready, but I pressed on. Thought that if I didn't give her time to overanalyze, she'd be fine. Well, you know how that ended. That was rushed. This"—he swings his spoon between us, wielding it like a sword—"isn't rushed. You're not pressing me into anything. I'm asking you."

"Okay." I still feel like I'm walking on eggshells. "Take some extra time to mull it over. Then, if you're still sure…"

"I don't need extra time."

I'm at a loss for words… I so didn't expect this.

"You want to know why I'm happy it's raining?" Richard continues.

Oh, so he *was* pleased by the awful weather. I nod.

"Rain means you spend the night. A sunny day means you go back to your place, and I'm alone. I hate sunny days."

"You hate the sun because of me?"

"Despise it."

A dumb smile appears on my lips. "Ah well, in that case…"

"Should I free a drawer?"

"Poor man. You've no idea what you just got yourself into. I'm going to need much more space than a drawer." My brain whizzes with all the technical, organizational steps. "I'd need to give Nikki some notice. I can't just stop paying my share of the rent and leave her out to hang. Plus, she hates the holidays, but…" I get up, another thought suddenly bolting through my head. "Wait here."

I retrieve my bag from down the hall and fish inside for something I haven't looked at in months. After some rummaging, I remember it's in my wallet. A piece of paper so crumpled and frail it might disintegrate at any second.

"What's that?" Richard asks.

Spreading the sheet on the bar, I ask, "You don't recognize it?"

"Is it the list?"

"Mmm-hmm. And there's just one item in there I haven't ticked off yet."

"Which is?"

"Don't move in without a ring."

"Oh, I never considered that angle. Does it bother you?"

"I always thought I wanted to be super traditional, but that was the old me."

Richard is still staring at the list, frowning now. "And when did you go skinny dipping, exactly?"

I blush and snatch the paper away. "I'm never telling you that."

"Hey." Richard makes to grab the sheet again.

I yank my arm away, crumple the list into a ball, and throw it across the hall. Richard doesn't need to re-read every insignificant item. Chevron woofs and runs after the paper ball. After catching it, she sits quietly in a corner, the ball between her front paws, chewing bits away. As I watch the poor piece of paper being shredded to confetti, I realize that the list, however wrong it was in principle, did come through for me in the end. Only not in the way I expected. With every item ticked off in reverse, life has never been better. Magical, spontaneous, and totally unplanned.

"That was naughty," Richard protests.

I round the bar and plant myself between Richard's legs, wrapping my arms around his neck. "You still in the market for a naughty roommate?"

Richard pulls me closer by the waist. "You don't care that it's Brooklyn?"

"I wouldn't care if it were New Jersey with you."

We both know I'm lying, but I quickly silence his rebuff with a kiss.

Mid-kiss, Richard tickles my sides. "When did you go skinny dipping?"

"Aaah, stop. *Stop!*" I struggle to get away. "I'm not talking."

"Yes, you are."

I wriggle free and make a dash for the bedroom.

"Gotcha." Richard pins me on the bed and starts the tickling torture again.

With him on top of me, my giggles soon die away, cutting off completely as his hands start moving in a different way on my body.

I smirk. "You're the worst interrogator ever."

"Being in love with the victim doesn't help, I guess."

"Shut up and kiss me, roommate."

End of Book Two

A Christmas DATE

A fake dating holiday romantic comedy
BY CAMILLA ISLEY

One

Christmas Is Coming

"Your mother called again," my assistant, Melanie, informs me as soon as I step foot into my office. "Third time this week."

I sit behind my desk and peek at the calendar placed next to my unopened laptop.

Tuesday, December 11

Only Tuesday and we're already on the third call of the week.

Bodes well.

"I'll call her back when I have a minute," I tell Melanie. "Anything else?"

Still standing on the threshold, she shifts on her feet, uncomfortable.

"Come on, I won't shoot the messenger," I promise her.

"Right, because she's asked me to read you this, word for word."

From the way Melanie is cowering, it can't be good. I lean back in my white leather chair, cross my hands in my lap, and sigh. "Go ahead."

"Nikki," she intones, "I spent thirty-five hours in excruciating pain to bring you into this world, and the least I deserve after nurturing you in a loving home for years is for my daughter to return my calls, especially at Christmas. I've already set my expectations very low, as I wouldn't presume you could pick up the phone and call your mother of your own free will..."

I grip the armrests of my chair until my knuckles turn white. "Can you skip the guilt tripping part and get to the core of the message?"

Melanie looks up at me. "Yeah, sure." Her eyes shift back to the note, and she scrolls through the words for what feels like ages. "Ah, yes," she finally sighs. "She demands to know when you'll be heading home for Christmas, how long you're staying, and if you're bringing someone."

I hate the holidays. And I hate when Mom uses the absent-daughter trope to shame me into doing what she wants. But what I hate the most is the two combined. And Christmas is the most inescapable holiday of all.

My stupid boss, along with millions of other idiots scattered around the planet, loves Christmas. So what does the prick do every year? He closes shop, forcing everyone to go on vacation. Which means that every December, without fail, I'm trapped visiting my family in Connecticut for too many days.

Even worse, this year Christmas falls on a Tuesday, meaning the agency will stay closed from the twenty-second to the twenty-ninth. Nine sanity-challenging days of hell in total. And my mother knows, and she's been on my case for a month now to make sure she'll get me for as many of those nine days as she can.

This must be punishment for something terrible I did in a past life, I swear.

I exhale. "I'll call her back when I have a minute."

Melanie is giving me the no-you-won't stink eye, but I have my mean boss poker face on, so she keeps quiet.

"Is that all?" I ask.

"Err, no. You have lunch with your sister today."

And my day isn't getting any better.

"I'll have to reschedule," I say, shuffling the notes from the morning's meetings. "Can you call Julia and tell her?"

"I could have… if you'd asked me this morning. But she's been waiting for you in the lobby for twenty minutes."

"What?!" I stare at my watch.

Half-past noon, already. Where did the morning go?

Well, no way out, then.

***

"Jules," I greet my younger, blessed with all the good Moore genetics, sister.

With natural blonde hair, blue eyes, and an angel face, she's the opposite of my dark hair, brown eyes, and sharp features. When people want to pay me a compliment, they tell me I'm interesting, unique, strong… never beautiful. Julia has always had the pretty-sister crown firmly glued to her head. Ever since we were babies, and her golden curls made her look like a cherub out of a painting. Even as a toddler, I was unimpressive.

"Nikki," Julia shrieks, pulling me into a hug in the middle of the lobby. Without leaving me time to react, she grabs my hand and drags me out of the building. "I can't believe we're really having lunch! I was sure you'd cancel at the last minute. When Melanie didn't call this morning, I was kind of surprised."

Guess the absent-sister guilt technique is another trait she inherited from our mother. And, okay, I'm not the best at keeping engagements… Or calling, or texting… And it's not that I don't love Jules… It's only that being around my baby sister is so hard sometimes…

"About that." I avoid looking at her by buttoning up the collar of my coat against the freezing air. "Can we go somewhere nearby? I have to get back to the office soon."

Hidden behind a curtain of flying hair, I watch as Jules struggles not to let her smile falter.

"Sorry," she says, linking our arms and dragging me to the edge of the curb to hail a cab. "I've already picked a place, and Paul is meeting us there."

A cab screeches to a halt in front of us seconds later, thankfully distracting Julia and buying me enough time to compose my features. Otherwise, my expression would've given me away. If being around Jules is hard, the combo Julia *and* Paul leans dangerously close to unbearable. Worse than family and holidays.

I open the cab's rear door and settle on the black leather seat. Not because I've accepted my fate, but because I really need to sit before I fall down. Julia squeezes in next to me.

Once the cab pulls into traffic, I casually ask, "If you're having lunch with your boyfriend, why do you need me to tag along? Don't you guys want to be alone?"

I'm still hoping I can escape. I could hop off the taxi at the next traffic light and grab a hot dog from a street cart on the way back… It'd be so easy. A perfect, quick, sans Jules & Paul lunch.

"Don't be silly," Julia says, laughing as she crushes my getting-out-of-lunch fantasy. "Paul loves you as a sister, just as much as I do."
Ah.
Whoever said words hurt more than actions was so right. I focus

on the tall city buildings sweeping by, fighting a losing battle with the lump in my throat. I don't utter a word for the rest of the fifteen-minute trip, and follow Julia out of the cab as it pulls up in front of... *No!*

I stare transfixed at the retro diner that used to be my and Paul's special place, now *their* special place. Behind the glass walls, Paul is already seated in a red vinyl booth, waiting for us at our usual table, now also *theirs*.

Nuh-uh, I don't think I can go in there. My feet are glued to the concrete. I can't move.

That is, until Jules pulls my hand forward, saying, "Come on, Nik, it's freezing out here."

She drags me the few steps to the door and pushes it open, pulling me into the past. Back to almost ten years ago when it was just Paul and me, when Julia was still in high school and living at home. Out of my life, never into his.

Big Mama hasn't changed since then: the black and white tiled floor, the red booths near the windows, and the row of metal stools with cushions of the same red vinyl along the bar on the other side. Even the air smells the same: of burgers and fries, vanilla, and coffee that never stops coming.

Paul and I have been friends since freshman year in college; we were both majoring at NYU in marketing, with a minor in design. Before we officially met—thanks to the Typography professor pairing us for the course project—I'd seen him around campus. It was impossible not to notice Paul. Blond, tall, with broad shoulders and a square jaw, he was a poster child for all-American wholesome handsomeness.

But before academic requirements forced us together, the idea of talking to him never crossed my mind, even if we shared almost every class. I didn't dislike him per se; I'd simply dismissed him as way out of my league, and someone who my parents would approve of too much.

They do, by the way.

I'm not sure how Big Mama became our regular meeting place. It could've been because here we could eat breakfast at any hour, or because the coffee was cheap and never ran out, or because the place was open 24/7... It just happened as our friendship happened: naturally.

One conversation with Paul was enough to make me go back on all my prejudices about him. Paul Collins wasn't just a pretty face in preppy clothes; he was smart, and fun, but also a creative genius—in short, a boy even more out of my league. Not that it mattered, as he had a girlfriend at the time: Marie, who, I suspect, barely tolerated our collaboration and following friendship.

For a long time, I believed Paul and I would be one of those couples who finally come together after an unfortunate mix of missed connections and bad timing. When he broke up with Marie, I was in another relationship, and when that ended, he'd started dating someone else. Then his first job out of college was in Chicago, where he lived for three years while I stayed in New York. But when he came back to the city single and called me to grab a coffee at our old spot, I thought, *This is it, we're finally going to happen.*

Little did I know that day would turn into the worst of my life instead. Whenever I try to pin down exactly how all my dreams of a future with Paul were crushed, I can't. My brain, probably suffering from a bad case of PTSD, has erased the details to protect me. All I remember is that while I was with Paul, Julia, who had also moved to the city by then, called me with some stupid emergency and joined us at the diner. Well, that was enough to erase me from Paul's dating map forever. If I'd ever been there at all.

From the moment Jules sat down next to me, it was as if I didn't exist anymore. Conversation just sparked between them, it was like there were fireworks coming across the table, while I remained invisible. That day, I officially became the old college friend who had introduced Paul to the love of his life. Big Mama ceased to be our special place, and instead became the special spot where they met.

Ten years of shared history wiped out by one of Julia's smiles.

Never, with any of Paul's previous girlfriends, had I experienced that sense of terrible loss, of a future that now could never be. Because even if they broke up, he would be my sister's ex: permanently off-limits. Sadly, that's also when I realized Paul meant more to me than an old crush or a romantic fantasy about a friend. I was in love with him. Had been for years. But on the same day I understood the depth of my feelings for him, they became forbidden.

As far as I know, Julia had no idea Paul wasn't just a friend for me. And by the time I figured myself out, they were already dating. Too late for me to call dibs on him. And no matter how much it hurt to sit silently by and watch them fall in love, I couldn't bring myself to ruin their relationship. I cared too much about both of them.

Now, as I walk back onto the crime scene, I'm all jitters.

Why has Julia dragged me here? Why are we having lunch with Paul? Let's hope at least it'll be quick. I mean, they both have jobs to go back to. Don't they?

The moment we sit, a server comes with menus. Like the diner, the menus haven't changed; the same big, laminated sheets barely legible through the years of grease that has seeped into the plastic. Not that I need to check the menu. I know what I'm getting, and also what Paul's ordering.

I leave my menu on the table and stare at Jules as she tries to decipher the writing under the dirty plastic to find something allowed by whatever diet she's following at the moment—not that she needs one.

When the server comes back, she turns to Paul first. He orders the fluffy pancakes, as I knew he would. Then, looking at me, he adds, "French toast with berries and cream?"

I can't help but smile and nod. He remembered.

"And you, honey?" Paul asks Julia. "What are you getting?"

All eyes are now on my sister.

"I'll take… Mmm…" Jules purses her lips. "The chicken salad without the chicken, eggs, bacon, and onions. Leave the dressing on the side, please."

Our server raises an eyebrow but doesn't comment, just writes Julia's order on her pad.

Paul sighs—half-amused, half-exasperated—and orders a round of Bloody Marys for everyone. Julia asks for hers to be virgin.

When the server's gone, Jules turns toward Paul with a complicit smile. "Should we tell her now?"

Paul shifts in his booth. "Maybe we should wait for our drinks."

"Tell me what?" I ask.

My sister smiles at me. "We have some very special news to share, and we wanted to do it here."

I don't like how this sounds. I look at Paul for reassurance, but he only shrugs in response. At once, my palms go clammy with sweat.

"This is where we met," Jules continues, "and if it weren't for you, it would've never happened."

Don't I know!

"So it seemed the perfect place to tell you…" My sister pauses for effect. "Are you ready?"

No!

Can I say, no, run out of the diner, and never see them again?

I swallow, grimace, and nod.

Julia takes a deep breath and says, "We're engaged!"

Something pulls tight in my chest, and I blab the first thing that comes into my head, "T-to each other?"

"Of course to each other, silly." Having thus handed down my death sentence, Jules launches into a wedding planning rant. "No need to say, you'll be my maid of honor. The main color scheme for the ceremony and reception will be cream and peach. But I'll need your visual expertise to make sure everything is perfect."

"I-I produce commercials," I manage to stutter. "I don't plan weddings."

"Yeah, but you have an eye for setting, wardrobe, photography… You're the ace up my sleeve. We're still debating over two different wedding planners, but as soon as we pick one I'll let you have their contact so we can all coordinate…"

I don't interrupt her a second time. I let her blab on and on about all her wedding ideas while I nod and mmm-hmm every now and then whenever I feel a pause in the conversation requires it. Conversation… more like a monologue. I should be glad my input isn't needed. There's too much of a strong buzz inside my head for me to be able to communicate anyway. Something like the loud ambient interference of a microphone standing too close to the speakers. I'm the microphone, and Jules and Paul's engagement is the amplifier making my brain explode and taking my heart with it.

Two

Blue Christmas

"You think I'm making a mistake?" Jules asks.

Her voice drags me out of the haze I've been in since my sister dropped the bombshell that she and Paul are engaged. I stare up at her, surprised to see we're both in my office. That I'm sitting behind my desk while my sister is perched on it and is eyeing me expectantly. I don't remember paying for lunch, or even if I said goodbye to Paul. Did I congratulate them? I hope my strict, uptight education kicked in at some point, and that I managed to be at least polite, if not overenthusiastic.

I'm not sure why Julia came back uptown with me after we left Big Mama. Or why she followed me all the way to my office. Or why she's now seated on my furniture asking very stupid questions.

"A mistake?" My words come out in a hiss. Julia is marrying Paul; how dare she not thank her lucky stars? "What do you mean, a mistake?"

"Only that Paul is so predictable sometimes, don't you think?" Jules doesn't let me answer before she continues. "Take the way he proposed. He made a romantic dinner at home with candlelight and roses and popped the question after dessert."

Red. I see red, and I'm not sure I can keep the anger out of my voice as I ask, "And what would a worthy proposal have entailed?"

"Something more original... More special. Take Amanda's boyfriend." Amanda is her best friend. "Joshua asked her on the summit of a wild mountain after they'd struggled to the top together. Paul's proposal was so cliché by comparison."

"I'm pretty sure that if Paul ever asked you to go rock-climbing, you'd dump him on the spot."

Jules shrugs. "Fair enough, but you're missing the point."

"Enlighten me."

"Sometimes I think Paul is a bit, you know, *boring*. Take his looks, for example, blond hair, blue eyes, square jaw... He's just so WASP-y; even his job is so proper and expected..."

I'm trying really hard not to start yelling what an ungrateful, spoiled brat she is. "I'm curious, how would a non-boring man look?"

Julia stares at the ceiling with a dreamy expression. "Don't you ever dream of an adventure with a tall, dark stranger? Someone with smoldering green eyes and full lips, and danger written all over his face. Someone who speaks Italian and doesn't own a car."

"And how would he get around? On the subway?"

The last time my sister took the subway, I was still in college.

"Ew, no. He would ride a bike, of course. One of those big, black monsters… We're talking about the kind of guy who sweeps you off your feet with just one look, who can make you fall hard and fast. Someone mysterious, intriguing…"

"And what occupation would this dangerous stranger have, since marketing is clearly so out of style with you?" I ask, even if I agree that Paul's job isn't exactly exciting. I've no clue why he decided to waste all his creativeness to go work in the driest, most Corporate America branch of marketing the city has to offer.

"You didn't get offended, did you?" Jules says. "When I said Paul's job is boring, I didn't mean yours, too. You do completely different things."

Her disrespect of my profession is the least of my concerns at the moment.

"Not at all," I say.

"Anyway," she continues, unfazed. I suspect I could've said I was mortally offended, and I would've gotten the same reaction. "My stranger would have to be some kind of struggling artist, someone who lives paycheck to paycheck, and who appreciates everything he has because he doesn't know if he's going to still have it tomorrow."

"So you basically want to marry a penniless, unemployed artist, who'd propose to you on top of a big rock with a plastic ring because he can't afford a real diamond?"

"I never said marry, I only said I'd like one last adventure. Is that so wrong?"

"I don't know. You're the one about to walk down the aisle."

I must've been scowling more than I realized, because Jules goes on the defensive. "No, you're right. I'm just being silly. But it's hard to think I'm done with first dates and first kisses… That Paul will be *it* for me for the rest of my life."

Considering the last few disastrous first dates I went on, I count Julia lucky she won't ever have to go on another one. "First dates are overrated, trust me."

She smiles. "Maybe you're right. But this is all so new; it's normal for me to have some wedding jitters, isn't it?"

I've had enough. "Listen, Jules, I don't mean to be rude, but I really have a ton of work to do…"

"Sorry." Julia hops off the desk. "I've already stolen too much of your time. Thank you for talking me down." She pulls on her coat. "I'll send you the wedding planner's contact as soon as I've picked one…"

"Whatever you need." I hug her goodbye and usher her out. "You know the way, right?"

"Yeah." She gives me another quick hug and goes.

I don't watch her get to the elevators; I shut the door to my office and pull down all the blinds. Back behind my desk, I drop my head on its cold surface and wait for the tears to come. Only they won't. After holding back for too long, my body is wired to resist and refuses to let go.

For the rest of the afternoon I stare blankly at my screen, finishing none of the work I was supposed to do—namely, the final revision of a lipstick commercial that starts shooting soon. A high-end gig with A-list models and a top-notch director. I just scroll through the art boards, casting pictures, and wardrobe selection without really seeing any of it. By the time Melanie knocks on my door to tell me she's leaving for the night, I've no idea what the plan is for the shoot the day after tomorrow.

Ah, hell. I decide to follow Melanie out. Take the night off, process the blow, and come back in the morning as good as new. The engagement doesn't really change anything. They already live together… Marriage won't make their relationship any better… Only more permanent… More unbreakable…

Kids are coming next, a vicious voice whispers inside my head.

As I walk out of my building, I try to imagine what a Jules & Paul baby would look like. Gorgeous, for sure, with blonde hair and blue eyes… Perfect, really. They're going to have perfect babies, to live in their perfect house, after their perfect wedding.

Despite the biting cold, my feet refuse to walk me to the subway station. Instead, I wander the streets of New York surrounded by a frenzied holiday crowd. Revoltingly cheery people going about their jolly business amidst colorful shopping windows and those sickening

Christmas tunes coming out of a thousand speakers hidden everywhere in the city.

A couple in front of me stops to kiss under a mistletoe wreath. Disgusted, I side-step past them, only to be assailed by a blinding display of red and green lights. Between the music, the lights, the colors, and the crowd, my head starts spinning. It seems like the whole city is bearing down on me. I need to get somewhere dark and quiet, *now!*

As I quicken my pace, my eyes catch on a shop window without even a hint of red or green, or of a single Christmas decoration. Instead of sickening jingle bells, modern lounge music is drifting out from under the glass door.

On impulse, I walk in.

An Asian guy with shoulder-length, platinum-blond hair welcomes me with an apologetic smile. "Sorry, dear, but we're almost closing. Did you have an appointment?"

An appointment? I take in the twin rows of black leather chairs in front of floor-to-ceiling mirror walls and realize I've walked into a hair salon.

"No, sorry," I say. "I just needed a break from all this holiday madness, and your place was so..."

The guy nods understandingly. "We pride ourselves in being the anti-Christmas types. So, my darling fellow Grinch, having a bad day?"

"Horrible." I walk toward one of the chairs. "Can I sit here for five minutes and breathe some un-festive fresh air?"

"Sure, sure." He gestures for me to sit, and I don't know if it's out of professional habit, but he starts combing his fingers through my hair. "Such a blank canvas," he says, pulling apart a few locks. "When was the last time you had it trimmed?"

"Honestly? I don't remember. It's been a while."

I like my hair as it is: long, dark, straight. And I haven't changed my style in forever. If it ain't broke...

"And are you feeling adventurous today?"

"No, *no!* Not at all."

I make to get up, but my host keeps me in place with a gentle pressure on my shoulders.

"Mmm, I'm not sure you've walked in here by chance, darling. Sure you're not ready for a change?"

I'm about to say "no" again, when the question really sinks in. Am I ready for a change? Do I want to keep spending my life pining after my sister's boyfriend—sorry, fiancé?

No.

Do I want to keep dreading the holidays and every visit home?

No.

So, am I ready for a change?

Hell yeah!

I meet the guy's eyes in the mirror.

"That's what I thought." He smiles knowingly. "I work only by appointment, but I will make an exception for you, little bird."

"Oh, no. You were about to close, I wouldn't want to make you stay late. I can come back tomorrow."

The stylist gives me a piercing stare through the mirror. "You walk out of that door now, honey, and we both know I'll never see you again."

He's right.

"Okay. Let's do this."

"Great!" He pats my shoulders. "Now, tell me how much of a radical change you want."

I lift my chin. "Make me a new woman."

***

After leaving the salon, I spend the rest of the walk home spying on my reflection in every shop window I pass. I barely recognize myself. Jiang—the genius hairstylist—basically turned me into Jaimie Alexander's secret twin sister. Think Nina Dobrev from the pilot episode of *The Vampire Diaries* to the series finale makeover. Only my new cut is shorter and more radical.

And so bouncy, and so fresh, and so not me.

As I unlock my apartment door, my phone pings with a new text. I drop my bag on the counter, take out the phone, and sag on the couch, exhausted.

What a day!

My fingers are so cold from my stroll around Manhattan that when

356

I try to unlock the phone, the touchscreen almost doesn't recognize them as warm, human flesh. Only after I blow hot air on my fingertips and swipe twice more does it work, and I can read the text.

It's from Blair, my best friend and roommate.

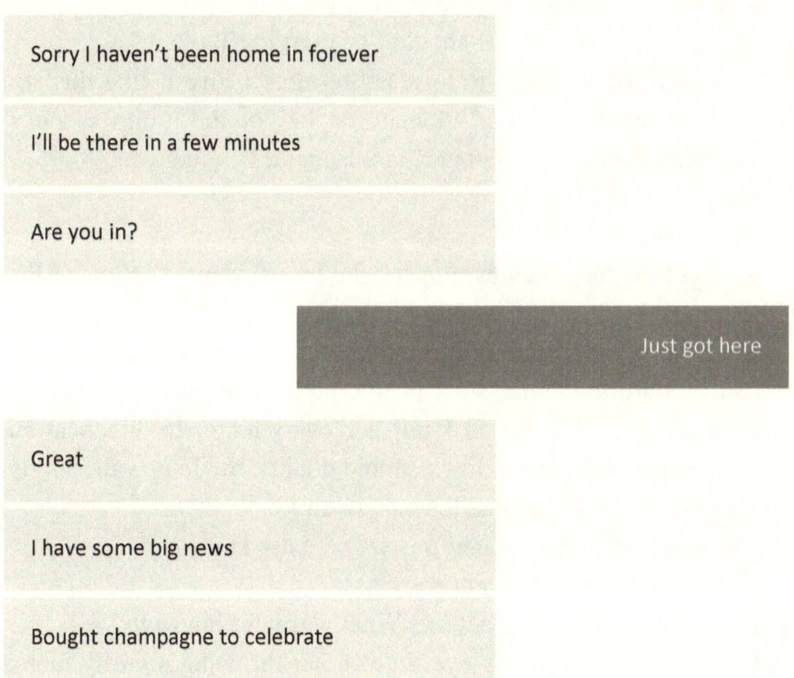

Champagne? Oh gosh, she's getting married, too. Richard proposed. I try to summon some altruistic joy, but I can't. There's only one thought drilling through my skull: I'm going to be single forever and die alone.

Just like that, out of nowhere, the tears come. My chest and shoulders spasm with body-wrenching sobs, and I don't seem to be able to stop the flood.

The frustration, the pain… the bitter jealousy, for my sister, for my best friend… they all come out in a downpour. Oh, gosh, I'm a horrible person who doesn't deserve love. Why would anyone love *me?* I'm dark and grumpy and stubborn—simply, utterly unlovable.

That's how Blair finds me a few minutes later: a sobbing, self-loathing mess sprawled on the couch.

"Oh my gosh, Nikki." She rushes into the living room, coat still on, dropping a bottle of bubbly on the coffee table, where she sits.

"Are you okay?"

I try to speak, but it's difficult when you're crying as hard as I am, so I only shake my head.

Blair does a double take and points at my face, shocked. "Your hair—it's gone! Are you crying about the haircut?"

"Noooooooo," I wail. "S-should I be c-crying about it?"

"No, no!" Blair jumps in to reassure me. "I love it like this! But it's a big transformation… I thought maybe you did it on the spur of the moment, then changed your mind. Is that it?"

I shake my head again.

"So what is it?"

After a few deep breaths, I speak the unspeakable. "Julia and Paul are engaged."

Blair doesn't respond. She removes her coat, kicks off her shoes, and slides onto the couch next to me, taking me into her arms. She pets me and cuddles me as I tell her everything: the lunch at Big Mama, the announcement, Jules' stupid doubts, my lone walk through the streets of Manhattan, and the hair salon.

"Do you really like my hair this way?" I ask at the end.

"Love it!" Blair smiles sincerely.

I hug her tighter. "Distract me. What was your big news?"

Out of the corner of my eye, I catch her throwing a guilty look at the champagne bottle. A thick layer of condensation now covers the dark glass. The wine's got to be warm by now. Great, I ruined her celebration.

"Oh, nothing," she says, brushing my question off. "Let's talk about it another night."

"You bought the bubbly," I insist. "Don't tell me it's nothing."

She chews on her index nail, undecided.

"Did Richard propose, too?"

"No," Blair says and, still biting her nail, adds, "but he asked me to move in with him."

I try to smile, I really try, but my lower lip starts trembling. I manage an, "I'm so happy for you," before I start sobbing again.

Blair pulls me back into her arms and tries to console me. "It won't be super soon. I told him we would need time to figure things out, and I'm not going anywhere until you're okay. Listen, I know the holidays are hard for you, and I'm here. Richard is going back to England over the break, but I'm staying in the States. We'll go home together, and whenever it gets too hard at your place, you can come and crash in my room, I promise. It'll be just you, me, and Chevron. A girls' club."

I calm down a little. Blair coming home to Connecticut with me is the lifeline I need to survive this Christmas. Knowing she'll be there is the only positive piece of news I've gotten all day. Also, for the first time, I notice Chevron—Blair's semi-golden-retriever dog—didn't come home with her.

"Hey, where did you leave Chevron?"

"At Richard's. I took the subway back. With traffic, it would've taken forever in his car, and it was too cold to walk, even for me."

"Oh, I could've used the extra cuddles."

Chevron is the most empathic and *only* dog I like.

"I thought you were a cat person."

"I am, but Chevron is basically a cat born in the wrong body."

Blair smirks. "If you say so."

"At least when the two of you move out I'll be able to adopt a real cat, body and soul."

The thought almost cheers me up, if not for the mocking voice inside my head announcing, *Ladies and gentlemen, I give you Nikki Moore: single, alone, and crazy cat-less cat lady.*

Three

The Perfect Man for Christmas

The next morning, I arrive at the office super early. Not only to catch up with work, but also to avoid the double-takes and possibly false compliments my impromptu makeover will spur.

I've just finished checking the wardrobe for tomorrow's shoot when Melanie walks in. She stops just inside the door and makes a shocked, "oh-I-walked-into-the-wrong-office" face. Then she blinks, realization dawning. Closing the door behind her, she approaches my desk slowly. "Your hair…"

"Is shorter," I say, making it clear that, no, I don't want to talk about it. "What can I do for you?"

"Your mother called again… I'm running out of excuses…"

"Arrrrrrrgh…" I let out an exasperated growl and drop my head in my hands.

"Mmm… Are you okay, boss?"

"No, I'm not okay." I lift my head and bang both fists on the desk. Not content, I brush off all the sheets of paper crowding it in a crazed swipe. The documents tumble to the floor, carrying a pen holder and my landline phone with them.

I stare at the mess with a small surge of satisfaction. Melanie, on the other hand, has gone pale.

"Sorry," I say. My reaction was atypical; I've never freaked out in front of her. "I'm not mad at you."

Still wary, my assistant sits in the chair opposite to mine. "Okay, boss, tell me what's going on."

Over the years, I've always strived to maintain a professional relationship with Melanie. But she's been with me from the start, and we've also developed a friendship-with-boundaries. This is one of the times I feel like testing those limits a little.

"It's the holidays and I'm single, while Julia just got engaged…" I skip the "to the love of my life" part, to maintain a shred of credibility in front of my assistant. "My roommate just told me she's moving in with her boyfriend. And in less than two weeks, I'll have to go home and listen to every single one of my relatives ask me why I'm still single. When what they really mean is, 'What's wrong with you? Why does nobody want you?'"

I huff. Aww… it felt good to let it all out.

Melanie absorbs all the personal info like a pro. "Is it the 'single at the holidays' part that bothers you, or is it your family?"

Good question. I don't particularly enjoy being single, and the prospect of dying a crazy cat lady is not very appealing. But why does the anxiety get so much worse near the end of the year? I'm fine with my life eleven months out of twelve, but every December I promptly turn into a train wreck. Does Christmas make being a spinster harder? Or is it the judgment in Aunt Betsy's thin-lipped smiles? The ill-concealed sadness behind my mother's eyes for my "condition?" Or the well-intentioned-but-deeply-insensitive jokes everyone spins me back home?

It's not me. It's them.

"My family," I tell Melanie. "They drive me nuts."

"Well, but that's an easy fix."

"Really? How?"

"You're an executive producer. Produce them."

"What do you mean?"

"There must be a gay best friend—possibly with the looks of Rupert Everett—you can ask to go home with you and pretend to be your boyfriend."

Sometimes I forget my assistant is still basically a child. At twenty-five, she's not jaded enough about life to accept not everything can be solved "Hollywood Style" and end in happily ever after.

Pity happily ever afters don't exist. Some genius in my profession invented them to sell romance to the crowds. That's all.

"Sorry, Mel, but I'm not Julia Roberts and this isn't a movie. No gorgeous gay besties in the picture."

"A straight friend would do, too. Anyone you can ask?"

Ironically, the one male friend I could've felt intimate enough to ask something so embarrassing would've been Paul. Isn't life funny sometimes?

"Not really," I say.

"Well, then hire someone!"

"Are you suggesting I hire a male escort?" And we've moved from *My Best Friend's Wedding* to *The Wedding Date,* maybe she has a thing for Dermot Mulroney. "Are you crazy? I'm not that desperate."

"I was thinking more an actor." She points at my computer. "You have a database full of them right there in front of you; you just have to pick and choose."

"That's even more absurd and unprofessional." To signify that this conversation is finished, I bend forward and start collecting the scattered documents from the floor. "Break's over," I say, pushing up the pen holder.

"All right, boss," Melanie says, getting up. She helps me clean the mess and places my office phone back on the desk, eyeing it meaningfully. "But your mom won't give up, you know?"

Don't I?

***

Another afternoon of staring into space earns me a late night at the office. I wish nothing more than to go home, change into a pair of sweatpants, and watch a silly romcom that will make me cry and despise my life even more. But I can't leave before every minute of tomorrow's shoot is mapped out. And I need to also check the ad sales reports on my holiday commercials and recheck the TV air schedules for the projects I'm following. So I trudge on, even if my eyes keep crossing over the endless Excel sheet lines and columns.

By 8:30 p.m. I'm so exhausted that, when my landline rings, I pick up without thinking.

"Nikki Moore."

"Nikki!" My mother sounds both astounded and utterly ecstatic she's finally cornered me. "I thought I'd get your voicemail. I'm not sure your secretary is passing along all my messages. What are you still doing at the office this late?"

"Working, obviously."

"Work, work, work. You work too much, honey, there's more to life than just work."

I could come up with a million retorts. But if I argue back, the conversation will spiral into a sermon from my mother. A lecture starting with a list of all the important things I'm neglecting, and ending in a praise of the perfect work-life balance Julia has achieved. So, instead of defending my right to be focused on my career, I give her the easy response.

"Mom, you know how busy it gets at the holidays, worst time of the year. I really need to finish up here, so…"

"I'll be quick, then." Now that she has me, she's not going to let me off the hook that easily. "I wanted to know when you're coming home for the break. Julia is coming on the twenty-second."

I peek at the calendar. The twenty-second is the Saturday before Christmas.

"Either then, or on the twenty-third," I say. "I'm sharing a car with Blair, and we haven't made a decision yet."

"But you'll definitely be here by Sunday night."

"Yes."

"And when are you leaving?"

"Not sure yet, Mom." I try to stall before she traps me up there for a full week. "Depends on what my plans for New Year's are."

"Oh, are you going somewhere?"

I twist the cord around my fingers and say, "I could." Which isn't an outright lie. I *could* go on a trip; I'm just not planning to.

"All right, we can settle that once you get home." I think she's finally going to cut me loose when she adds, "So, you've heard about Julia and Paul. Isn't it wonderful news?"

Peachy, I'd say, to keep in tone with the wedding color scheme.

"Yeah, I had lunch with them yesterday."

"Oh, great. So, I was wondering if you wouldn't mind swapping rooms with your sister?"

"And why should I do that?"

"Because your bed is bigger, and since Paul is spending the holidays with us—"

"WHAT?!"

"Isn't it marvelous? He's almost part of the family now, and it makes sense he'd want to be with us at Christmas."

"And what about *his* family? Don't they want to spend Christmas Day with their son?"

"I think his mom prefers Thanksgiving. Anyway, can I tell Julia she can have your room?"

"No."

"Nikki, don't be unreasonable. You're coming home by yourself, and they're two—they can't sleep in Julia's bunk bed."

The thought of Julia and Paul sleeping—*and doing who knows what else*—in my old bed blinds me with rage. I lost my virginity on that bed with my first boyfriend—senior year, one spring afternoon when both my parents were out. Julia can't have that, too. That bed has a lot of good memories, and I won't let Julia spoil those as well. She's already collected enough pieces of me.

"I'm not by myself," I say on impulse.

"What do you mean?" my mom asks, surprised.

"My boyfriend is coming with me."

And I'm digging myself a deeper grave with every sentence.

"You have a boyfriend? Since when?"

"Yeah, it hasn't been long, but I wanted you all to meet him."

Lie, after lie, after lie.

"Oh, Nikki, you're making me so happy! What's his name? How did you meet?"

"I don't have time to tell you the whole story now, Mom, but don't worry, you'll meet him soon enough."

"Sure. I'll let you go back to work… So many things to organize here. I love you, honey."

"Love you, too, Mom. Bye."

I hang up and drop my head on the desk over my crossed arms.

What have I done?

I should call her back and tell her it's all been a mistake. That Julia can have my man, my dream life, and even my bed. What does it matter, anyway?

Only it *does* matter. I can't spend a week at home, single and pathetic, sleeping in Julia's tiny princess bed while she shares my bed with Paul. Not possible.

I straighten up.

So, where do I find a boyfriend?

I throw a guilty stare at my computer.

No, I couldn't.

What if someone at the office found out?

Impossible.

No one would ever believe I've hired a fake boyfriend off the agency's database.

With a few quick clicks of the mouse, I close the Excel sheet I was studying and access the actors/models database.

A pop-up window prompts me to input filters to narrow down the search. I select "male" and then, before I know what I'm doing, I start creating an avatar of Julia's ideal man.

```
Eyes: green
Hair: dark
Height: 6'4" and above
Age: |
```

I'm undecided if I should include only the 30-34 range or expand it to 25-29 and 35-39. What if the perfect man is 29 or 35? I select all three, just to be on the safe side.

Languages: |

I check English and Italian and click Search.

With my heart in my throat, I wait for the results. Does such a man even exist?

The search engine lands three positive hits. Wow. Apparently, there are a lot more tall, dark-haired, Italian-speaking men in New York than I thought.

I open the first profile, and the picture of a beautiful man pops on the screen. I say "beautiful" because it's clear that this male model favors his feminine side. It's in the delicate pout of his lips and the graceful tilt of his head. No one would ever believe he's in love with me.

I close his profile and open the next one.

Jackpot!

Now, if a man could ever be described as dark, smoldering hot, and mysterious, this guy has nailed all three. The headshot is pretty simple: he's staring at the camera straight up, face forward. His wavy black hair is just long enough to be very sexy, as sexy as his full-lipped mouth, and his green eyes are piercing a hole through the screen. Tyra Banks would say he's smizing at the camera.

I study the picture a little longer… His straight nose is sprinkled with freckles that make him cute on top of sexy. And even the line of his neck is masculine and inviting. He is the perfect man. He's my guy.

His other pictures only reinforce my conviction. A profile shot: equally sexy. One of him smiling: heart-melting. And…

Whoa.

The last picture is a black and white bust shot. Mr. Tall, Dark, and Mysterious is wearing jeans and teasingly lifting a tank top to reveal his bare chest while he stares at the camera with a naughty expression—eyes alive with mischief and mouth curled up at one corner in a lopsided grin. The shot takes my breath away. This must be photoshopped; no real person could really have abs and pectorals that sculpted.

Reluctantly, I close the picture and open his profile.

Diego O'Donnell, age twenty-eight. Two years younger than me, but we live in a modern era where a two-year gap a cougar doesn't make. From his CV I see that the guy has done a few lesser gigs on Broadway and has a couple of high-level commercials under his belt. But nothing so big that it'll make him snub my proposal. Mr. O'Donnell still fits the struggling artist profile.

Mmm, let's see where you live.

The address listed on his file is far away enough from Manhattan to tell me he's not swimming in cash.

Good.

Because I need someone just as desperate as me to take this job.

Fueled up by adrenaline, I save his contact on my phone and press Call.

Four

Here Comes Santa Claus

Nothing.

The call goes to voicemail. I try a second time, with the same result, so I decide to try the other number listed on his profile. Maybe a landline?

"Hello?"

The voice is a letdown. Too creaky to match the man in the picture.

"Hello, Mr. O'Donnell?"

"Who?"

"Diego O'Donnell?"

"Oh, you mean Dunk. He's not home."

"You know when he'll be back?"

"Why?" The dude sounds suspicious.

"I'm calling about a job opportunity, something rather urgent. No chance you'd know where I can find him?"

"He could still be downtown. Dunk had a Santa Claus gig tonight, but it should be over by now."

Diego is in Manhattan! I can barely contain my excitement. "Do you remember where the gig was, by any chance?"

"No, sorry, some fancy mall downtown. You want to leave a

message?"

"No need, thank you, I'll call back."

I hang up and nibble at one of my nails. Damn. Now that my folly has gained momentum, I can't lose steam. If only that guy remembered the name of the mall…

Let's see if Google can help. A quick "santa claus wednesday december 12 manhattan mall" search and… Bingo! There's only one late-evening event today, and the address is not too far from my office. The program says the show ends at 9:30 p.m. If I hurry, I might get there just in time.

****

Fifteen minutes after the scheduled end of the event, I arrive at the mall worried sick I might've missed him. But, luckily, there's still a Santa seated in the winter wonderland booth at the mall's entrance. He's ushering a kid away, who an elf assistant promptly replaces with the last toddler in line, depositing the newcomer on Santa's knee.

As Diego listens to the little boy, I observe my mark to evaluate if he's as good looking in person, or if he's a cheat—aka a Photoshop-friendly model who doesn't understand that going to a casting looking half as hot as his portfolio is a lose-lose approach. But between the fake beard and fake belly, it's a hard one to call.

Once the kid has expressed all his Christmas wishes and taken the customary picture, my man stands up.

Mmm. Impressive. At least he didn't lie about his height.

"I'm getting hella out of here," his lady elf helper says. "You coming?"

"Nah, gotta get changed first. See ya soon, Jess."

They bump fists and the woman walks away, still wearing her red, white, and green costume.

In the few seconds I get distracted by watching the elf leave, Diego has opened a hidden door and is already disappearing backstage. Whoops. "Excuse me—!" I call.

"Sorry, Miss, the event's over," he says, without sparing me a second glance. And then he's gone.

What now? I could wait for him to get changed and come back out, but again, I'm impatient. And if I stay too long out here, I might chicken out, call my mom, and surrender my bed to Julia.

Never.

I throw a circumspect look around. No one's monitoring the booth, so I enter Santa World and follow Diego behind the hidden door into a tiny backstage dressing room. There's barely enough space for a locker and a small bench pushed against the opposite wall.

Diego has the upper half of the locker open, which screens him from my view.

"Excuse me?" I repeat.

"Hey." He closes the locker and throws me an angry stare. "This is personnel only."

He's still wearing the fake beard and Santa hat, but the upper part of the red suit is now dangling upside-down from his hips and the belly stuffer is gone, leaving his ripped chest and abs all too visible under a sweat-soaked white T-shirt. With muscles like that, he could win any wet-T-shirt contest.

I tear my eyes away from his chest, saying, "Yeah, I know. But I really needed to talk to you."

"Listen, lady, if your kid has missed his spot, I'm sorry, but it's late and I want to go home. We're doing another event in two days; you can come back then."

"I'm not here to see Santa. I'm here to see you, Mr. O'Donnell."

He starts at that. "How do you know my name?"

"Nikki Moore, nice to meet you. I work at KCU Advertising, and I'd like to talk to you about a job opportunity."

I don't usually name drop, but I need to gain some credibility before I present him with my crazy plan.

"The big agency on Madison Avenue?"

"Yes, but the job wouldn't be for the agency; you'd be working for me. Care to hear me out?"

He shrugs. "Mind if I keep getting changed?"

"No, not at all. Go ahead."

Diego turns around and pulls the wet T-shirt off his back in one fluid motion. I'm momentarily distracted by more male skin than I've seen in a long while. Gosh, even his back is ripped.

"I'm listening," he says, opening the locker again and blocking my ogling feast.

"Mmm, yeah, so." This is harder to explain than I thought. "It'd be an acting job. Nothing scripted… a lot of improv required. Sort of, you know, like a reality show, but with no cameras. And you might think I'm crazy for asking, but you must understand that the holidays can be a difficult period for many people. Single people, I mean. And people with a family that just won't back off, especially if they have a baby sister who's the poster child of perfection in their mother's eyes. You get what I'm saying?"

Back still turned, Diego says, "Not really." He rips off the rest of the Santa suit, rewarding me with an unobstructed view of his buttocks clad in close-fitting white boxer shorts. Mmm, those buns are so inviting I have to force myself not to reach out and squeeze one. Luckily, in a few quick moves, he pulls on a pair of jeans and a sweatshirt, and, closing the locker for good, turns all his attention to me.

For the first time I see his face without the beard, and one thing is immediately clear: he's no Photoshop user.

He fluffs his hair, which has been plastered to his head by the hat, and grins. "What's the job again?"

Guess there's really no other way to explain it. "I want to hire you to pose as my boyfriend for the holidays."

Diego opens his mouth to protest, but before he can, I stop him. "And before you say 'no,' please note that the pay is very competitive."

"How competitive?

"Five thousand dollars—twenty-five hundred in advance, and the rest at job completion. And our relationship would be strictly professional."

"While I pretend to be your boyfriend?"

"Exactly."

"I'm sorry, but—"

"Wait. Before refusing, please consider that if you say 'yes,' you'd be doing me a real solid, and I'd be happy to return the favor, professionally, of course, in any way you might need."

I saved the best bone for last. A struggling actor would do anything to have someone who matters in the industry owe him one. As expected, this offer gives him pause.

He scratches his head and studies me. "You're serious? This isn't a joke."

I shake my head. "Dead serious."

"And you work for KCU?"

I whip out my business card and present him with incontrovertible proof. "Mmm-hmm."

He eyes the card, thinking. "You guys are big on Super Bowl commercials. You even won an award last year, yeah?"

"Breath mints, that's us."

"Have you already cast this year's ads?"

"No, we start in early January."

"Can you get me a call in?"

"Into the castings, yes, but the rest is up to you. I can't guarantee a part."

A brief nod lets me know he understands. Then, out of the blue, he asks, "Why me?"

The question takes me off guard. I can't exactly say, *"Because I want my sister to rot with jealousy when I bring her dream guy home for Christmas."* He already thinks I'm nuts.

"We haven't worked together in the past, so there wouldn't be a conflict."

Diego keeps his eyes trained on me for the longest time. "Am I the only actor in your agency's database you haven't worked with before?"

What else can I say to convince him? Only one plausible reason I can think of. "No," I admit. "But you were the best-looking one."

I don't even think I'm lying right now.

My answer seems to have satisfied him. He smiles, forcing all the air out of my lungs. Now I get what *breathtaking* means.

Using basic yoga training to steady my respiration, I ask, "Then we have a deal?"

He offers me his hand. "Deal."

After we shake on it, he pulls on his coat and guides me out of the Santa closet.

"So how is this going to work?" he asks once we reach the mall exit.

The cold night air hits us the moment we step outside. It's

freezing, and I've already had enough excitement for one day. So I say, "It's late now. Why don't we discuss the details tomorrow over lunch?"

"Okay."

"You'll find a missed call from me on your phone from about an hour ago. I'll text you a place in the morning."

"All right, boss." As he says "boss," Diego winks at me. Then he turns around to climb on a monstrous black bike that he starts with a roar. "See you tomorrow."

I watch him put on a black helmet and speed away into traffic. I can't believe he even has a bike. I really picked the perfect man for the job.

***

The next day, I'm the first to arrive at the restaurant. I've picked a taqueria not too far from my office, but not too close, either. The last thing I need is to run into a colleague while I'm negotiating contract terms with my fake boyfriend.

Wow, I still can't believe I'm doing this, and that someone else has joined me in this crazy plan. I stare at the list of "hot topics" I've printed out, not sure Diego has grasped the full extent of what he agreed to yesterday. Might be my fault for being accidentally-on-purpose vague enough not to scare him away, but today I need to be one hundred percent assertive about what I want out of this deal.

A change of vibe inside the restaurant makes me lift my head. The normal tones of conversation have quieted down to be replaced by intrigued murmurs. At the table next to mine, the two women who've been bitching non-stop about their boss since I got here are now giggling, eyes fixated on the entrance door. I follow their stares, and my gaze lands on Mr. Tall, Dark, and Smoldering Hot.

Hair ruffled up in all directions, Diego is standing on the threshold scanning the tables, presumably to find me, and mostly unaware of the attention he's commanding from the entire room. Clad in a pair of light-washed jeans, a black leather biker jacket, and with the matching black helmet propped under his arm, he's the incarnation of the bad boy in every woman's fantasy.

I wave to attract his attention. He spots me and reaches our high table in a few quick strides—not surprising with that impressive leg span. While he sits opposite me with a quick, "Hello," I steal a glance at the two women sitting next to us and am ridiculously pleased with the vitriolic looks of pure envy stamped on their faces.

Ah, hell. For once I'm not the single lady having lunch alone, I'm the woman dating the hottest guy in the room—possibly the entire New York state—and who cares if I have to shell out a few thousand dollars for the privilege? Money well invested. I can't wait to stick it to my family for once. To have one glorious Christmas before I become the official family spinster forever.

"Hi," I greet him back. "Did you find the place all right?"

"Yeah." Diego settles his helmet on the empty stool between us. "Been here before."

We lock gazes for the first time since he arrived, and for a second, I have to steady myself. Today is a surprisingly bright day for December, and the sun is hitting Diego's face with just the right light, turning his eyes into two sparkly emeralds.

I clear my throat. "Err, great."

Good thing he's not my type at all. I prefer blue eyes and blonde hair, and guys with a stable job. Guys like Paul, in short. And Diego sits at the opposite end of the male spectrum. At least there won't be any risk of confusion on my part. And I'm sure on his, too. I don't know what kind of woman is his type, but she must be a few leagues above me in the looks department.

"Are you ready to order?" I ask.

"Yeah, I—"

"Hello, I'm Adalynn, and I'll be taking care of you today," an eager-looking woman interrupts us. She's sporting the smile of a server who's just won the table lottery. "Would you like to hear today's specials?"

Diego smiles back at her and says, "Sure."

"Wonderful." From the way she beams, you'd think he'd just agreed to go on a date with her. "Today's special tacos are the lobster with sweet corn, and fried duck with habanero honey. If I may suggest one, the duck is really something special."

"All right." Diego smizes, eyes as mischievous as in his pictures. "The duck one sounds great."

"Excellent choice. And to drink?"

"A beer, please."

After giving him another small smile, she turns toward me, her enthusiasm fading. "And for you?"

"A chicken taco and a Diet Coke, thank you."

"Perfect. I'll be right back with your drinks."

Adalynn isn't kidding; I haven't even struck up the nerve to broach the fake-boyfriend topic when she returns with our drinks. Setting them down, she throws Diego yet another smile and says, "Let me know if you need anything else."

Reluctantly, she walks away, finally leaving us in peace.

"So," I start, a little nervous. "Thanks for meeting me here today." Oh, come on, Nikki. No need to be nervous. Just treat him as any model or actor you would in one of your productions. Yeah, right. I've got this. "I wanted to go over the details of this job before we sign a formal contract… Did you have questions, or would you like to hear me out first?"

Diego leans his elbows on the table. "I might have too many questions. Best if you outline the ABCs first…"

"Oh, okay." I stare at the first item on my list: comp. "As I said, the compensation is a flat five thousand dollar fee, all included." Better remind him why he's here. "As for the specifics of the job, we need to script the basics: how we met, first date, a few cute anecdotes… stuff like that. And we have to familiarize ourselves with each other to improv the rest. Our interactions must be as natural as possible, and that's why I thought…" I hope he swallows this without protest. "…you should move in with me."

His eyebrows shoot high into his forehead. "Move in with you?"

"Yeah. We have to act as if we've known each other for a couple of months, at the very least." If I'm doing this, I'm doing it right. "I have to learn your tells, you have to learn mine, and living together is exactly the crash course we need. You would have your own room, of course." *Once I convince Blair to let you sleep in her bed, anyway.* But she's moving out soon, so it shouldn't be too hard for her to crash at Richard's until Christmas.

"You're a bit paranoid, you know? We don't need all that preparation to pass for a couple for one dinner."

"One dinner?"

"Yeah, the Christmas meal? Isn't that what we were talking about?"

"I'm not paying you five thousand dollars to have *one meal* with my family. You have to come with me to my hometown in Connecticut for a *week*." His eyes widen, and I already see him ready to backtrack and call everything off. But I can't let him. I'll never find someone as perfect. I mean, he even rides a bike! So I edge another sheet of paper toward him. "And as per the final part of our agreement, these are all the brands we're shooting Super Bowl ads with, and that I could get you castings for."

Diego stares at me with an appalled look, followed by a questioning side glare of who-is-this-crazy-person-I'm-having-lunch-with? Then he lowers his eyes to the list, and his expression switches to mmm-these-brands-are-really-cool-and-how-many-people-watch-the-super-bowl-again?

I've just delivered an exemplary carrot-and-stick performance. He's in.

"I still think moving in together is too much," Diego says, a tad too loud.

The ladies to my left look up at us open-mouthed for a second, and then snicker between themselves. And even our server seems to have a satisfied little smirk on her face as she deposits our plates on the table. Wow, this man can really bring female rivalry to a whole new level.

"Maybe," I say, pointedly lowering my voice. "But I can't risk either of us slipping up in front of my family, not even on the smallest thing. And what are you complaining about? I'm offering you a free stay in Manhattan for two weeks."

Before he has time to come up with a thousand plausible reasons not to move in with the crazy cat lady, I push my point. "And anyway, I'm at work twelve to fourteen hours a day, so we wouldn't clash too much. And you'd be free to come and go as you like, with no more long commutes. From my apartment, you can get everywhere in Manhattan in fifteen minutes on the subway. You can go to your Santa gigs, or go to castings, or whatever it is you do all day." I still read doubt in his eyes, so I end with a cocksure, "It's non-negotiable."

I try to keep a straight face as panic rises in my throat. If he bails, I'm fried. I will have to confess my lies to my mom and suffer the greatest humiliation of my life.

He stares at me for a second, back at the brands list, and then sighs. "Ah, hell." He grabs his beer and takes a long sip. "In for a penny…"

The air leaves my lungs, and I relax for the first time since I got here. At least now I know I have a potential second career as a poker player.

We eat our lunch in silence. It's one of the most awkward meals I've ever had. All the more reason for him to move in—this is exactly the sort of thing we need to fix before the holidays.

When the bill arrives, I slip my credit card into the folder and sign the receipt once the server brings it back.

"How was your taco?" I ask Diego, trying to break the ice.

"Bit too fancy. I should've stuck with the classic."

"Aw, don't tell our server, she's going to be crushed."

Diego gives me a brief smile, and then the awkward silence is back.

After a few eternally long moments, he asks, "When do you want me to move in?"

"Tonight, if you can. The sooner the better." I grab my phone and text him the address. "That's me," I say. "Whenever after 8 p.m. is fine."

"Great. Anything else?"

"Ah, yes." I fish a brown manila envelope out of my bag and slide it across the table toward him. "This is for you."

He looks skeptical again.

"What's this?"

"The first half of your payment," I reply, nonplussed.

Diego chuckles and shakes his head. "You brought an envelope full of cash?"

"Yeah, why? What did you expect?"

Still grinning, he says, "I don't know, PayPal?"

Oh. That would've made a lot of sense, actually. I guess I got a bit caught up in the movie stereotype. I blush and shrug, getting up. "I can do that if you prefer."

"Nah," Diego says, also standing. "Cash is fine." He makes the envelope disappear into an inside pocket of his jacket.

"Okay, then, see you tonight." I don't know if we should hug, or kiss on the cheek, or whatever… We'll need to decide what our thing is, but for now, I simply give him a professional nod and stroll out of the restaurant without looking back.

Five

Santa Claus Is Coming To Town

A new text from Blair.

Yeah, to get to know my fake boyfriend better.

So Blair will be home tonight. Good, as I need to catch her up on my crazy decisions of the past two days. And bad, as afterward, I need to convince her to traipse all the way back to Brooklyn on a cold December night.

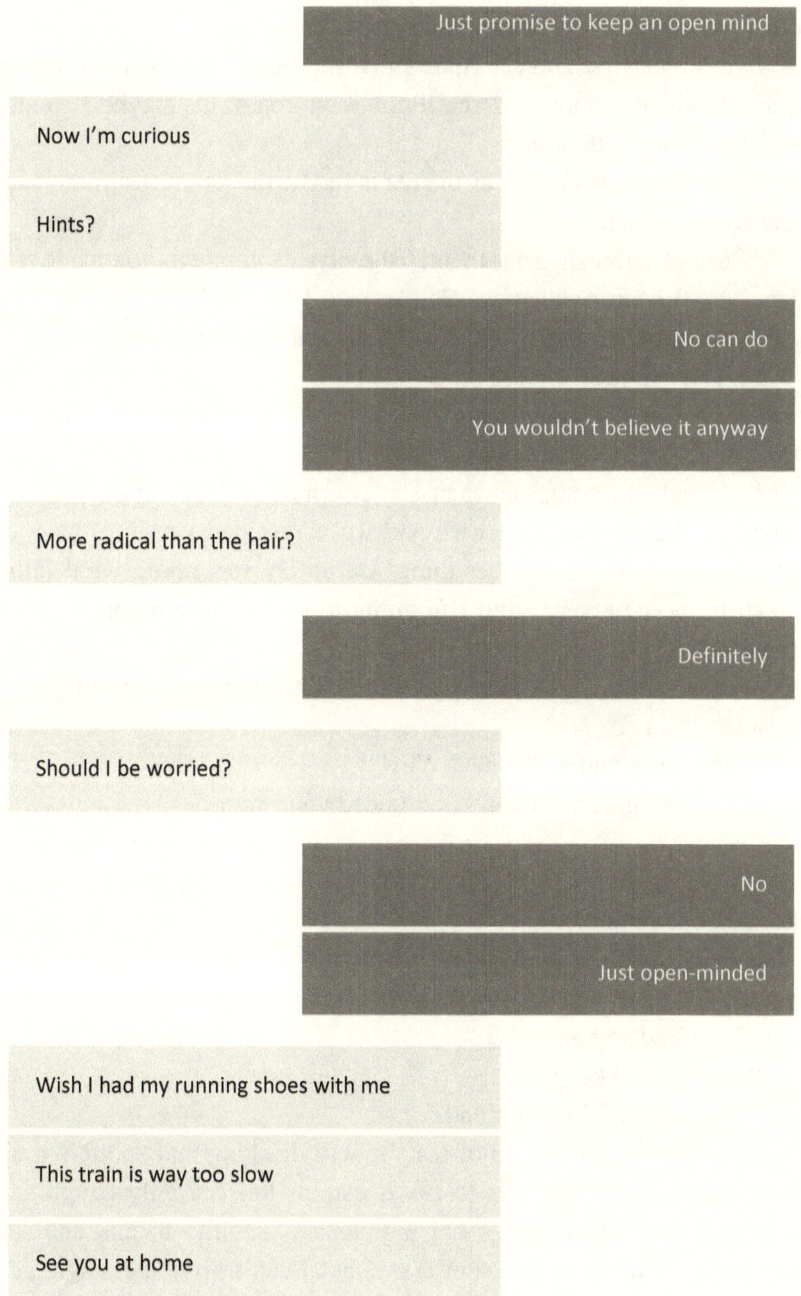

Blair is the only person I'm going to tell. A, because I can trust her, and B, because I have no choice if we're driving to Old Saybrook, our hometown, together. Our families live across the street from each other, so she'll need to corroborate my fake romance.

I get home first and set Blair's favorite herbal tea to steep. We're going to share a mug, and she'll come on board. Or maybe I should spike her mug with booze.

Five minutes later, just as the tea is ready, the key turns in the lock and Blair walks in.

"Gosh, it's freezing out there!" she says. "Oh, great, you made tea. Just what I need right now." She kicks off her heels, drapes her coat on the back of the couch, and takes a stool at the kitchen bar.

I fill two mugs from the other side of the bar and hand her one. She wraps her fingers around it to warm them and studies me. "So, my favorite tea, huh? What's going on?"

I'm ready to confess, when she continues, "But before you say anything, I spoke with Richard and we've decided we don't have to push the moving in together thing. Definitely something we'll think about in the new year. And I'm going to spend more nights home, I promise."

"Err, actually..." I take a sip of tea. "I kind of need you to do the opposite."

Blair's eyes widen. "What? Why?"

"I'm having a house guest and I need your room."

"Who?"

I plaster an innocent smile on my face. "This is the part where you keep an open mind..."

She narrows her eyes at me. "Nicola Addison Moore, what have you done?"

"I've hired someone."

"Like a housekeeper?"

"More like a fake boyfriend."

Blair chokes on the sip of tea she was drinking and sputters it all over the counter. She tries to ask questions but can only cough and spatter. I take advantage of her momentary inability to talk and say my piece. "And it might seem crazy, but I can't go home single and pathetic this year. Paul is going to spend the holidays at our place because he's *family* now, and I can't survive a whole week under the same roof with them by myself. My mom wanted to give them my room, my bed..."

Blair's face is still super red from the choking, and even if her eyes are still teary, I can tell she can speak now. Only she doesn't seem sure what she wants to say. She shakes her head, drops the mug on the bar, and starts massaging her temples. "Okay, let's pretend for a second I don't find this whole idea completely absurd, and that I'm keeping an open mind." She looks back up at me. "Who is this guy? Where did you find him? And you asked him to move in? In my room? Without even asking me?"

I lean back against the stove, keeping the bar between us in case she decides to throttle me. She's right, I should've at least asked her first, but I was desperate, and that's what I tell her. "I'm sorry, but I didn't know what else to do…"

"But why do you need to live together?"

"We have to fool my family for a whole week, and it needs to be a good act… so we need to appear comfortable around each other."

"But who is this person?"

"An actor. I hired him off the KCU's database."

"Have you worked with him before?"

"No."

"So you've invited a complete stranger to live with you?"

"Desperate times, desperate measures."

"But he could be a psycho, a rapist, a serial killer."

"I'm sure he's none of those things."

"Yeah? How sure?"

"You can tell for yourself. He'll be here in…" I check my watch. "Half an hour."

"WHAT?" Blair shoots up from her stool and starts pacing around, shaking her head. "He's coming over *tonight?* But where will he sleep?"

"The couch? I thought you were spending the night at Richard's."

"And what if I were? You would've let him sleep in my bed without even asking?"

"Oh, come on. We've always used each other's rooms to host friends and family when the other was away, *without* asking."

"Yeah, right. Friends and family, not complete strangers who—"

"Well, what was I supposed to do?" I raise my voice as tears of frustration fill my eyes. "Be the good girl, go home, and let Julia have everything she wants? Hasn't she taken enough from me? I won't let her win this time."

"Okay, let's calm down here." Blair's face softens. "The engagement and Paul joining your family for the holidays have been huge shocks. But is hiring this dude really the only answer?"

"If you have a better idea that will let me keep my sanity and my room back home, shoot…"

Blair goes to sit on the couch, and after a moment I join her. I can almost hear the wheels in her brain turning, trying to find an alternative solution. But after five minutes of scrunching her face and staring into space, she turns toward me, defeated.

"I've got nothing," she huffs.

"See? I'm not crazy."

"Apparently not. What do you need from me?"

"For you to get on board with the plan and pretend you've known Diego for a few months—"

"Diego?"

"Yeah, that's him."

"Surname?"

"O'Donnell."

She types both into her phone.

"What are you doing?"

"Saving his generalities in case you disappear and the police need them."

"Hey, you're the only person I know who ever got in trouble with the cops."

"I was a victim of the justice system, and we're not talking about me."

"I thought you were asking how you could be supportive."

Blair sighs. "I was. Anything else you need?"

I make big, Puss-in-Boots eyes at her. "Could you free some closet space in your room?"

***

When the doorbell rings, Blair is already packed and ready to go back to Brooklyn. She's called Richard, who'll come to pick her up in a bit—she's asked for enough time to make sure Diego is no Charlie

Manson, I suspect.

"He's coming up," I announce after buzzing Diego in.

"Good." Blair has settled with her butt against the back of the couch and is staring at the door with the same rapt expression of a hawk scanning the woods for squirrels.

I wait by the threshold, keeping the door half open and feeling ridiculously nervous.

When I spot Diego walking down the hall, I have a moment's hesitation. With his leather jacket, dark looks, and biker helmet, he really is a "bad boy" personification. I just hope Blair can get past first impressions.

"Hi," I call. "I'm down here."

He sees me and waves, quickening his pace. "Hey, boss," he greets me, more easygoing than he's been in all our previous meetings.

Good, I need him to be relaxed to withstand Blair's sure-to-come interrogation.

"My roommate's here." I give him a heads up on the situation before letting him in. "She's waiting for her boyfriend to pick her up."

"Oh, okay. Do I have to act boyfriendly, then?"

A thrill spider walks down my spine, making me wonder what his "acting boyfriendly" would entail, but I shake the thought away as quickly as it popped into my head.

"No need," I say. "She knows."

I finally nudge the door open all the way and let him in.

"Diego, this is Blair. Blair, Diego."

My best friend does a good job of dropping her jaw only for a second before resuming her studiously scolding expression.

"Hi, I'm Diego."

He offers her a hand, and she shakes it.

"Blair."

"Nice to meet you," he says, then turns toward me, asking, "Is there somewhere I can drop these?"

I take the helmet from him and place it on the bar. "You can leave your bag in Blair's room. This way." I beckon him to follow me.

He drops the bag on her bed, and before he can do or say anything, she's giving him the rules.

"I freed this side of the closet for you," Blair says, opening the door to show him. "And the nightstand. Everything else is still filled with my things, so please don't touch anything."

"I'm not diseased, you know?" Diego frowns, more jokingly than serious.

"No, I don't. Because I know nothing about you. For all *I know,* you could be a serial killer."

"I sense some hostility," Diego says, again not serious.

"Well, sorry if I'm not super-duper pleased about my best friend's idea to invite a perfect stranger to live in the house with her."

"Hey, don't take it out on me." He lifts his hands in a surrender gesture. "I tried to convince her it wasn't necessary."

We all move back into the living room. Diego sits on a stool while Blair walks into the kitchen. I lean against the back of the couch and observe warily as Blair takes a glass out of a cabinet and cleans it with a rag—even though it's perfectly clean already. Then she disappears into the bathroom and comes back with one of those plastic bags you have to use for liquids on a plane. Still holding the glass enveloped in the rag, she hands it to Diego.

"Hold this, please."

He takes it from her, looking rather puzzled. As am I.

"Okay, now put it in here," Blair instructs, keeping the plastic bag open.

Diego drops the glass in the bag and, just as he's looking back up with a questioning expression, Blair snaps a photo with her phone.

"What the hell?" he asks, blinded by the flash.

"All right, Mister, just be advised that if something happens to my best friend, I have your name, your picture, and your fingerprints." She dangles the makeshift evidence bag in front of him. "The police will find you in no time."

Diego seems more amused than offended. "Paranoid much?"

"I'm sorry," I say. "She's just being overprotective."

"You bet I am," Blair snaps. "And you should also be aware that I have a trained attack dog who'd chew you to pieces if you so much as harm a hair on her head."

To describe Chevron as a trained attack dog would be like saying Diego is a Danny DeVito lookalike—oil and water.

"And now..." Blair reaches into her bag, which is sitting on the stool next to Diego, and takes out a business card and a pen. She scribbles something on the blank side and hands it to him.

"What's this?" he asks.

"My business card," Blair says, nonplussed. "There's an address written on the back. We're casting a New Year's fashion photo-shoot. The screening starts at 10.30 a.m. on Tuesday. Don't be late."

Diego smiles. "Do you always invite presumed serial killers to job interviews, or do you only need an extra mug shot?"

Blair's answer dies on her lips as the buzzer goes off, and the only thing I can think is, *"Saved by the bell!"*

My roomie gathers the suitcase she's prepared for her ten-day stay at Richard's, and I walk her to the door. We pause just outside the hall to say goodbye.

"Thank you," I tell her. "I know you don't like this."

"Just be careful," she whispers. "And lock yourself into your room tonight."

I roll my eyes.

"Promise," she insists.

"I promise."

"All right." Blair hugs me. "Call me if you need anything. I'll keep my phone on."

"I will, but I'm sure it won't be necessary."

We hug again, and then I watch her go until she disappears inside the elevator.

So! Time to enjoy my first cozy evening with my fake boyfriend.

Filled with trepidation, I push the door open and walk back into my apartment.

Six

The Twelve Days of Christmas

Inside, Diego is standing in the living room, looking around as if he's afraid to touch anything.

"So that went well," I say sarcastically, shutting the door behind me.

"Are all your friends that feisty?" he asks.

"Forgive Blair, it's my fault. I totally blindsided her with"—I wiggle a finger between us—"this. Told her you were moving in only an hour ago."

"Smooth."

"Well," I snap. "Buying a boyfriend wasn't on my Christmas shopping list until a few days ago." That came out too harsh. "Sorry, I didn't mean to be rude, it's just that this whole situation is stressful for me, too. Can we pretend my best friend just told you *mi casa es tu casa* and move on?"

"Sure."

"Great. This is a spare set of keys." I grab it from the cabinet in the hall and hand it to him. "So you can come and go as you like. The blue is for the main door downstairs, and the big one opens this door here. The others, you won't need."

"Got it." Diego stashes the keys away in his jeans pocket.

Gosh, this is super awkward. Well, what did I expect? I don't know this guy, we've got nothing in common, and the situation per se is less than relaxing.

"So," I say, trying to loosen up the atmosphere. "What would you do if this was a regular night at home?"

"Probably play on the Xbox with my roommate."

"Sorry, no Xbox here, only that." I gesture to the small TV in the living room. "How about an old-fashioned chat?"

"Okay. You want to start scripting our relationship?"

"Nah, it's late, and I've no energy left. No creative juices flowing right now. Why don't we cover the basics for tonight? Where we're from, what our families are like, stuff like that."

"Yeah, great."

"You want a glass of wine?"

I need a drink. I'm definitely too nervous around this guy, and the feeling has to go quickly if my charade is to be believed by anyone.

"Yes, please." Diego nods and goes to settle on the couch.

"Red or white?"

"Whatever is fine."

I pick a bottle of red, grab two glasses, a corkscrew, and join him on the couch—sitting on the opposite, farthest end of it. I start maneuvering the corkscrew, damaging the cork more than I should in the process, when Diego says, "Here, let me."

I hand over the bottle and, in a couple of quick moves, Diego has the cork removed and undamaged. He pours two generous glasses.

"You're pretty handy with a bottle," I comment.

"Well, modeling and acting only pay for a small part of the bills. I'm a part-time server at a steakhouse downtown."

"When you're not busy being a Santa impersonator."

"Hey, I need all the money I can get. Wouldn't be here otherwise."

Yeah, right. We might need to get comfortable with each other, but I have to remember this is still an employer-employee kind of relationship.

"Is it going to be a problem for the restaurant—you not showing for a whole week over Christmas break?"

"Nah. I only work there three nights a week, and I've asked my roommate to cover for me. Screech could use the extra money, too, and the owner doesn't care as long as someone shows up to do the job."

"You guys call each other weird names. He called you 'Dunk' over the phone."

"Those are our gaming avatars."

"Oh, cool. Anyway, I'm glad I didn't mess with your work schedule."

"On the contrary." He flips Blair's business card between his fingers. "Is your friend's magazine legit?"

"Pretty new, but legit. Just a few months ago they did a fashion shoot with Saskia Landon."

Diego low whistles. "Then I'd better stay on your friend's good side."

"Blair is very friendly, usually. Earlier, she was just being overprotective. It's nothing personal."

"So, you two have been friends long?"

"Forever." I sip the wine, and its warm taste helps me ease into the conversation. "We grew up across the street from each other in Old Saybrook, a tiny coastal town a hundred miles north of here."

"Never heard of it."

"Small town." I shrug and take another sip of wine. "You from around here, too?"

"No, I'm originally from Chicago. My family still lives there."

"Is your family big?"

"Yep. I have three brothers, one older and two younger. And too many uncles, aunts, and cousins on both my dad and my mom's side to count. I guess that's what happens when an Irish man marries an Italian woman."

Oh, so that explains his uncommon name, the Mediterranean colorings of his skin and hair, and the fact that he speaks Italian paired with the Irish surname, green eyes, and freckles.

"What do your brothers do?"

"Johnathan, the older, is a cop, just been promoted to detective. Greg, the other middle child, is a fireman. And the baby, Adam, is a cop, too, but he's trying out for the FBI next year."

"Whoa, sounds like a committed public-service bunch."

"Well, my dad's been a cop for forty years…" He grimaces. "I'm the only one not to have followed in his footsteps, more or less."

"Do they give you a hard time about it?"

"Used to. I can't even remember how many sermons I had to hear about how acting wasn't a sound career choice. Now, I think they just feel sorry for me." Diego looks away in the distance. "My dream was easier to sell ten years ago. But after so many years without a breakthrough, they must wonder what I'm still doing in this city working as a server, and what my plan is."

"So, you're a member of the sibling-to-be-pitied club, huh?"

He frowns. "Why? Your parents aren't happy with your career?"

"Unfortunately, it has more to do with the lack of a diamond ring on my finger at the late age of thirty, and my inability to supply chubby grandkids."

"Oooooh, I know the drill," Diego sympathizes. "Two of my brothers are already married, and both have kids."

"Wow, you weren't kidding when you said you had a big family."

"Nope."

"You'll have to write me a family tree so I can learn their names."

"Why? It's not like you'll ever meet them."

"No, but my mom or sister could ask questions." Knowing them, they certainly will. "It'd be weird if I knew nothing about your family, at least the basics." I grab a pad and a pencil from the coffee table and hand them to him. "Just put down your mom, dad, brothers, and their spouses and kids' names."

Diego sets his almost-empty wine glass on the table and takes the notepad.

"Refill?" I ask, as he writes down the O'Donnell genealogy.

"Yes, please."

I top up his glass and wait for him to be done before asking my next question. "Why New York? Wouldn't LA have been the more obvious choice for an aspiring actor?"

Diego sighs. "Call me a romantic, but my heart is in the theater. Nothing can top performing in front of a live audience. The adrenaline of walking onto a stage, knowing you have to deliver every single time, and that if you make a mistake, there won't be a second take. It's priceless."

"So, what's your favorite show?"

"Ever, or recently?"

"Let's keep it recent."

"Then *Harry Potter and the Cursed Child*."

"Oh, I read the book—script, whatever—but it was a bit of a letdown."

"Of course, because it wasn't supposed to be experienced that way. You need to buy a ticket and go see the actual show. It'll blow your mind, I promise."

"Really? I don't know… I grew up reading Harry Potter… Do you remember the excitement when a new book was about to come out, and the desperation when you finished it and knew there'd be at least another two years to wait before the next one?"

"Yeah, it was the best and the worst."

"It's my favorite series ever, and I've read it so many times I think I've consumed the books beyond repair… so when *The Cursed Child* came out I was over the moon, but then I read it and… meh!"

Diego nods understandingly. "Nothing will ever top a new Harry Potter book, I agree. But if you approach *The Cursed Child* as a play and not a book, it's so much better. You won't regret watching it."

I smile. "Okay, maybe I'll try it…"

Diego's enthusiasm when he speaks about Broadway is contagious. This guy is turning out like nothing I would've expected from just looking at his picture. I thought he was going to be one of those vain, self-absorbed male models who pay more attention to their skin products than I do. But he's no egomaniac.

"What about you?" Diego asks. "Have you always wanted to work at an advertising agency?"

"I studied marketing and visual design in college, but I ended up in my line of work more by chance. I met my former boss at a recruiting event, and he gave an inspiring speech on what they did at KCU, on how they fostered new talent, and how a college graduate would thrive at their agency. So, I guess I chose a mentor more than a profession. And it worked out pretty well. I love what I do and the people I do it with, so…"

Diego grins. "Now you're only missing that diamond ring on your finger, and to pop out the standard two point five chubby babies before you turn forty."

I laugh. "Nailed it."

I'm not sure if it's the wine or the fact that we've been talking for a while, but I'm getting more relaxed around him. Same as if there was a regular person on the couch next to me, instead of an impossibly sexy hunk from another planet.

We chat a little more and finish the wine before I realize how late it is.

"Sorry," I say, getting up. My head is dizzier than I'd like. "I have an early morning tomorrow. You?"

"I switched my shifts at the restaurant to lunch, so I'll be free in the evenings."

"Perfect. Well, you have your keys, and the Wi-Fi password is on the back of the box." I point at the modem sitting next to the TV. "The fridge is stocked if you want to eat something; just beware of Blair's vegetarian crap."

"I will." Diego smiles and gets up. And I watch, astonished, as he gathers both our glasses and the bottle and rinses the former in the sink after throwing the latter in the recycle bin. Good looking, down to earth, *and* with perfect manners. *Impressive!*

"Mind if I use the bathroom first?" I ask.

He shrugs. "It's your house."

Feeling again awkward, I wave. "Good night, then."

"Night."

When I come out of the bathroom, Diego is in Blair's room, out of sight. I slip into my room, change into my PJs and, feeling a bit silly, I lock the door.

***

The next morning, my phone starts ringing the moment I resurface above ground from the subway station closest to work.

I lodge my earbuds in place and pick up.

"Are you alive?" Blair demands, as I begin the short walk to my office building. "Where are you?"

"I answered the phone; that should be a good indication I'm still breathing," I say, stopping at a red traffic light and wrapping the collar of my coat tighter around my neck. "I'm walking to the office. You?"

"Me, too. Sorry, I've just been so worried all night."

The light turns green and I cross the street. "No need to be; Diego is a perfectly nice guy."

"Nice or not, Richard agrees with me: you were reckless to invite a total stranger into our house."

"You told him?" I almost stop in the middle of the road, but the Manhattan pedestrian crowd prompts me forward.

"Of course I did. How else was I supposed to explain my late night pick up request?"

"Saying you wanted to spend time with him?"

"Oh, please, I'd just left him, he would've known something was up. He also said he wants to meet this guy before we drive home with him."

"Oh my gosh," I sigh, exasperated, as I open the door of my favorite Starbucks. "Richard is just as paranoid as you are."

"No, we're both responsible adults."

"Hold on a second..." I say, then mouth, "The usual," to the barista, switch my phone to the Starbucks app to pay, and go wait in line for my order. "Okay, Mr. and Mrs. Responsible Adults, you can both relax..."

"Yeah, why?"

"Diego's entire family is in law enforcement. He's hardly serial killer material.”

“Mmm, hello? Have you seen *Dexter?*”

“Dexter only zapped the bad guys, so I should be safe anyway, no?”

“Unless one of his serial killer buddies decides to take it out on the girlfriend.”

“*Fake* girlfriend, and, Blair, life isn’t a TV show. But if Richard really wants to meet Diego, tell your boyfriend to come to the casting on Tuesday. But please also tell him to be subtle and not to interrogate Diego, deal?”

“Oh, great, I wasn’t sure he’d come.”

“Why? Because you took his fingerprints? It’s a good opportunity for him. He’s a professional; why wouldn’t he come?”

“I don’t know… He could be busy planning his next murder?”

“I’m hanging up.”

“No, nooo. I was just kidding. So, how did your first night go? What did you guys do?”

“Skinny mocha vanilla latte for Nikki,” a barista shouts.

I shove the phone back into my coat pocket and grab the coffee, gladly wrapping my hands around the warm paper cup, before returning to the freezing temperatures of a New York morning in December.

“We opened a bottle of wine and chatted, you know, to cover the basics: family, education, career…”

“And how was it?”

“Pretty cozy; he’s an easy guy to talk to. I mean, for someone that looks so, mmm…”

Blair supplies the definition for me, “Freaking hot?”

“Yeah.”

“You’re not getting *too* cozy, are you? He’s there only because you’re paying him.”

“I’m aware, thank you. I was just saying that I expected a narcissistic showoff, and instead, he’s rather easy going, funny, even… But don’t worry, he’s not my type at all.”

“Yeah, about that… I was wondering why you picked someone so… *not you.* Isn’t your family going to get suspicious?”

I stop a few steps away from my building’s main entrance. “You want the ugly truth? The one I could tell only my best friend without being judged?"

"Yeah-ah…"

"He's Julia's type," I confess. "For once, I want her to be jealous of me, even if it's just for a second and it's all fake. Am I too pathetic?"

"No, you're not, and I don't have any siblings to compete with, so I'm really not an expert on the subject of sisterly envy. I can't even begin to think what I'd do if my imaginary sister was marrying Richard, so…"

"Thank you," I say, relieved she's in my corner no matter what crazy ideas get into my head. "Listen, I'm at the office, I gotta go."

"Yeah, I'm almost there, too. Okay, I'll talk to you soon, and please send regular texts to let me know you're alive."

I roll my eyes but smile. "I will."

***

I haven't been seated at my desk five minutes before my cell phone goes off again. It's Julia. Ugh, majorly not in the mood for another wedding planning rant. I let the call go unanswered. Three seconds later, my internal line rings, signaling Melanie is calling me.

"Yeah?" I say.

"I have your sister on line two."

I could tell Melanie to make an excuse for me—that I'm in a meeting, or not at the office—but I know Julia. If she's decided we have to talk now, she'll just pester me until I surrender and answer. Compared to my sister, my mom is a restrained serial caller.

I sigh. "All right, put the call through." Melanie hangs up. I wait for the external line's button to flash and push it. "Hello?"

"Mom says I can't have your room."

"Good morning to you, too," I reply. "And, yes, Mom would be correct."

"But Nikki, I'm bringing my fiancé home for the holidays. We can't stay in my room. Yours is bigger."

"Our rooms are exactly the same."

"Okay, but I can't make Paul sleep in my castle princess bed."

"I'm sorry about that, but when given the chance to choose a bed, you should've picked something more practical."

"I was eight."

"And I was ten. Didn't stop me from ordering a perfectly sensible queen bed."

Truth is, my only guiding principle at the time was to do the exact opposite of what Julia did. So, when she opted for a fairy tale bunk bed—pink, complete with turrets, crenellations, and tulle drapes—I went for the most serious, adult-looking bed I found at the shop.

"But Paul won't fit…"

"Then ask Mom to get rid of the princess bed and buy a replacement."

"But I love that bed."

"Well, sorry… You'll have to pick: either Paul sleeps in the princess bed, or the bed goes."

I take a little smudge of satisfaction in knowing Julia is not going to have exactly everything she wants.

"But why can't you switch?"

"Because my boyfriend won't fit in the princess bed any better."

"Oh, so you really have a boyfriend?"

"Yeah," I say.

"Since when? I thought Mom misunderstood."

Sure, because it would be so impossible for me to have a boyfriend. No matter that it sort of is impossible. The fact that Julia would just assume… Grrrrrrr. I bite the receiver before I continue.

"A few months."

"Why didn't you tell me? Who is this guy?"

"Jules, I'm just more private with my life than you, and right now I'm at the office, *working*. I don't have time to gossip."

"Work, work, work. You always have to work. I've been trying your private phone for an hour this morning, and it was always busy."

"I was talking to someone else."

"Who, your boyfriend?"

"No, Blair."

"Oh, the sister you wish you'd had."

I stare at the ceiling, trying to keep calm. It's definitely too early for one of Julia's dramatic scenes. "Why are you throwing a tantrum?" I ask.

"Because you're dating someone and didn't even think of telling me. I had to learn it from Mom!" she whines. "How long has Blair known him? It's like I don't exist for you."

Julia and I have never been close, and since she's been dating Paul, the distance has increased. I love her, she's my sister, and if she needed a kidney I'd give it to her without a moment's hesitation. But we're so different, and with her dating the guy I love… It's just hard.

"I'm sorry, Jules, but until recently I wasn't sure the relationship was that serious, or even worth mentioning."

"But why didn't you tell me the other day?"

"That was your moment, your big announcement… I didn't want to steal your thunder."

"Really?"

"Really."

"So who is this guy? When am I going to meet him?"

"At Christmas like the rest of the family."

"Why? We're both in the city; can't we meet up earlier?"

"I'm sorry, but no. I'm super busy until the agency closes, and Diego is super busy, too."

"Diego… Mmm, cool name. What does he look like?"

"Julia." I use my best older sister tone. "I don't have time to chat, but I'm sure you're going to like him." *Maybe a bit too much,* an evil little voice adds inside my head. "I really have to go now."

"You're a buzz kill."

"Love you, too. Bye." I hang up and lean back in my chair, massaging my temples.

Another twelve days to C-Day and I'm already about to explode. I just hope this mastermind plan of mine won't epically backfire on me.

Seven

Baby, It's Cold Outside

When I get home that evening, the house smells like… mmm… my mom's kitchen. For a second I panic, thinking she couldn't resist meeting my boyfriend and decided to drop by unannounced. But I let out a breath of relief as soon as I step out of the hallway and see there's only Diego seated at the kitchen bar, eating dinner.

"Hey," I say. "What smells good? Did you make dinner?"

"No, the chef at the restaurant always feeds me scraps. Sorry I didn't wait for you, but I was starving."

"Don't worry, I usually don't get home this late. What are you having?"

"Homemade lasagna, best in New York. There's plenty left, and it's still warm. Marisa always gives me way too much. Want some?"

My dinner plan was to order something from the Thai restaurant down the street, which is what I usually do when Blair isn't home to prepare a healthy dinner for the both of us. But homemade lasagna beats that a hundred to one.

"Sure there's enough for two?" I ask.

"Yeah, even three or four."

"All right, then."

I grab a plate, a glass, and a fork from the cabinets and sit at the kitchen bar next to him.

Diego scoops me a generous helping of lasagna out of the aluminum tray. "Here's the best lasagna you'll ever have—unless you meet my mom. No one beats my mom's."

I take a bite and... "Mmm... this is delicious." The lasagna is both creamy and rich, but not overwhelming. I could devour a whole tray of this.

"Told ya." Diego smiles. "So, how was your day?"

"Stupid, yours?"

"A regular shift at the restaurant, nothing exciting," he says, then smirks. "What happens on a stupid day?"

"Your boss poaches an unhappy client from another agency, and delivers the pitch but only brings the creative team with him..."

Diego finishes up his plate and rounds the bar to rinse his dish and drop it in the dishwasher. Gosh, he really is tidy. I would've dropped the dirty dish in the sink and maybe splashed water on it. I tend to postpone house chores until they become overwhelmingly necessary.

"So." Diego leans against the counter as I scarf down the last bites of lasagna. "Did the creatives drop the ball?"

"Oh, no, they wowed the client."

"And that's bad because?"

"Every creative pitch has to be vetted by a producer because we're the reality check. We understand what can be done in how much time, and at what budget… You leave the creatives free, and they'll go overboard."

"And they did this time?"

"For sure. The ad they pitched is brilliant and witty, but it's a production nightmare." I finish the lasagna and lick the fork before dropping it on the empty plate. "Too many actors, too many locations, and too little time. Not to talk about the budget; we'll be lucky if we break even on this one."

Promptly, Diego scoops up the plate, rinses it, and drops it into the dishwasher. "Where do you keep the dish soap?"

"There're pods under the sink."

He loads one, studies the dishwasher's buttons for a few seconds, pushes a couple, and the machine awakens.

"Your boss must really trust you if he put you on this assignment," Diego says, coming back to my side of the counter.

I stand up and move to the couch, where I kick off my shoes. "You have a future in management, you know?"

Diego joins me on the sofa, sticking to "his" end. "Yeah, why?"

"That's exactly what my boss told me to sell me the project, '…You're the only one who can pull it off… Can't trust anyone else… Blah, blah, blah…'"

Diego smirks. "Then it must be true."

"True or not, the bottom line stays the same: I'm screwed. There's even a cat in the ad. I mean, *a cat.*"

"You don't like cats?"

"I love cats. I'm one hundred percent a cat person. But on set, they're a nightmare. Trained animals are expensive, and a scene to turn out decent needs a million takes, meaning long hours and money and time I don't have. What about you, cats or dogs?"

Please say cats, please say cats…

"Cats…"

Yay! I do a mental victory dance. "How come? Guys usually go for dogs."

"Blame my mom; we've never had less than three cats in the house. And she keeps feeding all the neighborhood cats as well, stray or not. So I guess I was groomed into being a cat person."

"Great, I can't stand dogs."

"Why?"

"They lick, they're smelly… Ew, gross."

"Doesn't your roommate have a dog?"

"Chevron? She's different. She's a cat's soul trapped in a dog's body, know what I mean?"

Diego chuckles. "Not really."

"You'll see when you meet her."

He shakes his head, amused.

"What?" I ask self-consciously.

"You make little sense sometimes."

"Why?"

"A cat person who claims to hate dogs usually doesn't own one."

"Correction, my roommate has a dog. I've begged her to get a cat from the day we moved in together, but she always said the apartment was too small to have a pet. Then she found a stray puppy and suddenly we had enough room for a sixty-pound dog. So, really, it's her not making sense."

Diego nods. "Agreed."

"Hey, you want something to drink? Sorry I didn't offer. We have wine, beer…"

"Are you drinking?"

"No, my brain gets too scrambled if I drink two nights in a row, and I need to be on top of my game this week."

"Tomorrow's the weekend."

"Well, yeah, but thanks to my new assignment I have to drop by the office. You have your Santa thing tomorrow, right?"

"Yeah, the afternoon shift from two to six."

"That's perfect. We can go Christmas shopping together in the morning, work after lunch, and meet up again for dinner later. Sound good?"

"Christmas shopping?"

"Yeah, we need to buy each other presents. My family is big on present unwrapping on the twenty-fifth."

"Oh." He frowns.

"Don't worry, I'm buying my present. We just have to think of something smart, and unique, and romantic…"

Diego looks like he's just swallowed lemons. "Fine, but I should warn you: I hate Christmas shopping."

I laugh. "That makes two of us, but we gotta do what we gotta do… Anything on your letter to Santa?"

"Nothing you can put under wrapping paper…" he says, with that Broadway spark in his eyes.

"Know the feeling," I agree. My biggest Christmas wish has nothing to do with material things, either. And anyway, we're all supposed to be good at Christmas, so I can't really wish for my sister's life to crumble to pieces… But I could wish to feel less freaking alone all the time, or to forget Paul, or to fall in love with someone who loves me back for a change… Yeah, those would all be much better wishes…

"Are you okay?" Diego asks.

"Yeah, why?"

"You sort of went all glassy-eyed."

"Sorry." I massage my temples. "I'm just exhausted. What do you say we call it a night so we can start early on the shopping tomorrow morning?

Diego grimaces. "Ho ho ho," he chants in a deep voice nothing like his own.

"I never understood how you actors do that."

"Do what?"

"Change your voice on command."

"It's all diaphragm, throat, and nose work." With every word he changes his voice—throaty, nasal, husky—making me laugh. "And many hours of practice."

"That's amazing."

"All right, boss," he says, back to his normal tone. He gets up and offers me a hand. "Let's go to bed."

I take his hand and he lifts me up, and for a second we end up standing really close to each other. So close I can smell his clean soap scent… simple, but intoxicating. And I haven't had sex in too long to stand this close to the sexiest man I've ever met. And even if I don't like him that way, well… I'm still made of flesh…

"Okay, then," I say, sounding like an awkward teenager and trying hard not to blush. "Good night."

I move past him and go hide in my room. I barely hear his soft, "Night," reply before I shut the door and lock myself in.

***

I blink my eyes open to the sound of a blow dryer running.

What time is it?

A quick peek at my watch tells me it's already ten. So much for an early start. Sometimes I wish I could be one of those early risers, people who wake up at five a.m. on autopilot to go for a run. Someone like Blair. My roommate is so healthily annoying. But put me in a cozy bed and I could sleep in until noon every day. I don't know why I didn't set an alarm last night. Easy, because my phone has a weekly alarm programmed to let me sleep on the weekends.

I throw away the covers, get up, and swap PJs for a pair of sweatpants and a T-shirt. In front of the wardrobe mirror, I try to flatten my hair, preventing it from sticking out in all directions. I so wish it was still long enough to pull up in a bun. I miss buns.

Bun-less and still crazy-haired, I venture into the hall and almost collide with a semi-naked Diego. He's wearing only a towel around his hips, presenting me with the kind of naked chest usually reserved for steamy romance book covers. I try not to look, but my gaze gets drawn to the inviting V of muscle disappearing just below the towel, and I involuntarily bite my lower lip. I mentally slap myself, and my eyes snap back up to his face. His hair, fresh from the blow dry, is wilder than mine and gives him a tousled look that's hard to resist.

"Hi," I say.

"Morning."

"You been up long?"

"A couple of hours…"

"Why didn't you wake me?"

"I know you wanted an early start, but it didn't feel right to barge into your room to wake you, so I worked out a little instead."

A glorious image of him doing pushups and crunches bare chested is now permanently ingrained in my brain. And of course he'd be the kind of person who wakes up early on a Saturday to work out. A body like that just doesn't sculpt itself. I think of my soft belly and take back everything I just thought. Early risers are horrible people whose mission in life is to make us late sleepers feel guilty about our love for cushy pillows and snuggles under the comforter.

"No, you're right," I say. "I should've set an alarm… What do you say we go out for breakfast?" I stare at my watch. "It's too late to go shopping now, anyway. We can eat something and lay down the basis of our fake relationship instead."

"Yeah, I'm starving."

"Great, just give me time for a quick shower. Meet here in thirty?"

He winks at me. "All right, boss."

My stomach responds with a weird little flip. Maybe it wasn't the wink. Right, I'm probably just hungry.

We switch ends in the narrow hall, and I do my best to stick to the wall and not give in to the temptation to brush against all that bared muscle. Obstacle surpassed, I dive into the bathroom and hop into the shower.

One perk of short hair is that it takes less time to dry. So, in just under thirty minutes I'm all set and ready to go grab a coffee. Clad in black trousers and a gray knit sweater, casual-wear appropriate for the office, I go meet Diego down the hall and stop dead in my tracks again. Dressed Diego is no less heart-stopping than half-naked Diego. He's wearing a pair of light-faded jeans that fit his rear side so well they should be made illegal. And his biker jacket does nothing to tone down the sexiness. My mouth goes a little dry—too much sex appeal to handle on an empty stomach and without an ounce of caffeine in my system. I need breakfast.

We opt for the Starbucks around the corner. I order my usual skinny mocha vanilla latte and note that he goes for black coffee, super manly. As for food, we both get glazed donuts. At least he's not also one of those protein bars, healthy-eater types. I mean, nothing wrong with keeping a healthy diet and exercise routine, but I can't stand extremists. Julia sort of is a food extremist, but of course, I still love her. She's my sister; I have to.

"You always get black coffee?" I ask, as we sit at a table by the window.

"No, sometimes I venture into the wild lands of cappuccinos. Why?"

"Just trying to learn your habits. We should know these things about each other since we're"—I make air quotes—"dating. Skinny mocha vanilla lattes are my poison, and I prefer Starbucks."

"So you order fat-free milk, but a side of glazed, fried pastry is okay?"

I shrug. "Coffee tastes as good without the fatty milk and sugary syrup. Can't say the same about donuts." And to show my appreciation, I take a huge bite.

Diego smiles. "Duly noted." He rolls his coffee cup between his hands a few times, turning pensive.

"What?" I prompt him.

"Can I ask you one last time why you're doing this?"

"I already told—"

"Yeah, you need a date for the holidays. But… can I be honest?"

"Sure."

"Before getting to know you, I thought you had to have a major issue that scared men away or something, but spending the last few days together, you don't seem that…"

"Crazy?" I supply. "Well, thanks," I say, irritated.

"Don't get me wrong, I'm not trying to insult you. I only want to understand why a woman like you needs to hire someone to be her date."

My nostrils flare. "And by 'a woman like me' you mean?"

"Beautiful, smart, with a successful career, and with no clear social awkwardness… You shouldn't have any problems finding a man the traditional way."

That mollifies me a little… Did he really call me beautiful? I stop myself from asking for confirmation and answer his question instead. "The problem isn't that I *can't* find a boyfriend *ever*. It's that I'm single *right now* while my baby sister just got engaged, and that's going to point an even bigger bullseye on the lack of that diamond ring on my finger. And this year, I can't bear it." I leave out the why. "Also, I don't want to be in a relationship for the sake of dating, and my job makes it hard to put in the time to find that special person."

And being in love with my sister's fiancé doesn't help, I add in my head.

"So you prefer to hire your dates off a catalog." Diego tries to keep a straight face, but the corners of his mouth twitch.

"Now you're just making fun of me."

He finally lets the smile take over his mouth, and gosh if he isn't a sight to behold when he smiles like that. "Sorry. I thought my mom was scary with her constant nagging about me needing to settle down, but you make your family sound so much worse..."

"They are, believe me, and that's why we need to be prepared if we want to fool them."

"Okay, so what's the story?"

"Let's start easy. Our first date, how did it happen?"

"We met in a bar?"

"Nah, too prosaic. We should stick to reality as much as we can, like they teach in spy movies."

"What's your angle here? We can't say you picked me off a catalog."

My time to smirk. "Actually, we sort of can..."

"How?"

"You came to the agency for a casting, and that's where we met."

"And how did we move from the casting to the dating?"

"Ah, and the plot thickens... Any ideas?"

He frowns, concentrating. "You called me to say I had the job, and I told you I'd rather have a date."

"That sounds farfetched."

"Why?"

"Would you really have asked someone like me on a date?"

"And by 'someone like you,' you mean?"

"Someone who wouldn't look at home in a bikini catalog," I reply honestly.

He grimaces. "Ah, yes. Because we models can only date other models..."

"No, but..."

"But?"

"You're good looking, you know?"

Diego nods, serious, not one bit mollified.

"Above-average good looking..." I insist.

He nods again.

"So, it'd make sense you'd want to date someone as gorgeous as you."

"Why?"

"Because you can. Because why not?"

"Maybe because before I jump into bed with someone, I need a bit more of a connection. I'm not a horny teenager," he says harshly.

"Sorry, did I offend you?"

"Not really, I have thick skin. But don't assume I decide who to sleep with based only on how they look. Last time I slept with a woman only because she had a big rack, I was eighteen and in high school. So, when was the last time you slept with someone only because they had a nice ass?"

Totally against my will, an image of his perfectly round buns wrapped in white boxer briefs slips before my eyes. Those are buttocks that could definitely make me skip the need for an emotional connection.

I swallow, hoping I'm not blushing too hard. "I haven't... I mean... not really." At my visible embarrassment, his features soften a little. "Okay," I concede. "You've made your point. I won't make superficial assumptions about you from now on. Sorry."

He finally smiles. "Apology accepted, boss."

I try to bring the conversation back to its original track. "So, you asked me on a date. Why?"

"What do you mean, why?"

"What made you give up a job for me? If we tell that story, either my mom or my sister is going to ask why you were instantly smitten with me."

"Why? They can't accept a man could just ask you out?"

"We're women, we need details."

"Okay, I'll have an answer for when they ask."

"Can't you share it with me first?"

"No," he says, smirking. "It isn't ready yet."

I scowl at him.

"Don't worry." Diego leans forward in his chair. "I'll come up with something cheesy enough to sate your mom and sister's romance cravings."

I stare at him, unconvinced.

"Hey, I'm good at this stuff, I swear." He makes the Boy Scout salute.

I sure hope he is, with what I'm paying him. And if it turns out he sucks, I hope Mom and Julia will be too distracted by how good he looks to notice.

"Okay," I say. "I'm going to trust you on this. Oh, one last detail: What was the ad for?"

"Deodorant," Diego says without hesitation.

"Deodorant?"

"Yeah, what's wrong with it?"

"It isn't very romantic."

"We can say perfume or chocolate if you prefer, but deodorant makes it sound less staged, more real."

He has a point. "Deodorant it is."

An email flashes on my phone screen, and I get a peek of the time as well. "Wow, it's super late. Don't you have to be at the mall in like twenty minutes?"

He stares at his watch. "You're right."

We both get up, don our jackets, and exit the coffee shop in a hurry. It doesn't take long to be back at my building, where we stop outside to say goodbye.

"The subway is that way," I say. "I hope I haven't made you too late?"

"Nah, don't worry," Diego says, "it's only a ten-minute ride on the bike." He unlocks the saddle to take out his helmet. Then, as if on second thought, he adds, "Hey, you want a ride? Your office is on the way."

"No, no, you're already late, I don't want to make it worse."

"And you won't; we have all the time we need."

"I don't have a helmet," I protest.

"And I always carry a spare one." He opens a sort of detachable trunk and offers me a black helmet matching his.

"Err…"

When he sees me still hesitating, he asks, "You're not afraid of bikes, are you?"

"I wouldn't know," I say. "I've never been on one."

"Come on." Diego smiles encouragingly. "No girlfriend of mine, fake or otherwise, could skip a ride on my bike."

I quickly censor all the inappropriate scenarios my degenerate brain conjured up at the "take a ride on my bike" comment, and bravely nod, taking the helmet.

Eight

Sleigh Ride

The moment I climb on the bike behind Diego, I know I've made a mistake. This black monster is way too wobbly and unstable for my tastes.

At first, I try to keep my palms respectfully flat against Diego's sides while he backs the bike up. But the second he twists the accelerator, I wrap my arms around his waist as tightly as I can, my gloved fingers gripping his leather jacket for dear life. Especially when the bike stumbles off the curb with a roar of the engine, tires skidding on the road. The rumble is deafening; it vibrates up my legs to reach deep into my guts. I close my eyes, glue my head—helmet and all—to his broad back, and hope this ride will really only take ten minutes.

Diego works the clutches, making the bike gather speed, and I can't help but grip tighter as a little scream escapes my lips. Diego's chest starts to shake under my arms, and I have a strong suspicion he's laughing at me and my fear.

I couldn't care less. Right now, I'm focused on surviving the ride and getting off this death trap as soon as possible. Honestly, I don't understand how other women can find this sexy. Okay, I get the intimacy—physical, for how close the bodies touch, and emotional, for the trust one has to put in the driver to give away all control. And some women might like not being in control, or find the drop in their stomach at every acceleration thrilling, but I'm not one of them.

For the whole journey, I'm so pumped up with adrenaline I don't notice the chill. I'm sure riding a bike in December should feel colder than this, but right now my universe is made only of Diego's body and how hard I can cling to him. My chest is pressed so close to his back we might've been fused.

Every turn, incline, and acceleration makes my heart pound faster.

If this is what flying feels like, I'm glad humans were born without wings.

When we finally stop, I still hold onto him and keep my eyelids closed. It could be only a traffic light, and if I open my eyes now, I'm not sure I'll be able to handle the rest of the ride.

"Boss." Diego tries to turn back to look at me, but I'm holding on too tight. "We're here."

I'm still too scared to move.

"Nikki?" Diego calls again. "You can let go now."

Slowly, I release my koala grip on him and get off. I unhook my helmet and hand it to him, saying, "Let's never do this again."

"Don't say never, boss." Diego grins at me from underneath the helmet. I can tell he's smiling from the crinkles around his eyes. "It might grow on you…"

And with that he winks at me, pushes down on a pedal to revive the engine, opens the clutches, and disappears among the Manhattan traffic, leaving me standing on the curb in front of my building with legs still shaky from the sheer effort of pressing my thighs against his.

***

"I should buy you something for the bike," I say.

It's Sunday morning, and Diego and I are braving the holiday crowds to complete our Christmas shopping. I've already settled Julia with the fanciest wedding planner I could find in the mall's bookstore, Mom with a new recipe book, and Dad with the latest Ken Follett bestseller. Not the most original or thought-out presents, I'm aware, but I despise gift shopping.

I may or may not have also bought a novel for Paul a while ago. At the time, I wasn't even sure if I'd ever give it to him. But if he's going to spend the holidays at our house… I sort of have to. And, I mean, it's not like a thriller book—hardcover, special edition, signed by his favorite author—will send the message, *"I'm in love with you. Dump my sister and marry me instead."* Right?

"You need any new accessories?" I continue. "Gloves?" I couldn't help but notice his are a little worn out.

"Biker gear is expensive." Diego shrugs. "Why not get me a book like everybody else?"

"No, you're my *boyfriend*. I need to buy you something different, something special. You know a good biker gear shop?"

"There's one closer to your apartment; we can stop there on the way home."

"All right."

"We can go after buying my present for you. Have you decided what I'm getting you yet?"

I chew my lower lip. "I don't know."

Diego raises his brows. "A woman who can't choose her present. Impossible!"

"The best thing would be to get me a book. Or a cat. But I can't do the cat until Blair moves out, and it needs to be something showier than a book to impress my family."

"Remember, I'm a struggling artist." Diego grins.

"That's why we have to find a nice, thoughtful, but inexpensive gift." I stare at the shopping windows surrounding us, kind of lost. "See the problem now?"

Just as the words leave my lips, we pass in front of a jewelry shop, and I'm captivated by a glass cube showcasing three rings, identical but for the color: one in silver, one in gold, and the last one in rose gold. The design is simple: plain gold bands, but... *with ears!*

"See something you like?" Diego asks.

I smile, pushing the shop's door open. "How about a cat ring?"

A woman in a bright-red suit hurries up to us, making me wonder if she's wearing a special holiday suit or if they go 'round all year long wearing that almost blinding shade of red.

"Hello, how may I help you today?" She has a chirpy, honey-like voice, which fits the festive-bonanza décor of the shop perfectly.

"We're here to buy a ring," I say.

"A ring, how wonderful." She twinkles at me. "Christmas present?" Her big, it's-that-time-of-the-year, sparkly eyes set on Diego next.

Err... She thinks we're a real couple Christmas shopping. Well, why wouldn't she?

I glance at Diego for help—but he's staring around the shop, completely unaware. And there's no way I'm launching into the whole story of how Diego is only a for-hire boyfriend in front of a bunch of strangers—there are three shop assistants in total, all in eye-sore red.

"Yeah." I smile awkwardly. "It's a gift, I mean, sort of—"

"That's wonderful! I'm Evelyn, and I'll be happy to assist you today," Evelyn chirps. "Did you already have something specific in mind?"

"Yes," I say. "The cat rings by the windows."

"Oh." Another one of the women in red sighs. "They're so cute, aren't they?"

"Goodness." Evelyn takes my arm, steering me toward the showcase window, and leans in, lowering her voice to speak in a woman-to-woman tone. "The girls and I have a little contest every holiday season to find the cutest couple, and you've just knocked all competition out of the park! He's quite the catch. Lucky you!"

I should be proud of the admiration Diego is inspiring. After all, I've hired him to make sure my whole family shuts the hell up about my singlehood for one Christmas. But this is actually painful. What do I say?

"Err, thank you?"

"Oh, I'm sorry, I didn't mean to embarrass you," Evelyn says charmingly as she unhooks a bunch of keys from her neck and uses a tiny silver one to open the back of the glass cube displaying the cat rings.

She retrieves the dark-blue velvet tray holding the rings and sets it on a nearby glass cabinet. "These are our cat rings. They come in different materials, and are at different price points…"

Diego finally hovers next to me, listening in on Evelyn's explanation.

"…These ones here are all made of 10-carat gold: white, regular, and rose. And they cost \$99.99." She opens a white drawer under the glass cabinet and takes out two small, blue velvet boxes, which contain two silvery rings. "These are sterling silver, our cheapest option at \$29.99, and platinum, our most expensive at \$499.99."

"Better get the cheapest one," Diego chimes in. "Can't really tell the difference with the other ones."

Evelyn's next comment is cut off in a sort of gasp. "The materials may seem all the same right now, but the durability of platinum over time is superior by far. It's such a precious, timeless metal that will last a lifetime."

"Guess they can all make it to Christmas, though." Diego shrugs at her, and then, turning to me, he adds, "You can always tell your family it's platinum."

Gosh, he has *no* clue.

Evelyn's jaw has dropped to the floor by now, and I don't have the heart to look up at the other women. I'm sure I'd find equally crestfallen faces. There's nothing I can say.

"Sterling silver it is," I offer lamely. "Can I try it on for sizes? I should be a six."

For a moment, Evelyn seems unable to speak. "A size six! Right," she manages at last, sounding strangled. "In sterling silver, lovely. So pretty."

She collects the right size and offers me the ring.

I slip it on my finger and… "It's a perfect fit."

"It is!" Evelyn is obviously forcing herself to nod animatedly. "So nice!" She exchanges looks with the other red women, who all hastily chime in.

"Adorable!"

"Lovely choice!"

Their bright smiles *so* don't reach their eyes. One woman is actually blushing in mortification for me. I want to disappear.

"Would you like this gift wrapped?" Evelyn asks as she moves behind the register.

"Yes, please," I say.

"Maggie, can you take care of the wrapping?" she asks.

One of the women shuffles close by and grabs the box, careful to avoid looking me in the eye.

"With all our rings we also offer a care plan," Evelyn says. "For only ten dollars you get three cleanings and one re-sizing should you ever need it."

"A care plan on a thirty dollar ring?" Diego lets out an incredulous laugh. "That's such a rip-off."

"Just the ring," I hasten to say, before the situation gets any more awkward.

"Great." Evelyn taps the register keys, unfazed, almost

anesthetized by Diego's lack of romanticism. "Would you be paying cash or credit, sir?" she asks Diego pointedly, her bright smile frozen solid.

Diego raises an eyebrow at me.

"Credit," I mutter, lowering my gaze to pull my credit card out of my wallet.

"So… you'll be paying for the ring, madam." She can barely gather control of herself. "Wonderful! That's… wonderful. No problem at all." Evelyn is breathing harder and harder. "Absolutely fine." She processes the payment and hands me the receipt to sign, still trying to keep the smile on. It's obviously taking up all her energy.

The other woman comes back with my package, her expression now openly aghast and hands it to me with an almost apologetic nod of support.

I'm under a hot shower of mortification. I nearly melt with embarrassment.

Diego, of course, has noticed nothing.

"We wish you both very happy holidays." Evelyn makes a supreme effort to stay pleasant as she ushers us to the door. But just as Diego walks out, she holds me back, pulling me by the elbow. "I know this is none of my business, hon," she whispers urgently in my ear. "But looks aren't everything, trust me."

As I finally exit the shop, Diego is waiting for me in the least over-packed corner of the hall, looking impatient.

"What was that about?" he asks. "Everything okay?"

"Yes! Super!"

I'm still flushed, and I just want to get out of this damned mall. A quick glance back toward the shop reveals Evelyn and the other women talking animatedly and gesticulating out the window toward Diego with outraged looks on their faces.

"What's up?" Diego frowns. "That shop assistant seemed a little weird—"

"She was," I confirm, rolling my eyes.

Can he really be this clueless? Yes, he's a man. So I spell it out for him. "She thought you were my boyfriend making me buy my own Christmas present."

Light slowly dawns on Diego's face, and he bursts into laughter. "So that's why they were all giving me the stink eye."

"Sorry, they all assumed you were a cheap bastard. I feel horrible."

Diego looks lost again. "Why? I don't care what three shop assistants think of me."

"Not even a bit?"

"Nope."

His face is relaxed, calm. He really doesn't care. How can he not care what other people think?

Well, that's probably why I'm the one hiring a fake boyfriend, and he's not.

Nine

A Purrfect Christmas

Mr. Fluff will run, jump, sit, and cuddle on request. He's a quick learner, and in just a few hours this magnificent exemplar of Silver Tabby British Shorthair can be trained to perform just about any task. At Le Paw Animal Talent Management Agency, we strive to provide our clients with the perfect animal for any job. We will provide you with expert advice and coordination to make all your productions spectacular.

I click on the casting video that shows Mr. Fluff playing with a plumed cat wand, chasing after a mechanical mouse… Then he eats, jumps, runs up the stairs, and the video ends with a close-up of the cat resting on a white couch while purring loudly. He seems indeed like a wonderful actor.

I grab the landline receiver and dial the agency number.

"Le Paw Animal Talent Management Agency," a female voice says, picking up on the second ring. "How can I help you?"

"Hi, hello, this is Nikki Moore from KCU Advertising. I was calling to inquire about one of your actors…" And, yes, I feel stupid saying this, but pet agencies can be a tad sensitive, and I've learned that if I don't refer to the animals as "professionals" or "talent" they can get pretty prickly. "Err… Mr. Fluff?"

"Oh, sure, Mr. Fluff is one of our best performers, always in demand. Needs a month's advance booking at the very least."

"A month?" I gasp. "You mean he wouldn't be available this Thursday?"

"As in, the day after tomorrow?" the woman asks, appalled.

"Yes?"

"Sorry, ma'am. He's fully booked through January. Cats are very popular for Valentine's Day commercials, you know?"

Yes, I *do* know. It's my job to know. "Thank you very much anyway," I say, discouraged.

Third hole in the water today.

"You're welcome. And if you ever need our services in the future, don't hesitate to call us back. Le Paw Animal Talent Management Agency wishes you a purrfect Christmas."

Did she really just wish me a purrfect Christmas? I smash the receiver on its case three times, imagining it to be the face of the creative who suggested a tabby cat would suit the commercial better than the Russian Blue I'd hired.

It's Tuesday afternoon, and I'm losing a battle with time to wrap up this last-minute job that Teddy—my stupid holiday-loving boss—dumped on me. I'm about to click the link for the next animal "talent" agency when my personal phone starts vibrating somewhere on my desk. I can't see it; it must be hidden under some sheets of paper, so I ignore its insistent buzzing and let the call go unanswered. Five seconds later the vibration starts again, disrupting my concentration. If I keep ignoring whoever's calling, then curiosity would just bug me for the rest of the afternoon, slowing my progress even further. So I unceremoniously shuffle the piles of documents aside until I find the phone.

It's Blair.

Except for my "still alive" texts, we haven't talked much since she's moved out of the house, so I pick up.

"Hello?"

"Guess what I'm looking at right now?" she asks.

I sigh. "I don't have time for games, I'm swamped with work."

"Oh, what are you doing?"

"Watching cat videos. I'm trying to find a tabby cat that rolls on its back on command. Apparently, a monochrome gray cat doing everything exactly as it was told at every take wasn't pretty enough for the commercial we're shooting."

"You're watching cat videos and complaining?"

"It's not the cats; it's their trainers who drive me mad. Not to mention my creatives. So, are your eyes better occupied?"

"Oh, yeah. Right now I'm staring at the best six pack ever."

"Is Richard performing a mid-afternoon office striptease for you?"

"No, we hired Diego for the campaign." A vision of Diego clad only in a white towel flashes before my eyes, and I understand why Blair felt compelled to call me. Diego bare-chested is not an everyday sight. "The moment Angelika Black set eyes on him, it was game over for everybody else."

"Oh, great." I'm genuinely happy he got the job, and that, if nothing else, posing as my boyfriend will help his career. I guess one can't put "played fake boyfriend for a desperate single lady over the holidays" on one's résumé.

"So…" Blair says suggestively.

"So?"

"You've seen what I've seen?"

I can picture her waggling her eyebrows.

"Yes, it's in his portfolio," I lie. For some reason, I don't want her to know I had a real-life show. Two, counting the Santa World backstage.

"And?" she insists.

"And nothing."

"Are you telling me you're not even tempted?"

"To do what?"

"Oh, come on… You sleep in the candy shop every night, and you want me to believe you've never thought of tasting the candies?"

I massage my temples as the first signs of a cat-talent-plus-stupid-questions-from-my-best-friend induced headache start pressing on my skull. "Blair, we're in a *professional* agreement. I'm not going to hit on the guy." As if I had a chance, anyway. No matter what Diego says, guys like him don't end up with regular women like me.

"Why not? He's so hot, and he seems like a nice guy; couldn't you at least have some fun with this crazy pantomime of yours?"

"Why are you suddenly trying to push me into his arms? Only last week you were convinced he was a serial killer."

"Well…"

I can hear the guilt in her tone.

"Blair, what did you do?"

"Oh, nothing, really. But in order for us to hire him, he had to give us his social security number, and I told you how Richard wanted to meet the guy before we drove home with him… So, he sort of had a PI friend of his run a background check on Diego."

"You guys didn't," I hiss into the mic.

"We did, and you should thank us. Diego is squeaky clean. No criminal record, and his identity checked out. His credit score could be better, but that can be expected of a struggling artist."

"Oh my gosh." I close my eyes and intensify the massage. "He won't find out, will he?"

"I don't think so. And even if he does, we can always say it's a standard employee background check we carry out for all new hires."

"How wonderful," I say, hoping she'll catch the sarcasm.

"Stop being such a Scrooge. I just wanted to let you know that I approve."

"There's nothing to approve."

"If you say so. Anyway, that's not the only reason I called… Richard has booked his flight to London. Do you mind if we leave for home on Sunday instead of Saturday?"

"And skip a day in the torture pit? No, I don't mind."

"Okay, then. Richard will drop me and Chevron by the house early Sunday morning before he drives to the airport. Can you rent the car?"

"Sure, I'll book it when I get home from work." *If I ever leave this place,* I add in my mind. "When do you want to come back, on the twenty-ninth or the thirtieth?"

"Twenty-ninth?" Blair suggests. "So we get that extra day to recuperate before New Year's Eve?"

"Big plans?"

"No, just a party at Richard's friend's house. Want to come?"

"Is it all couples?"

"Err… I don't know. I can check if you want."

"Yeah, please." The last thing I need is to be the only sad loser at a party with no one to kiss at midnight. "So, I'll pick up the car Saturday night and schedule the drop off for the next Saturday." This way I can shave two whole days off my homestay and blame it on Blair and her British boyfriend with my mom. She loves Blair; she's not going to hold it against her. "A clean one-week rental. I hope they have discounts for that." Gosh, a full week at home. Fake boyfriend or not, the thought still makes me nauseous. "Anything else?"

"Just make sure the rental company allows for pets in the car."

"And maybe that they check their plates before doling out cars." I chuckle. "Wouldn't want to get arrested."

"Ah, ah… very funny."

"I'm still so sad they didn't take a mug shot of you," I say, referring to Blair's incident with law enforcement last summer. "I really gotta go now. See you on Sunday?"

"Yeah, bye."

"Bye."

***

Whenever I imagined low points in my career, delivering a sales pitch on all the qualities of Russian Blue cats never made the list. Nevertheless, the impossibility of finding a replacement "actor" forced me to do exactly that. I had to support my argument with adoption statistics, substantiated research on the most-loved cat breeds, and a small focus group's—made of the office secretaries—approval ratings for the specific cat performance.

In the end, I convinced the client to keep the Russian Blue. But this job is killing me. I have to treat myself to something, and since Diego and I also need more shared experiences, I ask Melanie to buy two tickets for *Harry Potter and the Cursed Child*. I'm sure Diego won't mind seeing it a second time.

When my assistant delivers the tickets to my desk the next day, she eyes me inquisitively. "Two front-row seats for tomorrow and Friday's shows," she says. "Solved that boyfriend issue, have you?"

I instantly regret having shared too much personal information with her. "Don't be ridiculous, I'm going with a friend."

"Oh, you seemed so much happier in the past week… I thought you'd met someone."

Happier, me? How, when I've been swamped by my usual workload, plus an impossible project, a rogue team of creatives, and had to deal with kitty-gate. I feel more stressed than ever, definitely not happier.

"What made you think that?" I ask.

"Nothing, really, but you seem more lively lately… more energetic. Usually happens to people who are in love."

"Didn't have much of a choice if I wanted to deliver everything Teddy asked for."

"Hey, don't get defensive, I was only saying you look better. Maybe it's the hair. Anyway…" She taps the tickets now resting on my desk, taking the hint my happiness level isn't a topic I care to discuss with her. "Both Part 1 and 2 start at 7:30 p.m. The ticket lady advised getting there a little early just to be on the safe side."

"Thank you, Mel, that'll be all," I dismiss her.

I stash the tickets away in my wallet and take a moment to stare out the window.

I'm not happier.

Why would I be?

Ten

Bossy Much

The show is everything Diego promised. Definitely a much better experience than reading the script, and sharing it with him has made it even more special. The moment my fake boyfriend set foot on Broadway, his whole demeanor changed. The passion he has for the theater is contagious, and now I get why he can't surrender his dream and give up on being an actor. Getting a regular nine-to-five job would kill Diego's spirit. Pity it's so difficult to have a breakthrough in his field. I wish I could do something more to help him than sneak him into a few castings.

A frantic work schedule and two nights in a row spent on Broadway make the weekend and the imminent departure advance in no time. On Saturday, I indulge in a late morning and a lush brunch while Diego takes his last shift at the restaurant. Before I know it, it's time to get everything ready for the trip home. Come Saturday evening, I can't help feeling as jittery as an actor before opening night. Tomorrow, the biggest performance of my life will kick off, and no matter that all the technical details have been set, I'm still tense.

I do a mental recap.

Rental car, check!

Luggage packed and ready to be loaded, check!

Fake boyfriend, check!

But what about my nerves? Will I really be able to pull off this farce in front of my family? Will they believe Diego and I are together? I should've picked someone less hot than Diego; a guy more in my league. They're going to bust me the moment I step over the threshold. Why did I do this? This whole idea was crazy. I should call it all off.

No, no, Nikki, you just need to stop panicking and calm down.

Still, even with all the details of my fake relationship laid out, I can't settle. One final review can't hurt.

I sit on the coffee table in front of Diego, who's sprawled on the couch. I can tell he's tired after a day of waiting tables. But this won't take long.

"We should go over each other's backgrounds one last time," I announce.

"Boss, relax. We have it covered, went over it a million times."

"Also, you need to stop calling me 'boss.' When we're with my family, I'm Nikki."

"Or I could tell them I call you 'boss' for how bossy you are."

"I'm not bossy." I hand Diego his cheat sheet of information about my family and keep the one about his. "So, backgrounds."

"Bossy." He grins.

I scowl. "Be serious, we can't make mistakes. My family really needs to think we know each other."

Diego leans forward, dropping his elbows on his knees. "But we do, and better than most couples. We've been together all the time for two weeks." *Never this close, though.* His nose is only a few inches from mine. "Doesn't matter if you forget my third uncle's name."

"You think you know me?"

"I do."

"Prove it," I challenge him.

"Name: Nicola Addison Moore. Birthday: April 24. Born and raised in Old Saybrook. NYU graduate with a degree in Marketing and Visual design. Father: Jason Moore. Mother: Dora Moore, maiden name Appleton. Only one sibling, Julia, soon to be married to Paul Collins. And it doesn't matter if I don't remember your Aunt Laurel's middle name"—he pauses to peek at the sheet—"is Clara, and that she's the one allergic to nuts."

"It matters! You could offer her the wrong cookie and kill her," I say, somewhat annoyed that he's basically memorized the whole sheet, while I still struggle to remember all of his nephews' names.

"No, it doesn't. This list isn't that important; not when I've learned everything else about you."

"Like what?" I cross my arms pettily.

"You only have a few friends, but the ones you have, you would die for. Harry Potter is your favorite series, but you refuse to pick a single favorite book like everybody else because the story wouldn't exist without all seven novels. You never leave the house before spraying yourself head to toe in Flower by Kenzo, the same perfume you've used since you were sixteen..."

I gape at him. "How do you know that?"

"Blair told me." He winks.

Oh, so the two buggers talked about me behind my back.

"Anything else?" I ask.

"Yes. You like to paint your nails in the most obnoxious, shocking colors." I stare down at my fingers, and the tips are in fact neon pink. "But you'd never use a lipstick shade other than nude. Pity, because a bold red would look killer on you, if I may say."

"You may..." I mock-scold him.

Eyes never leaving mine, Diego continues, "You refuse to dress more casually at the office, even if your boss has probably told you a million times you could lie low on the suits..."

He has.

"...When you're concentrating, you reach out to twirl a lock of hair around your finger, only to lower your hand, disappointed, because you've forgotten you've chopped it all off..."

As he keeps talking, it's hard not to notice how green his eyes are, or how close our faces are hovering. Also hard to ignore is that, in just two weeks, he's mapped me out better than any boyfriend I've ever had. And I don't like the kind of fuzzy sensation his words are putting in my stomach, so I interrupt him, "Okay, you're very observant. Noted."

He leans back on the couch, arms behind his head, leaving a huge bubble of empty space in front of me. "Comes with the job," he says. "Every good actor needs to notice how other people behave."

Right. Remember, this is only a job for him. Also, I might need to take a cold shower.

I lift my butt from the coffee table and, pointing at the list in his hands, I say, "Just read it one more time before you go to bed. Blair will be here super early tomorrow morning."

"Aye, aye, boss."

"And stop calling me 'boss.'" I scowl again and am rewarded with a devilish grin.

Definitely need that cold shower.

***

At eight sharp the next morning, Blair walks into the apartment, Chevron in tow. Diego and I are just finishing a quick breakfast of coffee, milk, and cookies, when I'm assaulted by sixty pounds of enthusiastic dog.

"Yeah, yeah." I stroke Chevron behind the ears as she yaps away frantically, shaking her tail in a mad frenzy and trying to jump in my lap. "Good girl, I've missed you, too."

Diego leans against the kitchen bar column and eyes Chevron skeptically. "Is this supposed to be the trained attack dog?" he asks Blair.

"Hey," she says apologetically. "You were a perfect stranger living with my best friend. I had to use every possible form of intimidation."

Diego lets out two low whistles in sequence to attract Chevron's attention and crouches down.

Blair's dog, never one to shy away from cuddles or to be wary of strangers, responds to the call right away. She yaps happily and barrels into Diego with renewed enthusiasm, almost knocking him on his butt. Chevron keeps yapping for a while and then rolls on her back, paws in the air, offering her belly for Diego to pat.

"Well." Diego laughs. "If her strategy is to kill strangers with cuddles, she might succeed."

Twenty minutes later, we're in the car, me driving, Diego sitting shotgun, and Blair and Chevron in the backseat. We're heading north on FDR Drive toward Old Saybrook, and the traffic doesn't seem bad. We should get there in good time.

"So, Blair," Diego says, after a stretch of road spent in silence. "Are you, at least, happy to go home for the holidays?"

"Fifty percent," Blair replies.

Diego throws her a questioning look from the rearview mirror.

"I'm happy to see my dad," Blair explains, "but dreading seeing my mother."

"She a tough cookie?"

"More an insufferable snob, and she's not very happy with my latest life choices."

"Like?"

"Like quitting a career at a glossy magazine to work at a startup. And she's still trying to convince me that my cheating Manhattan lawyer ex was better than my perfect Brooklyn startup-owner boyfriend."

"Really? Why?" I insert myself into the conversation. "How can she?"

"Oh, you know Mrs. Walker, queen of suburbs living. Gerard is New York WASP old money elite, my mother's son-in-law wet dream."

"You should tell her Richard is royalty," I say. "That should shut her up."

"It probably would, but then she'd also expect to have tea with the Queen sooner or later, so you see how that could backfire."

At that moment, Blair's phone chimes, and she says, "Speaking of the devil, it's Richard."

"He's taking off?" I ask.

"No, says his flight is an hour late, and that he's ordering a coffee from my former suitor."

"What former suitor?"

"No idea," she says, and types away into the phone. "Ah," she yelps after a few seconds. "He's talking about Mark."

I've never heard of a Mark. "And who is this Mark guy?"

"A cute bartender who works at JFK."

"Walker, you kept secrets," I mock-complain. "Why does Richard think this guy was your suitor?"

"Remember when we went to California last summer?"

"To Christian Slade's charity gala? Hell yeah. You flew off to meet the sexiest man alive and left me at home to take care of the furball."

"*Woof,*" Chevron comments.

"You know Christian Slade?" Diego asks, visibly impressed. Guess that kind of fame is like the oasis mirage in the desert for him.

"My boyfriend does. They went to boarding school together back in England. Anyway, Richard and I weren't together at the time," she explains to Diego, "and I was so nervous about going on a trip with my boss—"

"Who she had a huge crush on," I intervene.

"Who I had a huge crush on," Blair confirms. "That I poured my heart out to this bartender guy, and we became sort of friends, and Richard—"

"Who was in denial about not having feelings for her back then," I helpfully supply.

"—who was in denial about not having feelings for me back then, thought I was flirting with the guy. Should I tell him the whole discussion was about him?"

I say, "No," just as Diego says, "Yes."

"Explain yourselves, both of you," Blair orders.

"Keep Richard on his toes," I say. "Make him see how lucky he is you're with him."

"Diego?" Blair asks.

"You guys are in a serious relationship?"

"Yeah."

"He loves you, and you love him?"

"Mmm-hmm."

"No need to play games, then. For a guy, what you say is what you mean. If you say you were flirting with this dude, Richard will believe you. He won't think you were really obsessing over him the whole time, and only telling him it was a flirt to *keep him on his toes...*" Diego throws me an overcritical side stare. "He's not going to realize how lucky he is to have you; he'll just assume you weren't that into him at the time of the trip. My suggestion is to tell the truth and give the guy's ego a little boost. You'll send him to London happy with a big, goofy smile on his face."

I hear Blair tapping on the phone and narrow my eyes at her in the rearview mirror. "Are you taking his advice over mine?"

She shrugs. "He's a guy."

Her phone chimes back a second later.

"So, what did Richard say?" I ask.

"Sent me the 'cool' emoji with the sunglasses, and a shower of kisses, and says he loves me."

"I'm getting diabetes," I say, smiling, and change the subject. "Before we get home, you need to be up to date on our narrative."

"What narrative?" Blair asks.

"How Diego and I met, our first date, how long we've been together, and so on..."

"Oh, so we're not telling people you picked him off a catalog?" she jokes.

"Blair, be serious, you have to memorize everything we tell you, and we only have about two hours."

She pokes her head between the front seats to speak to Diego. "Don't you hate her when she's this bossy?" she asks him.

His only response is to throw back his head and let out a throaty laugh.

This is going to be the longest week of my life.

Eleven

There's No Place Like Home for the Holidays

Too soon for my cranky nerves, I'm pulling onto my street. The neighborhood in which Blair and I grew up resembles the perfect Christmas dream fairy tale at this time of the year—or nightmare, depending on one's feelings toward the holidays. Rows and rows of perfectly-curated townhomes and gardens coated in dusty snow, mercilessly decorated to the death.

My house, in particular, could win the go-absolutely-nuts-with-fairy-lights competition. There isn't a single tree or shrub that isn't supporting some kind of illumination contraption. And on the lawn, they've scattered sparkly reindeers and a huge light-up sleigh. Even in daylight, the house is blinding, I wonder what it'll do at night. Guess my mom ran off the bat with her daughters bringing home a fiancé and a new boyfriend, respectively.

I kill the car's engine and turn back toward Blair. "Here we are." She lives just across the street. "Are you coming over tonight after dinner?"

"Definitely," Blair says, clipping on Chevron's leash.

"All right." I button up my coat, and we all get out of the car.

Diego helps Blair unload her bag and does the same with ours.

"Say hello to your parents," Blair says, hugging me. "See you later."

I watch her cross the street and then turn back toward my house, filled with dread.

I look up at Diego. "Ready?"

He nods.

"Let's do this."

I hook my travel bag over my shoulder next to my regular bag and walk up the driveway to the porch. My gloved finger has barely touched the doorbell when the door swings open to reveal Mom, Dad, and Julia crowding the threshold. If Diego was a real boyfriend, and not one paid to endure my family, I'd be dying of shame at their ill-concealed eagerness. Mom and Julia look like wolfhounds with the scent of a bone fresh in their nostrils.

Mom is poring over Diego in awe. I don't think she even notices how hot he is; she's just overwhelmed he's the first boyfriend I've brought home since high school. Julia, on the other hand, is staring at him slightly slack-jawed. Ah, ah. Bet she was expecting me to introduce them to someone boring and possibly balding, not Mr. Tall, Dark, and Mysterious. Take that, little sis.

"Hi, everyone," I greet them, walking inside and taking notice of how the interior of the house is no better than the outside. Looks like a

Christmas Tree Shop has opened in here. Every square inch is covered with a decoration, wreath, or Christmas light, and the tree they bought this year is so massive it almost touches the living room ceiling. "Mom, Dad, this is Diego," I make the introductions. "Diego, this is my mom, dad, and my sister, Julia."

They all do the "nice to meet you" handshake dance—or, at least, my parents do. Julia just stares at Diego, speechless, as he shakes her hand.

Something brushes against my legs, and I bend down to pick up the only being I'm actually excited to see over this break: Mr. Darcy, the family tomcat. Dad found him hiding under his truck when he was just a tabby kitten in my junior year of high school. Even if we only lived under the same roof for two years, I still consider him my cat. In fact, the moment he's in my arms, he starts purring and bumping his head under my chin.

In the three seconds I've been distracted by Mr. Darcy, my mom has closed in on Diego and is bombarding him with questions.

"Mom," I interrupt her, saving him. "Let us at least drop our bags before you start with the third degree."

Then I make the mistake of using my cat-free hand to pull my beanie off.

Mom gasps. "Darling, your hair!"

Oh, I forgot they haven't seen my new haircut yet.

"Yeah." I ruffle it up to remove the flattening effect of the hat. "New style."

"But your hair was so pretty."

Mom uses the same tone she'd strike up if someone in the family had died.

"Well, I wanted something different. I need to drop these off," I say, tilting my chin toward the bags dangling from my side. Between them and the cat, who's no feather-weight, my arms are getting heavy. "Can we discuss how I ruined my hair later?"

"That's not what I meant, honey, of course you look gorgeous."

Dad takes the opportunity to give me a side hug. "Love the new cut, baby."

"Thanks, Dad." I kiss him on the cheek. "So, we'll pop upstairs and be right back."

"Great," Mom says. "Lunch is almost ready. You two go freshen up and come back downstairs whenever you're ready. But don't take too long," she adds in a shrill voice. "I've made mac and cheese, and it needs to come out of the oven soon."

Diego gives her the perfect future-son-in-law answer. "Can't wait to taste it, Mrs. Moore. I've been told your cooking is the best in the entire state."

He's worth every single penny.

Mom blushes, and coos, "Oh, please, it's just something I threw together in five minutes." She's lying. Her secret recipe for mac and cheese requires at least five different cheeses and a complicated double-baking timing. And sometimes, besides baked breadcrumbs, she also adds shrimp or lobster, which of course she has to cook separately first, and then add later in the oven. Hardly a five-minute meal. "And please, call me Dora," she concludes.

"I will." Diego flashes her a bright smile, making his conquest final and absolute.

Mom scurries back to the kitchen happier than I've seen her in years.

"This way." I guide Diego up the stairs, still holding Mr. Darcy in my arms.

On the landing, my heart almost stops as I find myself face-to-face with Paul.

"I heard some noises," he says, smiling, his blue stare piercing a hole through my soul. "Thought you might've arrived." Then his eyes widen. "New haircut, huh? Looks great on you."

I try not to blush, and keep a detached, sister-in-law-appropriate tone. "Paul," I greet him, and give him a quick hug, squishing Mr. Darcy between us. My nostrils immediately fill with his cologne; he was wearing CK One the first day I met him, and I've never smelled anything else on him. Guess we both stick to a perfume when we find one we like. "You guys got here last night, right?"

"Yeah."

"Have my parents scared you off already?" I joke.

"Nuh-uh."

"Not even the princess bed?"

Paul grins. "That almost did it, but IKEA saved me. We shipped a bed and mattress here before leaving New York, and we assembled everything yesterday."

"Oh, I never thought Julia would give up her pink castle."

"Your dad and I brought it down to the garage. The decision on what to do with it is still pending."

"What are the options?"

"Your parents want to give it away to charity, but Jules point-blank refuses. She wants to keep it in case we have a daughter."

Ice courses through my veins. "You guys are... mmm... expecting?"

"What? No!" Paul laughs the question off, and I can breathe again. "She's just thinking future tense; *way* future tense."

"Err-hem," Diego clears his throat behind me.

I had completely forgotten he was here.

"Oh, right." I turn sideways in the hall to give him room to climb the last two steps. "Paul, this is Diego, my boyfriend. Diego, Paul, Julia's soon-to-be husband."

Another handshake, and Paul is on his way downstairs.

So far so good. Operation "Fake Boyfriend" is proceeding well. Nobody looked at Diego and me and screamed "Imposters!"

In my room, I drop Mr. Darcy on the bed, the bags on a chair, and finally remove my coat. I was overheating; it must be eighty degrees in the house. Once Diego is inside, I close the door behind him and whisper, "What do you think?"

He looks at me sheepishly. "Of what?"

"Did they look suspicious?"

"Relax, b—" I give him such a fierce scowl that he changes words mid-sentence. "Nikki. We've talked to them for only five minutes. No one suspects anything."

I take his jacket and hang it next to mine. "Good. Great job buttering up my mom," I say. "Nicely done."

He grins. "Hey, I have a mom, I know how to handle those. Your sister is a different story, though, she didn't seem to warm up to me."

"Julia was probably just surprised." I do an evil laugh inside my head. Yeah, surprised that her dream man just materialized before her eyes as my boyfriend. "You're not exactly my type."

"You have a type?"

Yes. Tall, blond, blue eyes... engaged to my sister...

"I do."

"And why am I not it?"

Because you're not Paul.

"You're too dark," I say instead, gesturing at his hair.

"So why pick me again?"

"You had the best face, I've already told you."

"So I was chosen solely because of my face?" He gives me a long and penetrating stare, prompting quick flashes of the other photos in his portfolio—where his face definitely played the extra—to invade my mind.

I break eye contact and manage to mumble, "Among your other very respectable assets."

"Oh, so now I have assets?" He chuckles. "What assets?"

"You know, stuff?"

"What stuff?"

I huff, exasperated. "You have a nice ass, happy?"

"Very." He laughs. "Likewise, boss."

I hide my blush with an angry pout. "Don't call me 'boss.'"

"All right, all right. You want to go downstairs?"

"No?"

I'm terrified.

"Well, unless you want your family to think you're up here playing with some of my *assets*... we'd better go."

I try to ignore the sexy pun, even if my cheeks heat up, and ask, "Are you ready? Do you remember everything?" I fire one nervous question after the other. "Do you need to meditate? Take a few moments to get into character?"

"I've had two weeks to get into character. I'm ready if you are."

"Okay." I hold out my hand and he takes it. It's nothing romantic, just human solidarity. Even if his hand is warm and dry and really big and it feels kind of good in mine. "Let's go do this."

And shame on me because, as we exit the room, I peek behind my shoulder at the reflection of my butt in the wardrobe mirror. I never thought of myself as a nice-ass girl; I never really gave my buns much consideration. Still, there's nothing I can do to hide the small, satisfied smile that hasn't left my lips since Diego's comment.

When we arrive downstairs, everyone is already seated at the dining table and gossiping—probably about us, seeing how the conversation dies off the second Diego and I enter the room. Could they be any more obvious?

Mom and Dad are sitting at opposite heads of the table, with Julia and Paul occupying one of the long sides between them. So I sit next to Dad in front of Julia, and Diego takes the seat next to Mom, facing Paul.

An embarrassed silence lingers for about thirty seconds before my mom gets up. "Everyone's here," she says, moving toward the kitchen. "I'll go get the food."

In sixty seconds she's back with a steaming oven dish filled to the brim with delicious and super-creamy-looking mac and cheese.

And, yes, the lobster and breadcrumbs topping. Yum!

Mom sets the dish in the center of the table and disappears back into the kitchen, returning with a smaller, round dish that she lays in front of Julia. My sister's special preparation seems like a smaller tureen of mac and cheese, but the color is slightly off—a sad, dirty white instead of rich cream—and there is no lobster or breadcrumbs on top. Also, the pasta is different; looks kind of gummy.

"You having a different menu?" I ask Julia.

"The wedding is in only six months; I'm on a vegan diet until then."

"You're vegan? Since when?"

"Since I need a pre-wedding detox. For the next semester, I've sworn off meat, dairy, seafood, sugar, gluten, and all other poison foods."

"Good for you," I say, trying to keep the sarcasm from my voice and doing my best not to roll my eyes. Secretly, I'm thanking the Christmas spirits she hasn't convinced Mom to cook the vegan version of her mac and cheese for everyone.

"Guests first," my mom chimes in. Eager to end the vegan discussion, I'm sure. She serves Paul and Diego, and then me and Dad. "Well, everyone, enjoy your meal… Bon appétit!"

"Bon appétit," we all reply. Well, all except for Diego, who goes for a slightly different version, saying, "*Buon appetito.*"

"Is that Italian I hear, young man?" Dad asks.

"Yes, sir, I'm part Italian from my mother's side."

"Please, call me Jason," my dad says. "So, you speak Italian?"

"*Bene come l'Inglese.*" Diego smiles.

"Oh," Julia gasps. "I've always wanted to learn Italian."

I think of my sister's secret list of qualities for her perfect man, and mentally check off "speaks Italian." I should also check off tall, dark, and with smoldering green eyes. She's seen that.

"So, Diego, what is it that you do in New York?" my mom asks. "Nikki hasn't told us much."

"I'm an actor," Diego replies.

The declaration is followed by a prolonged moment of silence.

"An actor?" my dad repeats. "What kind of acting?"

"Theater on Broadway would be the dream, of course, but for now I scrape by with whatever I can get. Commercials, modeling… Christmas is always good, so many Santa gigs are available."

"Y-you play Santa at the mall?" my mom asks.

My parents are still a bit too "middle class" for this kind of future-son-in-law. I'd feel sorry for them, if not for the years of pestering me about settling down. This is like a small, sweet revenge.

"Yeah, but I mainly work as a server to pay the bills. Until my big break comes, I'm living paycheck to paycheck."

Julia is openly gaping right now. I mentally check "struggling artist" off the list. I can't wait for Diego to tell her he rides a motorcycle.

Dad, on the other hand, isn't impressed. "How old are you?" he asks.

Guess we're not over the "lack of a proper enough career to date my daughter" topic.

"Twenty-eight," Diego answers.

"And do many actors have big breaks when they're close to thirty? I thought they all had to start much earlier…"

"Depends on—"

"Diego's job is actually how we met," I interrupt. "We bumped into each other at the agency." Then, wanting to make it clear the third degree is over—I might be paying Diego, but no one deserves to be grilled this hard—I turn to Mom. "Mom, you've outdone yourself. It's like your mac and cheese gets better every year."

"Yeah, truly delicious." Paul and Diego echo my compliments. "Amazing recipe."

"And how is yours?" I ask Julia.

She narrows her eyes at me. "Healthier, for sure."

Uh-oh, someone sounds a little sour…

Twelve

Better Eat Your Vegetables

Luckily, lunch continues with no further interrogations. But when the meal's over and everyone has had coffee—except for Julia, who opted for a fennel infusion—I've already had enough of the family reunion, so I take the excuse of showing Diego around town to get the hell out of the house.

"Congratulations, you survived the first drill," I tell Diego as we exit the car and stroll toward the town's center.

Downtown is not that impressive, just a road with shops and restaurants on either side. But with the snow crunching under our feet and fairy lights dangling from every tree and shop window, I have to admit the Christmas flourish makes it prettier than usual.

"Mmm, I don't think your dad was a fan of my job," Diego says, offering me his arm.

"Don't worry, he won't have time to try to turn you into an accountant," I reassure him, linking our arms together. "Five more days and you'll never see him again."

"Right." Diego's face doesn't look relieved.

"Come on, I promise I'll keep my dad off your back." I pull him toward the main shopping street. "Ready to dive into my past?"

Diego nods and follows me obligingly around town as I show him all the local attractions.

***

"And I worked at that café for two years when I was sixteen to eighteen," I say about half an hour later. I kept my favorite coffee house for last. "Hot chocolate? They make the best in town with melting marshmallows and a side of cookies.”

Diego rubs his hands in a warming gesture. “You had me at *hot*.”

Old Saybrook is only two hours north of Manhattan, but the climate is considerably more frigid up here; even a short time outside is enough to freeze one’s ass over.

I push my way into the shop, making the little bell over the door chime in greeting. If the atmosphere was Christmassy outside, in here it looks like a drunken elf threw up all over the place. But not even the Christmas overload and cheesy tunes can keep me from enjoying the best chocolate ever brewed.

“Nikki,” Mrs. Cravath, my former employer, greets me. “So good to see you! And who is this young man?” She eyes Diego from behind the counter with sparkly eyes.

“Hello, Mrs. Cravath. This is Diego, my boyfriend,” I introduce.

“Oh, how wonderful. See? I was right, and they were wrong,” she says, and I have absolutely no clue what she’s talking about. “Dora owes me one of her famous pumpkin pies.”

“Excuse me?” I say.

“Your mom and your old crone of an aunt always complain you’re never going to find a man. But I told them how wrong they were and bet Dora a pie you’d be married before forty, which is the new thirty.” She winks at me.

Again, if Diego really was my boyfriend, I’d be dead from the shame. Now I’m just livid. I’m not sure what makes me angrier: the fact that my mom openly discusses my dating life with the whole town or that, apparently, the prize of my happiness is a pumpkin pie. I’m almost tempted to turn on my heel and get the hell out, but then I get a whiff of cacao and can’t help myself. No gossiping old ladies will keep me from my hot chocolate.

“Still ten years to go,” I point out, putting on a sterner and definitely less cordial tone. “I’m sure you’ll get your pie, eventually.” I rejoice in knowing that my lifelong spinsterhood will at least deprive Mrs. Cravath—who I honestly liked until five minutes ago—of her pie.

“So, what can I get you two lovebirds?” she asks, unaware of my shifted demeanor.

“We’ll take two hot chocolate specials, thank you.”

"Go sit… I'll be right there with your order."

We choose a table by the window, and I can't help but notice how Diego's mouth keeps twitching.

"You have something to add?" I hiss.

"No, sorry." He finally lets the smile dance on his lips. "It's just that I grew up in Chicago, and now I live in New York…"

"So?" I ask, impatient.

"I never got that whole 'small town where everyone knows everyone' thing. But now I do."

"Welcome to my personal ho-ho-hell." I roll my eyes. "See why I needed you here?"

"I'm starting to."

***

When we leave the café, it's already dark outside. We hop into the car and I take Diego to the final spot of our tour.

We cross a stretch of open water toward Lynde Point, and I pull over on the other side of the bridge. "Our famous lighthouse is over there, but I can't get any closer with the car. Want to take a stroll? It's really pretty at night."

"Sure," Diego says.

I open the car door, and a freezing blizzard attacks me. "On second thought," I say, pulling the door close again. "It's too windy out there. Another day?"

"At least we'll still have an excuse to get out of the house." He grins.

"I see you're getting into the right Christmas spirit." I glance at the car's clock. "Oh, and it's late, anyway. My parents like to eat dinner early."

Diego massages his belly. "If dinner is anything like lunch, I'm all in. Your mom is an amazing cook."

"Yeah." I reverse the car and hit the road again. "The food is one of the few perks of coming home for the holidays."

As we drive, I keep up my role of improvised tour guide whenever we pass a building of interest, like the local brewery, or the Katharine Hepburn museum and the cultural arts center. "And that's my high school," I say, pointing. "And right there, under the ledge near the entrance, is where I had my first kiss."

"And who was the lucky guy?"

"Michael Connell, a real jackass. The jerk dumped me for Rebecca Miller three weeks later."

"Ouch."

"Yeah, my first heartbreak. Took me a whole month to get over him," I joke. "What about you? Who broke your heart for the first time?"

"Ah, freshman year. Sally Parker agreed to come to the school dance with me only because her parents knew me, then she ditched me to go make out with a senior all night."

"So, you weren't a ladies' man in high school?"

Looking at him now, I find it hard to believe.

"I was a late bloomer. In the ninth grade, I was your typical skimpy kid: skinny and short. Then the summer between freshman and sophomore year I shot up a foot and started playing basketball, packed on some muscle."

"Did Sally Parker ever regret her decision?"

Diego shrugs. "Don't think so. We never talked much after that night."

I don't know why, but I'm pretty sure old Sally *did* curse herself for not sticking with the ugly duckling until he turned into a swan.

***

When we get back home, the house smells like kale and rotten eggs.

"Mom," I call. "We're back."

"Great." She comes out of the kitchen, looking a little frazzled. "Dinner is almost ready."

"Yeah, what is this smell? What did you make?"

"Your sister…" She lowers her stare to the floor for a second before answering. "She's offered to cook us dinner tonight."

"Julia's cooking?" I ask, horrified.

"She swears we could all use the detox, and she's put a lot of effort into making dinner, so don't you dare be nasty about it."

Of course, we wouldn't want to hurt poor Julia's feelings.

"Now, go sit at the table," Mom orders.

Filled with dread, I step into the dining room and stare at the laid table, aghast.

I quickly turn toward Diego and whisper in his ear, "I'm really sorry for what's about to happen. Please pretend you still like me after this."

But if anyone wanted to know what real terror looks like, they should watch my father's face as Julia presents our multi-course vegan dinner. To my credit, I'm trying to keep a neutral expression, as is Diego, while Paul has the resigned look of someone who has listened to this speech multiple times. The only one showing an ounce of enthusiasm is Mom.

Jules is lecturing us on all the benefits of abandoning unhealthy eating habits to cleanse our bodies of toxins, clear our minds of food-induced headaches, and save our stomachs from bloating… and our arteries from clogging… and our skin from breaking out… and on, and on, and on…

I've lost count of all the damages I'm inflicting on my person with my daily diet when my dad asks, "But is a little meat really that bad?"

"Yes, Dad," Julia confirms. "Do you know that we have an herbivorous digestive system, and not carnivorous?"

"Aren't we omnivorous?" he asks, hopeful.

"Not in origin. In fact, the human intestine is twenty-eight feet long. A lion, for example, only has ten feet. A long intestine is a characteristic of herbivorous animals. That's why we can't digest meat properly. It takes too long for it to journey through our guts, and it starts to putrefy while it's still inside our bodies. And I don't know about you, but I prefer to keep my intestines free of rotting corpses."

"Sure, honey," Dad concedes, defeated.

I don't even want to know where she gets her information. And from the various expressions around the table ranging from disgust to despair, it seems my fellow diners are of the same mind.

When the introductory speech is over, Julia finally presents the first course: pumpkin soup with chia seeds.

Pumpkin soup doesn't sound that bad; I love soup. As Julia sets the bowl before me, I'm even encouraged by the color: a deep, rich orange. And the smallish brown seeds she's used as a garnish don't seem too scary. I'm actually kind of enthusiastic as I grab my spoon to have a taste.

When everyone is served, Julia claps her hands. "Tuck in, everyone."

I take a large spoonful, and wince. "Julia," I protest. "The soup is cold."

"It's not cold, it's lukewarm," she says, her tone of voice implying I just said something really stupid.

"Well, I prefer my soup hot," I say, getting up. "I'll microwave it real quick. Does anyone else want me to microwave theirs—"

"You can't microwave it!" Julia shouts. I freeze in place as she explains, "First of all, microwaves are really toxic." She turns toward Mom. "You should get rid of that death trap." Her focus shifts back to me. "And second, you can't warm the pumpkin. Keep it at two hundred degrees for even a minute and you lose half of all the thermolabile vitamins."

"I think I can live with fewer vitamins if it means I can eat hot soup."

"Suit yourself, but that's not how it's supposed to be eaten. You might as well go out and order a burger."

That actually sounds like a great idea.

"Why don't you give Julia's cooking a try," my mom intervenes. "She's put so much effort into preparing this lovely dinner for all of us." She gives me a long, now-be-good-and-eat-your-disgusting-cold-soup stare.

I sit back down, resigned, and do my best to force a few more spoonfuls of this cold poultice down my throat. Cold soup in December! This is a madhouse.

Unfortunately, the main course—tofu steak—doesn't prove any tastier or more filling. The only saving grace is the salad side. Not really much you can do wrong with a salad, even if Dad isn't allowed to use his favorite ranch dressing as it has dairy in it, which is supposedly even worse than meat. Cow Milk & Co are guilty of containing lactose—we don't possess the enzymes to digest it—as well as casein, a dreadful animal protein capable of causing cancer, respiratory problems, inflammation, bloating, headaches…

Makes me wonder if at the agency we should put side-effect warnings at the end of our food commercials like we do with pharmaceuticals.

As for me, I'm happy I'm allowed to use olive oil to dress the salad, even if the salt gets rationed down—it's bad for blood pressure.

The cherry on the cake of the most horrible dinner ever is the dessert: an oatmeal pudding made with maca root powder, so dense it has the consistency of glue. Of course, not a pinch of sugar in it.

I really try to finish mine, but I can't; each tiny spoonful I ingest makes me want to gag more than the previous one. Diego, definitely a much better sport, manages to finish all his pudding, and even has the poker face to compliment Julia, gaining an appreciative nod from my mom.

And so, after an hour and a half of suffering, we're all allowed to retire for the night and go lick our wounds in private. I don't know if this is a behavior typical of herbivorous or carnivorous species, but right now, I'm only hoping I can find a cereal bar hidden at the bottom of my bag.

Thirteen

Pizza Gate

Later, in my room, Diego and I are lying on opposite sides of the bed, wrapped in utter misery. Mr. Darcy, who wasn't forced to eat a vegan cat dinner, is curled up at our feet, much more contented. Barely half an hour since we left the dinner table and I'm already famished. So much so that my stomach grumbles loudly, prompting Diego to turn toward me.

"Hungry?" he asks.

"Yeah, you?"

"Starving. Does your mom have any of that mac and cheese left?"

"Even if she did, we can't go downstairs and heat it up in the evil microwave. If Julia found out, she'd throw the tantrum of the century."

"Right now, I'd gladly eat it cold."

"Nah, I've had enough cold food for one night." I sigh as my belly complains again.

I can't go to sleep on an empty stomach. There must be a way to get a proper dinner without Julia finding out…

"Wait," I say, and grab my phone to text Blair.

Where are u?

U coming over?

Yeah, just finishing walking Chevron

Be there in ten

Any chance you'll pass near the pizza place by the corner?

Standing right in front of it now

Why?

Can you order two giant pizzas to go?

Sure

I ♥ you

When you get here come in through the back door

It's open

Come upstairs immediately and be stealthy

> No one can see you

???

> I'll explain once you're here

> But Julia can't catch you

> Make sure she's nowhere in sight before you enter

> And hurry

> We're hungry

Half an hour later the door of my room bursts open and Blair enters in a blur, balancing two giant pizza boxes in one hand while trying not to stumble over Chevron. The dog has barreled into the room, slaloming between her legs.

"I've made it," she says.

I get up to relieve her of the pizzas, and carefully close the door behind her.

"Did anyone see you?" I ask.

"Your dad, but he's promised to keep quiet." Blair bites her lower lip. "But I suspect he might come over and ask for a pizza bribe in exchange for his silence. He was looking at the boxes like he's never seen pizza before. Did you guys all skip dinner or something?" She removes her coat and goes to sit at my desk.

I jump back on the bed, handing Diego a box and opening mine while Chevron sniffs every corner of the room. When she gets near the bed to sniffle out Mr. Darcy, the cat's only reaction is to lift his head and throw the dog a disdainful stare. Subdued by this display of animal hostility, Chevron lets out a low whine and settles on the rug by the bed.

Before answering Blair, I can't resist a quick bite of pizza. It tastes delicious. The place by the corner makes a thick dough and always puts loads of extra cheese—*real, made with milk that came from cow's cheese*—on top. But it's not just that; this pizza is the taste of my youth. I can't even remember how many Blair and I shared over the years.

When my grumbling stomach is somewhat placated, I finally show enough restraint to stop scarfing down pizza and talk. "Worse than skipping dinner," I explain. "Julia cooked."

"Oh, is she that bad?"

"No idea, but tonight she made us a vegan meal." I switch my tone of voice to talk like a yoga teacher. "To help us cleanse our bodies before the coming days of unchecked indulging." I go back to my normal voice. "And half of it was *raw* vegan cuisine, in the middle of December. Can you believe it?"

"Mmm… But you like it when I make you vegetarian dinners…"

"Yeah, because A, you can cook, and B, you actually cook your vegetables. Plus, vegan is extreme: no cheese, no eggs, no butter. And she only allowed gluten-free bread. The entire dinner was disgusting, and we were both hungry again half an hour later."

Blair laughs. "Yes, I guess vegan eating can be hard."

"Thanks for the pizzas." Diego lifts a slice toward her as if he was toasting a glass of wine. "You're a life saver."

"Wouldn't want anyone to starve." She smiles, then lowers her voice conspiratorially. "So, how did today go? Did 'the family' buy your story?"

I'm about to reply when there's a knock on the door and my dad quickly sneaks into the room.

"Ah." I look at him. "Come to exact payment for your silence, I see."

Dad puts on an innocent face that doesn't reach his mischievous, twinkly eyes. "Would you refuse an old man a slice of pizza?"

"Here." I grab a napkin and place a big slice on top, handing it to him.

And, old man or not, he looks like an excited kid as he takes it from me.

Dad hasn't finished his first bite when the door opens again and

Paul slips inside, clearing his throat. "Err… I heard there was black-market pizza here."

I throw a killer stare at my dad, who promptly justifies himself. "Found him in the kitchen scavenging for food. Couldn't let the poor fella starve."

I roll my eyes and hand them my box with the remaining half of my pizza. Diego, the saint, nudges his box toward me and I gladly take another slice.

That's when Mom arrives. She stares at us, asking, "What are you all doing up here?"

Why no one ever knocks in this house…?

Dad swiftly ushers her inside and closes the door behind her. "Shhh, Dory. You want to get us caught?"

Mom scowls at him. "Your daughter worked so hard to cook you dinner, and if she were to find you all eating pizza behind her back she'd be crushed."

Dad keeps eating, unperturbed. "And that's why I ate my dinner in silence like a good father would. But if my other daughter decides to sneak pizza into the house later, it's only fair I accept all of my offsprings' culinary offerings."

"Two dinners are too much at your age," my mom insists.

"Oh, come on, Dory dear. Only a slice." He turns the open box toward her tantalizingly. "Get one yourself and relax; it's Christmas."

Mom stares at the pizza for a while, indecision clearly written on her features. She's just reaching for the slice when the door opens again and Julia enters, saying, "Nik, do you know where everyone went?"

We all freeze, caught in the act.

Julia takes in the scene, and her jaw drops just before her eyes go all watery. "If you didn't like dinner, you could've said so," she wails dramatically. Then her gaze narrows on Mom, who's standing immobile, arm still stretched forward, reaching for the box. "I could've expected it from them." Julia points at me and my dad. "But I hoped for better from you." Then she turns toward Paul, points an accusing finger at him, and hisses, "And you."

With that, she turns on her heel and flees the room. Mom retracts her arm and runs after her. "Julia, baby… Wait."

Paul, on the other hand, shrugs and serenely finishes his slice. "She'll get over it," he reassures us, before going after his fiancée.

Dad, equally nonplussed, says, "Well, since we've been busted, I can go finish this downstairs." And he, too, leaves, bringing the pizza box with him.

"So," Blair says, when it's only the three of us left in the room—five, counting pets. "I guess it's been a regular day in the Moore family and no one suspects anything."

"Pretty much," I confirm. "What about you? How were your parents?"

We complain about our respective families for another hour or so, before Blair lets out a very loud yawn. "Sorry, guys. I'm beat. Time to go home."

"I'll walk you downstairs," I say.

She and Diego say goodnight while I check the hallway to make sure my sister isn't around. I know she'll make me pay for the pizza stunt, and I'm not looking forward to the moment she'll decide to take her revenge. Luckily, she seems to have already retired to bed, and Blair and I don't meet anyone on our way to the front door.

"How much do I owe you for the pizzas?" I ask, unhooking my bag from the entrance rack.

"Oh, please. Pizza's on me tonight."

"Are you sure?"

"Yeah. Good night, honey. I'll see you tomorrow."

We exchange a quick hug, and I'm about to draw away when she pulls me back in to whisper in my ear, "Oh, and enjoy your first night in bed with Diego." There's plenty of mischief in her voice.

"Blair," I hiss, outraged. "It's not like that."

"I'm just saying that if your hands happened to wander a little under the sheets in the middle of the night, no one could really blame you."

"Only sue me for sexual harassment."

Blair finally lets me go and, with a wink, she adds, "You should try to have more fun."

I shoo her out of the house without comment, taking a moment afterward to rest my back against the door, her words still ringing in my ears. Am I nervous about sleeping in the same bed with Diego? A little… but we're both adults and professionals. The situation might be awkward, but we don't have to make a big fuss about it.

When I get back upstairs, Diego is not in the room. He probably followed me downstairs to go to the bathroom to get ready for the night. He and Paul are using the guest bathroom downstairs, while Julia and I share the one on this floor, and my parents have an en suite.

Did he overhear Blair and me talking? No, impossible. We were whispering.

While he's gone, I shed my clothes at the speed of light and quickly change for bed, feeling glad I opted to bring un-sexy, warm PJs. The thought of bringing lacy lingerie instead *had* crossed my mind as I was packing, but then I decided that my butt would've frozen in skimpy underwear. And, honestly, the embarrassment of wearing close to nothing in front of Diego would've been too much. And anyway, it's not like I have to seduce him or anything.

The door opens, and he walks in wearing only a black T-shirt and gray sweatpants—guess he doesn't need special lingerie to look hot.

He eyes my outfit, the corners of his mouth curling up. "You're sleeping in that?"

I stare down at my plush black hoodie, complete with kitty ears, and the matching mint leggings covered in a black cat print. "Yes, why? You don't like it?"

Diego shakes his head. "Actually," he says, as if he can't believe his own words, "it's kind of cute."

So now I'm cute?

No, Nikki, the PJs are cute, not you.

Right.

"Well, thanks," I mumble, trying not to blush. "And you're sleeping in that?" I ask, pointing at his clothes.

"I don't usually keep the sweatpants on, but I can tonight if it bothers you. I mean, am I even sleeping in the bed?"

"Mmm, yeah, where else would you sleep?"

"I thought you might send me to the floor."

"No, no. There's plenty of space in the bed, unless you… want to sleep on the floor?"

"No, definitely not."

"Great," I say, still feeling awkward. "I'll go brush my teeth. Be right back."

In the bathroom, I also splash my face with cold water. Why am I feeling so nervous? It's ridiculous. And okay, I'm about to share a bed with a relative stranger, but there's no romance involved, no expectations… *So please, Nikki, stop being such a wuss and go sleep with the guy.*

Diego is already under the covers when I get back to the bedroom, and the first thought that crosses my mind is: *Has he kept the sweatpants?*

Easy to find out…

I circle to the left side of the bed and slide under the sheets next to him, casting a furtive glance at his legs—the sweatpants stayed.

"Is the cat sleeping in bed, too?" Diego asks.

"Yeah, Mr. Darcy always sleeps with me when I'm home. You don't want him?"

He squirms a little in the bed. "It's just that he's right on my feet. I don't think I can sleep with him there."

I bend forward and gently move Mr. Darcy to the foot corner on my side of the bed. He regards me in outrage, incredulous that I would dare disturb him. But then he starts kneading the comforter and settles down without further protest.

"Better?" I ask Diego.

"Yep, thank you… So, I guess it's goodnight."

I kill the lights. "Night."

I feel Diego shifting under the covers, probably to sleep on his side, but I keep rigidly supine and immobile, careful not to touch him even with a toe, and also attentive not to disturb Mr. Darcy. I'm never going to fall asleep this way, too many variables. I stare into the dark for a long time. But then Diego's breathing becomes low and regular, and Mr. Darcy starts purring, and both sounds kind of lull me into sleep because I feel my lids getting heavier and heavier and…

***

What time is it? Where am I? What's this thing between my legs? And what's pushing me from behind?

With horror, I realize that it's morning, and I'm at my parents' house. That the thing between my legs is Diego's right thigh, and, if I had to guess, I'd say the weight pushing at my back is Mr. Darcy.

The new position is all the cat's fault. During the night, Mr. Darcy decided to expand into my area of the bed, prompting me to leave his feline majesty all the space he required and to shift toward Diego. But what prompted me to wrap myself around Diego like a baby koala remains a mystery.

I look up at him and find two crinkly green eyes staring back at me. "Morning," he says.

I make an effort to ignore how good it feels to have my body pressed against Diego's, and instantly thrash away from him, retreating to my side of the bed and sending Mr. Darcy tumbling down to the floor. I'm so embarrassed I don't even care about the indignant, *"Meow,"* and the kitty evil eye the cat throws me.

"So sorry," I babble. "I don't know what happened. Usually I'm not a hugger."

"Relax, boss." Diego smiles. "It would've been worse if you were a snorer."

"Yeah, right. Sorry anyway." And with that, I get up. "I'm heading down for breakfast. Join us whenever you want."

Even the thought of having to face my sure-to-be-angry sister can't keep me in this room right now.

Weird.

At breakfast, Julia at least waits until after my first cup of coffee to punish me for the pizza.

I'm reaching for my third slice of toast when she snaps, "Shouldn't you be watching how many carbs you eat at your age?" I'm still debating if she's calling me fat, old, or both, when she adds, "I mean, after all that pizza last night."

I stop buttering the toast to look at her. "I'm not the one getting married, so, no, I don't need to go on a neurotic diet."

To make my point, I take another generous slab of butter and spread it on my slice.

"Well, even if you're *not* the one getting married"—she says it in a nasty, *as if* tone—"you still need to fit in your bridesmaid dress."

"Are you really being this petty over pizza?"

My mom is not at the table, leaving only the male population to witness this exchange. My dad doesn't seem to care; he's used to our bickering. He's reading the paper, face hidden behind it, while Paul and Diego are doing their best to stare at their plates, pretending they don't exist.

"If you didn't like dinner, you should've just said so, instead of being dishonest and eating pizza behind my back."

"Dishonest? I was hungry, and I ordered pizza. Big deal! You want honesty? Your vegan cuisine sucks, as do all your other eating habits."

"What other eating habits?"

I start talking in a mock shrill-posh voice. "No sugar, no dairy, no meat, no gluten, no salt…"

"Maybe you shouldn't be my maid of honor after all."

"Ask another one of your friends with an eating disorder; I'm sure she'll look stunning in her dress."

"Girls…" My dad intervenes without lowering his paper, using his "enough" tone.

"Dad, she started it," I say, realizing I've successfully reverted to being a sulky teenager.

Dad lowers the paper just a few inches and arches an eyebrow at me from behind his reading glasses.

"Fine," I snap. "Take her side. It's what you always do." And with that, in true adolescent fashion, I leave my breakfast unfinished and storm upstairs to my room, slamming the door shut behind me.

Fourteen

Frosty the Snowman

When Diego joins me in my room, I'm pacing around it in circles, fuming with suppressed rage.

"That was an interesting breakfast," he says.

"See what I have to put up with?" I rant. "How spoiled she is, and how my parents always take her side?"

"Your dad didn't take anyone's side."

"You only say that because you can't recognize the subtleties. And then, what did I do, anyway? I ordered a pizza. Big deal. It's not like I forced her to eat fried chicken, so why should I eat tofu?"

"Can't you see your sister is just jealous of you?"

"Jealous? Why would she be jealous?"

"Because she spent hours cooking and nobody liked her dinner, whereas everyone came to you to get contraband pizza."

"That's ridiculous. And even if it were true, that doesn't justify her calling me fat and old. She's so petty."

"I don't remember Julia calling you fat or old."

"But she did, in female code language."

"You ladies have a secret language?"

"All gals do; it's Bitchenglish. Most of the time, when a woman tells another woman, 'Your new haircut looks lovely,' what she really means is, 'Gosh, who is your hair stylist? Better make sure I never go to that butcher.'"

"And how do you recognize when someone is talking to you in Bitchenglish?"

"Instinct, and years of faring in the lipstick jungle."

Diego drops his hands on my shoulders to steady me before I dig a trench in the floor with my pacing. "Relax," he says, pinning me in place with those wonderful eyes of his. "You need to get out of the house."

"Yeah, you're right, we should go out," I agree, trying to ignore the warmth spreading from my shoulders downward. "Where do you want to go? Yesterday was pretty much the whole tour. There's not much else to do here in winter. I guess we could go to the brewery and get drunk."

"At ten in the morning?"

"It's Christmas Eve, I'm sure getting wasted is socially accepted, regardless of the hour. How else would people cope?"

"I was thinking of a more wholesome Christmas tradition..."

"Like what?" I ask suspiciously.

"Want to build a snowman?"

"What?" I step back, shrugging free of his hands. "You know I hate all things Christmas, not to mention it's freezing out there."

"Cover up, then." He smiles encouragingly. "Come on, I always make snowmen with my brothers when I'm home. It's a tradition."

I notice a hint of sadness in his voice. "Are you sorry you can't spend the holidays with your family?"

He shrugs. "A little, but I told them it was work. They understand. And I promised to go visit as soon as I can."

"Okay."

"To the snowman?" Diego asks hopefully.

"No."

"Come on, I promise the fresh air and hard work will make you feel much better afterward. Plus, what else would you do all morning?"

"I brought a book; I can stay in bed reading with Mr. Darcy. Better use of my time than freezing my ass off in the snow to build a stupid puppet."

"Right, especially if you want everyone to think you're hiding up here."

"Hiding? Why would I be hiding?"

Diego shrugs. "People with a dirty conscience usually do."

"I don't have a dirty conscience. I did nothing wrong…" I'm about to start on a tirade when I notice his foxy grin. "Oh, I see what you're trying to do here. Sneaky you."

He puts on an innocent expression that doesn't reach his mischievous eyes. "Me?"

"Yeah, you, Mister."

Diego lets all pretense go and flashes me a dashing smile. "Did it work?"

How can anyone say no to that face?

Nonetheless, I scowl. "Snowman it is. Are you equipped for the snow?"

"I have my biker boots."

"Those will get soaked in a second. I'll see if we can borrow an old pair of my dad's. What's your size?"

"Eleven, eleven and a half?"

I solemnly swear that I'm not thinking about big socks.

"Mmm, Dad's boots won't fit, then. But maybe we still have something left from Bill, Julia's ex. He was a half-giant. You have pants?"

"I can use my riding pants, they're waterproof." He fishes them out of his bag.

"Great. Go get changed in the bathroom and wait for me downstairs."

"Aye, aye, captain."

I open the door and push him out, hissing, "I'm not bossy."

"Sure you're not." Diego winks, before turning on his heel and heading for the bathroom.

I close the door behind him, then search my old closet for snow-appropriate clothing. I find an old pair of cyan and pink snow pants, and an equally old gray fleece. A heavyweight one, so thick you can go outside wearing no jacket.

I smell it to make sure it's still wearable. A bit stale, but it'll do. And the pants have a distinct nineties vibe, but I can't make miracles. If Ron Weasley couldn't conjure better clothes out of thin air, neither can I.

I swap the cat-hoodie PJs for a sweater, change my leggings, and put the fleece on. Dressed like a sixteen-year-old version of myself, I go scavenge in the garage for my old snow boots and gloves, and any footwear that will fit Diego… which I find at the bottom of the shoe closet.

These were definitely once Billy's boots; the poor kid used to practically live here before Julia dumped him to move to the city. They're not in particularly good shape, but they seem solid enough to wear.

"Here." I hand them to Diego five minutes later.

We're standing in the small hallway next to the back door, pulling on layers of snow gear: hats, scarves, gloves, boots… It's sunny outside, but the temperature is in the low twenties.

"Wow," I say, stepping out as a cold gush of air blows on my cheeks. "Refreshing for sure. So," I ask, turning toward Diego. "How are snowmen made?"

"First, we need to find the right spot," he says, advancing along the walkway that cuts the garden in half. Dad has plowed the way until about three-quarters into the backyard, leaving only the last stretch untouched. "Here." Diego stops near the giant hemlock that towers over the garden. "We should build it under the shade of this tree so it doesn't melt right away."

I'm thinking that in this freezing cold, we could build our

snowman in the sunniest spot and still it wouldn't melt, but I don't comment.

"I'm going to make the bigger body snowball," Diego instructs. "And you can work on the chest ball."

"Okay, show me what to do."

He gathers some fresh snow in his hands and starts compacting it into a ball. When the globe is big enough, he starts rolling it on the ground, making it bigger and bigger. I imitate him and come up with a decent-sized, if not as perfectly round, sphere. Diego adjusts the misshapen bits, and then puts my ball on top of his.

"I'll make the head," he says. "Can you find some twigs for the arms and something to make the eyes and the mouth?"

I move into the wood shack to scavenge the twigs, collect two small pinecones for the eyes, and strip a curvy line of bark off a log to use for the mouth.

"Perfect," Diego says, assessing the final result. "We just need a carrot for the nose."

"I'll go ask Mom for one."

I jog back to the house, and I'm about to enter the kitchen when I overhear my mom and sister talking, so I stop just behind the open door.

"They look cute," Mom says.

"They look weird," Julia hisses.

"What do you mean, 'weird?'"

"Come on, he's not her type at all. No stable job, probably no education, dark hair... Nikki prefers blonds."

Mostly true, but how dare she?

"Oh, honey... love is blind," my mom sighs. "You can't control who you fall for."

"Love, sure," Julia snaps.

"What do you have against Diego?"

"Nothing, he's absolutely fine. But doesn't it seem strange to you that out of the blue"—she snaps her fingers—"Nikki suddenly has a boyfriend no one has ever seen or heard of, and suddenly she's bringing the guy home for Christmas?"

"What are you suggesting?"

"I don't know. Maybe she didn't want to be the single older sister for yet another year, and she asked a friend to do her a favor. I mean, it must be hard for her with me getting married before her…"

It takes all of my willpower not to go in there and strangle Julia on the spot. I don't need anyone's pity, and especially not hers, thank you very much. And what she's saying stings even more—not only because it's true that Diego is not my boyfriend, but more so because he isn't even a friend. He's just a guy I'm paying five thousand dollars to pretend he likes me.

"Don't be silly, Jules," my mom says. "They're not friends. Have you seen the way he looks at her?"

What? How does he look at me?

"No," Julia says, echoing my thoughts. "Does he have a special look?"

"Yes, he stares at your sister the way your father used to look at me when we were young."

"Mom, that's absurd." Unfortunately, I agree with my sister here. "And Dad still looks at you that way."

"True." Mom giggles. "And trust me, love, I can tell when a young man is in love."

"Mom, I think you want to see Nikki married off so much that you've put your pink glasses on and are ready to swallow whatever bullshit she feeds you."

"Don't swear, dear, it's not becoming for a bride. And don't treat me like an old lady who doesn't understand how the world works anymore. With age comes wisdom, and I can see a lot more than you think."

"I don't know. I'm not convinced. Have you even seen them kiss, like, ever?"

"Maybe they're just private people. Look how cute they are… they're building a snowman. When did you ever see Nikki build a snowman?"

I can't see what my mom's doing, but I can imagine her pointing out the kitchen window to the backyard.

"Where's Nikki?" Julia asks, alarmed.

With the speed of the best undercover agents, I quickly backtrack to the rear door, slam it shut with a loud bang, and call, "Mom? Are you inside?"

"In the kitchen, baby," she shouts back.

I walk in, plastering a big, fake smile on my lips. My heart is still beating super fast. "Can you gals spare a carrot?" I say, struggling to keep my voice even. "We need a nose for our frosty man."

"Sure, honey," she says a bit over-brightly. "You want it peeled?"

"No, I'm sure Frosty won't mind."

Despite my best efforts, I can't bring myself to meet Julia's eyes. I take the carrot from Mom and hurry back outside as quickly as I can.

"Here's your carrot," I snap to Diego.

"Whoa, what happened to you?" He stops leveling the main body snowball and gets up from his crouch. "You went inside a cute, hopping bunny and came out a roaring tiger."

"My stupid sister is putting weird ideas into my mom's head."

He sticks the carrot in the middle of the head ball, making our masterpiece complete. "What weird ideas?"

"Like we're not together, and you're really just a friend doing me a favor pretending to be my boyfriend."

Diego flashes me his impossibly sexy grin. "How absurd."

Out of the corner of my eye, I catch two heads staring from the kitchen window. Panicking, I quickly grab Diego by the hips and pull him toward me.

"And what's happening now?" he asks, the smile never leaving his face.

"They're spying on us from inside the house. We need to appear… mmm… affectionate."

"Mmm, boss, is it just me?" Diego taunts me. "Or are you taking the opportunity to discretely grope my *assets?*"

Accurate, unfortunately. My hands are wrapped around his lower back, well within ass-groping territory.

"Sorry," I say. "Emergency situations call for extreme measures."

"In that case…"

And with a devilish sparkle in his eyes, he lowers his hands on my back to return the favor.

I scowl, although I'm not at all convinced I don't like the close contact.

"Want to know what I think, boss?"

"No."

"I think there's a much better way of convincing your mom and sister we're legit than discreetly groping each other's assets in the backyard."

"What way?"

"You should kiss me."

If the cold hasn't turned my cheeks bright red already, they sure are now. "I-I should... what?"

Diego stares up at the sky. "I mean, we're not standing under the mistletoe or anything." He looks back at me, his eyes teasing. Is he flirting with me? Or is he just a really good actor? "But we should make an exception; extreme circumstances and all..." He pulls me closer.

"I'm not forcing you to kiss me," I say. "It wasn't in our contract, and I promised you no physical interactions, and—"

"Nikki," he interrupts. He's never said my name with such intensity. "Shut up."

And to make sure I do, he presses his lips onto mine. And it's no stage kiss. There's tongue, and there's heat. So much heat I'm afraid poor Frosty will melt after all.

Gosh, how long has it been since someone kissed me like this? Has anyone *ever* kissed me like this? I can't remember... Right now I can't remember anything; my brain is melting, and my knees are turning into a wobbly mess. I remove my hands from his butt and wrap them around his neck—to pull him closer, or to support myself, I'm not sure.

"Err-emm," someone clears his throat behind us.

I quickly detach myself from Diego and turn around to find Dad staring at us from the backyard threshold, arms severely crossed over his chest.

"Lunch is ready," he announces.

Oh my goodness! I can't believe my dad just did that! Worse than when I was a teenager and he would signal my date that making out time was over by turning on the porch lights.

"Guess they bought the show." Diego winks at me and affectionately pats my rear end before preceding me into the house.

So it was all just for show?

I can't help but feel disappointed as I follow him inside.

But for the rest of the day, Diego keeps throwing me flirty stares, which I find myself willingly reciprocating. What's happening to us? What's happening to *me?*

I feel different. I don't hate Christmas that much anymore. And I don't miss work at all. And whenever I stare at Paul and Julia together, I no longer feel a stab through the heart.

Today has been so weird. Like, take this afternoon. Dad roped Diego into going with him to the store to get more firewood, and Mom and Julia went out grocery shopping because Mom's pantry wasn't equipped to meet all of my sister's vegan needs. So Paul and I were left home alone for a couple of hours. We hadn't been alone for that long in ages, and after only fifteen minutes of him talking about his job non-stop—as I said, he's drifted into the most boring, corporate, figures-oriented branch of marketing ever invented—I found myself zoning out more often than not. Whereas, back when we were in college, I used to hang from his every word.

Could it be that after such a long time apart, I no longer know Paul? That the man I thought I loved no longer exists? I mean, what happened to the boy who used to stay up all night discussing politics and higher ideals with me when I didn't have class in the morning and he did? Or to the guy who used to fall asleep in my bathtub on the weekends because he was too drunk to aim for the couch? Or the dude who forced me to crash strangers' parties just because it was fun? The man standing before me earlier today just seemed so *boring*... Oh, did I just call Paul "boring?"

Really, what's happening to me?

I can't say, exactly. I just know that tonight I'm a lot more nervous about sharing a bed with Diego than I was yesterday.

Fifteen

The Night Before Christmas

In my room, I change into my cat PJs while Diego is in the bathroom and wait for him to come to bed already stashed under the sheets. And, I'm not sure why, but I even go as far as picking up Mr. Darcy from the comforter and relocating him to the armchair in the corner.

Unhappy with the move, the cat curls up and stares at me in resentment.

"Sorry," I whisper.

When Diego comes in, the absence of the cat from the bed is the first thing he notices.

"So his royal highness is not gracing us with his presence tonight?"

I shrug. "Sharing a bed with us is an honor he doesn't bestow easily. Mr. Darcy likes to keep his subjects on their toes. Don't you?" I add in a silly voice.

The cat throws me a you-traitor stare, whips his tail in the air once, and then settles his head on his paws, probably deciding that ignoring me completely is punishment enough.

"Oh, you're such a sourpuss," I tell him.

But as Diego climbs into bed next to me, the cat drama is quickly forgotten. My whole body tenses under the covers for no reason. There's enough free space between me and Diego that not an inch of our bodies is touching. Still, there's a strong warmth emanating from his side of the bed, as if the air surrounding him was shimmering. Or maybe I'm making the air shimmer with heat whenever I think about that kiss today.

"You want to read or something?" I ask.

"No, I'm good."

"Should I kill the lights, then?"

"Yeah."

I turn to switch off the bedside lamp, and burrow deeper under the covers. "Good night."

"Night," comes Diego's whispered answer.

I lie there, with my arms along my sides rigid as a mummy, staring into the dark with all my senses on high alert. From the utter silence on my right, I can tell Diego isn't sleeping, either. Not a single breath coming out of him. What is he doing? What is he thinking?

Something brushes against my right pinky. At first, the touch is so light I think I've imagined it. But then Diego's fingers tickle mine again in an unmistakable move, his thumb sweeping over my knuckles in a soft caress. And the simple skin-on-skin contact is enough to make me experience a charge like a static shock. A flow of current that shoots up from my hand to my arm, then to the rest of me.

Swallowing my sudden agitation, I return his touch, keeping my movements just as gentle and light. Until our fingers are intertwined in a firm lock. Diego's thumb massages my palm in slow circles. I never thought of my hands as erogenous points, but I was wrong. This seemingly-innocent fondling is doing the weirdest things to me.

Our feet touch next. Just a tentative exploration at first, and then another joining of limbs.

I can't stand this tension any longer. I gently tug Diego toward me, and he doesn't seem to need much more encouragement to partially roll on top of me, the pressure of his body on mine divine. With his free hand, he cups my left cheek and... He doesn't kiss me. He teases my lips with his, never allowing them to stay in contact for long. Nibbling at me with his teeth, and kissing me everywhere—cheeks, jaw, neck—but on the mouth.

Just when I think I won't be able to stand this sweet torture any longer, he finally gives in to my silent prayer. The kiss feels much more intimate than the one we shared this morning, but no less heated.

We make out for hours. And I don't know if it's the fact that we're in my old room and have to be careful not to make too much noise or to keep the bed from squeaking, but I feel like a high school junior exploring boys for the first time.

Why don't adults spend more time kissing? Once we discover the main act—sex—we forget everything that used to come before. How good it is to just kiss. How intimate. How soul-baring. But now I'm back to being sixteen, and kissing Diego is all I want to do tonight. I'm not sure if he feels the same way, because we don't say a word to each other the entire time. But he never tries to go further than kissing, and a very chaste version of second base. In fact, every roaming of our hands on our bodies is strictly clothes-on, with no skin coming in contact except for our hands, feet, and lips.

We kiss, kiss, and kiss, until my lips are so swollen they hurt. Still, I wouldn't want it to ever stop. But at one point my body seems to have expended all its energy. I let Diego's mouth go and burrow my head in the nook between his neck and shoulder, wrapping my legs around his in a tight embrace. I fall asleep almost immediately.

***

For the first time in I don't know how many years, I wake up happy on Christmas Day. I'm smiling even before I can remember why, which doesn't take long considering I'm sleeping all over him.

"Hey." I shyly lift my head to look at Diego.

He has his arms wrapped around me, and gently pushes a lock of hair away from my forehead to kiss me there. "Morning."

I blush and hide my face back into his neck.

Last night, in the dark, it all seemed simple. But right now, I don't know what to tell Diego. We kissed. Real, non-job-related kissing. What does it mean? Are we dating for real now? Am I still his boss? What the hell is happening to us?

"Last night was…" I start tentatively.

"I know." Diego holds me closer and kisses my head again.

I'm gathering enough courage to ask the hard question—*What did last night mean to you?*—when an explosion of Christmas bells from one of Mom's favorite old songs invades the relative quiet of the morning.

My mother's shouting quickly follows. "Come on, kids, time to get up! The buns are just out of the oven, come down before they get cold… and Merry Christmas, everyone!"

This is my mom's idea of a jolly wake up call. She pumps holiday tunes at top volume on the stereo and calls us down to all have breakfast together with her famous cinnamon rolls. Usually, this treatment turns me into Miss Cranky MacGrumpy right away. I'd drag myself out of bed, join the breakfast table with a frown, only half-appreciate the deliciousness of my mother's buns, and ready myself for a day of misery spent defending my dating life—or lack of thereof.

But not today. Today, I'm ready to gorge on buttery cinnamon rolls, I want to unwrap the presents, eat the turkey, and I might even start humming holiday tunes under my breath. Not even Aunt Betsy can ruin my mood.

"Better not make her wait," I say, sitting up, glad I have an excuse to postpone *The Conversation*. "And the cinnamon rolls are worth it, I promise."

We get up and awkwardly bump into each other as I side-step him on my way to the door. "I'll meet you downstairs in just a few minutes," I tell him.

In the bathroom, I take extra care to make myself as pretty as possible without giving the impression of trying too hard. I wash my face, brush my teeth, fluff my hair, and pinch some color into my cheeks. My lips are already red and plump, so they don't need any extra pinching—a night of making out will do that for you. I'm tempted to apply some concealer under my eyes but decide against it. Julia might notice and call me out on it in front of everyone.

I hop down the stairs, skipping steps, and promptly barrel into Diego on the landing just as he comes out of the guest bathroom.

"Whoa, careful there." He catches me by the waist and kisses my temple, whispering, "Merry Christmas, by the way."

"Merry Christmas," I repeat, out of breath.

We walk into the dining room holding hands and smiling like two fools.

"Morning." I beam at everyone.

My mom immediately starts fussing around, serving coffee and placing two trays of cinnamon rolls on the table.

"Which ones are mine?" I ask.

Mom points to the tray on the left. "These are half raisin-free regulars." For me, I hate raisins. "And the other half is the vegan version," she adds for Julia.

Gosh, we're two spoiled-rotten kids. At this moment, a surge of appreciation for my mom swells in my chest. I'm an awful child. I never call, I come home the bare minimum, and always try to avoid my family like the plague. True, whenever I talk to Mom she finds a way to work my non-existent love life into the conversation, driving me mad. But I know she does it out of real concern for my well-being. I should try to be more patient with her, and call her more, and visit more often.

But this year I can enjoy all her maternal love, with no discussions. I dread the moment I'll have to tell her Diego and I broke up.

The thought hits me in the stomach like a punch with more force than I could've ever expected. To stage a fake breakup with my fake boyfriend has always been the plan, but after last night... What are we going to do? Are we still going to break up at the end of the week? Can you really break up if you've never even been officially together? Are we together?

The questions that have been swirling inside my head since I woke up, keep on spinning, chasing one another around my poor brain. I fend them off with a bite of warm roll and a sip of steamy coffee. Today's my first chance at a merry Christmas, and I'm not going to waste it roasting in self-doubt all day. *Que será, será...*

Sixteen

Santa Baby

On a whim of daughterly love, I offer to help Mom in the kitchen after breakfast, sending her over the moon with joy and a bit of shock. My standard MO for Christmases past had been to hide in my room until all the guests had arrived and get as little involved in the preparations—*ahem, and celebrations*—as I could.

Although my offer of help is welcomed with warmth, poor kitchen skills relegate me to vegetable-peeling duty. But I don't mind. The task is easy and repetitive; it has a steadiness to it that's keeping me Zen. I'm so at peace with the universe today. I even manage not to roll my eyes whenever Julia takes Mom's perfect recipes and mangles them with her new vegan creed. Thankfully, the special menu will apply only to her today—and to any volunteers. I doubt there'll be any. Maybe Paul will taste something out of sheer love—or duty.

I wait for the usual pang of the heart, or the tightening in my chest, that I get whenever I think about how Paul is in love with my sister. But it doesn't come. Zero. Nada. No pain. No wistfulness. Was one night with Diego really enough to make me forget Paul? Okay, it wasn't really just one night. We've been living together for two weeks, learning everything about each other...

A sudden rush of heat spreads over my cheeks. Oh gosh, the guy knows so much about me. Too much. Like my non-existent romantic track record. I can't date someone who knows all my secrets. I need a consultation ASAP.

"Mom." I throw the last peeled carrot into the bowl. "The vegetables are ready; you need something else? I wanted to drop by Blair's house and wish her Merry Christmas."

"No, sweetheart, you go right ahead. And please wish Mr. and

Mrs. Walker happy holidays from us."

"Will do."

I wash my hands, put on my jacket and boots, and march across the street.

***

I barge into Blair's room. "We need to talk."

"And Merry Christmas to you, too." Blair smirks at me from the mirror on her dressing table, then turns around in her chair to look me in the eye. "Did Julia make you eat cold mashed potatoes or something?"

"No, way worse."

"Worse than when Ross says the wrong name at the altar?" She starts playing our usual game of comparing situations to things that happened in TV shows and movies.

"Worse. Everyone hated Emily."

"Mmm… Better or worse than when Ben Stiller rescues the wrong cat in *Meet the Parents,* sprays his tail with paint, and then gets caught?"

"Funny one." I chuckle. "Worse."

"Okay." She concentrates. "Better or worse than when Patrick Dempsey was killed off of *Gray's Anatomy?*"

"Ah! Dead McDreamy, that's a low blow. Better."

With a smug smile, Blair orders, "Tell me what happened."

I bite my lower lip. "I made out with Diego all night."

"Oh, that doesn't sound bad at all. Why the pout? Is he a bad kisser?"

"No, it's not that." I drop on her bed. "The kissing was great. Epic."

"So?"

"You don't understand." I sigh. "The man knows too much."

"What does he know?"

"That I'm such a screw-up with men I needed to hire a fake boyfriend for the holidays…"

"And apparently he doesn't care; he wouldn't have kissed you otherwise… Did you start it, or did he?"

Well, he brushed his hand against mine first. And he was the one who suggested we kiss in the garden, too.

"He did, I think."

Blair flashes me an evil grin. "Was it only kissing?"

"Yeah, same as I used to do with Jackson Spencer and you with Andy Bryant before, you know, we discovered sex?"

My best friend stares at the ceiling in awe. "Those were the most romantic afternoons of my life. I don't think anyone ever kissed me like that after junior year."

"Not even Richard?"

"Richard is a great kisser, the best, really. But we never spent a whole night *just* kissing."

"Try it when we get back to New York. Last night, I was sixteen again."

Blair's face lights up. "I'm so happy for you."

I scoff. "There's nothing to be happy about. Do you really think Diego could like me?"

"He spent the night kissing you silly… Seems like a good hint."

"But he's so good looking, and we're so different. Could it ever work between us?"

"Wait, you want this to get serious? So you're not just having fun?"

I hesitate to answer.

"Oh, gosh, are you falling in love with him?"

That's too scary a thought to even consider, so I deflect the question. "I'm definitely falling in lust."

Blair narrows her eyes at me. "And what about Paul?"

"See, the weird thing is, the more time I spend around him the less I see him that way…"

"Seriously? Just like that, you're not in love with him anymore?"

"Was I ever?"

Blair's face turns smug.

"What?" I ask.

"Nothing." She shrugs. "You came here to hear my wisdom, and I'm going to give it to you. The thing between you and Diego is great. Don't you dare go all insecure about it and try to sabotage yourself for no reason. He's a wonderful guy, and he's clearly into you. And, no, he's not too hot for you, because there's no such thing."

"You're forgetting a little detail…"

"Which one?"

"I'm still paying him to be here."

Blair waves me off. "I'm sure he'll give you the money back on the first occasion. And once you're back in the city, you can start dating like two normal people. Who cares how you met? On the record, you two met through work; doesn't matter if the job setting wasn't exactly conventional."

I stare at her still half-unconvinced, but also relieved.

"Have I been persuasive enough?" Blair asks.

I nod.

"Great," she cheers. "Now that I've got you all wised up, you want to open your Christmas present?"

***

Comforted by Blair's words, I return to the house just in time to shower and get ready for the big day. Alone in my room, with my hair still damp, I pull on the dress I brought for today: black, simple, not a hint of cheer anywhere on it.

Mmm… I stare in the mirror, unsure. My habit of dressing more for a funeral than for Christmas Day doesn't seem appropriate this year. But I didn't bring any other dresses elegant enough for the occasion. I could ask to borrow something from Julia, but would her clothes even fit me? And I'd gladly skip the chance to try one on and not be able to close the zipper. Yeah, it'd just give her another opportunity to tell me how I should cut back on carbs. So, black dress it is. Unless…

I open the closet and shuffle all my old clothes to the side until I find what I'm looking for. At the back, hidden behind everything else, rests—abandoned and forgotten—my last attempt at joining my family's festivities with any real enthusiasm.

Blair forced me to buy this dress five or six years ago. She's a fan of Christmas like everybody else and had me convinced the bright red fabric would help me get into the holiday spirit. The dress was gorgeous, and it fit me perfectly, so I bought it and brought it home to wear on Christmas Day. Then, my mom—or my sister, I can't remember—majorly pissed me off with a stupid remark, which put me off any attempt of "joining in" the celebrations. And so my dress-for-a-funeral-on-Christmas-Day tradition was born.

I take out the dress and press it against my body, studying the design. Square-cut neckline with cap sleeves, and a high, fitted waist with a peplum frill detailing. The cut of the skirt is midi length, and the whole shape has a tailored fit. Too much? And more to the point, will it still fit me? Only one way to know.

In a fluid motion, I shed the black dress and replace it with the red one, glad the zipper closes all the way up. Still, it fits a little tighter than I remembered. To make sure the seams won't burst apart the first time I sit, I try a couple of squats. Not exactly comfortable, but doable. Actually, the snug fit has the positive effect of pushing up my boobs, making them seem bigger. Yeah, not bad. Not bad at all.

I'm about to take it off when the door opens and Diego walks in. He's wearing camel chinos and a deep-green sweater that makes his eyes pop. With his hair all messy as if he's just finished drying it, and still slightly damp and curly around the nape, he's breathtaking.

Insecurities gnaw at my flanks; this guy can't possibly like me. I wish I was still wearing the black dress; I'd feel less exposed. Diego, however, doesn't seem to mind the red one. He gives me a once-over and low whistles. With two quick steps, he closes the distance between us, wraps his arms around my waist, and pulls me in for a kiss as if it was the most natural thing in the world.

So, kissing each other is fair game now, apparently. No complaints here. Still, as we pull apart, I can't help but blush and, not knowing what to say, I use the first lame excuse to avoid saying anything. "I... err... need to go dry my hair."

"Sure." He winks at me and gives me a gentle push toward the door. "I'll catch you downstairs; your dad asked me to help him bring in logs for the fire."

I nod and, still equally randy and embarrassed, I make my way to the bathroom, glad I don't have to hurry. Julia called dibs on first use and showered and did her makeup while I was at Blair's. So I can take my time to style my hair with the blow dryer and flat iron and to carefully do my makeup. I pause only when I have to choose the lipstick. I'm about to go for my usual nude shade when one of Diego's remarks about my grooming habits pops into my head:

"...You like to paint your nails in the most obnoxious, shocking colors, but you'd never use a lipstick shade other than nude. Pity, because a bold red would look killer on you..."

I stare down at my nails, which are painted black. Not a shocking color, but still a fierce one. I raise my gaze back to my lips in the mirror. Could I really pull off red lipstick? Why not? Today, I feel like there's nothing I can't do. Only problem is, I don't own a red lipstick... but maybe Julia does. I shuffle through her beauty case until I find an almost new stick of Dior Addict lip gloss in a cherry shade.

Bingo!

Red takes longer than usual to apply. With natural shades, I can get away with sloppy technique, but with the red, I really have to be careful how I contour everything if I don't want to end up looking like a clown.

Once I'm done, I study the result in the mirror and almost don't recognize myself. Between the short hair, lips that look ten times plusher than mine, and a healthy glow that probably comes from not having spent the last few days stuck in front of a monitor—but could as well be the consequence of a night of adolescent making out—I'm a different person. Confident, sexy, and edgy.

That's exactly how I feel as I walk down the stairs. I stop with one step to go when Diego comes out of the living room, splinters of wood clinging to the fabric of his sweater. He freezes mid-step and stares up at me, wide-eyed.

I reach for the largest chip of bark on his chest and pull it off. "Be careful," I say. "You'll ruin your sweater."

"The only thing in ruins by the end of the day will be my sanity. Are you trying to kill me with those lips?"

"I thought you liked the red?"

"I like it too much." He pulls me closer and brushes his nose against mine. "I want to kiss you."

"You can't; it took forever to apply, and I don't have time to re-do it."

"See?" He kisses my forehead instead. "You're killing me."

"I'll make up for it later," I whisper.

He throws me a burning stare, which promises he'll hold me to my word.

My knees go weak under the intensity of his gaze, and I smile wider and brighter than ever before… My transformation from Grinch to Santa Baby is complete.

Seventeen

Rocking Around the Christmas Tree

The first, and least-welcome, guest arrives at noon: Aunt Betsy. As I hug her, I do my best not to wince at her usual smell of dust and mothballs.

"Nicola." She's the only one of my relatives who in thirty years has stubbornly refused to let go of my full name. "You're almost unrecognizable this year; what happened to you?" Then she delivers the first jab. "Have you finally decided it's time to find a man?" And the second. "Has Julia's engagement lit a fire under you?"

I force my eyes not to roll. "Actually, this is my boyfriend." I give Diego a slight push forward.

Earlier, after a brief moment of shock at my merry and bright appearance, Mom decided that this year I looked Christmassy enough to be in charge, together with Diego, of answering the door and welcoming the guests in. Julia is still helping her in the kitchen— more supervising nothing contaminates her precious vegan food. And Paul and Dad are tending the fire.

"Diego, this is my aunt Betsy," I use the diminutive she hates on purpose. "Aunt Betsy, this is Diego."

"*Elisabeth* Appleton," she corrects, throwing me a displeased look as she shakes Diego's hand. "Nice to meet you, young man."

"Diego O'Donnell. The pleasure is all mine, ma'am."

They shake hands and, even at the ripe age of ninety, I can tell the woman in Aunt Betsy is not insensitive to Diego's sex appeal.

Unfortunately, she recovers quickly enough from her initial stupor. "So, Diego, what is it that you do?"

"Acting is my calling."

"Oh." An evil little smile plays on her lips. "And does that pay the bills?"

"Not much. I work mostly as a server to make ends meet."

"I see." Turning to me, she adds, "Your parents must be thrilled to have both their girls settled down." The malicious glint in her eyes sends a completely different message. In two seconds sharp, she's nailed the one thing my parents don't approve of about Diego: his job.

I plaster a fake smile on my lips. "They are."

"Well," Evil Betsy continues. "I'm sure we'll have plenty of time to talk later, Mr. O'Donnell. Now, I need to go sit down. My old limbs are not what they used to be."

Oh, she's such a drama queen. She should've been an actress, too. Aunt Betsy is the most independent ninety-year-old I know. She drove here in her car, and she's never needed to use a cane to help her walk in her life. I'm convinced she's going to bury us all.

"Dad's in the living room with Paul," I say. "We'll join you later."

We watch her make her way down the hallway, spry as a bunny, and Diego waits for her to disappear around the corner before whispering in my ear, "Are all your relatives this charming?"

"No." I lean back into him. "You've met the worst; it's all downhill from here."

As if on cue, the doorbell rings again.

Diego goes to open the door, revealing my cousin Mandy struggling to keep a hold of two huge bags filled with wrapped gifts.

"I don't know you," she says to Diego with a cheery smile.

Diego is about to introduce himself when her three boys barrel into the house, screaming like crazed gremlins.

"BOYS!" she yells after them. "How many times do I have to tell you not to ruuuun?"

An ominous crashing noise is the only reply.

"I'm sorry." Mandy walks past us to run after them. "Nikki, love the new haircut, we'll catch up later…" And she's gone, too.

"You were saying?" Diego grins.

"At least she's nice."

Mandy's husband, Peter, comes in next, carrying as many bags as his wife. From then on, it's a steady flow of people: my dad's brother, Uncle Tom, with his wife Debra, their kids Michael and Sarah, who are about my age, their spouses and kids; and just as many relatives on my mother's side. Aunt Betsy's forty-five-year-old bachelor nephew is the last one to arrive at one o'clock.

There are too many people to have a proper meal all seated at the table—*thank goodness*—so the Christmas feast is consumed more buffet style. The older crowd takes over the dining room, while us younger folk claim the living room, sitting on the couch, armchairs, or on the pillows Mom has scattered around the huge rug for exactly this purpose. The kids have their reserved dining area set up in the kitchen.

There are about ten of us seated around the Christmas tree, ages ranging from twenty-eight to forty-five. Mom comes and goes, bringing new trays of food which quickly get emptied—except for Julia's special trays. All the vegan platters are still half-full by the end of the meal, scattered atop the furniture surrounding her. I spot Cousin Michael take a bite of one of her brownish tarts, and discretely spit it into his paper napkin two seconds later. But otherwise, it seems everyone has quickly learned to steer clear of whatever platters Julia is grazing from.

We make it all the way to the mini desserts stage before the questions about my new boyfriend start.

"So," Mandy asks, "how did you and Diego meet?"

"Through work," I say, keeping my answer vague, as planned.

"Yeah, you said that," Julia intervenes. "But how, exactly?"

I launch into our fake narrative. "Diego was auditioning for a commercial I was producing, and when I called him in to tell him he got the part…"

"I told her I'd rather have a date," Diego ends the story for me.

I love that we appear like one of those couples who can end each other's sentences. It's cheesy and soppy, but it's making me feel all warm and fuzzy, as if what Diego and I are saying was actually true.

Julia arches an eyebrow. "Really?"

Diego casually twirls his finger around a lock of my hair and stares right into my eyes. "Couldn't let the prettiest producer I've ever met slip through my fingers."

Okay, this is not the lengthy and super-detailed list of all the reasons he wanted to date me I'd asked him to come up with, but strangely, it's more than enough. It's the way he says it, and the way he looks at me as he speaks. *I'm sold.* And so, it seems, is everybody else.

"What was the ad for?" Julia asks.

"Deodorant," we say in unison, sharing a secret smile.

"MOM!" One of Mandy's boys—Jarred, Jake, Johnathan, I don't know, they all have J-starting names—barrels into the room. "I want to open my presents."

Mandy's sitting next to the tree. She wraps one arm around his legs and pulls him toward her to kiss him on the cheek. He can't be older than four or five. "Go call your brothers and cousins and we can all open our presents together."

"Yaaayyyy," he yells, running away.

I can't help but think, *Tasmanian devil. How does she handle three of them?*

The kids flood into the room shortly after, followed by the old folks. Those of us who were perched on the sofa or armchair leave the more comfortable accommodations to them and find new spots on the rug, so that almost every inch of the living room's floor is now occupied.

Once everyone's settled, the complicated gift-distribution operation starts. All the packages under the Christmas tree get passed around, along with the presents my relatives brought with them. We don't each buy a gift for everybody else—Mom buys the presents for the extended family circle, with one gift per family plus a toy for each of the kids. Still, there are a lot of wrapped boxes passing hands, and delirious quantities of colored paper being torn and scattered around.

I reach into the red-and-white-striped plastic bag where I stuffed my presents for everyone and start handing them out. Now I feel super silly for having spent so much time researching the perfect gift for Paul. Luckily, I didn't go too overboard with it. He's still getting a book like everyone else, only a bit more special.

I collect my family's gifts in return, and am surprised when Diego hands me not one, but two wrapped bundles. One I recognize as the ring box from the mall. The other is a mystery. I tear into that one first.

I push the wrapping paper aside to reveal a hardback copy of *Harry Potter and the Sorcerer's Stone*. I flip the cover open, and gasp at the tiny writing printed on the copyright page:

Printed in the U.S.A.23
First American edition, October 1998

I stare up at Diego, astonished. "This must've cost you a fortune."

"Nah." He shrugs. "Found it in a used bookstore in Brooklyn. I don't think the owner realized it might have any value."

Still, I don't know what to say. I keep looking into his eyes, speechless.

He must read the unasked question in my gaze, because he leans in and whispers in my ear, "Everyone deserves a little surprise at Christmas."

Before I know what I'm doing, I turn my head to the side and kiss him. A deep, non-PG-rated kiss.

"Ewww," Sarah's five-year-old daughter protests. "Mom, they're kissing."

I pull back, smiling, and say, "Thank you."

"You might want to open your other present, too," Diego says, in a voice so low only I can hear. "Would look a bit suspicious if you didn't." He grins at me.

A minute later, I'm pulling on my cat ring when the inevitable happens. From the other side of the fireplace, Paul opens his present from me and exclaims, "Nikki, wow. Liam Grady's new book." And then he asks the deadly question. "How did you manage to get a signed copy? I thought those were super rare."

They are, damn me.

"Oh, really?" I play dumb. "I just picked it up at the store from the new releases booth. Guess I got lucky."

Next to me, Diego tenses. He knows I'm lying; he was with me when I bought all the other books, and Paul's book wasn't among them. Let's hope he won't read too much into it.

Eighteen

All I Want For Christmas Is You

My hopes are in vain. Diego is cold and detached with me for the rest of the day. He does nothing overtly hostile, but by now I can pick up on his moods as well as if I'd known him a lot longer than two weeks. And I can tell he's pissed.

It's written all over his curt, monosyllabic answers. In the way he does his best to avoid meeting my eyes after we've been eye-flirting for days. And in the way he avoids even the slightest contact with me.

I just know it has to do with Paul and his gift. Diego is no fool, and if I got to know him so well in such a short time, the same must be true for him. But even if I'm pretty sure why he's upset, I say nothing. I'm too much of a chicken. So I let this new distance between us fester until we're both in bed that night and there's nowhere left to hide. Not even in the oppressive silence weighing down on us both.

When I can't stand it any longer, I burst out with, "Are you mad at me?"

Diego doesn't turn his head toward me. He just keeps staring at the wall, arms crossed over his chest. "I don't know; should I be mad at you?"

"No, why would you?"

"I feel like I don't have all the info here."

"What info?" I ask innocently.

He finally meets my eyes. "Mmm, for example... Let's see..." He scrunches his face in a mock-interrogative expression. "How long have you been in love with your soon-to-be brother-in-law?"

I'm *so* busted. "Paul and I have been friends since college. That's all."

Diego throws me such a seething, don't-bullshit-me stare, that I'm compelled to admit, "I thought I had feelings for him for the longest time, but I'm past that now."

"Is that why you went to such trouble to get him the perfect Christmas present? I checked the author's website. It's almost impossible to get a signed copy of a Liam Grady book. The only way is to attend one of his book events and queue in line for hours, and his New York gigs are always the busiest."

True. True. And True.

With no intelligent reply to offer, I get petty. "So what?"

"You bought everybody else's presents with barely a week to go before Christmas, not giving two cents about what you were getting, but for Paul, you just happened to stumble across the release event and… what? You decided waiting in line for hours to get a signed book for your sister's fiancé was a good way to spend the afternoon? Do you go through all that trouble for all your ex-crushes?"

"No, but—"

"Is that why I'm really here?" Diego interrupts me. "To make Paul jealous?"

"No, of course not."

Diego keeps staring at me, clearly unsatisfied with my answer. Taking a deep breath, I try to explain the big mess I've gotten myself into. "Okay, fine, I used to have a crush on him. That's why I worked so hard on his gift." I cringe at how easily I'm now downgrading my previous obsession with Paul to a silly crush, but that's really all it feels like now. "And yes, he was a big part of the reason why it was so difficult for me to come home alone this year. Julia had just announced the engagement, and that she was bringing Paul home for the holidays, and I thought I still liked him, and that Julia had sort of stolen him from me, and it was too much to handle on my own as the spinster sister."

I watch Diego as he tries to digest all this new information.

"But now you're over him?" he asks.

"Yes. One hundred percent."

"Is there anything else you haven't told me?"

"No," I say.

Diego keeps quiet next to me for the longest time, and I have no idea what's passing through his mind as he stares down at the comforter. When he finally lifts his gaze again, his eyes are burning. "When did you stop liking him?"

There's only one honest answer I can give him. "The first time you kissed me, in the garden. It's like you erased everything I ever felt for—"

He doesn't let me finish. His face contorts into an almost animal snarl, a primordial expression of male possessiveness, and he kisses me, imprisoning my face between his hands and pressing his lips to mine with such passion I might faint. Thank goodness I'm already in bed.

We kiss for a long time, just like last night. But when he looks me in the eyes and tenderly brushes the hair away from my forehead, I know tonight is not going to be kissing-only. I haven't been with a man in forever, and I've never wanted anyone the way I want Diego right now. My body wants him, my mind wants him… I want to give myself to him, and I want all of him in return.

Diego has been in my life only a short time, and we haven't spoken about the future or where we stand with each other. But looking into the green of his eyes, I can't help but trust him with all my heart, with all of my body, with everything that I am…

Making love to Diego is a soul-wrenching experience. It shatters me to pieces, before bringing me back together in his embrace. We make love all night until we're both too exhausted to keep going, and we fall asleep clinging to each other.

When I wake up still wrapped in his arms, I experience a brief moment of pure ecstasy. Then a sheer terror engulfs me, making my chest clench under the pressure of its tendrils. I'm terrified that I'm flying so high I wouldn't survive a fall. Terrified, because I realize I've fallen hard for a man I barely know. A man whose ideas on the future I ignore. Is he looking for a relationship? Does he want to get married? To have kids?

Okay, maybe I'm jumping the gun a little here. But I can't get rid of the cloud of doubts circling my head even if nothing about last night feels like a mistake.

That's why I sneak out of bed before he wakes up. I'm not sure he would've wanted to talk right away, but I'm too scared of learning the answers to all my questions. All I need now is to shower and clear my head first; we'll have plenty of time to talk later. Now, I just want to be happy and cherish what happened.

Nineteen

Do You Hear What I Hear?

There's a long-standing Moore tradition I need to submit to on the day after Christmas. Since we were old enough to be safely left alone in the kitchen, Julia and I have been in charge of lunch. With us busy preparing the food, our parents can spend the morning visiting their neighbors to exchange late best wishes. The tradition originated mainly to give Mom a rest after the cooking marathon of the previous day, but also because, since we're basically rearranging scraps, it's impossible even for the two of us to screw up the meal.

Julia has been uncharacteristically quiet, but I don't mind. I'm too tired for conversation. Even if I got up super late, I'm still experiencing the after-effects of a sleepless night. And I might be unable to stop smiling, but the bags under my eyes are blossoming. I hope we didn't make too much noise. What if my parents heard us?

Another yawn turns to a half-smile as a memory from last night plays in my head.

Enough, Nikki.

Right, I need to concentrate on the practical tasks and stop reliving every second of my night with Diego. Not that what I'm doing requires any extent of brainpower. Right now I'm busy revamping the leftover coleslaw by adding more sauce and transferring it into a serving bowl. I'm sprinkling a generous amount of sauce over the vegetables when Julia bangs a metal spoon on a platter, making me jump.

I turn toward her. "What's up?"

"Nothing. It's only the third time I've asked you to pass me a wooden spoon."

Someone is cranky today. I grab the biggest spoon from the utensil jar on my side of the kitchen island and hand it over. "This one okay?"

"Yeah."

Julia snatches it rather violently.

"Hey, what's wrong with you?"

"Nothing's wrong with *me,*" she hisses.

I set aside the coleslaw for a second and turn to face her. "You have a problem?"

"Why would I have any problem? Relax. You can keep smiling and humming under your breath, not caring about anybody else but yourself."

"Is it a crime to be happy now?"

"No, but you could be a little less selfish."

"Why? What did I do?"

Julia brutally mixes her mashed potatoes as she answers. "The fact that you can't even see it should tell you enough."

"See what?!"

"That just for once." She drops her spoons and points at her chest. "This Christmas was supposed to be about me. About my engagement. About introducing my fiancé into the family. But, of course, you couldn't let me have that. No, you had to bring a new boyfriend home and steal everyone's attention."

"Me. Me. Me. Oh, pooh-pooh, poor Julia had to share the attention with someone else, what a tragedy. You sound like a five-year-old. Grow up!"

"And you sound like a bitch."

"Better a bitch than a brat," I snap, satisfied to get the last word in.

I get back to the coleslaw, but as I'm unloading a generous serving into the new bowl, the spoon slips from my grip and cartwheels in the air. I dash to catch it mid-flight, but as I grip the handle, a big glop of coleslaw flies away and lands on the side of Julia's face.

Startled, she brings a hand to her neck. "You didn't."

"I'm so sorry!"

I'm so focused on finding a rag for her to clean up with that I miss the mashed potatoes projectile headed for my face. It hits me in the right temple, sliding down my hair.

"Are you crazy?" I glare at her. "I didn't do it on purpose."

"You think I'm stupid?" Julia screams, and reaches for the mashed potatoes again.

"Don't you dare," I threaten.

She ignores me and—*squish!*—I'm hit near the collarbone.

After that, it's mayhem. I grab the first thing within my reach on the table—cranberry sauce—and throw it at her. She retaliates with a greenish vegan slop, and we keep going until we're both panting hard and drenched head to toe in goo.

"Can you tell me why you're so mad at me, really?" I ask.

"Maybe because I find it strange that a boyfriend no one had ever heard about suddenly appeared the day after I told you I was engaged," Julia yells, still panting. "And it's even stranger that he just so happens to look and act exactly like the fantasy man I told you about when I came up to your office!"

"You said you wanted someone dark and mysterious, someone

dangerous. I don't see Diego that way."

"I also said he would have to be tall, with smoldering green eyes, and full lips… Ring a bell? I said I wanted him to speak Italian, and to ride a bike. That he would have to be some kind of struggling artist, someone who lives paycheck to paycheck. And who buys cheap rings. That's basically Diego's identikit. You really failed to notice?"

"So what if I did? You're just jealous I stole the attention for five minutes, preventing everybody in the family from drooling over your one-carat ring the entire time."

"Oh, so now I'm the jealous one?" Julia brushes a slab of muck that's dripping down her forehead away from her eye. "That's rich, coming from you!"

"What's that supposed to mean?"

"That at least now you can stop being jealous of me dating Paul."

The accusation hurts like a slap. "Why would I be jealous of you dating Paul?"

"Oh, please. I've always known you had a thing for him."

I freeze at that. My first instinct is to deny it, but an irrational rage takes over and, calm as a snake before it attacks, I hiss, "So why did you go out with him if you knew?"

Julia lowers her eyes, looking momentarily guilty, before her usual flippancy is back. She shrugs, and says, "I liked him."

That could be it: she saw something she liked and took it, no matter whose feelings she had to trample in the process. But that fraction-of-a-second guilty stare gave her away.

I narrow my eyes at her. "Did you go out with Paul specifically to piss me off?"

"Don't be ridiculous." She waves dismissively, but I see how she flares her nostrils, like she does whenever she's lying.

"You're lying." The realization hits me in the gut like a sucker punch. "You knew I liked him, and that's the only reason you went out with him." My voice goes up a notch. "You're such a bitch!"

Blind fury takes over again, and I make a grab for the first offending substance I can find—chocolate pudding—and throw a handful at her, aiming for her face. I miss and hit her below the shoulder.

"Aaaaargh!" she screams. Not even trying to clean herself, Julia grasps a bowl full of whipped cream and slashes it in my direction, covering my entire torso in white slime. "I hate you!"

"*You* hate *me*? After what you did? Why?" I fling a saucer filled with cold gravy at her. A brown, shoulder-to-hip, gooey welt appears on her clothes. "Why would you do something so mean on purpose? What did I ever do to you?"

"You've always looked down on me!" Julia shrieks. "But now I realize you're just a loser who spent the past two years drooling over her younger sister's boyfriend. How pathetic is that?"

"At least I don't think Paul is plain and boring and without imagination. And I'm not marrying someone only to spite my older sister. Now, that's pathetic!"

"Is that what you really think of me?" a male voice asks.

Both our necks snap to the kitchen entrance, where Paul is staring at Julia with an unreadable expression on his face.

"No, of course not!" Julia hastens to say, panic written all over her face.

"And what about the rest?" I've never seen Paul so eerily calm. "Did you go out with me just to get back at her?"

"Paul, I can explain." Julia wrings her dirty hands. "It's not... I'm not..."

Paul lifts his hands to stop her. "I don't want to hear it." His gaze shifts to her clutched hands. "Keep the ring, take it off, I don't care... We're not getting married."

Then he turns on his heel and marches out of the kitchen.

"Paul, please." Julia runs after him.

Two seconds later, the main door bangs shut. Julia reopens it and screams Paul's name again and again, until everything goes quiet. She walks back into the kitchen, her tear-streaked face red and blotched, her hair wild, and her clothes all dirty from the food fight.

"He took the car." Julia throws me a withering look. "I hope you're happy now." She looks like she's about to add something, but a sob makes her whole body shake, and she runs up the stairs crying without sparing another look in my direction.

I stand in the kitchen breathing heavily, still shocked by everything I just learned. A blob of whipped cream slides down from my forehead to land on the island, reminding me I'm covered in food. I make a quick dash into the guest bathroom, removing my pants and sweater and washing the slime out of my hair and face the best I can. All the while, my brain keeps racing with contrasting thoughts.

Part of me thinks Julia got exactly what she deserved. She stole Paul from me willingly and knowingly, and now she deserves to suffer, to have her wedding canceled, to try being the single sister for a while and see how much she enjoys it. But there's another, protective piece of me that feels guilty for what happened. That wants to fix the situation for her. No matter how or why her love story with Paul started, I know her feelings are real now. Julia's stupid complaints are irrelevant; she didn't mean any of them. She and Paul are perfect for each other. But taken out of context, the conversation Paul overheard could really ruin their relationship forever if not set right.

I have to find him and bring him back home.

My mind set, I crunch my dirty clothes in a ball and hurry out of the bathroom wearing only a tank top and panties to go get a fresh change of clothes from my room. I freeze at the bottom of the stairs. Diego is sitting halfway up them, and when he sees me he throws me a stare pretty much equal to the one Paul used on Julia.

"Hey," I say tentatively. "I've made a mess."

"Yeah, I've heard," he replies, his tone glacial.

Worry wraps around me. "How much did you hear?"

"All of it."

"Diego, I can explain everything, but not now." I find the courage to climb up the stairs and walk past him and into my bedroom.

The moment I walk in, the door clicks shut behind me.

"Sorry," Diego says. "I want answers now."

"Well, now I can't." I drop the dirty clothes in a plastic bag and open my luggage to find new ones. "I have to go find Paul."

"Paul, right." Diego snarls. "Last night you swore you didn't have any more secrets."

"And I don't."

"Oh, so you just forgot to mention that I'm basically a product of your sister's imagination? When I asked you why you picked me for this job, you said it was because *you* liked me. How many other lies have you spun me?"

"None."

"Really? First, I find out you're in love with your sister's fiancé. Then, that you've chosen me to be her secret dream guy. What did you do? Did you put all her requisites in your agency's search engine and wait for the best match to pop up?"

My face goes on fire. That's exactly what I did, but I don't think confessing it to Diego now would do any good.

I squeeze into a clean pair of jeans and button them up. "It's not like that."

"So you say. Why should I trust anything that comes out of your mouth?"

Socks, I need socks.

"Because you can. Ask me anything you want later, but now I have to go."

"Because you have to run after Paul."

Shoes… where are my boots? Ah, there under the bed. "Yeah, I have to find him and talk to him before it's too late."

I pull a knit sweater on, barely hearing what Diego says next.

"Guess now he and Julia are no longer an item, everything's changed. Was this your plan all along? To bring me here to break them up?"

What did he say? I don't have time to ask him. I search for the car keys, finding them under a T-shirt on my desk. I need to go and fast.

"Listen, I know you're upset." I stop a second to look at him. "But right now I need to find Paul and bring him home. Then we can talk all day if you want."

Diego is still blocking the door, so I wait for him to step aside. He doesn't.

"Please don't go," he says.

"I have to."

Without another word, he steps out of the way, leaving the exit free. I pause on the threshold and turn back toward him. "I'll be back as soon as I can."

Diego says nothing. He doesn't even look at me as I walk out of the room.

Twenty

Let It Snow! Let It Snow! Let It Snow!

Outside, it has started snowing. I trudge my way to the rental car and start the engine to get the car warm while I rid the windshield of ice. There's a pit of anguish in my stomach. Partly for the mess I've created with Julia and Paul, but mostly for the hurt look on Diego's face as he begged me not to go.

I wish I could've stayed and talked to him, or listened to what he was saying, but right now finding Paul has to be my priority. Diego can wait for an hour; he's already so mad at me, it won't make much of a difference. I've screwed up, big time. But even if I haven't been one hundred percent honest with him, he must know how I feel about him after last night. Once the initial shock has passed, he will forgive me.

If how Julia and Paul started dating isn't relevant, the same is true for Diego and me. Feelings matter; the rest is dust in the wind.

When the windshield is clear enough, I hop in the car and pull off the road, not sure where I'm headed. Where did Paul go? He could've gone straight back to New York, but knowing him, I doubt it. Paul isn't that impulsive; I don't see him driving away to the city without a word to anyone. He must've gone searching for a quiet place to think and I know exactly where to look. No point in calling him, he wouldn't pick up.

Driving slowly in the sudden blizzard, I head for the coast. I pass a few panoramic pull-over spots without success, before spotting Paul's gray SUV sitting alone in the parking lot overlooking Harvey's Beach. I pull up next to him, get out of the car, and knock on his passenger window.

Paul turns toward me, startled. He must recognize me even through the condensation-covered glass, because he leans forward to open the passenger door for me. I hop in, glad to escape the biting wind that's whipping the coast.

"How did you find me?" Paul asks.

"The ocean. You always come near the water when you have to think. At NYU, I could always find you by the Hudson after a breakup."

Paul snorts. "Julia had no clue where to go, did she?"

"That's not fair, Paul, I have ten years of knowing you on her."

He stares back out the windshield at the dark sea. "Why are you here?"

"To bring you back home. You and Julia need to talk... Clear things up."

"Why?"

"Because you love each other, and a stupid argument shouldn't—"

"No, why are you here advocating for her?" Paul asks. "After what she just told you."

"She's my sister."

"Yeah, and half an hour ago you were throwing food and yelling how much you hated her."

"So, we fight. Doesn't mean we don't care for each other."

"Is what she said true? Were you really into me?" Paul turns toward me. "Are you?"

I look at him, imagining how differently this conversation might've gone only a couple of days ago. "I was for the longest time," I say, surprised at how sure I am of my words. "But not anymore."

"I never knew. You never said anything."

"Paul, you were my best friend, and the timing never seemed right. Either you were dating someone, or I was, and then you moved to Chicago. Then you came back to New York..."

"And started dating your sister."

"Exactly. Until that day, I'd always thought something was bound to happen between us, *eventually*. But after you and Julia got together, I knew it would be impossible. Didn't... didn't the thought of us being more than friends ever cross your mind?"

Paul smiles an enigmatic smile. "It did... But I never thought you were interested, and when you introduced me to your sister, I took it as my final answer. You didn't see me that way, and never would..."

I stare into his blue eyes, into the life that could've been... Paul and I, we would've made each other happy. That much, I'm sure of. But that thread of destiny has been lost forever; it was never meant to be. It's another man who makes my heart beat now, Diego. And another woman who Paul loves and wants to marry, Julia. I just have to remind him.

"Maybe we should think about working on our communication

skills." I chuckle. "Which brings us back to Julia. Paul, you have to forgive her."

"I really don't understand how you can sit here defending her after she's told you the only reason she and I are together is that she wanted to hurt you."

"Because she didn't want to hurt-*hurt* me—bug me a little, yes, but that's all. I'm sure Julia didn't realize how much I cared for you, or she wouldn't have done it."

"Are you sure you no longer…?"

"One hundred percent," I say firmly. "I'm in love with Diego." The ease with which the words came out of my mouth surprises me. Not a doubt in my mind about their truth. "And you're in love with my sister."

Paul scoffs. "Yeah, for all the good that will do me. Seems clear she doesn't really love me; that our entire relationship is a big, fat sham."

"Paul, it doesn't matter how it started. If Julia really only wanted to annoy me, she would've slept with you once and dumped you the next day. She wouldn't be marrying you."

"Great, that makes me feel so much better about my future wife." Paul sighs. "I've always known she could be a little spoiled, but I never imagined her to be so mean and petty."

"That's only because you're not a woman."

"Thank you, I guess? What do you mean?"

"Female psychology is more complicated and"—I lift one hand in small increments—"layered. What she did wasn't great, but it doesn't mean she's all bad. One mean action doesn't define who she is as a person. You shouldn't punish her for something that has nothing to do with the two of you."

"But it does. We wouldn't be here if she hadn't randomly decided one day to piss off her sister."

"But does it really matter?"

"Shouldn't it?"

"Not really. How many times do people get together for all the wrong reasons? Is dating a guy because you saw him in a bar and found him attractive really any better or more profound?"

"No idea; I don't date many guys."

I playfully swat him. "Come on, you know what I mean. First dates are superficial and meaningless most of the time. It's what comes later that matters. Julia is in love with you, and you're in love with her. The rest, you can work out."

"Even if I'm plain and boring?"

"Oh, you know Julia, my sister doesn't mean half the things that come out of her mouth."

"So, Jules doesn't really want to date a tall biker with green eyes and dark hair?"

"I guarantee you she doesn't. She only wants you…"

Paul's phone rings from inside the small compartment between our seats.

He picks the phone up and stares at the screen. "It's her. She's already called a million times."

Paul lets the call go unanswered.

"Please text her," I say. "Tell her you're coming home to talk. She's suffered enough."

He considers this, then starts typing.

"Why are you smiling?" I ask.

With a devilish grin, he says, "After today, I have enough leverage never to touch a vegan meal again."

And at that moment, as he makes the joke, I know he and Julia will be all right. A huge weight lifts off my chest… only to be immediately replaced by another. One relationship salvaged, but there's still another I have to mend. I give Paul a hug, then climb out and brave the cold back to my own car.

On the drive home, all I can think about is Diego and what I'm going to say to him. There are no excuses for what I did. I can only apologize and hope he forgives me.

***

At home, Paul makes the mistake of going in through the front door. We pulled up in my street only seconds apart, but as he walked up the main walkway, I snuck around the house to use the back door.

The short trek through knee-deep snow proves worth the hassle as I gingerly open the rear door and hear my parents assail Paul with questions.

"...the kitchen looked like a war zone," Mom's saying. "You and Nikki were gone."

Dad chimes in. "And we couldn't get Julia to stop sobbing and come out of her room..."

I don't wait to hear how Paul is going to dig himself out of this hole. Walking on tiptoes, I slip inside the house and up the stairs to my room with no one noticing me.

Diego isn't in my room. And I can't help but notice the space seems half-empty.

Because it is.

All his stuff is gone. His clothes, his bag, his jacket. I take in all the empty spots where his things should've been, until my eyes land on a crumpled brown envelope lying on the bed. Propped on top of it is a set of keys—the spare for my apartment that I gave Diego.

I toss the car keys on my desk and sit on the bed, clutching the envelope in my hands. I know what's inside; still, I open it and shuffle through the wad of cash. A tight pull in my chest makes it hard to breathe. Even as my face flushes with heat and my palms pool with sweat, I feel cold.

Diego is gone. The message he left couldn't be clearer. Nevertheless, I jump off the bed and ransack the room in search of a note or anything else that would explain his absence. But there's nothing.

I shouldn't have left without talking to him. No, I was right, I needed to find Paul and fix things. Diego is the one who should've waited for me. No matter how mad he is with me, running away isn't the answer.

I fish my phone out of my bag and call him.

The call goes unanswered.

I dial his number again and wait in vain.

On my third attempt, I get sent straight to voicemail.

Avoiding me, are you?

Oooooh, but he's not going to get out of this so easily. Nuh-uh. I mean, he doesn't have a car or his stupid bike; how far could he have gotten? Not very far. I can still catch him, wherever he is.

The sinking realization that I knew exactly where to find Paul, but have no idea where to look for Diego, hits me like a hard blow. It doesn't matter. He has to be around Old Saybrook somewhere. This is a small town; there are only so many hotels he could've gone to.

Fueled by my new purpose, I march down the stairs, forgetting to be stealthy.

"Nikki!" My mom spots me the second I set foot on the landing. "Are you all right?"

"Yeah, I-I just need… Diego and I…"

"Oh, yes, darling. Such a pity he had to go back to New York early. He told us about the casting call for the big job."

At least he had the decency to cover up his sudden disappearance with my family, leaving me to explain the fight—the breakup? What is this, anyway? Doesn't matter; this is not the time to label things. My only concern is to find Diego, explain everything, and beg him not to go.

Right, finding him. Mom is my best chance at fresh intelligence.

"Yeah, Mom, he texted me to tell me. He was really sorry, but he couldn't miss an opportunity so big. I just wish I could catch him before he goes and say goodbye in person."

"Oh, he took a cab to the train station only fifteen minutes ago. If you hurry, you should get to him in time."

"Thank you, Mom!" I pull her into a bone-crushing hug and kiss the top of her head. "You're the best."

I let her go and rush back outside. I need to get to the station before Diego leaves.

After ten minutes of frantic driving, I skid to a halt in the Amtrak parking lot, not caring that my car is strewn halfway through two parking spots, or that I could get fined for leaving it like that. There's only one thing on my mind. Only one man.

Inside the station, I stare at the departure board and see that the next train to New York is at 5:15 pm. The big, round clock dangling from the ceiling says it's only a quarter to four. I've made it with plenty of time to spare. Now I just have to find him.

Slightly less panicked than before, I search around the station. The place is almost deserted. There's no one near the tracks, or in the waiting room, or in the area near the vending machines. I even go as far as checking the men's room. When I come up empty-handed again, I walk back to the main entrance and up to the ticket booth.

"Excuse me," I say to the man behind the thick glass.

"Where would you like to go, miss?"

"Oh, no. I'm not here to buy a ticket. I was wondering if you sold one to New York to a friend of mine; he must've come here only minutes ago."

"Tall guy, dark hair, leather jacket?"

My chest swells with hope. "Yes, him. Did you see him?"

"Hard to miss; it was my only sale of the day."

"You know where he went?"

"He left with the 3:32 train to New York, darling."

My heart sinks. "Oh. *Oh.* Thank you."

"It was nothing, dear. And happy holidays."

Yeah, happy indeed. Holly jolly merry freaking bright!

"To you, too."

I walk away and collapse on the nearest bench, staring blankly at the empty tracks. Diego left. He's gone. He wants nothing else to do with me. I was too late. I lost him…

***

I sit on the bench for the longest time. The snowstorm eventually gives way to a timid, pallid sun that starts disappearing under the horizon soon afterward. When it's all gone, the chill of the station becomes unbearable, and I find the strength to get up from this frozen bench and go back to my car.

On the drive home, my head goes strangely blank. It's empty. As empty as my chest feels. When I walk into the house, I lie to my mother and tell her I managed to catch up with Diego and say goodbye. And that, no, I'm not hungry, I just want to rest a little. Thankfully, she doesn't ask questions about the kitchen fight, or what happened with Julia. I have no idea what Paul told her, and right now I don't care.

Mr. Darcy rubs against my jeans, arching his back and raising his tail, wanting me to pick him up. I oblige him and bring him upstairs with me. In my room, I change into PJs and try to coax the blood to flow back to my red toes, rubbing my feet in a blanket and putting on a pair of clean, warm socks. Then I hide under the covers.

It's a mistake.

The sheets still smell of Diego. Against my better judgment, I grab his pillow and press it to my nose, inhaling deeply. I'm exhausted, ironically, because I spent the night awake making love to Diego, and I can't wrap my head around how much has changed in such a short time. How can one person go from waking up so perfectly happy, to ending up back in bed less than twelve hours later so utterly destroyed?

I smell the pillow again, and that does it; tears streak down my cheeks uncontrolled. Mr. Darcy is purring next to me, but the sound's usually soothing effect is lost on me today. I can't help but resent the cat a little at how content he looks; he has his half of the bed all back to himself.

All I want to do is sleep, but my brain is too jacked up to let me. But as my body begins to warm up after being out in the cold for the better part of the afternoon, the heavy blankets and hypnotic purring sound start to win. Weariness takes over, and I doze off.

When I open my eyes again, there's a faint light coming in through the windows. How long did I sleep? The bedside table clock tells me it's half past six in the morning. Oh, so I was out cold all evening and night. I sit up in bed feeling slightly sick and dizzy, my stomach protesting loudly. Figures. I've had nothing to eat since yesterday at breakfast, when the world still seemed like a good place.

I sneak down to the kitchen, brew a pot of dark coffee, and eat a leftover cinnamon bun. Before anyone wakes up, I go back to my room. Unfortunately, caged up in here, my brain starts obsessing again. I'd like to be one of those proud women who can flip a switch and immediately move on with their lives after being dumped. But I'm not. So, less than an hour later, I text Diego. No reply comes. I call him once, twice, with no result. I write him an email begging him to pick up the phone. Text him again. Call.

Nothing.

There's only silence on the other side.

By midday, my depression is turning into seething anger. How dare he sleep with me and then run away the next day without a word? So, yeah, I made a mistake. I wasn't one hundred percent honest with him from the start. But our relationship became something neither of us expected, and at least I was ready to stand and face my mistakes.

Like an adult would. He's just a child running away.

Or maybe it was all in my head. He never promised me anything; our being together always had a deadline. Diego just pulled the plug three days early. He probably never imagined a future for us back in Manhattan. He had a little side fun on the job while he was here, and that was it.

But he gave the money back.

It doesn't matter. It's an insignificant detail. All his other actions speak volumes. He doesn't want to be with me? Well, then, I sure as hell don't want to be with him! I've been perfectly happy without a man for the longest time, and I was a fool to bare my soul to a perfect stranger.

I only need to seal my heart back into its bunker and go back to being the rational, sensible woman I was before. Cold, professional, detached.

Determined to erase any trace of Diego from my life, I rip the sheets off the bed and replace them with fresh ones. I drop everything in the laundry basket and take a long, hot shower, trying to scrub him off my skin. Unfortunately, as I soap up, the light catches on the tiny silver band adorning my left hand. I pull the ring off and eye the shower drain uncertainly. It'd be so easy to let it slip down the tube and make it disappear forever, but silly me, I can't get myself to throw the band away.

What is it anyway? A present I bought myself, Diego had literally nothing to do with it. I have witnesses. There are three angry shop assistants ready to corroborate my version. And I like the ring. I slip it back on. The ring stays.

What about the Harry Potter first edition?

I'll sell it off on eBay and make plenty of money off it. That's what I'll do.

I rinse the shampoo off my hair with a vengeance and step out of the shower.

Wrapped in a towel, I brace my hands on the sink and give myself a little motivational speech, reminding myself I'm a strong, independent woman. So that by the time Mom calls everyone down for lunch, I'm a logical, put-together person again.

Throughout the meal, I notice Julia seeking to catch my eye, but I stubbornly avoid her gaze. Sooner or later, we'll have to talk. A food fight can't be our last interaction. But it's not a conversation I'm looking forward to having. What I said to Paul is true—one bad action doesn't make her a bad person. But still, the thought that one of the people who should always have my back was out to get me instead is unsettling.

Oh, come on, get off your high horse, a little voice inside my head sneers. *You were just as bad when you picked out a fake boyfriend specifically to make Julia jealous.*

I shut my annoying conscience off and excuse myself as soon as I'm done eating. My plan is to spend the rest of today and tomorrow holed up in my room, working, until on Saturday I can finally go back to my real life and to sanity. As far away from family drama and fake-boyfriends-turned-real-runaway-boyfriends as I can.

Twenty-one

Silent Nights

I've barely sat down at the desk in my bedroom, ready to fire up my laptop, when a knock on my door disrupts my plan of isolating myself from the world for the foreseeable future.

"Yeah?" I call.

Julia walks in, the image of a repentant sister. "Can we talk?"

Well, we had to face off at some point. Better to just rip off the Band-Aid, I guess. I'll still have plenty of time to be alone. The rest of my life, actually.

"Sure." I shrug and shift my chair so that it's facing her.

Julia sits at the foot of the bed. "Let me start by saying I know I can be petty and insufferable at times, and that I'm aware I have a serious problem with not being the center of everyone's attention."

My mouth dangles open. I'm shocked. This is the first time in twenty-eight years I've heard Julia admit she has flaws, and that she isn't always one hundred percent right about everything.

I narrow my eyes at her. "Who are you, and what did you do with my sister?"

"Why did you run after Paul to save my ass yesterday?" she asks, ignoring my joke. "After the way I treated you."

"Because I know Paul; never let something fester with him. He needed to hear the other side of the story, and that couldn't come from you, not while he was still so mad. Also…" I pause here, undecided if I should say what I'm really thinking. But if we have to have one big, clarifying talk, it wouldn't make sense to leave my hurt feelings out. "…I'm not in the business of ruining the lives of the people I love on purpose."

Tears well in Julia's eyes. "I never meant to ruin your life or hurt you."

"Really? Because dating a guy only because you knew I liked him seems like a pretty good way to achieve exactly that."

"When I said 'yes' to that first date with Paul, I did it only to annoy you a little. I thought we would've gone out once, flirted some, and then the fling would die there. I wasn't prepared to fall in love with him so completely after only one date. And after that, I didn't have the strength to call it off because of you. And I hated myself for putting an even bigger wedge between us. In the past two years, you've become even colder and more detached."

"Well, can you blame me? And why did you want to annoy me so badly in the first place, anyway?"

"Because I wanted you to pay attention to me. For twenty-six years, you never so much as—"

"Please, Julia, not the neglected sister act again," I interrupt. "I've always been there for you when you needed me."

"Technically, yes, but was it out of duty, or because you wanted to? I always felt like the sister you were stuck with, as opposed to the sister you wanted, or…" Julia stares out the window across the street. "…the sister you chose."

I follow her gaze to Blair's house. "Is this about Blair again? Julia, I can have a best friend and still love my sister. The two are not mutually exclusive."

"Yeah, but since we were kids, you two have always shoved me to the sidelines of your cool lives."

That's such a distorted view of reality, I'm appalled. "Julia, I hate to break it to you, but teenagers don't like to hang out with younger kids. Two years might seem like a short gap, but it's not when you're in high school. And I'm not saying it was very mature of me or right not to spend time with my little sister, but it's the way teenage girls act. And Blair and I were never such cool kids; you've always been more popular than us, even when we were seniors and you were just a sophomore. You were Prom Queen, for goodness' sake!" I take a breath. "Plus, I don't share parents with Blair, which makes it a lot easier to be around her."

"Why?"

"Because whenever I look at Blair, I don't feel like I got the shallow end of the gene pool."

"Meaning?"

"Meaning you got Mom's blonde hair, the better looks, the bubbly personality... I've always been the shy introvert, and it didn't help that whatever I did, you had to go and prove you could do better. Ballet as kids, swimming in high school, life in New York, and then Paul."

"I didn't do it to prove I was better, I did it to prove I was worthy. That we could be friends, that we liked the same things."

That shuts me up all right. "I never saw it that way," I confess. "I've always assumed you were competing with me."

"No. And, Nik, you didn't get the shallow end of the gene pool. You have bigger boobs..." *And a bigger ass,* I comment inside my head. "...and you won't believe how much I envy your dark, straight hair. I hate my golden curls."

"That's the stupidest thing I've ever heard. You're a natural blonde; half the women on the planet would kill for hair like yours, including me."

Julia grimaces. "Guess we're hard-wired to want what we don't have."

"Are you really saying you've never wanted to compete with me?"

Julia smirks. "Maybe a little, but everything I did was mostly to impress you."

I stare at my sister as if I'm seeing her for the first time.

"Wow, we should've had this conversation ages ago."

"I know. And I'm sorry for everything..."

"Me, too."

"Well, you did nothing wrong, whereas with Paul... I screwed up big time. But I'm so happy you're over him now. And I'm also over the moon for you and Diego."

A small knife jacks its way into my heart at the mention of Diego's name.

"Are you?"

"Yeah, I was so relieved when you brought him home." Julia chuckles. "I mean, I was also a little jealous, to be honest, because he's really a guy out of a fantasy. I even went as far as accusing you of not really being together, and of having brought home a friend to play your fake boyfriend just to steal my thunder… How absurd."

"Ha, ha, ha…" I chuckle along with her. "Crazy, right?"

"But Mom made me see how much you two love each other."

The knife in my heart twists, and the wound I've been trying so hard to seal starts bleeding again.

"I hope he gets that job in New York," Julia continues. "And we should all go out to dinner once we're back in the city."

"That would be wonderful."

I don't have the strength to tell her Diego and I are over, finished, caput. Once the scar is a little more healed, I'll come up with a credible breakup story. I can't deal with the unavoidable family's sympathy that would follow such a revelation; not in person, at least. Better to break the news to my parents over the phone once I'm safely back in Manhattan. And I can go out with Julia in the city, and lie to her for the last time, as soon as I'm a little better. But not today, not this week, not when the memory of Diego's lips on my skin is still so fresh…

"Sisterly hug?" Julia gets up, stretching her arms wide and bringing me out of my mental reverie.

I lift my butt from the chair and pull her into a tight hug. "Love you," I whisper.

"I love you, too," she replies, choked.

We hang on to each other for the longest time, closer than we've been in years. If nothing else, something good came out of this dreadful holiday break.

***

After my heart-to-heart with Julia, the rest of my stay at home passes rather uneventfully. I try my best not to think about Diego, even if every time I catch sight of the snowman adorning our backyard, it's like a million arrows puncture my chest at once.

Diego really picked the perfect spot; the damn thing is not going to melt, ever. It'll probably still be there come spring. More than once, I'm tempted to march outside and kick the wretched thing back to powder. But then I'd have to explain to my family why I've suddenly turned into a snowman-killing maniac. So I just cope by avoiding the windows that overlook the backyard.

During the day, I keep myself busy with work. But it's the nights that are the hardest. There's no escape in the dark and silent witching hours, when all the demons tormenting my heart are let loose. This room is haunted by the ghosts of our kisses and touches and... *I shouldn't be thinking about that!*

I hope that once I get back to my apartment, I can finally shake off every last, painful memory of Diego. We never shared a room in New York, and I'm so grateful for that now.

It's that expectation alone that allows me, two days later, to leave my parents' house filled with a decent amount of self-imposed optimism. After loading the trunk of the rental car with my luggage, I honk twice to signal Blair it's time to go. I've already hugged my family goodbye, and I'm ready to get back to New York and turn the page on the worst December to date. The new year will help with that. I'll write a list of resolutions and try to stick to them for once. First item on the list: avoid memories of a certain dark-haired, green-eyed person at all costs.

I watch as Blair and Chevron burst out of their house. The dog is wearing paw booties and looks absolutely ridiculous. But we're trying to keep the rental car as clean as we can, so as not to forfeit the deposit.

Chevron, however, has different ideas. Halfway down the walkway, she strays into the front garden, drops to her back, and rolls in the snow. If she were human, she'd be making angels. Blair drops her bags and runs screaming after her, but the damage is done. Dirty paws are the least of our problems right now. There's a head-to-toe wet mutt Labrador to transport.

My parents, who must've followed the scene from the windows, promptly come to the rescue. They help me line the backseat with trash bags, which we lock in place with duct tape. It's not the best cover job in the world, but it should do the trick.

"I'm so sorry," Blair pants, dragging a now-leashed Chevron behind her. "I don't know what got into her."

We both turn to stare at the dog, who tilts her head and gives us a first-class show of contrite puppy-dog eyes.

"I'm not buying it, Miss," Blair chides. "You knew exactly what you were doing."

Chevron whines and uses a paw to cover her eyes.

"She's good," I say to Blair.

"Too good," she agrees.

"On with you." She opens the car's rear door. "Get in."

"Oh, don't scowl at her," I defend Chevron, and scratch her behind the ears. "She's too cute to be told off."

"Woof." Chevron lets out a grateful bark and takes her seat in the back of the car. She's now the picture of a well-behaved, educated dog.

We say our last goodbyes to the crowd of parents and neighbors that has gathered around, hop in the car, and drive out of town. I can't believe this break is finally over!

Blair keeps quiet for the whole of fifteen minutes before she puffs her cheeks full of air and blows it all out in one annoyed huff. "So, I guess we're not talking about why Diego isn't in the car with us, or why you've been avoiding me for the past two days?"

"Nope, I'm not touching that."

"Are you all right, at least?"

"Super," I snap.

"That's total bullshit."

"Woof," Chevron agrees.

"Hey." I stare in the rearview mirror. "I was the one defending you just moments ago; you should side with me."

Chevron howls in response.

"What do you think that meant?" I ask Blair.

"That she is on your side, and because of that, she wants you to open up with us and tell us what the hell happened because it's the best thing for you."

"And you got all that from one howl."

"Absolutely."

"*Awooooh.*"

When I still keep quiet, Blair snaps, "Oh, come on, do I have to beg?"

"I can't." I shake my head. "It's just too raw still."

Blair thinks for a second. "Better or worse than when Bambi's mother dies?"

"You can't use Disney parents being killed off; it's too sad, and against the rules."

"Oh, we have rules?"

"Mmm-hmm. No Disney deaths."

"Okay." Blair concentrates on the road ahead for a couple of blocks. "Mmm… Better or worse than when Bridget Jones finally gets Daniel to sleep with her, and he discovers her granny underwear?"

Despite myself, I chuckle. "Worse. That wasn't such a bad moment. Kind of cute and romantic, actually."

"Yeah, it was cute. Hugh Grant was so hot in that scene."

"Way too hot."

"So… so… so… Aha!" Blair hoots. "Better or worse than when Kristen Wiig brings the bridal party to the Mexican restaurant before the dress rehearsal, and everyone ends up with food poisoning, and there aren't enough restrooms in the dress shop, so Lillian ends up taking a dump in the middle of the street while wearing a wedding dress?"

I laugh at that. *Bridesmaids* is one of our favorite movies. "That was *funny*-tragic; my situation is *tragic*-tragic. But, yeah, you could say I feel as humiliated as if I'd just pooped in the middle of the street."

"Why? What happened?"

"Diego and I had sex on Christmas Day." I can't bring myself to say we "made love," even if that's what it felt like. "And the next day he bailed on me without as much as a note and returned none of my calls afterward."

"Just like that? Nothing happened between the sex—How was it, by the way?—and him leaving?"

I ignore the sex question. "A lot happened before and after."

"So tell me!"

I do. I start with Paul's Christmas present, the argument with Diego about my feelings for my sister's fiancé, and our night together. Then I tell her about the food fight with Julia, and Diego overhearing that I picked him to be Julia's fantasy and not mine. I end with the second fight about Paul, with me leaving to set things right between him and Julia and coming home to find Diego gone.

"And you really don't see why he left?" Blair asks, a bit exasperated.

"No! You do?"

"Let's try on the situation in reverse. Imagine you were dating this wonderful guy, and were falling for him…"

Easy.

"…Then, when things get serious, you find out that until a few days ago, he's been madly in love with a woman who's already taken by his brother."

"'Madly in love' seems like a bit much," I protest.

"Would 'mildly in love' work better?" Blair asks, sarcastic. "Point is, you've been obsessing over Paul for years."

"I don't see where you're going with this."

"Be patient. Get back in the story: You're dating this guy, and things are going great until you find out he's had feelings for this woman for the longest time before meeting you. Still following?"

"Yeah."

"Then you overhear this big argument between him and his brother, and you also discover you're not exactly his type. That he went out with you only to piss off his brother. You're super mad and want to understand where you stand with him. But in the meantime, the other woman breaks up with the brother. So, she's now technically free and available. Now, once the fight between the brothers is over, you ask your guy to talk with you, and he blows you off to run after this other woman… What is your first thought?"

I try to censor my answer before it even pops into my head, but there's really no point. "That he still cares about her more than he does about me."

"See? Diego could've misinterpreted the situation in a million different ways."

"There was nothing up for interpretation. Yes, I ran after Paul, but only to make him go back to Julia."

"Did you mention that *specifically* to Diego? Or did you just go on one of your incomprehensible rants: Paul-Paul-Paul-I-have-to-find-Paul-we'll-talk-later-bye?"

I want to say I made it clear why I was chasing Paul, but... "I'm not sure if I spelled it out, but it seemed obvious to me."

"To you, yes. To Diego, maybe not so much."

"Okay. Let's say, for the sake of arguing, that you're right. Diego assumed the worst about me running after Paul. So, what? Should his first reaction really have been to give up? Step aside. Run away."

"Did you two ever talk feelings?"

"No, it all happened so quickly. And then he was gone."

"So he's a little impulsive. Shouldn't you give the guy a second chance?"

"Me? He doesn't want a second chance, Blair," I say, exasperated. "I called him, texted him, wrote him an email basically begging him to pick up the phone. Nothing. He ignored me. Shut me out completely. Our night together was probably a one-night stand while on a job to him, and nothing more."

"Then why leave and not stay to finish the job if he didn't care?"

"Maybe he really had a better offer back in the city, I don't know. This isn't a fairy tale, Blair, there wasn't an evil queen who forced him to leave. He left because he wanted to, and the story doesn't have a happy ending. Happily ever afters don't exist in the real world."

"But—"

"Don't you dare say you found yours with Richard, and it's only a matter of time before I find mine. It's what coupled people say to singles, and we hate to hear it."

"Okay, I won't, but I'm still not convinced Diego left because he doesn't care. Did he give the money back?"

"Yeah, why?"

"See? He cares."

"It changes nothing. The only positive fact I can see out of this whole situation is that I won't start the new year broke."

"I don't know." Blair plays with her hair as she thinks. "Seems to me you guys are just being two stubborn idiots."

"Arrrhf-woof."

"You agree that I'm being an idiot?" I ask the dog.

Chevron gives two positive barks in response.

"Well, what am I supposed to do, in your mighty opinions?" I ask. "I already tried calling him and texting. I'm not going to knock on his door to beg him to talk."

"No, you're right." Blair nods. "It shouldn't be you," she says, and spends the rest of the journey staring out of the window, deep in thought.

Twenty-two

New Year's Eve

On the last night of the year, I sit on the toilet lid and watch Blair do her makeup as we chat. I'm not quite able to squash my resentment.

"When is Richard picking you up?" I ask.

Blair peeks at her watch. "Should be here in less than an hour. Gosh, I have to hurry." She gives another brush to her lashes with the mascara wand. "Could you please plug in the flat iron for me?"

"Sure," I snap.

I catch her throwing me a side stare in the mirror while I comply with her request.

"Are you sure you're not mad I didn't invite you to the party?"

"Blair, I'm not mad."

I'm so mad I want to strangle her.

"It's just that it's all couples," she repeats for the hundredth time. "You would've felt awkward, I'm sure. What with being the only person with no one to kiss at midnight?"

True, I would've hated it. And I also would've rather cut off my right arm than go to an all-couples New Year's party. But that's not the point. As my best friend, she should've begged me to go with her, and insisted that I go at least a few times after my every stubborn "no."

"Really, it's no trouble," I lie. "You know I hate couples' dinners."

"Well." Blair coats her lips in a bold shade of burgundy, smacks them together, and stares in the mirror, satisfied. "It's not going to be exactly a boring dinner. Richard's friend is famous for throwing the best parties."

Oh, I gasp inside my head, *what a bitch!*

I get that her life is perfect, and she has the perfect boyfriend, and that they're going to the best New Year's party in the city. But does she really have to rub it in my face? Tonight, I don't recognize my best friend. Not as the kind and loving person who has been super supportive since we came back to New York. No idea what happened to turn on her mean girl switch, but it'd better turn back off quickly if she wants us to still be friends next year.

Pretending I'm busy with the flat iron cord, I turn away from her to hide my seething look of outrage.

"Cool party or not, it's still going to be a cheesy PDA shit show," I say, harsher than I meant.

"Right," Blair agrees. "I'd so rather spend the night in watching TV than having to get all dressed up and go out in the cold for a whole night of partying."

As she says this, she pulls on the expensive new dress Richard brought her from London and admires how it perfectly hugs her figure in the mirror. She doesn't look like someone who'd rather spend the night in and order takeout pizza for dinner.

She twirls around once, and then turns toward me. "Mind getting the zipper?"

"Not at all." I pull the back of her dress together and slash the zipper up in one rough movement.

"Hey," Blair protests. "Careful there, I don't want to rip the dress off." Then she winks at me through the mirror. "Not unless it's Richard doing it later tonight."

I swear, I want to take her head and smash it in the mirror until she shuts the hell up.

"I'm hungry," I say, as an excuse to leave the bathroom. I can't stand her presence right now. "I'm going to order pizza."

I've just hung up with the delivery guy when Blair comes marching into the living room surrounded by a cloud of perfume. With high heels, her new dress, perfect makeup, and a stylish coat on, she looks one hundred percent like a character from *The Devil Wears Prada.*

"Richard just texted," she trills. "He's downstairs. Is your pizza arriving soon?"

"No," I sulk. "Apparently there're a lot of people spending the night in and ordering pizza."

"See? I told you it's the best way to spend the night." She smiles, and sighs. "New Year's is *so* overrated, really."

My eyes turn to slits. "Absolutely."

"I really gotta go now." She shrugs. "I'm staying at Richard's tonight, so don't wait up for me."

"I won't."

"Well, don't have too much fun without me." Blair opens the door and waltzes out of the apartment. "See yah."

I slam the door shut after her and lean against it. *What the hell? Bitch.*

She made me want to smash everything in the house. I need to relax.

The pizza boy said the wait would be well over an hour, so I might as well take a bath in the meantime. I go back to the bathroom, fill the tub to the brim with hot water, and happily empty half of Blair's super expensive perfumed oils in it in petty revenge.

When the doorbell rings a while later, I've just finished changing into one of my favorite cat PJs—about eighty percent of my PJs feature cats—and am much more relaxed.

I push the speaker button on the buzzer. "I'm up on the fourth floor," I inform the pizza boy.

"I know," a voice I recognize instantly says back.

Diego! I hate the way my heartbeat immediately speeds up. What is he doing here?

"What are you doing here?"

"Expecting someone else?"

"Yeah, pizza. What do you want?"

"To talk."

"Now? What about a week ago, when I called you a thousand times and begged you to pick up the phone?"

"I'm sorry. Can you please let me in and insult me in person?"

No, because the moment I see his eyes, I know my brain will fry and logic will fail me. No, because I've just barely started feeling like a human again. And no, because this apartment is free of painful, Diego-related memories. Yeah, he lived with me for a while, but nothing cathartic or intimate happened while he was here, and I don't want to make this place haunted, too. This is my safe haven.

"Are you still there?" comes his voice from the buzzer.

"Yeah. Listen, Diego, you slept with me and then ran away the next day without a word… That's not… There isn't a single thing you might say that will make me open this door."

"Err-hem." He clears his throat. "I have a rescue kitten here that I was hoping to drop off with you. He's sort of freezing his tiny tail off."

A cat bribe? *A cat bribe?*

Bastard!

But I can't resist; cats are my kryptonite. Or maybe Diego is. So I buzz him in.

I wait by the door, trying to steady my heartbeat, but my heart wants to jump out of my chest and run off to meet Diego down the hall. I compromise by opening the door and waiting for him propped against the threshold.

Mr. Tall, Dark, and Smoldering Hot comes out of the elevator in all black—black hair, black jeans, black leather jacket—carrying a carton transporter box with a cat silhouette on the side and cute, cat-shaped holes for air.

It might be the coldest time of the year, but I'm suddenly all hot and bothered. When did it become so hard to breathe? As Diego stops a few inches away from me, I find it almost impossible to inhale and exhale properly. The air between us seems charged with electricity, and I'm doing my best not to notice his clean and masculine scent mixed with the smell of night winds. And, damn me, the only thing I want to do right now is throw my arms around his neck and kiss those lips.

Instead, I extend one arm toward the carton box, saying, "You can leave the kitten and go."

"No, I can't," he says seriously. "At the shelter, they said I should spend at least an hour with him before leaving him with someone else. They did the same with me before they let me take him." He's trying really hard to maintain a somber and contrite expression, but I can see the ghost of a smile dancing behind his eyes. Oh, I shouldn't have looked him in the eyes. I could get lost in there, and I need to stay grounded now more than ever. "That way, he'll have the time to adjust to his new home and owner," Diego concludes.

One hour.

Can I survive that long?

Without a word, I step aside and make room for him to enter the apartment.

"Is your dog home?" he asks.

"No, Chevron is staying at Richard's for a while. He missed her over the Christmas break."

Diego nods and walks in, heading for the living room with a familiarity I don't like. I watch him move the coffee table against the wall, freeing the rug in front of the couch, and set a bunch of pillows down with the same ease as if he were at his place. I hate that I let him so far into my world.

I shut the door and join him. He's seated on one side of the rug and has placed the carton box, still sealed, in the center. From a plastic bag, he unloads a series of different items: a soft blanket that he spreads over the rug, a plastic box that he fills with litter, a bowl in which he empties a small bag of dry cat food, and finally another bowl that he lifts toward me.

"Can you fill this with water?" he asks.

I make a quick dash to the kitchen, fill the bowl, and carefully place it next to the food. With nothing else left to do, I sit on the opposite side of the rug—as far from Diego as the reduced square footage of New York living space allows.

Diego turns the carrier box toward me, placing his hand on the latch. "Ready?" he asks.

I nod.

"A word of warning." The grin he's been suppressing since stepping on my landing finally appears in a half-smile. "He's very cute."

I scowl at him and wait for him to open the box. As soon as he does, two tiny, half-white paws step into the light, followed by the cutest furry face I've ever seen. The kitten is a brown-gray tabby, but with a streak of auburn fur that covers his nose and spreads in a small inverted triangle between his eyes. His paws and underbelly are white.

If my heart wasn't melted before, it is now. Like with Diego, my first instinct is to take the mini cat into my arms and hug the little furball to my chest.

The urge must be written all over my face, because Diego warns me, "Let him come to you."

We watch patiently as the kitten walks out on the blanket and sniffs the surrounding air.

"Hello, you," I say.

I'm already in love.

"*Mew,*" he meows in response.

The kitty follows his sense of smell to the food bowl, eats a little, drinks, and then he climbs over my left knee to land in my lap, purring. Oh, he's a cuddler. I can't resist any longer; I plunge my hands into his soft fur and give him a full-body scratch. The kitty seems to appreciate the contact, because he starts making muffins on my leg, then curls into a tiny ball and goes to sleep.

"Seems like you two are a good fit," Diego says.

I look up, startled. For a moment I'd forgotten he was here.

The smile he'd been trying to hide before is now wide and warm and… *heart-shattering,* unfortunately for me.

"I'm in no way mollified," I tell him.

The grin now turns foxy. "Of course you aren't."

"So." I pause for effect. "What are you doing here?"

Before he can answer, the buzzer goes off again.

"It's the pizza," I say. "Do you mind getting that?"

I don't want to disturb the cat.

Diego gets up and comes back two minutes later carrying a family-sized pizza box.

He places the box in front of me and eyes it suspiciously. "Are you sure you're not expecting company?"

"No," I reply, and to justify the disproportionate pizza, I add, "I thought I'd warm some for lunch tomorrow."

So not true. Left to myself, I would've scarfed down the whole thing tonight. I mean, single and alone on New Year's Eve, a girl deserves her pizza.

I open the box and, with the aid of a few paper napkins, bring the first slice to my mouth. Mmm, it's delicious.

Diego watches me, not making any attempt to touch the pizza, but with a clear longing in his eyes.

"Did you have dinner?" I ask.

He shakes his head.

"Get the Cokes from the fridge"—I jerk my chin backward toward the kitchen—"and you can have a slice or two."

We establish a sort of pizza-truce and eat dinner mostly in silence, but not without an extensive amount of non-verbal eye communication. Not a single serious word has been spoken, and yet I feel as if I've already lost. I've tried to lock my heart behind a steel cage, but between Diego and the kitten, all my defenses have melted.

The pizza disappears alarmingly quickly, and once it's gone there's no more circling around the famous pink elephant in the room.

I take one last sip of Coke, and say, "So?"

"So."

"Why are you here? Why now?"

"There's a certain magic in the air tonight."

"And you just assumed I'd spend New Year's Eve home alone."

Diego's sexy-and-infuriating smirk makes another appearance. "I might've had a little tip-off."

I tilt my head questioningly.

"Blair called," he confesses. "She gave me a half-an-hour pep talk explaining all the reasons why I was being an idiot, and then told me that if I came to my senses, I'd find you here all alone and majorly pissed off that you weren't invited to her friend's party."

That sneaky bitch.

I can't help but smile. Oh, she got me good this time.

"Care to repeat them?" I ask.

"What?"

"All the reasons why you've been an idiot."

"No," he says. "You go first."

"Me?" My mouth dangles open. "If this is your way to apologize—"

"I've always been honest with you. You've been the one keeping secrets. Paul first, then your sister…"

I want to get up and shove him out of my house, but the kitten is forcing me to stay put and talk. "You already know everything there is to know."

"Did you really run after Paul only to make him go back to Julia?" Diego asks.

"Yes. Why else would I go after him?"

"I thought you wanted to break them off for good."

"What? What kind of horrible person would do that?"

"The same kind who would hire a guy she's mapped to her sister's every fantasy to play her fake boyfriend."

Touché.

"I'm not an angel; so what? I just wanted to annoy Julia a little."

Diego shakes his head. "And look how well it ended the last time she just wanted to annoy you a little. She made you miserable for two years."

"Well, she's not perfect, either. Anyway, my relationship with my sister has nothing to do with us. You left me," I accuse him.

He shifts his butt on the rug so that he's now sitting next to me, both our backs leaning against the couch. Diego takes my hand into his and starts drawing small circles on my palm with his thumb. "I'm sorry," he says.

"It's not enough." I try to get my hand back, but he keeps it imprisoned in his. "What if Blair hadn't called you? Would you still be here?"

"Maybe." He lowers his gaze. "I received the casting calls for the Super Bowl ads this morning. I didn't think you'd keep your word on those. Made me feel like shit that you'd still be kind to me after the way I left."

Truth is, I'd set up the castings before Christmas and completely forgotten about them. If I'd remembered, I might've had a petty fit at the office today and deleted his name from the call list.

"I usually keep my promises." I play the saint. "But a casting call is no better than a call from my best friend. Will somebody have to call you every time we argue, otherwise you'll disappear off the face of the Earth?" He smiles at that, driving me mad. "Why are you smiling now?"

"Because if we're going to argue in the future, it means we're going to be together…"

I force myself to look him in the eye. "If that's what you wanted, why disappear? I get you might've been mad at first, but why not return any of my texts or calls?"

"I've misread a situation once before," he says, his gaze open and sincere. "Only that time, I trusted a woman who told me her feelings for her ex were dead, until they weren't. So when I saw you wanting to run after Paul so bad you couldn't spare ten minutes to talk to me first, it all came back in a rush. I thought, fool me once don't fool me twice. So, rather than having to hear you tell me you'd realized you were still in love with Paul, I ran away. Stupid, right?"

"*Very* stupid," I agree, and wait for a little more groveling.

"But since I've left, I haven't been able to stop thinking about you." As he says this, he gently cups my face and turns it toward him. Diego's hands are too warm, his eyes too green, and his mouth too close. "And I don't care if you picked me off a catalog based on your sister's preferences," he continues. "I'm just glad someone in your family has decent taste; otherwise, I would never have met you."

I remove his hands from my face—too distracting—and lower them to our legs without letting go.

"And you realized all of this today?"

"No, today's just the day I realized how much of an idiot I've been… And after Blair's call…"

"You decided to adopt a cat and bribe me with him?"

"The cat strategy seems to have worked pretty well." He smiles down at the little cutie. "Have you picked a name yet?"

I stare at the tiny streak of auburn fur on the kitten's face. "Cinnamon. I want to call him Cinnamon."

"I like it."

Diego squeezes my hand, making me look back up at him.

"So, what happens now?" I ask.

"This is the part where you forgive me and give me another chance." He scrunches up his face in a cute, irresistible, pleading expression.

"I still don't know if I can trust you not to run away at the first difficulty. We were only together for two days, and when you left I was so crushed… I don't think I could survive you leaving again."

One of his hands sneaks back up to my neck, his fingers caressing the sensitive skin just behind my ear. "I won't leave you again. I promise I'll face every fight like a man, without running."

I frown. "You expect many fights?"

The foxy grin is back. "If you keep on being so bossy, I don't see how we won't."

"I'm not bossy—"

"Yes, you are. You're bossy, and stubborn, and impossible to deal with sometimes. But you're also beautiful, and kind, and smart, and that's why I love you so much."

My heart stops. "You what?"

"I love you, Nikki," he repeats, and my name on his lips sounds like the softest caress. "And I think you love me, too."

"Really? How do you know that?"

He bends forward to whisper in my ear. "From the way you call my name when we make love."

The last ounce of resistance I had evaporates. Tears streak down my cheeks, but I can't stop smiling. "Diego, I…"

"Yes, just like that," he breathes down my neck.

"I…" I'm too choked to speak.

"Shh." He massages my shoulders to soothe me. "It's okay."

Diego pulls back to look me in the eyes for the longest time. Then he leans forward and kisses me.

As our lips touch, an explosion of cheery noises and sounds invades the apartment from outside, above, and below.

And so, at the stroke of midnight on New Year's Eve, my happily ever after becomes true.

End of Book Three

Note from the Author

Dear Reader,

I hope you enjoyed the first three books in the *First Comes Love* series. The next book in the series will feature six-times-in-a-row Sexiest Man Alive and Hollywood superstar Christian Slade as he struggles to find a woman who's not after him just for his fame. I can't wait to get started on this new novel, set in sunny Los Angeles. California, here we come!

Now, I have to ask you a favor. If you loved my story, **please leave a review** on Goodreads, your favorite retailer's website, or wherever you like to post reviews (your blog, your Facebook wall, your bedroom wall, in a text to your best friend…) Reviews are the best gift you can give to an author, and word of mouth is the most powerful means of book discovery.

Thank you for your constant support!

Camilla, x

Acknowledgments

Thank you to my street team, and to all of you who leave book reviews. They're so appreciated.

Thank you to all my readers. Without your constant support, I wouldn't keep pushing through the blank pages.

Thank you to my editors and proofreaders, Michelle Proulx, Helen Baggott, Hayley Stone, Alison Jack, and Jennifer Harris for making my writing the best it can be.

And lastly, thank you to my family and friends for your constant encouragement.

www.ingramcontent.com/pod-product-compliance
Lightning Source LLC
Chambersburg PA
CBHW022013300726
48970CB00003B/863